GRAVE WATER LAKE

ALSO BY A.M. STRONG AND SONYA SARGENT

Stand-Alone Psychological Thrillers

The Last Girl Left

The Patterson Blake Series

Never Lie to Me

Sister Where Are You

Is She Really Gone

All the Dead Girls

Never Let Her Go

Dark Road from Sunrise

I Will Find Her

GRAVE WATER LAKE

A THRILLER

A.M. STRONG
SONYA SARGENT

This is a work of fiction. Names, characters, organizations, places, events, and incidents are either products of the author's imagination or are used fictitiously. Otherwise, any resemblance to actual persons, living or dead, is purely coincidental.

Published by Thomas & Mercer, Seattle

www.apub.com

ISBN-13: 9781662518393 (paperback)
ISBN-13: 9781662518409 (digital)

Cover design by Faceout Studio, Elisha Zepeda
Cover image: © Gremlin, © Andrzej Ploch / Getty; © Denis Belitsky / Shutterstock

Printed in the United States of America

To H and I, whose joyful exploration of the world around them is always an inspiration

PROLOGUE

Adria

The Day She Found Out

There wasn't much time before he came back, and Adria couldn't take it any longer. She had to know. This was her only chance.

She clutched a screwdriver and hammer in one hand. In the other, she held a flashlight from the junk drawer in the kitchen. The beam lit up the darkness, playing across the foyer and casting long shadows that danced and bobbed as she hurried toward Peter's study.

The power had gone out twenty minutes ago, as it often did during blizzards. When it didn't come right back on, her husband had grabbed his thickest coat, grumbling under his breath all the while, and headed out into the storm toward the utility shed housing the decades-old generator he sarcastically called *the beast*. She figured it would be at least another fifteen minutes before he got the finicky generator working and returned to the house. They had talked about replacing it when they'd first bought the remote lakefront retreat in the north of Vermont, but there had been better things to spend their money on, so the unreliable generator had stayed. Now she was glad of its vagaries. They bought her time.

Reaching the study, Adria pinched the flashlight between her rib cage and arm, then tried the handle. She half expected it to be locked—Peter valued his privacy above all else—but it wasn't.

The door swung inward.

Relieved, she stepped inside and glanced around. To her left was a floor-to-ceiling panoramic window that looked out over the lake she knew was there, even though it was currently shrouded in darkness. The night was thick with falling snow that settled on the wide deck they had built the previous year. A pair of Adirondack chairs positioned to take in the natural majesty of their surroundings were already turning into formless white lumps. They wouldn't be getting out of here anytime soon, which wouldn't have bothered Adria normally. She liked nothing better than curling up in front of a roaring fire and snuggling on a frigid winter's eve. But not tonight. Not if she was correct.

But where to look?

A bookcase occupied the room's far wall, its shelves packed with volumes, mostly nonfiction. Peter was an avid reader. But there wouldn't be anything there, she knew. No proof that he had been deceiving her since the day they'd met. He wouldn't leave such incriminating evidence in plain view.

Which left the desk.

They had found it in a booth toward the back of an antique mall on one of their many local explorations. The desk was made of solid red oak and scarred from almost two centuries of use. Peter had fallen in love with it instantly. It would be, he had told her, the perfect addition to his study. It was also a great place to conceal evidence of his lies. Things he didn't want her to see.

Adria sat down, placing the screwdriver and hammer on the desktop.

There were three drawers on each side, all with brass-rimmed keyholes. She tried the top left drawer. It slid open to reveal a stack of paperwork held together by a rubber band, mostly utility bills inside their envelopes with *paid* written across the front of each in black pen.

The next drawer contained an assortment of pens and pencils, a push-type staple remover, and more rubber bands of various sizes. The bottom drawer was empty.

She turned her attention to the drawers on the other side. The top one contained more papers. She leafed through them but found nothing of any interest. The second contained a spiral-bound notepad and some assorted cables.

The bottom drawer didn't open.

She tugged again, just to make sure it wasn't stuck.

It still wouldn't open.

This must be it. Adria looked around on the desk and in the other drawers for the key but came up empty. Not a surprise. If there really were something incriminating inside that drawer, Peter would keep the key hidden. It might even be on his person at that very moment, tucked into his pants pocket, out of harm's way.

Adria wasn't going to let that stop her. She had come too far and spent too long living with the creeping fear that she didn't actually know the man she had married. One way or the other, she needed to find out.

Wedging the flashlight under her arm again so that it pointed toward the desk, she picked up the screwdriver and forced it into the gap between the drawer and the surround. The blade was thin, but it still required some effort. She was about to pry up on the blade to pop the lock when she hesitated.

Peter would know what she had done the moment he saw the desk. There would be no hiding the damage. Even if there was nothing worth finding in that drawer, she would have revealed her hand.

But not looking in the drawer would leave her forever wondering. She had no choice.

With a deep breath, Adria pried up the screwdriver.

The blade slipped on the wood, threatening to slide out, but she pushed against the resistance and managed to keep it steady. Her hand shook with the effort. She wondered if the lock was too strong. Then, with a splintering crack, the drawer popped open.

She peered inside to see a single item. A black metal safe box of the kind used to store cash and other valuables. With trembling hands, she reached down and gripped the handle, pulling it out of the drawer, then set it upon the desk.

It was locked, of course.

As before, there was no key.

Adria glanced toward the study door. In her haste to search the desk, she had let time slip away from her. How long had Peter been tending to that generator? The power wasn't back on yet, so that was a good sign. But it wouldn't stay that way, she was sure.

Turning her attention back to the box, she studied the lock. It didn't look too hard to break. She picked up the screwdriver again and placed it against the rim, then brought the hammer down. Once. Twice. Three times. On the fourth whack, the lock barrel gave way.

Adria lifted the lid.

The first thing she saw was a small red jewelry box with the name of a jeweler printed on top in gold lettering. She lifted it out and opened it. There were two items inside. A wedding ring and an engagement ring. The wedding ring was inscribed with initials: *R & J*. She set the rings aside and turned her attention back to the contents of the larger box.

There were more items. Lots of them.

An expired California driver's license in the name of Nick Blakely with her husband's picture on it. He was younger, but it was clearly him. She rummaged deeper. Another driver's license, this one from Oregon in another name she didn't know. Again, her husband's face peered back at her from the thin piece of plastic. There was an old speeding ticket from Connecticut, the writing faded to obscurity. A bill of sale for a truck, also not in her husband's name, dated a few months before she'd met Peter.

Adria lifted out the items, placed them on the desk, saw that there was more underneath. A yellowed newspaper clipping about a missing couple, Jess and Rob Cody, dated twelve years earlier. There were other articles too, all about the same couple. They had vanished from their Santa Barbara home under mysterious circumstances. The police suspected foul play. Underneath the articles was a stack of postcards from places like Orlando, New York City, and Niagara Falls. There were ones from farther afield too. Rome. Paris. London. They were all blank except one, depicting the Southernmost Point buoy in the Florida Keys. That had been written out but never addressed.

She picked it up.

Having so much fun here in Key West! Not sure when we will be back. Please take good care of Charlie Cat for a little longer!

Love, Jess and Rob

Adria stared at the message, read it again just to be sure, even as a prickle of fear inched up her spine . . . because she knew what all this meant.

"You shouldn't be looking at that stuff. It's mine."

Adria jumped and dropped the postcard, startled by a voice from behind her. Peter's voice. She turned to find him standing in the doorway, anger etched on his face.

"I'm sorry. I was just . . ." She struggled to keep her composure. Why was he back when the power was still off? Had he even tried to get the generator running, or was he lurking out of sight, watching her all this time?

"Snooping." Peter finished the sentence. "You were just snooping."

Adria sprang to her feet, her need to know overcoming the cold terror that twisted her stomach. She looked down at the box and then back toward her husband. "You killed them, didn't you? That couple. Jess and Rob. That's why you have those rings. You killed them."

"That was a long time ago and nothing to do with you." Peter stepped into the room and started toward her, his blue eyes turning to steel.

Adria shrank back, bumping into the desk, even as she realized that there was nowhere to go. And in that moment, her previous bravado fled, leaving her with nothing but a hollow, terrible certainty. She was trapped, and there was no way Peter was going to let her walk out of this alive.

1

A thousand frigid pinpricks needle the bare flesh of my arms, neck, and face. The sound of lapping water accompanies a sensation of movement against my body, of rolling back and forth.

I force my eyes open. At first, I cannot make sense of what I see—or rather, the lack of it. Above me is nothing but impenetrable blackness, broken only by swirling flecks of white that tumble down and land on my skin, where they melt. With each comes another brief twinge of icy discomfort. But it's nothing compared to the deep chill that seeps through my clothes and down to my very bones.

The reason becomes obvious when I cajole my aching body to respond.

It's night. I'm sitting at the edge of a vast body of water surrounded by pine trees that push toward a leaden sky bloated with heavy falling snow. Gentle waves lap at a sandy shore and break around my feet and legs.

I'm so cold. My clothes are soaked through. I lift a hand to my hair, discover that this too is wet. It sticks to my scalp in flaccid, tangled strands.

I stare at the lake, and a strange thought comes to me. That I had been one with that expanse of water. That it took me into its depths and welcomed me. Embraced me. At least until it spat me out and deposited me here. Rejected me like flotsam washed ashore by the tide.

I feel a momentary tug of anxiety accompanied by a vague memory of slipping beneath the surface that quickly fades back into the vast blankness of my mind.

And it's then that I realize . . . I don't know where I am—other than being beside this water—or what happened before I woke up dripping wet and shivering.

The anxiety turns into full-blown panic. My heart races. A thought crashes through my mind. *How did I get here?*

I still have my hand pressed to my hair, the wet strands soggy and cold under my fingers.

I draw in a deep breath to calm myself. Lower my arm. When I do, a bangle bracelet slips down to my wrist. Dainty. Made of silver. It curves around my wrist like an old friend. A glimmer of familiarity dances beyond the edges of my comprehension, but then it's gone, and the bracelet becomes strange again.

I turn the slim ribbon of silver, desperate to recapture that brief moment of vague recognition, and in doing so, make a discovery.

An engraving. One simple letter etched into the pale metal.

A.

An initial perhaps. The first letter of my name? But if it is, I don't remember, because my identity is as much a blank as everything else.

A new glut of terror envelops me. I don't know who I am. *How can I not know who I am?* Everyone knows who they are. It doesn't make sense.

I rack my brain, trying to glean a morsel of information about myself. Something. Anything. But it's no use. My memory remains a stubborn blank.

I want to scream in frustration. Or maybe fear. But that won't do me any good. I need to keep calm, and then maybe everything will come back.

Except it doesn't, even when I force the swell of panic back down. Swallow it.

But it does clear my mind enough to let me think.

I stare at the bracelet, and the initial, even more sure than ever that it's the first letter of a name. The only tangible clue to my identity. The question is, What name? Alison, or Annabel, or Astrid? None of those shake anything loose in the empty well of my mind.

I try again, run through more names in my head. *Amy. Alice. Anastasia.*

That last one sounds like too much, even to me.

I give up and turn my attention outward, toward my surroundings. The water still laps around my legs. Goose bumps rise on my arms, and my teeth chatter. I can't stay here like this. I'll freeze to death.

I stand up, look down at myself, and am surprised to see that I'm hardly dressed for a night such as this. A pair of blue jeans and a thin cotton blouse, both soaked through. A slipper clings to one foot. The other foot is bare. I pull the unsheathed one up like I've stepped in fire, shocked by the stab of frigid discomfort when it sinks into the thin covering of snow that blankets the ground.

The sudden movement awakens a dull throb that pulses at the back of my skull. I touch my scalp again, pushing aside my hair to probe the spot where it hurts, and find a lump. The pain explodes at my touch. I pull my hand away quickly, but a pulsing headache remains, like a souvenir of my inquisitiveness.

The lump explains why my memory is a blank. I must have hit my head. But on what? I look around and see a dark finger of wooden supports and planks jutting out into the water.

A dock.

Is that how I ended up here? Did I slip on a wet plank and fall into the water? Plunge under that impenetrable black surface, only to crack my head on a submerged rock?

It's impossible to know.

But I know a few things. I'm all alone in this strange place with no memory of who I am or how I got here. I'm not wearing a coat despite the weather, which is odd. I'm also clearly on the edge of hypothermia.

I have a head injury, which means I also could have a concussion. And I'm wearing a slipper, so I clearly did not intend to go outside.

And now the fear sets in. A swell of panic that washes over my momentary calmness and sweeps it away.

Caught in the grip of a frantic terror, I turn and scan my surroundings, praying for a way out. And all the time, one thought rolls through my mind. *I could die here.* Freeze to death in this snowy, bitter landscape without ever knowing how I got here or why.

And then I see it. Blessed salvation. A pale oblong of light between the trees. A window.

I stumble toward the glow, ignoring the frosty ache that accompanies each fall of my single bare foot upon the snow, and soon the dark outline of a house comes into view. It sits a couple of hundred feet behind the dock at the point where the woods meet the shore. A walkway connects the dock to the building.

Panic morphs into hope. This must be where I came from.

I quicken my step, eager to be out of the elements. Desperate to be warm again. My feet leave impressions in the snow. I notice that there are no footprints going in the other direction, leading *away* from the house, but that doesn't mean anything. Fresh snow might have covered them while I was unconscious. Or maybe this isn't my house after all. Maybe I came from somewhere else entirely.

The answer could lie inside that building.

Drawing closer, I look for anything that might trip my memory. Nothing does, but I get my first good look at the building. The house is two stories tall, with a wide deck overlooking the lake. Thick, dark wood beams form a pattern along the outside in sharp contrast to the lighter colored stone of its walls. The light is coming from a window on the first floor. The curtains are drawn. There's no other sign of life from within. If I fell off that dock, then I might be the only person who lives here.

I cross the deck to the back door. Try the handle. It doesn't open. Locked. *Oh shit.*

I raise my hand to knock, but my fingers are so cold that I can barely move them. When I finally close my hand into a fist, it hurts, even though my fingertips are numb.

I bang on the door, praying someone will answer, because I'm not sure how much longer I can endure being out in the frozen night air.

At first, nothing happens.

I'm so cold that it hurts.

I wrap my arms around myself and try to control the new wave of panic that rises inside me.

I reach out to knock again.

But then a floodlight snaps on, bathing the deck in a cool white glow. I hear movement on the other side of the door before it opens.

The man who stands there is as much a mystery to me as everything else. He is tall and muscular, with a two-day shadow darkening his chin. He wears jeans and a navy cotton shirt with the sleeves rolled up. His eyes are piercing and blue. I don't recognize him, which isn't surprising.

He doesn't recognize me either, judging by the look of bewilderment that passes across his face. A look that quickly turns to shock.

I want to speak, to ask this man for help, but I can't. Instead, I'm overcome by dizziness. Darkness closes in at the edge of my vision. My legs give way. I slump forward into his arms, even as the world around me fades to black.

2

Warm. I'm so warm and cozy.

My head hurts. A deep, pulsing ache.

I groan and open my eyes. The light makes the pain in my head worse. The first thing I see is an enormous stone fireplace and a roaring fire. The flames send flickering shadows leaping across a honey-colored wood floor partly covered by a rustic red shag rug.

My gaze drifts upward past the mantel to a large abstract oil painting in an ornate gold frame that contrasts with the bright colors and bold brushstrokes that weave across the canvas in swirling, almost organic patterns. Higher still is a ceiling supported by thick wood beams. A floor lamp with a Tiffany-style glass shade stands in the corner near the fireplace, emitting a soft glow. A scent of pine mixed with lavender hangs in the air.

I shift and realize that I'm lying on a soft leather couch with a blanket covering me. I'm also dry. My hands are stiff, and the tips of my fingers burn. A leftover remnant from being out in the cold for so long, I am sure. I lift the corner of the blanket to peek underneath. My wet clothes are gone, replaced by a pair of blue flannel PJs sporting a tartan pattern. The fabric is soft against my skin.

"Well, hello." A voice, deep and soft, interrupts my discovery. "You're back in the land of the living."

I let the blanket fall back into place. My savior stands at the end of the couch. The man into whose arms I collapsed. A complete stranger, at least as far as I know. I'm not sure if I should be comforted or scared. Fear wins. I scoot back on the sofa, just a little, and ask the question burning through my mind. "Where am I?"

The man observes me for a long moment, then clears his throat and asks, "You don't know where you are?"

I shake my head.

Another short silence. "How about me? Do you recognize me?"

Another shake. Before he answered the door and caught me in his arms, I'd never seen him before, which isn't saying much, given my disturbing lack of recall.

The man studies me with those piercing blue eyes I noticed earlier, right before I passed out. "What's your name?"

Good question, if only I had an answer. "I don't know."

"You don't know your own name?"

"No." Panic overwhelms me when I admit that, as if voicing my predicament makes it more real.

"Do you remember anything?"

"No." I fight back tears.

"Hey. Take it easy." My savior comes around the couch and perches on the edge. He reaches a hand toward mine, hesitates, then thinks better of it and pulls back. "We'll figure this out."

It takes a huge effort to stifle the tears. I sniff. "You asked if I know you."

"Yes."

"Do *you* know me?"

The answer is instant. "I've never seen you before tonight."

"Oh." So much for figuring out who I am. But there is one thing I can learn. "What's your name?"

"Gregg."

I force a weak smile. "Hello, Gregg."

"Hello."

I glance around. "Is there a Mrs. Gregg?"

"No. Just me."

I let this sink in, and all at once, a disturbing thought occurs to me. "My clothes. I'm not wearing them anymore."

"They were soaked through. Couldn't leave them on you."

"If you're the only other person in the house, then . . ." A rush of heat touches my face.

"I changed you out of them. You'd have probably caught pneumonia otherwise. I don't know how long you were out in the elements, but your skin was practically blue." Gregg looks away, then back to me. "I did my best not to look. Promise."

I can't see any way he didn't look. Even my bra and panties are gone, probably because they were soaked like everything else. A deep sense of unease edges my panic aside. I ask the obvious next question. "Why am I here?"

Gregg tilts his head to one side. He looks a bit like a puppy trying to understand its master. In other circumstances, his expression might be cute. Not right now. "You came to my door."

"I get that. But if you don't know me, why didn't you call the police? Call for an ambulance?" My voice rises in pitch despite my best efforts to stay calm. "Why am I still here? Something obviously happened to me. I'm hurt. There's a bump on the back of my head."

"I noticed."

"And you didn't call for help?" Even in my addled state, I know that when a stranger shows up at your door, frozen and disoriented, you don't just plant them on the sofa and do nothing.

"I can't call for help." Gregg glances toward a bay window on the other side of the room overlooking the water. The curtains are mostly drawn, but not quite. In the darkness beyond, snow is falling, thick and heavy. "We're cut off. Cell phones don't work up here, even when there isn't a storm. The house has a DSL connection for the landline phone and internet, but the line's down right now, so we don't have either."

That's convenient. "Then why didn't you put me in your car and drive me somewhere? To a hospital. The police. There must be a town close by."

“There isn’t.” Gregg shakes his head. “Closest town is Culver, almost fifteen miles away, and we’d never get there. The road is impassable because of the blizzard. It could be days before we can get out of here.”

“What about other houses?” I ask, clutching at straws. “This can’t be the only home in the area.”

“It’s not. There are a bunch more, all summer cottages, which means they’re closed down for the winter.”

I wonder how he’s so sure of that. “You’re here.”

“I like my solitude.”

“Maybe I’m the same. Maybe I came from one of those other houses.” A twinge of hope pulses inside me. “There might be someone out there right now who’s looking for me.”

“I doubt it. I’ve been up here for several days, and I haven’t seen anyone. This isn’t the kind of place you live year-round. Too remote.”

I want to remind him again that he’s here, so someone else could be, but he sounds so confident. Still, I didn’t just materialize on his doorstep from thin air. “If all the other houses are empty, where did I come from?”

“That’s the million-dollar question.” Gregg places a reassuring hand on the blanket, and my knee beneath. “Maybe your car broke down somewhere close by, and you found your way here.”

That doesn’t sit right. “I was in the water. I bumped my head.”

Gregg shrugs. “I wish I had an answer for you.”

I’m about to press him further, but at that moment I hear a shrill, escalating whistle from somewhere else in the house.

He glances toward the living room door. “Kettle’s boiling. I’m making tea. Figured you might like something hot when you woke up.”

He turns to leave.

“Wait.” I struggle to sit up. The blanket falls to my lap. I scoop it up and hold it against my chest, conscious of my state of undress beneath the partially buttoned flannel top. It’s a pointless modesty under the circumstances, but one that I cling to. “Do you have any painkillers?”

Gregg observes me, perhaps trying to decide if medication is wise for a person who likely has a concussion.

"Please? My head aches."

"I'll see what I can find." Then he's gone, leaving me alone with the hollow emptiness of my mind.

3

"Here. Drink this." Gregg hands me a steaming mug of tea, then drops two small white pills into my palm. "And take these too. Acetaminophen. They're safe to use with a concussion."

"What are you, a doctor?" I ask. His house is certainly big enough.

Gregg laughs. "No. But I did play ball in high school. Got my fair share of knocks to the head."

"Thank you." I take the pills, wash them down with a gulp of tea. It's hot and good. Just a dash of milk. It's sweet. I might not remember who I am, but apparently, I like hot tea with sugar. One less thing to worry about, right? If only I could fill in the blanks regarding everything else. I wrap my hands around the warm mug, which soothes the ache in my cold, stiff fingers. I look up at Gregg and once again ask, "Where am I? I mean, where is this place, exactly? The water out there."

"Gravewater Lake."

The name doesn't shake anything loose. All it does is send a shiver down my spine. It sounds . . . ominous.

Gregg continues. "We're in northern Vermont. It's January. Ring a bell?"

"No." Northern Vermont in January doesn't sound like a place I would want to be. Then again, how would I know? Or, more accurately, how do I *not* know? I want to scream at the blank wall that is my mind. This all feels so wrong.

Gregg waits for me to elaborate. When I don't, he adds, "The clothes you were wearing . . . they were expensive. Designer."

I stare at him blankly.

"You really don't remember anything?"

"No," I say again, overcome by a sudden gnawing panic. "Don't you think that if I remembered anything, even the tiniest glimmer of what happened before I woke up on the shore of that lake, I'd tell you? For God's sake, I don't even know my own name."

"Hey, it's okay." Gregg's voice is soothing. Calm. The opposite of mine. "I didn't mean to upset you."

"I know." I make an effort to control my swirling emotions. "Where are my clothes?"

"Laundry room. Figured I'd wash them, but I'm not sure they're salvageable. The jeans were stained, and your top had a tear in it near the shoulder. You probably caught it on something when . . ."

"When I was in the lake."

"Or afterward, before you arrived at my door."

"Before I fainted in your arms."

"Yes."

"How long was I unconscious?"

"About an hour. I was beginning to worry. Thought you might be worse off than you looked. Concussions can be tricky."

"That probably accounts for the memory loss," I say, the words triggering a fresh surge of raw panic. I swallow a rising sob. "At least, I hope it does. It's awful, not knowing who I am. It's like there's a dark pit in my mind. A blank void where my identity should be."

"We do have some clues," Gregg says, nodding toward my wrist. "You're wearing a bracelet. There's a letter engraved on it."

"I saw that." It was one of the first things I noticed when I woke up. "I figured it might be an initial."

"Shame it's not an entire name."

"It's a start."

"We could try some names that start with *A*, see if any of them feel familiar."

I almost tell him that I've already done that, that I ran through names in my head when I first saw the bracelet, but he dives right in, repeating pretty much the same ones.

After a list of at least ten monikers that start with *A*, he pauses. "Anything?"

I shake my head, then add, "You forgot *Anne*."

"And its cousin, *Anna*," he says. "Short for *Anneliese*."

"That's a bit obscure, isn't it?" I wonder where he came up with such a random name. "Wouldn't *Annabelle* be a better fit?"

"I knew an Anneliese. I like the name."

"I don't think I'm an Anneliese."

"How do you know?"

"Fair point." I *don't* know. That's the problem. "It just doesn't feel right. Too stuffy."

"Well, I think it's perfect, and we have to call you something. At least until you remember who you really are."

"It's a bit of a mouthful." If I'm going to have a pseudonym, I'd like it to be easy. "How about we keep it simple? Like maybe just *Anna*."

"Fine. We'll go with Anna."

"That works." I yawn, suddenly exhausted. It's dark out, but I have no idea how late it is. "What's the time?"

Gregg glances at his watch. "Almost one in the morning."

Guess I'm not a night owl. I slide back down on the couch. Yawn again. "I'm not sure I can keep my eyes open much longer. Sorry."

"Don't worry about it. I shouldn't have kept you talking. You've been through an ordeal." Gregg stands up. "There's a guest bedroom with an en suite upstairs. We can pick this up in the morning. Maybe you'll remember something by then."

"I hope so." I'm almost too tired to move. The thought of lugging my aching body up a flight of stairs makes me feel even more exhausted. "I can just sleep here."

"Not a chance. That couch might be comfortable right now, but your back will kill you by morning. Trust me, I know. I've slept on more than a few couches. You need a proper bed." Gregg offers me his hand. "I can carry you up if you want."

"I'll walk," I say, pushing back the blanket and swinging my legs off the couch. I stand up and am hit by a moment of dizziness accompanied by another flare of pain inside my head. I almost sink back down.

Gregg takes my arm, holds me up. "I think it might be best if you let me help you."

I'm too weak to argue, so I let him.

A minute later, I'm climbing the stairs into an unknown as dark as the one filling my head.

4

The house is enormous. I don't realize just *how* big until we are on the wide oak staircase that rises from the foyer toward the second floor. Gregg guides me along, a steadying hand on my elbow, and leads me down a dark hallway to the guest bedroom. Then he takes his leave.

Alone now, I crawl into the king-size bed, slip between the crisp sheets with the heavy comforter pulled up to my chin, and listen to the wind beyond the lead-paned window on the far side of the room. It howls and whistles, almost as if the night beyond that thin barrier of glass is alive.

The curtains are open a crack. I watch snow flurrying sideways in the gale, only to loop downward out of sight whenever there's a sufficient lull.

I can't believe I was out in that weather, lying frozen on the shore of Gravewater Lake. If I hadn't woken when I did, found shelter, that dark body of water would have lived up to its name and become a real-life watery grave. Even now, snug and cozy, I'm overcome by a bone-deep chill that I just can't shake. A phantom memory of that frigid ordeal weaves through every fiber of my being.

I shudder and slip lower under the covers, cocoon myself in their warm embrace, then lie there and resist the tears that threaten to flow. Because I'm in a strange place with no memory of who I am or where I was before I woke up at the edge of the lake. I press against the fog of amnesia that clouds my mind, cast some light into the void, but all

I get is stubborn blankness. Maybe tomorrow my mind will offer up a morsel. Some clue to my identity. Or maybe it won't. The only thing I can do is wait and see.

I close my eyes and force my panicked mind into quietude, but sleep remains elusive. And finally, just when I've lost all hope, I fall into a dreamless slumber . . .

◆ ◆ ◆

At least, until I'm jolted back awake sometime later by a thud.

I jerk upright in the bed. The covers fall away and crumple in my lap.

What the hell was that?

I strain to listen, heart pounding against my ribs.

It's still dark. The middle of the night.

I'm not alone here in this house. It was probably Gregg visiting the bathroom and closing a door too loudly. But I'm in a strange place, and Gregg is a stranger to me. Hell, I'm a stranger to myself. My brief slumber hasn't fixed whatever broke in my brain to deprive me of a past. Damn it. That in itself is enough to put me on edge. And now I realize something else. My bedroom door isn't even locked because, in my exhaustion, it never occurred to me.

I feel suddenly vulnerable. All I can think about is that door, and how easy it would have been for someone to enter the room while I was sleeping. Maybe that was what I heard. Not Gregg stumbling from his bed to answer the call of nature but slipping into my room and watching me while I slept.

The sudden thought surprises me, and I'm not sure why it even enters my head. After all, he's been good to me. Saved me from hypothermia. Provided me with a comfortable bed to sleep in. He doesn't seem like a creep. On the other hand, I know nothing about him. He could be a weirdo or, worse, a serial killer. Why is such a good-looking man sitting in a house all alone in the middle of nowhere? It's a little strange.

I suppress a shudder.

It's a ridiculous notion, right? After all, there was no one in my room when I woke up. I was alone. The bump I heard must have come from somewhere else in the house. But I want to lock the door all the same. It's the only way I'll feel safe now.

Pushing the covers back, I climb out of bed, shivering when the cold night air worms its way inside my flannel PJs. A faint ache pulses inside my skull. My muscles are sore when I stand. Reminders that something bad happened to me in the hours or minutes before I lost my memory.

The wind is still howling outside. The storm shows no sign of letting up. If anything, it's gotten worse. Snow is coming down harder than before.

I pad barefoot across the room to the door. There's a privacy lock on the handle. I go to push it but then stop and listen. Because I hear something else. Muffled voices. I can't make out what they are saying. It's like when you hear the slight murmur of a TV in another room. The sound travels, but the distance strips away everything but the low register, reducing the words to nothing but rhythmic noise.

Except I don't think this is a TV. There are no other sounds. No laugh track or background music. It sounds more . . . present.

Is it Gregg? I don't see how, since he claimed to be alone in the house. I wonder if he's on the phone, but then I remember what he told me.

Cell phones don't work up here, and the landline is down.

My hand is still on the handle. I turn it and open the door a crack. The hallway beyond my room is dark and empty.

I pull the door wider and poke my head out. Gathering my courage, I step into the hallway and start toward the voices, treading lightly. I still can't make out what they're saying and quicken my pace. Then, just when I think I'm getting close, my foot lands on a loose floorboard that shifts under my weight, emitting a tortured creak.

The voices cease as if on cue.

Silence hangs like lead in the air.

I stand stock still, terrified to move forward. Afraid to retreat. What exactly did I hear? Was it Gregg talking to someone, or just the sound of a TV after all? Did he turn it off when he heard the creak? Is he listening for me to make another noise even now as I listen for him?

I wait, praying that he won't come to investigate. I don't want him to catch me here, sneaking around his house in the middle of the night.

When he doesn't appear, I breathe easier and retrace my steps, careful to avoid the creaky board this time, and hurry back to my room.

Safely inside, I push the door closed and engage the lock, then return to my bed. But I don't fall back to sleep. Not now. Instead, I listen for those voices to return because I know what I heard, even if I can't make sense of it. And outside, providing an eerie backdrop to my insomnia, is the wind, which now sounds more alive to me than ever.

5

Adria

One Week Before

The day that Adria Rhodes set in motion the chain of events that would put her life in danger came two years, five months, and fourteen days after the one when she said *I do* to the man she once thought she would spend the rest of her life with.

But it didn't start out that way.

It was an unusually crisp and bright Saturday afternoon in January. The kind of glorious sunny day that made the rest of the frigid and snowy Boston winter tolerable.

She had spent the morning working from her home office and catching up on paperwork. Her husband, Peter, had told her more than once that she worked too much, and perhaps it was true. As president of the charitable foundation her grandfather had established over fifty years ago to give back some of the millions in profits from their family's business enterprises, she could work as much or as little as she wanted. When she had stepped into the role, everyone expected her to be more of a spokesperson for the foundation, a figurehead who would leave its day-to-day running to the board. After all, she was already wealthy in her own right, thanks to the substantial trust fund that had kicked in on her twenty-first birthday. But Adria had other ideas. She didn't want to be seen as some rich socialite with nothing better to do than attend fancy galas, jet off to exotic locales on a whim, and party the night away in exclusive clubs.

Instead, she was on a mission to prove that being wealthy wasn't the same thing as being entitled. Which was why she often ended up working longer hours than anyone else at the foundation. Some might have called her a workaholic, but Adria liked to think of herself as driven.

But not today, because she had the afternoon to herself. Peter had left their condo in the upscale suburb of Cambridge an hour earlier and climbed into a cab headed for the Charlton Club, which had occupied a brownstone overlooking Boston's Public Gardens since 1898. He would probably spend the entire afternoon and evening there, rubbing shoulders with the rich and powerful and drinking port so expensive that one bottle could pay the salary of the person serving it to him for an entire month.

Adria preferred to spend her free time engaged in a less stuffy pastime: shopping. Which was how she found herself at Harvard Square, bundled up in a thick wool sweater, jeans, and a pair of brown leather boots that were swiftly becoming her favorites. She strolled from store to store, ducking into a boutique here and there to browse racks of chic clothing under the hopeful gaze of the store clerks, who could tell the difference between a wistful browser and someone who could afford the high-priced fashions on display. If they were hoping to earn a nice commission, Adria disappointed them. She had more than enough clothes already, and eventually grew bored with looking at crop tops, denim jeans with holes in the knees, and short skirts.

Which was why, after popping into a coffee shop for a midafternoon caffeine hit, she ended up in a bookstore, wandering through the aisles in search of a perfect companion for the bottle of wine that was in her future just as soon as she returned home.

Except she never got that far, thanks to the girl in the black leather jacket.

Adria was standing at the table in the middle of the store, browsing through piles of recently released books, when she first noticed her. The young woman looked to be in her midtwenties. She wore a pair of faded and ripped jeans that were nothing like the trendy boutique offerings Adria had been perusing not long before. A black T-shirt peeked out from under the leather jacket. Her blond, highlighted hair was shaved on one side of her scalp and left to grow long on the other, giving her the strange appearance of two people in one. A snake tattoo wound its way up her neck and curled around the back of her ear.

She was observing Adria across the table with a gaze of such intensity that it sent a chill up her spine.

Adria put down the book she was looking at and stepped away from the table, walked back between two bookcases full of thrillers.

The exit was up ahead, beyond more tables of artfully arranged fiction. Bestsellers, works of critical acclaim, and new releases placed close to the front of the store to attract buyers.

When she looked back, the girl had moved and now stood near one bookcase with a book in her hand, watching with a sideways glance that she didn't bother to hide. Why was the woman staring like that? Her gaze felt menacing and deliberate.

Adria picked up the pace and reached the door. She fumbled to pull it open even as an older man wearing a black peacoat tried to enter. They got caught up and danced around each other for a moment, each trying to move aside for the other. Mumbling a quick apology, Adria sidestepped him and hurried out onto the street.

She turned toward her condo, which was a good fifteen-minute walk away, all thoughts of shopping now forgotten. The encounter with the woman in the bookstore had left her shaken, and all she wanted to do was get home and lock her door to the outside world. An Uber would take too long to get there, and when she looked around, there were no cabs in sight, so she started walking briskly. But then a thought occurred to her. What if she was being followed? The last thing Adria wanted to do was lead a dangerous stranger to her doorstep. She slowed and looked back over her shoulder toward the bookstore, relieved to see that there was no one behind her. The girl in the leather jacket was nowhere in sight. Even so, Adria walked faster, her hand resting on the cell phone in her jeans pocket. If anything happened, she could whip it out and phone 911 in an instant.

That made her feel a bit better.

But what made Adria feel really good was when she turned down a side street and saw the building that housed her third-floor condo ahead on the left.

She breathed a sigh of relief and hurried along, approaching the steps that led up to the front entrance even as she pulled from her pocket the key card that would open the front door.

At that moment, a dark shape stepped out from behind one of the pillars that supported the portico, blocking the steps and her entry into the building.

It was a man, thickset and unshaven, wearing a pair of grease-stained jeans and a faded black jacket. He looked as out of place standing under the portico of the exclusive Baldwin building as a penguin would in the Sahara.

Adria suppressed a scream and took a step back.

And there was the girl in the leather jacket, who had appeared out of nowhere and was now standing behind her, blocking Adria's retreat.

Adria glanced sideways down the street, but there was nobody around. Only the occasional car that paid them no heed. She summed up her chances of flagging down a vehicle.

The man shook his head. "I wouldn't if I were you," he said in a low voice.

"And keep your hands where we can see them," said the girl, noticing how Adria's hand still rested on the cell phone in her pocket.

"What do you want?" Adria forced herself to remain calm despite her unease. "I don't have any cash on me."

The woman grimaced. "This isn't a robbery. Is that what you think we are? Petty thieves?"

"Why else would you be following me?"

"We're looking for your husband," the man said in a brogue that sounded almost Irish. She recognized it as what the locals called a Southie accent, mostly associated with the roughest areas of South Boston, where it originated.

Adria shrank back. "Peter's not at home right now."

The man's gaze darted toward the lobby entrance. "You sure about that?"

"Quite sure."

"Well, then, how about you take us inside where it's more comfortable, and we'll wait for him to come back." The man's lips came together in a thin smile that almost looked smug.

"I don't know how long that will be, but it won't be soon. Maybe you should come back later."

"I don't think so." The man took a step forward. As he did so, his jacket shifted, and Adria glimpsed the unmistakable bulge of a concealed firearm. "We'll wait. I'm in no hurry."

"No!" Adria's throat tightened. The last thing she wanted was these people in her home. "How about I call him instead, and let you talk?"

The man nodded slowly. "That would be acceptable."

Thank God. Adria fumbled for her phone. Pulled it from her pocket and dialed Peter's number, waited while it rang four times before going to voicemail.

Shit.

She tried again, praying he would answer this time.

When it went to voicemail again, her visitor made a tutting sound. "Looks like we'll have to come inside, after all."

"One more try." Adria's throat was dry. She swallowed and dialed a third time.

One ring.

Two.

Three.

This was *not* good. If he didn't answer now, she would be powerless to stop the man with the gun and his female companion from forcing their way inside the condo. And after that, who knew what would happen? A slew of scenarios flashed through her mind. The strangers taking her hostage. The man raping her to pass the time while they waited. Worse, Peter coming home to find her lifeless corpse sprawled on the foyer tiles in a pool of blood. Or maybe he would just bide his time and use the gun on her husband instead. Surprise him with a bullet when he walked in. She considered hanging up. Dialing 911. But that would be pointless. Even if she got through, asked for help before the man at her door took the phone away, the cops would take too long to arrive. She would already be dead.

Just as she thought it would click over to voicemail yet again, a familiar voice filled her ear.

"Hey, baby, what's up?"

"Peter! Thank heavens. I was starting to think you weren't going to answer."

"It's loud here. I didn't hear the phone ring."

Then put it on vibrate, she thought. *For the love of God, put it on vibrate.* "There's someone here to see you."

The stranger reached out, snatched the phone from her hand, and lifted it to his ear. "Good afternoon . . . *Peter*. It's been a while."

Adria strained to hear her husband's response but couldn't.

After a brief pause, the stranger spoke again. "Well now, that's not a nice way to greet a buddy. This is a friendly visit, nothing more. A couple of old friends catching up. How about we keep it that way?"

Pause.

"Never mind how I found you. We need to talk."

Pause.

"Not over the phone. In person. I can wait with this pretty little thing at your house until you get here."

Another pause, longer this time.

"Fine. Our old meeting spot, then, but you better show up." The stranger met eyes with Adria, his gaze sending a chill down her spine. "Or I'll be forced to come back and pay another visit to this cutie you're shacking up with, and next time, I won't be making polite conversation."

He cocked his head to one side, listening to Peter's answer. Then he grinned. "I knew you'd come to your senses. See you in one hour. Don't be late."

The man hung up without waiting for Peter to say anything and handed the phone back to Adria.

"Much obliged," he said, then turned and strode away with the woman by his side.

Adria wasted no time in hurrying inside and closing the lobby door behind her. Then she made another call. But not to Peter. Instead, she dialed the one person who could find out why a man with a gun was looking for her husband.

6

Anna

Day One

I eventually fall asleep again. Or at least, I doze fitfully. When dawn breaks, I rise and go to the en suite, where I look at myself in the mirror.

The face of a thirtysomething stranger with hazel eyes, wavy dark brown hair that falls just past her shoulders, and a pert, upturned nose stares back at me. I'm pretty. Not beautiful, but certainly attractive enough, even if my face is marred right now. Because there's a fat ugly bruise above my left eye to go along with the lump on the back of my head. Whatever happened to me must have been violent.

I stare at my reflection for a moment longer, unnerved by the strange sensation of looking at a countenance you know is your own but cannot recall. Then I snap out of it and splash water on my face. My hair is a mess. I run my hands through it because I don't have a brush. The strands are thick and matted, probably because of my ordeal. I should take a shower, wash away the grime and dirt I picked up out on the lakeshore.

But not right now. Instead, I take care of my morning business and return to the bedroom.

Now another problem presents itself.

I have nothing to wear.

Gregg took my clothes the night before. The thought of him peeling them off my unconscious body, lying there naked to his gaze, makes my skin crawl, but what else was he going to do? I was drenched and could hardly do it myself under the circumstances. Better a little embarrassment than hypothermia. For all I know, he saved my life.

Somehow, that doesn't make it any better.

Neither does the fact that the only clothes I have might be ruined. He said my blouse was torn and my jeans were stained. If only I could remember where I came from, I might be able to get some fresh clothes. Of course, if I had my memories, I wouldn't have just spent the night in the house of a man I don't know.

On a whim, I go to the bedroom closet, pull the doors open. It's empty save for three wire hangers dangling from the rod. The dresser is the same. Four empty drawers.

But really, what did I expect?

If I want some clothes, I'll have to ask Gregg.

I close the dresser drawers and make my way to the bedroom door. I open it and peek outside. The hallway beyond is empty, but I hear faint noises drifting up from the floor below.

He must be up already.

I step from the room, close the door behind me, and go downstairs.

I find him in a huge kitchen with a center island the size of a small country. There are two French-door Viking refrigerators side by side, a six-burner gas stove, and a pair of expensive-looking ovens set into the wall. A wine cooler taller than me caps off the luxury. He is standing at the stove with a frying pan in front of him and a spatula in his hand. A carton of eggs is open on the counter. The aroma of coffee fills the air. It smells heavenly, and I learn another tidbit about myself. I like to drink coffee.

"Good morning." He turns at my approach, taps the index finger of his free hand to his forehead, and furrows his brow. "Any luck?"

I purse my lips and shake my head. "Still a blank."

"Ah." Gregg observes me with narrowed eyes. "I'm sorry."

"Me too."

"How are you feeling this morning? Do you still have a headache? Any nausea, or sensitivity to bright lights?" Gregg lays the spatula on the island and looks at me, his eyes resting on the bruise above my left eye.

"I still have a little headache, and the back of my head and the bruise on my forehead hurt if I touch them, but no, I don't feel sick or have any issue with bright lights bothering me."

"Good. Then it's unlikely that you have a concussion, or if you do, it must be mild." He turns around and opens a cabinet door, pulls out a bottle of ibuprofen, then slides it across the island toward me. "Here, take these and use them as needed. They will help with the headache and the tenderness as well, I expect."

"Thank you." I grab the bottle and move it so that it will be within easy reach when I have my coffee. Then I fold my arms and press them to my chest, feeling vulnerable and exposed. "I don't have anything to wear."

It must take a moment for my predicament to sink in; then his shoulders slump. "Of course. How silly of me. I put your clothes in the wash last night."

"Yes."

"They should be dry by now. I can fetch them, but you might not be pleased. They aren't in great condition. Your top is a goner, I'm afraid. That rip got bigger. I'm not sure it's still wearable."

This is bad. I can't wear nothing but flannel pajamas twenty-four hours a day. I cling to a hope that it isn't as awful as he says. "I'll have to make do."

Gregg turns the burner off and slides the pan to one side. He looks me up and down. "I can help."

"You can?"

"Yup." He takes off toward the stairs.

When I don't move, he turns around. "Well, are you coming?"

"You don't need to give me your clothes." Maybe the PJs aren't so bad, especially since Gregg is at least six inches taller than me and muscular. A shirt might work, but there's no way anything else of his will fit.

"I'm not. Just trust me."

"Okay. Fine." I follow behind, curious to see where this is going.

We climb to the second floor, where he leads me to what turns out to be a main bedroom so large, you could live in it. There's a sitting area with a sofa and two chairs, a king bed even fancier than the one in my room, and a stone fireplace with a pair of leather chairs facing it.

There's also what turns out to be an enormous walk-in closet with a bench down the middle. On one side are men's clothes arranged by pants, button-down shirts, and polos. On the other are women's clothes. Whole racks of them. Summer dresses in light cotton. Jeans. Skirts. Shirts. A shoe rack low to the floor loaded with every conceivable type of footwear.

I stare at the dizzying array of clothes in confusion. "I thought you lived alone?"

"I do." Gregg pushes his hands into his pockets and takes a long breath. "These belonged to my wife. She died."

"I'm so sorry."

"I can't bring myself to get rid of them," he says at length. "Now I'm glad because you have something to wear. They look to be about your size."

I'm not sure I want to wear a dead woman's clothes. It's weird, especially around Gregg. Some of these items probably hold memories for him. "Are there any clothes you want me to avoid?"

"Not really. They're only going to waste sitting here on hangers. Help yourself." Gregg backs up toward the door. "I should get back to the kitchen. The eggs are getting cold. I'll leave you to get dressed. Breakfast will be ready when you come down."

"Thank you." I watch him leave, then turn my attention to the closet. I start with the drawers. I find undergarments. As much as the idea of wearing another woman's underwear creeps me out, I'm not wandering around a strange house with a strange man without wearing panties. *Ick.* Thankfully, I spot several pairs and matching bras with the tags still attached. These will do nicely.

Next, I examine the heaving racks of clothes. There are so many choices. I flip through them, pulling items down and holding them against myself in front of a full-length mirror standing near the back wall of the closet. I come across a gorgeous cream-colored cashmere sweater. The fabric is so soft, I can't help but run my hands over it.

This is a keeper.

I slip it off the hanger and grab a pair of navy-blue linen pants, mostly because I figure they will fit better than the jeans, which all look tailored. When I put them on, I'm surprised. They could be made for me. Even the length is perfect. Maybe I should try the jeans. But I'm dressed now and too hungry to bother swapping clothes.

I fold the flannel PJs and step out of the closet, carrying them under my arm, then make my way toward the landing and my bedroom, where I intend to drop them off for later. Assuming I'm still here then, that is. But when I reach the stairs, I see a figure descending quickly.

It's Gregg.

I stop and watch him, confused. He was supposed to be going back to the kitchen to finish making breakfast, so why was he upstairs? My thoughts turn to the previous night, when I got the feeling someone might have been in my room, watching me sleep. I'd quickly dismissed the idea as crazy, but now I wonder. Because I can think of only one reason that he would still be upstairs. To spy on me while I got dressed.

Again, the rational side of my brain kicks in. There must be a reasonable explanation. Maybe he forgot something and came back up. After all, I didn't sense anyone lurking out in the bedroom while I was in the closet. And it is *his* house. He's allowed to walk around it if he so pleases. Yet as I watch him disappear back into the kitchen, I can't shake a sense that something is not right. But what it is, I have no idea.

7

When I enter the kitchen, a plate of scrambled eggs topped with blistered cherry tomatoes and toast is waiting for me on the island, along with a steaming mug of coffee. A carton of cream and a bowl of sugar sit next to the mug. I'm impressed. And hungry.

Gregg is already digging into his own breakfast.

"Wow," he says as I approach the island. "You look . . . different."

I drop my gaze, uncomfortable with his attention. An image of him standing outside the closet, of those piercing blue eyes watching me through the gap between the door and the frame, flits through my head. I decide to get some answers.

"I heard noises last night," I say. "A bump and what sounded like voices. They woke me up."

Gregg puts his fork down. "I went downstairs around two for a bottle of water. I was thirsty. Maybe that's what you heard."

"And the voices?"

"No voices. You're the only other person in the house. Maybe you dreamed them."

"I was awake."

"Then I don't know." He shrugs. "But you had a nasty knock. Actually, more than one knock, judging by that bruise on your forehead. Maybe you only thought you heard them."

"Is that even a thing?" I have no idea if a knock on the head makes you hear noises that aren't really there. It doesn't sound plausible. Then again, I'm not an expert, and even if I were, I wouldn't remember it.

"Beats me." Gregg dives back into his eggs.

"How did your wife die?" I ask. He's so young to be widowed—probably no older than forty.

"Cancer." He looks away when he answers. "I'd rather not talk about that."

None of my business. Got it. Still . . . "It must get lonely, living here all alone so far from civilization, especially in winter."

"I like solitude. And I don't live here all the time. It's mostly a summer home, just like the other houses around the lake. I only drive up when I want to get away. Feel closer to my wife. She loved it here in the winter. We used to spend the holidays here."

"I thought you said the road was impassable because of the storm."

"It is right now, but it wasn't a few days ago."

"I guess I'm lucky the storm didn't blow in earlier, then; otherwise, the house would have been empty, and I would have frozen to death." If this is his second home, how big is the first one?

"I guess."

"Where do you live the rest of the year?"

Gregg finishes the last of his eggs. "Look, I don't mean to be rude, but can we talk about something else?"

"Sorry. I didn't mean to pry."

"That's okay." Gregg's tone softens. "And besides, I'm not the only person who was here before the storm. You were too, even if you can't remember it."

"I've been trying to remember." The blank slate of my mind infuriates me. It also worries me. What if my memory loss is permanent? What if I have brain damage? I wish we weren't snowed in, so Gregg could take me to the nearest town to get medical help. I'm trying not to panic, but it's hard. "Are you sure you don't recognize me?"

"I would have told you last night if I did."

"Maybe I came from one of the other houses. You must know some of the other residents."

"Not really. I keep to myself. That's the point of having such a remote home."

"You don't know anyone?" I can't keep the surprise from my voice.

"I'm not the social type. And anyway, most of the other owners rent their houses out when they're not here, so people are always coming and going, especially in the summer. Short-term renters don't care much about making friends." Gregg looks at my food, which I've been pushing around the plate. "You should really finish that."

"I thought I was hungry, but I've lost my appetite." My situation is getting the better of me. I don't like not knowing who I am, and even though it's probably just my imagination, I feel like Gregg is holding back. I slide the plate away. "I'd like to go down to the lake. To see where I woke up."

Gregg takes the plate and drops the half-eaten eggs into the trash. "You think you'll find a clue to your identity out there?"

"Maybe. It was so dark last night, I wouldn't have seen anything even if I was thinking straight. Especially with the storm."

"Makes sense. But I wouldn't get your hopes up. It's been snowing all night. There probably aren't any footprints or anything left by now."

"I'd like to go, anyway." I hop down off my stool and gulp the last of the coffee. Even if I don't feel like eating, I'm not turning down caffeine, especially since I still feel a bit lightheaded.

Gregg observes me for a moment, then nods. "Okay. But I'm going with you."

"You don't have to do that."

"I know." He glances down at my feet, which are currently snug inside a pair of thick wool socks I found in a drawer inside the closet. "We'll need to find you some decent footwear first, though."

"There were shoes upstairs. I don't know if they fit me. I didn't try any of them on."

"I can do you one better." Gregg is already on his way toward the foyer. "There are boots in the mudroom. And you'll need a coat too."

I follow him past the stairs to a small room next to the back door—the same door I came to the previous evening—where he finds me a pair of boots that fit surprisingly well. He also hands me a thick winter jacket. Then we're off into the bleak winter landscape that waits on the other side of the door.

8

The storm has mostly passed. Snowflakes still linger in the air but only fall in light flurries now. We trudge toward the lake, our feet sinking deep into a blanket of virgin snow. My footprints from the night before, when I stumbled up to Gregg's door, are gone, covered as if they never existed. Once or twice, I spot what I think might be a vague foot-shaped depression in the great white expanse, but I can't say for certain if I made it or it's just a random feature of the landscape beneath the snow.

One thing is for certain: I won't be following a trail of footprints back to wherever I came from. Not that it was likely, anyway. I was in the lake before I woke up. My drenched clothes and sorry state were a testament to that fact. Also, there's the vague recollection that flashed through my mind the night before of slipping beneath the surface of what I have since learned is Gravewater Lake. It was only a momentary fragment that I'm not sure can even be called a genuine memory. It was more of a vague feeling than anything tangible. But it's the one clue I have regarding my life before I was reborn on that frigid shoreline.

"You okay, there?" Gregg asks, glancing sideways at me. His misty breath hangs in the air before being snatched away on the breeze. "You're very quiet."

"I'm trying to remember," I reply as my gaze drifts over the scene ahead of me. The lake is flat and calm, surrounded by trees that cluster together to form a dark and impenetrable wall of evergreens. Here and there, I glimpse a house close to the shore. Nothing is familiar. My surroundings are as much a mystery now as they were the previous evening. I look at the dock. Is that where I fell into the water? It doesn't seem likely, considering the occupant of the only house within walking distance of the dock doesn't know who I am. Yet I turn my head to look back at the house, anyway, hoping it will spark recognition.

And in that moment, I'm overcome by a wave of dizziness.

I falter, almost go down, but Gregg is fast. He grabs me. Keeps me upright.

"Whoa. Easy there." His arm is around my waist, hand flat against the bottom of my rib cage. He brings us to a halt. "Maybe we should go back. You're obviously still suffering from that knock to the head."

"I'm fine. Just give me a moment." The dizziness is fading, but I'm not sure that I trust my legs just yet. We stand there for another minute with Gregg supporting me. Then I nod and ease myself away from him.

"All good?" he asks.

"Yes." I continue toward the lake, trying to gauge exactly where I woke up. Just like my footprints, the snow has covered the spot where I was lying, but I see the vaguest of depressions where the land meets the water, which I assume to be the place. Apart from that, the area is pristine. There is nothing here that would tell me who I am or where I came from. Not even my missing slipper is there. It probably came off in the water and is at the bottom of the lake by now. Not that it would be of any help, anyway.

"This is the spot?" Gregg stands with his hands on his hips and looks around.

"Right here, next to the lake. My legs were still in the water." I shiver at the memory despite the warm coat and boots I'm wearing.

"No wonder you were frozen. You're lucky you didn't get frostbite."

"Tell me about it." I walk to the shore and stare out over the water. There is a house sitting directly opposite me on the other side. It is tucked in between the trees and barely visible. I can just make out a wooden dock in front of it but can't tell if a boat is docked there. For a moment, I wonder if this is where I came from, but it doesn't seem likely. It's such a long distance across the lake that I surely would have drowned long before I washed ashore on this side. I look away, dropping my gaze, and in doing so, I catch a brief glint of something at my feet, caught among the pebbles and sandy loam.

I bend down, reach toward the object, and am surprised to see a small round white pearl with a sliver of silver chain attached to each side. It looks like part of a necklace.

I pick it up.

The chain is dainty and thin. The pearl shimmers as the sun breaks through the clouds and bathes us in a soft, wintry glow.

"You found something?"

I turn to Gregg and hold my hand out for him to see. "A necklace. Or at least, a part of one."

"You think it's yours?"

"It must be." I can't see any other way it would be right here, so close to where I woke up.

"Looks expensive." Gregg reaches out, pushes the collar of my coat aside, and pulls the sweater away from my neck.

"What are you doing?"

"Checking something." His fingers brush the skin beneath my ear ever so lightly, sending a tingle down my spine. "If the chain got ripped off, it might have left a mark."

"Did it?" I don't remember seeing anything when I was looking in the mirror earlier that morning.

"No." He withdraws his hand. "Your neck is fine."

I look down at the ground, wondering if more of the necklace is close by, but see nothing.

Gregg paces along the shoreline for several feet in each direction, conducting his own search. Then he turns back to me. "There's nothing else here, and it's freezing. We should go back to the house."

I don't want to go back. I want to figure out who I am, and this is the only place that might give me that answer. But he's right. There's nothing else here. Just that fragment of a pearl necklace that I now clutch in my hand. I have a feeling it's important. But I can't fathom why.

9

When we get back to the house, Gregg leads me to the sofa and insists that I sit down. The dizziness hasn't returned, but apparently, he's taking no chances. I have a light headache, though, and I ask him for more painkillers.

He obliges, saying he'll grab the bottle I left in the kitchen and a mug of hot tea, which he appears to think is a cure-all for both my headache and the wider side effects of whatever happened to me last night. He returns five minutes later and watches me take the pills, then says that he's stepping back out.

This surprises me, and I ask where he's going. He's already told me that the road to town is impassable because of the storm.

"Figured I'd take a look around," he replies. "Maybe you had an accident. Went off the road in your car, or even into the brook that feeds the lake."

"If I had an accident on the road, how did I end up beside the lake?" I ask.

"I don't know. Maybe you were looking for help and got lost."

"Or maybe the road isn't as bad as you think."

Gregg shakes his head. "I tried to drive into town yesterday before you showed up, but the snow was already too deep, and there's been no sign of the plow. It's probably even worse now. I'll have to walk. I'll be gone for a couple of hours. Will you be okay here all on your own?"

I tell him I will.

He tells me not to go anywhere, to stay where I am and rest. Then he departs.

I'm alone in the house now. And I'm curious.

Ignoring Gregg's advice, I stand and look around the living room. Something has been bothering me ever since the previous night. He said the house made him feel closer to his dead wife, yet I don't see a single picture of her anywhere. No photos of them together. No portraits on the mantel. Nothing. The living room is gorgeous, with fine furnishings, but it feels . . . sterile.

I find that odd, especially since he hasn't been able to part with her clothes. And now that I think about it, I don't remember seeing any photos of her in the main bedroom either. A space where they would have shared their most intimate moments.

I want to confirm my suspicions.

A minute later, I'm upstairs in Gregg's room. I was right. Apart from the clothes and shoes in the closet, there are no other outward signs of a female presence anywhere. The least I would have expected was a photograph on his nightstand.

I leave the bedroom behind and go back downstairs. I wander through the rest of the ground floor. There is a study behind the living room. A desk sits in the middle. There are bookshelves and a wingback chair in the corner near the window, but no obvious personal items. Once again, no outward sign that Gregg ever had a wife. On the other side of the foyer is a dining room that connects to the kitchen. I wander through it and soon find myself on the other side of the island where Gregg was making breakfast earlier.

Now I see another fridge sitting under the counter. Like the taller wine fridge, it has a glass door, but instead of wine bottles, I see rows of cans behind the frosty glass.

I open it—wondering just how many refrigerators one kitchen needs—and pull out a can, which turns out to be a cheap domestic beer. The kind a gas station or grocery store might sell. I root around some more, coming up with another brand of domestic light beer. They are an anomaly. Not the sort of beers I would expect the owners of a house like this to drink. Especially since the wines in the other fridge look expensive. At least, if the row of bottles standing at forty-five degrees on an exhibition shelf is any indication.

I don't know what to make of it, but Gregg is clearly drinking these beers, because when I open the cupboard next to the fridge, I find a slide-out trash receptacle with two bins. The first one is full of assorted kitchen waste. The other bin is for recycling. It is almost full and contains crushed empties of both brands of beer.

I close the cupboard and look around. There is a butler's pantry on the far side of the kitchen, the shelves stocked with provisions. I see nothing else of interest and wander back into the foyer and past the stairs toward the front door.

I notice another closed door in the hallway, which I open to find the laundry room. There's a small pile of folded clothes on top of the dryer. My clothes. I pick up the shirt, unfold it, and look at it. It has a tear across the front from the shoulder down to the waist. Despite the shirt being washed, dirty smears still stain the white fabric. I feel no connection to the garment, no glimmer of recognition, which is disappointing. Then I unfold the jeans. They are cute, with a drop waist and a slight boot-cut flare. She . . . I . . . have good taste. But they don't feel familiar any more than the shirt. *Come on. These are mine. I chose these clothes, shopped for them, wore them. Why can't I remember them?*

I toss the jeans aside in frustration. I'd held some hope that seeing the clothes would jog my memory. Under the jeans are my undergarments. A pale blue, lacy bra with a little bow in the middle and matching underwear. I involuntarily shudder at the thought of a stranger touching these, removing them from my limp body. I pick up the bra, finger the little bow and delicate lace, and finally, something feels familiar. I recognize the pattern, the color. I hold the garment tighter, squeeze my eyes shut and try to latch on to the feeling. If I can capture this moment, maybe a single memory can pull all the others forward. But even as I think this, the feeling fades and is soon gone.

I open my eyes and stare at the bra, now just a pretty lacy thing that has no meaning. I drop it on top of the other clothes, walk out, and slam the door behind me harder than necessary. The crack of wood on wood sends a stab of pain through my head, and I instantly regret my display of frustration.

I turn toward the front door. Opening it, I peer out into the wintry expanse beyond. There is a circular driveway that hasn't been plowed. The snow lies thick in an unbroken sheet of crystalline whiteness. There is a three-bay garage to my right. Snow has drifted up against the doors. I see no footprints leading away from the house. Gregg must have gone out the back door and across the deck, just like when we went down to the lake earlier to look around.

Retreating into the house, I return to the living room, eager to warm up in front of the fire. There's a reading nook with a bench beside the bay window that overlooks the lake. Built-in shelves on each side of the fireplace hold an eclectic assortment of decorative items and hardback books.

Still no photographs of Gregg and his wife, but for the first time, I see a woman's touch.

The books are a mixture of thrillers that I can imagine a man like Gregg reading and historical romances that I'm sure he wouldn't. I browse the shelves, clueless regarding my own reading habits, and pull down several volumes only to put them back again. Eventually, I settle upon a domestic thriller, which I take to the reading nook. I sit with the book open on my lap and wait for Gregg to come back—hopefully with news about where I came from and who I am.

10

Adria

Five Days Before

When Adria entered the coffee shop, Harvey Lang, head of corporate security for both the foundation and her family's many companies, was already waiting at a table near the back.

She went to the counter and ordered a drink, then made her way toward him. As she reached the table, he stood and shook her hand.

"Adria," he said with a smile. "It's been a while since we last talked."

"Too long," Adria replied. She liked Harvey. He'd been around since she was a kid and was about as close to a family friend as anyone outside her father's elite social circle could ever be. He was loyal, trustworthy, and knew more than a few family secrets she was sure he would take to his grave. "I'm so grateful that you agreed to meet with me like this. I know it's unusual, but I didn't know who else to call."

"Not at all." Harvey sat back down and waited for Adria to do the same before continuing. "I'm always here for you. Now tell me, what's all this about?"

"I don't know where to begin." Adria shifted in her seat, tapped her fingers nervously against the side of the disposable coffee cup. "I'm worried about Peter. Something's wrong. I've had this feeling in my gut for a while. I tried to ignore it at first, figured it was just my imagination, but . . ."

"I'm listening."

"Now, I'm not so sure, and it scares me." She took a trembling breath. "I don't think Peter is the man I thought he was. I think . . ." She hesitated, almost as if saying the words out loud made them even more true. "I think he's been lying to me."

"Why?" Harvey narrowed his eyes. "Do you have any proof?"

"No. Like I said, it's just a feeling, but I can't shake it. And then yesterday afternoon, this couple showed up at our condo looking for him. A man with a Southie accent, and a woman with a snake tattoo going up her neck. And . . ."

"And what?"

"The guy had a gun. He was carrying it under his coat, like in a shoulder holster. I didn't actually see it, but I saw the bulge, and there's nothing else it could have been."

Harvey rubbed his chin. "And you've never seen this man before?"

"No." Adria shook her head. "I would have remembered."

"Okay." Harvey nodded. "Tell me what happened."

Adria did. She told him about the man wanting to wait for Peter. About the conversation on the telephone—or at least the side of it she could hear. Then she told him about the threat to come back if Peter didn't show up at wherever they had arranged to meet.

Harvey waited for her to finish before speaking again. "Did you ask Peter about this?"

"Of course I did. He blew it off. Said that the guy was an old college friend looking to catch up, which is ridiculous. This guy never stepped foot anywhere near a college. I'd bet a million bucks on it. And certainly not Cornell, where Peter says he went. The guy was so . . . lowbrow." Adria bit her bottom lip. "I don't know how it got to this, Harvey. Peter has changed. He was so charming when we first met."

Adria looked down at her coffee and barely heard Harvey's reply as her mind drifted to another place and time.

◆ ◆ ◆

The gallery was full of the kind of people Adria despised. Pretentious people who talked in hushed whispers about the art hanging from the walls as if they had some personal insight into the artist's mind. Which they didn't.

If anyone knew the mind of the recent art scene sensation Frederick Lange, it was Adria. They had been friends since childhood. They went to the same private school, then found themselves at Harvard together. She'd even introduced him to his wife, Laura, at a party during their senior year more than a decade ago. Adria knew him better than anyone, and she certainly knew that the prattling collectors and art investors drinking champagne and pontificating about the hidden depths and meaning of his abstract works were spouting hot air to convince themselves that a square of unframed canvas covered with swirling patterns of dense impasto oil paint was worth the money they were about to shell out for it.

Not that his paintings weren't good. Adria liked them well enough, but she didn't buy into the hype. The same couldn't be said for Frederick. Right now, he was holding court and lapping up the compliments and comments about the depths of his artistic talent. She couldn't blame him. Who didn't like their ego stroked? And Frederick certainly had one of those.

She smiled to herself, thinking back to a few weeks ago when she, Frederick, and Laura were hanging out at his studio, drinking way too much wine on a Saturday night while he worked to finish up the final piece needed for the exhibit. Frustrated with the way the painting was turning out—declaring that it lacked depth and emotion—he handed a brush to Laura and another to Adria, then told them to have at it. The women drank and splattered paint on the canvas. Swished and swirled and laughed their way up and down, side to side.

Her gaze swept across the room to the finished piece dominating the opposite wall. He'd named it Joyful Friends with Pinot. *There was a little red dot next to the outrageous price. Sold.*

Her attention wandered toward the door. She sipped her drink and wondered how long politeness dictated she had to stay before slipping out and returning to her condo on a quiet side street a few blocks from Harvard Square. Curling up with a good book and a hot cup of tea sounded divine. Duty done. Friend supported. Enjoy the rest of the night in.

"You look about as eager to be here as I am," a voice said from somewhere to her rear.

She turned to find a tall stranger with striking blue eyes, a square jaw, and dark hair standing there. He held a glass of champagne in one hand and a brochure for the art exhibit in the other. Maybe the book and tea could wait a little longer.

"I'm just here to support my friend," Adria said, tipping her head toward Frederick, who was still surrounded by a gaggle of admirers on the other side of the room.

"Doesn't look like he knows that." The man tucked the brochure into his jacket pocket and held out a hand. "I'm Peter."

"Adria."

"Pretty name." He smiled. "It suits you."

"Thanks." A tinge of heat reddened Adria's cheeks. She turned away briefly so he wouldn't see it. When she looked back, he was still looking at her, a mildly bemused expression on his face. She tried not to blush again and said the first thing that came to her. "I should probably go mingle or something."

"Or you could leave with me."

"What?"

"You're clearly bored, and I'd love an excuse to sneak out. These gallery events are all the same. It would be a mutually beneficial arrangement."

"Ah. We're using each other as cover. I see." Adria placed her empty champagne glass on the tray of a passing server. "What do we do once we're outside? Shake hands and go our separate ways?"

"Not unless you want to." Peter glanced around. "I was thinking we could grab a bite to eat. Get to know each other better."

"At nine thirty on a Saturday night in Boston? Good luck with that unless you want a burger and fries."

"I know a place we can go."

"Where?"

"Wait and see. It's not far."

"Everywhere is far in the city."

"Is that a no?" Peter finished his drink and set the empty glass down.

"Can I trust you?"

Peter smiled. "I'm inviting you out to dinner in public, not back to my lair. You'll have fun, I promise. And afterward, I'll get you safely into a taxi."

"You have a lair?" Adria couldn't help but laugh.

"I have a town house in Back Bay if that counts." Peter glanced toward the door. "What do you say?"

Adria gave Frederick one more look, noting that his admirers still distracted him. She was not sure he even knew she had shown up. "Sounds good. Let's go."

Adria took a sip of her coffee, struggled to focus on the present, but the past refused to release its grip on her. She just could not understand how Peter, once so kind and thoughtful, had turned into a man she barely recognized. The night when they first met felt like a century ago. It was hard to believe it was less than three years earlier.

When they arrived at the place Peter wanted to eat, Adria was taken aback. Pierre-Jacques was one of the finest French restaurants in the city, and just down the street from the swanky gallery they had just escaped. "This is where

you had in mind? We're never going to get in. It's almost impossible to get a reservation, let alone walk in right off the street."

"Have a little faith." Peter pulled the door open and waited for her to enter, then stepped up to the maître d' station, where he talked in hushed whispers with the man who held the rest of their evening in his hands. A minute later, Peter returned. "All set. They were happy to fit us in."

"How?" Adria wasn't sure what to think. She had eaten at Pierre-Jacques twice before, and both times she was forced to make a reservation more than three months out, despite her status as the daughter of one of the city's most prominent figures. If a wealthy socialite couldn't get the restaurant to bend the rules, she could hardly see how Peter managed such a feat. And a walk-in, no less.

He shrugged. "I just explained who we are, and since it's so late, he was able to find us a table."

"And exactly who are we?" Adria wondered what Peter had said to get them such swift service.

"That's not important. What matters is that we're not going to starve tonight." Peter motioned for her to follow the maître d', who showed them to a small table near the back of the restaurant.

After they settled down, Peter ordered a bottle of merlot and stared across the table at Adria. "I was dreading going to that stuffy art opening, but now I'm glad that I did."

"Are you an art collector?"

"Sometimes. Mostly in an amateur capacity." Peter unfurled his napkin and placed it on his lap. "But not tonight. I was just there as a favor. The gallery owner is an acquaintance of mine. We've done some business together before. He likes the place to look full. It encourages the buyers to move fast."

"Ah. Then if you're not an art collector, what is your business?"

"Oh, this and that." Peter waved a hand in the air. "I'm sure you'd find it boring."

"No, really, I'm interested," Adria said. The man had a town house in Back Bay. Whatever he did for a living paid well. Actually, it paid more than well. Not to mention that he had convinced the maître d' of a fancy restaurant that was booked for months to let them in just like that. Peter intrigued her. In her circle, it was not unusual for a date to show off his wealth and influence, but somehow, this felt different. Like it was natural for him, not for show or to impress her.

"I'd rather not talk about business tonight if you don't mind. Not when I'm in the company of such a beautiful woman."

"I already agreed to have dinner with you." Adria looked away quickly, then back to Peter. "You don't need to keep flattering me."

"It's not flattery if it's true." Peter reached across the table. His hand brushed hers. He touched the silver bracelet on her wrist, turning it to reveal an inscription. "A. For Adria."

"My father gave it to me for my sixteenth birthday." She slid her hand back, subtly breaking contact. "It's silly, I know, but even after all these years, I still like to wear it."

"It's not silly." Peter met her gaze across the table, his eyes under the restaurant's lights appearing even bluer than before. "I think it's fantastic that you have something that means so much to you."

Adria stared back at him, wondering just who this dark, handsome stranger really was.

"Adria." Harvey's voice cut through the fog.

She snapped back to the present. "Sorry. I was miles away. What were you saying?"

"This isn't really my area of expertise. I handle corporate security. Cyber breaches. Industrial espionage. Arranging security to make sure you and your family are safe when you travel. That sort of thing. You might be better off with a private detective."

"And making sure we're safe at home too," Adria countered. "I don't feel safe there. Not anymore."

"I can't provide security to protect you from your own husband. How would that even work?" Harvey sat back in his chair and folded his arms. "If you think Peter is a threat, perhaps you should speak to the police."

"No." Adria shook her head. "I need you. Not a private eye. Not some detective who won't do anything until it's too late." She leaned forward. "I just want you to do some digging. See what you can find out about Peter. See if he's in some sort of trouble. If anyone can get to the bottom of it, you can. Please, I'm begging you . . ."

Harvey sighed. "Look, I'll do my best. Reach out to some of my contacts in the business, people who will find more answers than I can on my own, and see what they tell me, okay?"

"That's all I'm asking." Relief washed over Adria. "Thank you."

"Don't thank me yet. I can't guarantee I'll find anything, and if I do, you might not like what you hear."

"I'll take that chance."

"Very well." Harvey reached into his jacket and brought out a phone, which he pushed across the table to her.

"What's this?"

"A burner. I use them sometimes to keep in contact with sources without going through regular channels or arousing suspicion."

Adria looked at the phone. "Isn't this a little much?"

"Maybe. But I don't like to take chances. That's why I'm so good at my job. I try to anticipate all eventualities. You live with Peter. Your regular phone is too much of a risk." Harvey met Adria's gaze. "Look, I know it's probably unnecessary, but if there really is something shady going on, we don't want to tip your husband off that we know, do we?"

"I guess not." Adria took the phone.

"Good. Keep it close, but don't let Peter see it. Understand?"

Adria nodded.

"Good. And don't forget to set a passcode. Something he won't guess. No face ID. That's important. It'll be too easy for him to make you open it under duress."

Adria nodded again. Would Peter really do such a thing? She didn't want to find out.

"Fantastic. I'll make contact as soon as I have something." Harvey stood up, gripping the coffee he'd barely touched in one hand. "Give me a few days on this, okay?"

"Okay." Adria examined the phone, which was identical to the one she used for work. It was one expensive burner, and even better, it wouldn't raise suspicion if Peter saw it. Unless she had both phones out at the same time, which she didn't intend to do. She touched the screen, saw that it was bare bones with hardly any apps installed. Only the essentials. Likewise, there was only one number in the address book. She went to the settings, created a passcode that Peter couldn't possibly know. The combination of her locker in high school, which had stuck in her mind all these years. Random enough not to be guessed, but simple for her to remember.

When she looked up, Harvey was gone.

Adria gathered her purse, slipped the burner phone inside, and headed for the door. She stepped outside and started toward her car, which was parked two blocks away on a side street. And then she saw it. A dark red Mercedes SUV with tinted windows that looked an awful lot like Peter's vehicle crawling past in the clogged Boston traffic, its license plate hidden from view by other cars. Her chest tightened. It couldn't possibly be him. How would he even know where she was? But even so, she stopped and watched as the Mercedes reached an intersection and turned from view, too far away now for Adria to read the plate and know for sure.

She watched a moment longer, trying to reason away the sighting. There were plenty of red Mercedes SUVs in the city, right? Except *that* red was a custom-color option, which meant it wouldn't be anywhere near as common. She remembered Peter complaining about the time it took for the dealership to deliver the car after they'd bought it. Still, there must be at least a few other Mercedes in that custom red somewhere around town. Just seeing one shouldn't give her cause for concern. It was probably nothing but a coincidence. Yet as she hurried toward her own vehicle, she couldn't shake the sense of unease and a feeling that her life was going to get a lot more complicated . . . and dangerous.

11

ANNA

Day One

Gregg returns an hour after I settle down to read. When I hear him come in, I jump up. By the time he removes his coat and boots and exits the mudroom, I'm waiting in the foyer.

"Well, did you find anything?" I'm eager to hear what he has to say.

He rubs his hands together, then blows on them. "No. I walked along the road all the way to the bridge that crosses the brook but didn't see anything. If you came here by car, I didn't find it."

My heart falls. If there was a vehicle out there somewhere that belonged to me, the mystery would be solved. There would be a registration document with my name on it. I would know who I am, even if I still don't know why I came here. Damn it. Gregg's failure to find anything leaves me in limbo, as much a stranger to myself as before.

Gregg has more bad news. "It gets worse. The bridge is out."

"Oh no." I bite my lip. "That sounds bad."

"It is, but not unexpected. The brook swells when it snows. There's nowhere else for the water to go. A few years ago, it got washed away during a storm. And it doesn't look like they've sent a plow to open up the road yet. They probably don't even know the bridge is damaged. We could be stuck here for a while."

"For how long?" Panic rises within me. I want to get out of here. I *need* to find out who I am.

"Well, the last time the bridge got washed away, it took them three weeks to rebuild it, and that storm was nowhere near as bad as this one."

"You were stranded here for three weeks with no way to get out?" My panic turns to horror.

"Not quite. We weren't here at the time. But the caretaker couldn't check on the place for over a month. It was a concern, but luckily, the house came through undamaged."

"You really think we'll be stuck here that long?" The house is remote, and it doesn't even have a working phone line. There's no cell service here either, according to Gregg. We are truly cut off from the outside world. "What if we run out of food? What if the power goes out?"

"Don't worry. We have a well-stocked kitchen and a thirty-two-thousand-watt backup generator that can run the entire house if we lose power. The water is from a well, and the pump runs off the same generator. We'll be fine."

It doesn't feel fine. "Why would it take them so long to fix the bridge? They must know there are houses around the lake."

"I'm sure they do, but like I said, most of them are closed up in the fall and not reopened until the following spring, so it's just not a priority. Especially since there isn't any skiing or other winter recreation nearby. No one has much incentive to spend time here out of season."

"But you do." Regardless of what he said earlier, I find it odd that Gregg would choose to spend his time here in winter if it's so inhospitable.

"I told you already, I like the solitude."

"And it makes you feel closer to your wife."

"Yes, it does. She grew up in southern Vermont. Loved the snow. Said it made the world a more peaceful place."

"What did she look like?" My mind is still on the lack of photographs around the house. "Your wife?"

"She was beautiful. A ray of sunshine." Gregg hesitates. "I have to admit, I was taken aback when you showed up at my door. For a moment, right before you passed out in my arms, I thought it was her come back to me."

"You think I look like your wife?"

"There's a passing resemblance. Kind of freaked me out last night, to be honest. I'm getting used to it now, though."

It might not be a photograph, but at least I know what Gregg's wife looked like now—sort of. And it's unsettling. On the other hand, he might just be projecting. Looking for a resemblance where there isn't much of one to allay his lingering grief. Since we're on the subject of his dead wife, I ask the next obvious question. "What was her name?"

For a moment, it's like time has frozen. Gregg doesn't react. Doesn't reply. He just stares at me like a schoolkid asked a question on a test he didn't study for. Then his face softens. "Look at me, putting all this stuff on you. Saying that you look like her. Whatever am I thinking? You have enough to worry about."

"It's fine," I say, taken aback. He clearly doesn't enjoy talking about his wife. Have I pushed him too far? I was just curious. Then again, he's the one who said I looked like her. I'm not sure what to say next.

Dead air hangs between us until he claps his hands together. "You must be starving. It's been hours since breakfast, and you hardly ate a thing." He glances toward the kitchen. "How about I rustle us up a late lunch?"

I'm still not hungry. I'm also a little tired, which I attribute to my ordeal. "Actually, I'd really like to go lie down for an hour before we eat, if you don't mind."

Gregg smiles. “Hey, whatever you need to do. Go have a nap, and I’ll be ready to make us dinner when you come down. Deal?”

“Deal.” I head for the stairs. As I climb to the second floor, my thoughts are still on the way he backed off after I asked his wife’s name. I wonder, *Was Gregg really concerned about making me uncomfortable, or is it something else?*

12

I head straight for my bedroom and flop down on the bed. Beyond the window, the winter sun is sinking low on the horizon and casting a golden-hued glow into the room through the partly drawn curtains. The snow has stopped falling—at least for now—and the landscape is serene and quiet. It looks like something out of a fairy tale. *Or a scene from a Christmas card,* I think. How is it even possible that I can remember such things and yet have no idea who I am? The world around me is not new, and yet my face, my body, my life before yesterday is a complete unknown.

I yawn and close my eyes. Just an hour of rest, and then I'll go back down and join Gregg for dinner.

It isn't long before I fall into a deep sleep.

When I wake up, the bedroom is mired in darkness. The only illumination comes from a night-light that shines through the open door of the en suite bathroom. I've slept much longer than an hour. A clock on the nightstand tells me that it's almost 8:00 p.m.

Crap.

I jump up, alarmed. I was out for almost four hours. I never meant to sleep for that long. Gregg must be starving. Assuming he hasn't already eaten without me, that is. I rush to the door and out into the hallway. Then, at the top of the stairs, I hesitate.

Farther down, on the other side of the hallway, is Gregg's room. I decide to pop in and grab some more clothes for tomorrow before going downstairs.

I step into the main bedroom and hurry straight to the walk-in closet, where I browse through the clothes, marveling at the number of high-end designer brand names. The contents of this closet must be worth thousands. And what luck, all of it fits me. I grab a couple of pairs of jeans, some tops, and a wool sweater, then head back into the bedroom.

And then I spot it. A huge TV mounted on the wall near the couch in the sitting area. I didn't notice it before because it faces away from the door. Maybe there is a logical explanation for those voices I heard last night.

My gaze settles on a remote control sitting on the arm of the couch. Maybe he has satellite TV, and I can find a news station and see if the storm has blown through or if there's more bad weather out there. That way, I'll know how long it might be before I can get out of here. Get to a doctor who can tell me what's going on inside my head and why my life is a blank.

I juggle the clothes in my arms and pick up the remote, press the power button, and wait for the TV to turn on.

"There you are."

Gregg's voice makes me jump. I turn around to see him standing in the doorway.

"I didn't have anything to wear tomorrow," I tell him, holding up the clothes. "You said I could borrow whatever I needed."

"Of course." His eyes dart toward the TV.

"I was looking for a weather report." Does he think I'm invading his privacy? I hope not. I shut the TV off. "I didn't see a television downstairs."

"That's because there isn't one." Gregg doesn't sound annoyed, which is a relief. "I was coming to wake you for dinner. I'll starve if we don't eat soon."

"I slept for longer than I intended."

"That's what I figured." Gregg nods toward the television. "I checked the phone downstairs about an hour ago, and the DSL is still down, so no TV either."

"Oh." *Well, that answers my question. Apparently, everything in the house connects to that DSL line. Crap.*

We stand there in silence for a moment. Then Gregg motions toward the door. "You hungry?"

"Yes." I follow him out of the bedroom and into the hallway.

When we reach the top of the stairs, he asks, "Do you like pasta and red sauce?"

"Um . . ." I ponder this and realize that my mouth is watering, which probably means that I do. My stomach growls, as if to confirm my suspicion. "I think so."

"How about grilled chicken? You didn't seem overly keen on those eggs this morning. I'd hate for your memories to come back only for you to discover that you're a vegetarian." He laughs at this, maybe trying to lighten the mood. It sounds forced.

"Don't vegetarians still eat eggs?" I ask. "And chicken is fine. If I turn out to be vegan or something when my memories return, I'll deal with it."

"Got it." Gregg nods toward the clothes I'm holding. "Why don't you put those in your room?" Then he starts down the stairs without waiting for me to answer.

13

After dropping the clothes off in my room, I hurry downstairs and join Gregg in the kitchen. I settle on a stool and watch him go back and forth from the stove, the refrigerator, and the butler's pantry, gathering the ingredients for his pasta meal. He grabs a couple of pots from a cupboard, fills one with water, then puts them both on the stovetop.

He works in silence, and I can't help wondering if he's secretly annoyed that I was in his bedroom with the TV on or if he's just concentrating on his task. Eventually, after dumping pasta into the pot of boiling water and throwing a jar of sauce into the other, he speaks.

"How does your head feel now?" he asks.

"It's fine," I reply. The lingering headache that has plagued me since the previous evening is gone. The bump on the back of my head still hurts when I touch it, but not enough to complain about. If a concussion caused my amnesia, maybe my memories will come back soon. I hope so. I don't like the emptiness inside my head. It's like the road ahead is clear, but when you turn to look back at the route you traveled, there's nothing but swirling white fog. At least I must not have permanent brain damage because my memories are fine from the point when I woke up on the lakeshore. No haziness there, which is a relief.

Gregg appears satisfied with my answer. He nods and starts slicing a precooked chicken breast from the fridge into strips, then adds it to the sauce, which is now simmering. The aroma makes my stomach rumble again. I'm about to compliment him on how good it smells, even though the sauce came from a jar, when a knock at the back door interrupts me.

Gregg turns toward the sound, the knife still in his hand.

Another knock. It might be someone looking for me. I feel my pulse quicken with anticipation.

"You want me to get that?" I ask. I'm excited to discover who I am. Maybe someone reported me missing, and it's the police working their way around the lake and going door-to-door. My absence can't have gone completely unnoticed.

"No. I can't imagine who would come to the door at this time of night. Stay here." Gregg is already coming around the island and heading toward the foyer. "I'll see what they want."

I'm about to argue with him, but he's gone before I can reply.

A moment later, I hear Gregg open the door, followed by a murmur of voices. It sounds a bit like the muffled conversation I heard the previous evening, except that this time one voice sounds different. It's a woman.

I hop down from the stool and rush into the foyer.

Gregg is standing with his back to me at the door, blocking my view of our visitor. The knife he was using to slice the chicken is still in his hand, which he holds behind his back. He obviously forgot to put it down and didn't want to answer the door while waving a knife around.

I approach him and catch my first glimpse of the woman standing on the doorstep. She looks to be in her late twenties or early thirties, with long dark brown hair, short bangs, and a chunky figure. She's wearing a heavy coat and a wool hat pulled down over her ears. She carries a sturdy flashlight that she points downward to create a tight circle of light on the snow-covered deck.

Her gaze shifts away from Gregg, and for a moment, I think she recognizes me.

"I'm sorry to interrupt," I say, my heart racing. I might be about to find out who I am. "But do you know me?"

"What?" A flash of confusion crosses the woman's face.

"Do you know who I am? If you do, please tell me."

"I, um . . ." The woman takes a step away from the door, her gaze darting back to Gregg. "What exactly is going on here?"

Gregg looks about as uncomfortable as our uninvited guest. "This is Anna. She got caught in the storm and had an accident. She's staying with me for a while."

"What kind of an accident?"

"I wish I knew," I say as disappointment washes over me. This woman obviously doesn't recognize me. "I can't remember anything before last night. But I have a bump on my head, so something happened to me."

"You've lost your memory?"

"Yes."

"And you just stayed here instead of getting help?"

"Don't have much choice," I say. "The bridge is out. There's no way into town."

"The storm took it out," Gregg says quickly. "Washed away the supports. The brook always swells when there's a bad snowstorm. It's happened before. The road into town is impassable right now. We're all going to be stuck here for a while."

"Oh dear. I guess that explains why the road hasn't been plowed." The woman nods. "I hope we won't be stuck up here for *too* long."

Gregg says nothing.

"What's your name?" I ask, jumping in.

Again, I sense a slight hesitation. "Helene. I'm renting a cabin directly across from you on the other shore."

"Pleased to meet you, Helene," I say, even as a thought occurs to me. "I don't suppose you have internet or a working phone line over there. Ours isn't working."

Before she can respond, Gregg chimes in. "I wouldn't get your hopes up. All the houses around the lake run off the same main DSL line. If one home goes down, they all do."

Helene pauses a moment, then nods in agreement. "That's right. No service at my place either. Sorry." She studies me with narrowed eyes. "Now, can I ask you a question?"

"Sure." I nod.

"If you've lost your memory, how do you know that your name is Anna?"

"I don't, but I can't go around nameless until I get my memories back." I lift my arm to show her the bracelet. "It's inscribed with an *A*. We figured it must be a first initial and picked Anna."

"Ah."

"If you aren't looking for me, why did you come over here?"

Helene shifts the flashlight from one hand to the other. "I noticed your lights last night from across the lake. I didn't think anyone else was around. Figured I should come over and make my presence known. You know, so we can look out for each other if need be."

There are fresh footprints in the snow leading across the deck. "You walked all the way around the lake?"

Helene tips her head toward the dock, where I now see a boat with a small outboard motor tied up. "Heavens, no. That would be beyond crazy in the dark. Probably trip and crack my head open."

I'm about to ask her if she's seen any other lights around the lake, but before I get the chance, Gregg jumps in.

"We appreciate you checking on us," he says. "Very neighborly."

I wonder if he's going to invite her to join us for dinner, but he doesn't. Instead, he puts his free hand on the front door. A subtle clue that he wants the conversation to be over.

Helene takes the hint. "I'll be off, back to my side of the lake, then. It was nice to meet you, Anna."

"You too." I try to hide my disappointment that Helene doesn't recognize me, but it's hard. "Maybe we'll run into each other again soon."

"I'm sure we will," Helene replies. Then she turns and starts back across the deck toward the dock and her boat, leaving a second trail of footprints in her wake.

Gregg closes the door. "I'm sorry that you're no closer to finding out who you are," he says, finally letting the hand holding the knife drop to his side.

"It's okay." I glance down at the knife and see something I hadn't noticed before. He was gripping it so tightly that his knuckles had turned white.

14

After Helene leaves, Gregg goes back to cooking the meal and serves it in the dining room. Despite the interruption, the pasta ends up perfectly al dente. Gregg also brings a bottle of wine and two glasses to the table.

"Should I be drinking when I have memory loss?"

Gregg pours two glasses of wine, hands me one, and takes a seat at the table opposite me. "I'm sure it will be fine. But if you want me to put it back into the bottle—"

"No." I really don't want that, and when I sip the wine, I'm sold. It has a deep smoky taste with hints of blackberries and spice. In short, it's fantastic. And probably expensive, given the ridiculously large wine fridge in the kitchen. You don't spend that much on storing your wines only to buy cheap swill.

I eat heartily, my appetite having returned since breakfast. I wonder if this is partly because now that the initial shock has worn off, I'm getting used to my reality, even if I don't like it.

The company isn't bad either. Gregg is easy to talk to. When I compliment him on the food, he tells me he once thought about becoming a chef.

"Why didn't you?" I ask.

"Because I didn't think I was good enough," Gregg replies, with no hint of bitterness.

"My stomach would beg to differ."

Gregg chuckles. "Pasta from a box and red sauce from a jar are hardly haute cuisine."

Now it's my turn to laugh. "Don't be too hard on yourself. I bet you cooked the chicken from scratch."

"That much I can claim, although it probably would've been better if I'd cooked fresh chicken breast today rather than using leftovers."

"It's delicious," I tell him, finishing up the last scraps of pasta. "So, if you aren't a world-famous chef, what is your chosen profession?"

"You really want to spoil the evening by talking about what I do for a living?"

"I'm curious, that's all." I wave a hand around the room. "Whatever it is, you must be pretty good at it to pay for all this. Especially since you said it's a second home. I can't imagine how big your other house is."

My wineglass is empty. He pours me another. "I *am* good at what I do, but my work is boring and hardly what I want to talk about with such enjoyable company."

Is he flirting with me? I look away. When I look back, our eyes meet, and my breath quickens.

Gregg mistakes my silence for unease. "I'm sorry. I didn't mean to make you uncomfortable."

"You didn't," I say quickly. "I'm just not . . . I mean . . . this is a strange situation."

"I understand." Gregg gets up and gathers the empty plates, then takes them into the kitchen. He comes back a few minutes later but doesn't return to his chair. Instead, he picks up his wineglass, comes to my side of the table and grabs the bottle, then tops me up.

"That's better," he says, taking a sip of his wine, and I notice he's barely drunk any.

My mind wanders to the fridge full of light beer, and I wonder if he would have been happier with a cold one. But I say nothing because I don't want to spoil the moment. Especially when he takes my hand and suggests that we go into the living room and finish our drinks in front of the fire.

I'm not sure exactly what's going on, but I go along with it anyway, letting him lead me through the foyer. It's nice to be distracted. And the wine helps. It takes the edge off. Lowers my inhibitions to where I'm willing to see what will happen next.

We reach the living room, and Gregg motions for me to sit on the sofa. He puts his glass down, then goes to the fire and adds a log. He stokes it with a poker. The flames leap and crackle. I feel a rush of warmth as he replaces the poker in its cradle on the hearth and comes back to the sofa.

"That's better." He sits down next to me. "Nice and cozy."

I agree. The room is lit only by the Tiffany-style floor lamp in the corner and the warm glow of the fire.

I sip my wine.

Gregg observes me for a moment and then says, "Let's play a game."

"What kind of game?" I ask, surprised. This isn't where I thought the evening was heading. I hope he won't pull out a pack of cards or, worse, a board game.

"Word association," he answers. "I say a word, and you reply with the first thing that comes into your head. I know it sounds silly, but maybe it will help you remember."

I think that's a big if, but I go along with it, anyway. "All right."

"Excellent." Gregg smiles. "First word: *dog*."

"Cute."

"Okay." Gregg nods. "Next word: *skiing*."

"Hot cocoa."

"Interesting. How about . . . *lighthouse*."

"Nantucket." I shift on the sofa. "This isn't working."

"On the contrary, we know more about you than we did a few minutes ago. You think dogs are cute."

"Who doesn't?"

Gregg ignores my comment. "And you associate hot cocoa with skiing, which means not only might you ski, but you hang out at the lodge."

"That's a stretch."

"Is it? My wife's favorite part of skiing was a cup of hot cocoa after a day on the slopes."

"Still more of an assumption than a memory."

"Hey, it's a start."

"And what about Nantucket?" I ask. "How do you explain that?"

"Maybe you spent time there, like a vacation. Or maybe you live there. Even if you can't remember your past, I'll bet it's still locked away somewhere in your subconscious."

"All right, Dr. Jung. I'll give you the benefit of the doubt . . . for the time being." I grin. Despite myself, I'm starting to have fun. "Another one. Hit me."

"Hmm. Let's see." He furrows his brow. *"Baseball."*

I open my mouth to say "Red Sox," but at that moment, there's a loud crash from the direction of the kitchen.

I jump. "What was that?"

"I don't know." Gregg is already on his feet and heading toward the foyer.

I hurry to catch up with him, and we enter the kitchen together. I look around but don't see anything amiss. The dishes are right where he left them beside the sink. The saucepans are still on the stove. There's nothing broken. But then my gaze settles on the butler's pantry and a dark red puddle expanding across the floor tiles and running into the grout lines. The items on the lowest shelves are splashed with crimson. At first, I'm not sure what I'm looking at, but then it hits me.

Blood.

There's blood all over the pantry floor.

I take a step back and scream.

15

ADRIA

Five Days Before

When Adria arrived home, Peter was waiting for her. He wore a slim-fitting black tux and paced back and forth in the living room with a hard scowl on his face.

"Where were you all afternoon?" he asked. "The charity gala is tonight. Or did you forget?"

"I didn't forget. I had some work to finish up at the office, so I stepped out for a few hours, that's all." An image of the red Mercedes flitted through Adria's head. If it had been Peter, he would know she was lying. "I'll run up and change now. We have plenty of time."

"You'd better. We're major donors. It won't look good if we show up late." He tugged at his jacket, smoothed it out.

"I know." So far, so good. He hadn't mentioned the coffee shop. Maybe it really wasn't him in the Mercedes. Adria turned and hurried upstairs, then went to the bedroom.

She went straight to the closet and hid the burner phone in her underwear drawer, pushing it all the way to the back, where she was sure Peter would never look. Her clandestine task completed, she removed the dress she'd picked out earlier that day and a pair of complementary shoes. Placing them on the bed, she undressed and changed into a white strapless bra and matching panties. Then she headed for the en suite to fix her hair and makeup.

When she stepped back into the bedroom twenty minutes later, Peter was there, standing in the middle of the room with his arms folded.

Adria stopped in the doorway.

He stared at her with an expression as hard as concrete.

The unease lurched back anew. In that moment, she was sure, as sure as she had ever been, that he knew about her afternoon excursion to meet Harvey. She swallowed, waited for the confrontation that was about to come.

But it didn't. Instead, Peter's expression softened. He smiled and picked up the gown, unzipped it, and held it out for her. "Want some help with this?"

"Um, okay." Adria nodded and walked over to him. Had she imagined that look he gave her?

"Here. Stand still." Peter lifted the dress and slipped it over her head, careful not to mess up her hair and makeup. Then he pulled it down into place and zipped it.

Adria took a deep breath to quell her nerves. She was terrible at keeping secrets, and having Harvey look into Peter's past was a big one. She slid on her shoes, then went to the floor-length mirror. The dress was perfect. A simple semifitted slip style with a deep V neckline, a layer of cream silk, and beaded silver netting over the top. As she turned to the left and right, admiring herself, the garment sparkled in the soft bedroom light.

"You look gorgeous." Peter came up behind her, peered over her shoulder, and studied her reflection. "That dress is stunning. Why haven't you worn it before?"

"I bought it last month when I was in New York," Adria said, turning away from the mirror.

Peter watched her for a moment with narrowed eyes. "It needs something else."

He went to the walk-in closet and the tall jewelry armoire standing at the back on the side where Adria's clothes filled the racks with nary an inch to spare. Opening the top drawer, he withdrew a slim, oblong, dark red jeweler's box and stepped back out of the closet before opening it. Inside was a delicate silver chain dotted with pearls. A necklace he had given her back when they first started dating.

She stared at it, surprised that this was the piece he wanted her to wear, then raised her eyes to meet his.

Peter stepped close. "Turn back around."

She turned to face the mirror again.

Her husband was so close that she could feel the tickle of his breath on her nape. He lifted the necklace, slipped it around her neck, and clasped it. Then he pushed her hair aside, his fingers brushing the skin beneath her ear in a light touch that meandered down to her collarbone, and finally to her cleavage, where a large pearl rested. He straightened the chain, his hand lingering on the soft swell of her breasts as he locked eyes with her in the mirror.

"Perfect," he said in a voice barely above a whisper, even as his lips curled into a thin smile that somehow contained more menace than mirth.

Adria forced herself not to pull away. Not to twist from his embrace.

He knows, she thought, her earlier suspicions racing back. There was something about his demeanor. A vague underlying threat beneath the charm, subtle but menacing, that only hardened her conviction. *He knows where I was this afternoon and why. That I'm onto him, or he would never have chosen this necklace. He's trying to remind me of that night. The night when we truly became a couple.*

And it had worked.

◆ ◆ ◆

When Adria entered the bedroom the night he'd given her that necklace, her eyes had been drawn to the oblong jeweler's box sitting on the pillow. She paused in the doorway, surprised. They'd been dating for several weeks, but Peter had never given her a gift before. He'd shown up with flowers once, but that really wasn't the same thing. Did this mean their relationship was moving to the next level? Did she want that?

Peter came up behind her, wrapped his arms around her, and pulled her back against his chest.

"I see you spotted my little gift," he murmured in her ear before playfully tugging at her lobe with his lips.

She turned and planted a kiss on his cheek. "To what do I owe the honor?"

"It's just a little trinket I came across the other day. Thought it would suit you."

"A little trinket?" She glanced again at the box on the pillow. "Looks expensive."

"Nothing more than you deserve." Peter nudged her toward the bed. "Go on. Open it."

Adria sat down on the edge of the mattress and lifted the box. It was crimson velvet with the name of a high-end Newbury Street estate jeweler embossed in gold on the lid. When she opened the box, a delicate silver chain dotted with small iridescent pearls gleamed in the light. It came together in a Y, *with a single larger pearl centered at the bottom. She removed the necklace and held it up.*

It was stunning. And Peter was right: It would look great on her. She loved it.

"Here. Put it on." Peter joined her on the bed and took the necklace, then waited while she lifted her long brown hair away from her neck before reaching around and clasping it.

The necklace fell into place, the large pearl sitting snug in her cleavage.

Peter exhaled. "Breathtaking. Just as I imagined it would look on you."

"It's perfect."

"You're perfect." Peter moved closer and stroked her neck, sending shivers racing through her body. Then he kissed her, starting at her forehead, then moving down to her lips, her neck, her collarbone.

"What I really want to see is you in just *this necklace. This and nothing else." Then he leaned back on the bed, waiting for her to do as he asked.*

Adria hesitated. They'd been sleeping together for about a month, and the sex was fabulous. Maybe even mind-blowing. Some of the best she'd ever had. And of course, he'd seen her naked, brief glimpses at night when they made love with the lights turned down and the curtains drawn. But to strip bare right here, right now, while he watched? A faint heat touched her cheeks. She felt . . . vulnerable, exposed. And excited.

"What are you waiting for?" Peter demanded. His eyes—those same deep blue eyes that had captured her attention on the day they'd first met—burned with desire. "Do it. Undress for me, Adria."

Adria rose to her feet, butterflies swarming in her stomach. She touched the top button of her shirt, drew her hand away. The overhead light was too much. She crossed the room and turned it off, leaving just the light filtering in from the hallway casting a soft glow over the room. This felt better. She went back to the button, undid it. Then the next and the one after that.

Peter's eyes bored into her, his face lit with amusement at her discomfort.

The last button popped free. She slipped the garment from her shoulders, let it fall to the floor. Then she reached around and unzipped her skirt, pushed it down over her hips, until it joined her discarded top.

Now she stood in front of him in nothing but her bra, panties, and the necklace. Cool air from the AC vent in the ceiling swirled around her, lifting goose bumps on her bare skin.

"Now the rest, Adria," he said in a confident, commanding voice she had never heard him use before. Always independent and self-assured, she was surprised by her body's response to his sudden take-charge attitude, and her forced vulnerability. It was delicious. Sexy. And suddenly, she realized she liked this feeling, releasing control and allowing him to take charge.

"What are you waiting for?"

Adria didn't reply. She wet her lips, tried to ignore the growing heat between her legs, and reached around to unclasp her bra. She slid the straps off her shoulders and let go. Then she glanced down at herself. At the swell of her naked breasts and the pearl necklace that nestled between them. At the V-shaped scrap of pink fabric that covered the one part of her body—the most intimate part—still not exposed to Peter's gaze.

When she looked back up, Peter's expression had changed from amused to intense with desire. Spurred on by those dark eyes and the promise that they held, Adria hooked her fingers into the sides of her lacy underwear and slowly drew them down.

Now she stood in front of Peter wearing only the necklace.

He gazed at her without saying a word, desire burning in his eyes.

Adria let him look. Her nipples grew hard. The necklace caught the soft light shining in from the hallway and sparkled around her neck.

A minute went by.

Adria thought she might burst with desire. She had never realized how erotic a gaze could be until this moment.

Another minute passed, her anticipation growing with each passing second.

But Peter made no move. He just stared. Was he playing with her? Trying to drive her crazy? When she could take it no longer, she went to the bed, climbed up, and straddled him, one arm looping around his neck.

"Well?" she asked, toying with the necklace. "What do you think? Is this how you imagined it on me? Does it suit me?"

He locked his eyes with hers. Then his gaze moved slowly, exquisitely, down her body. He took in the sight of her, kneeling above him with legs open wide. She shivered again, but not from the cool air this time. This was a shiver of anticipation. She wanted him to touch her. No. She needed him to touch her.

Finally, he raised himself up so that their bodies were almost touching as he unbuttoned and removed his shirt. She could feel the heat from his bare skin inches from hers. When he reached up and stroked her hair, the touch made her moan.

"My imagination didn't do it justice," he finally murmured. "You are so beautiful."

Then his lips were on her breast, his tongue playing over the swollen mound of her nipple. His hand trailed down her abdomen, then lower, finding her wet and ready for him. Adria moaned, the touch igniting a fire hotter than she'd ever experienced before. She began to move against his probing fingers, begging him to go deeper, faster. When he finally pulled away, she was panting and dizzy with desire. He quickly unzipped his pants and freed himself. She pushed him back onto the bed, slid down on top of him. And then their bodies joined at last.

"Adria?" Peter snapped his fingers at her, shattering the memory. "You with me?"

"Yes. I was just . . ."

"What?"

"I was remembering the night you gave me this necklace." Adria forced the memory back down. If Peter was toying with her, trying to control her, well, two could play that game. She could pretend to be the devoted wife, unaware of the deceit she now suspected lingered just below the surface of their relationship. Deception she had sensed so many times before and ignored, tucking the uncomfortable feelings away and hoping they would vanish, and he would be the man she thought he was when they met. Yes, she could do that. At least for a little while longer.

She smiled up at him and planted a kiss on his cheek before grabbing her handbag and heading for the door.

"Come on, we don't want to be late."

16

Anna

Day One

The scream is barely off my lips before Gregg sidesteps me and rushes into the pantry. He bends down, examines the blood, then straightens up and turns to me.

"Take it easy. It's just beet juice," he says. "Be careful. There's broken glass here too."

"Beet juice?" I repeat, my heart still racing from the shock.

"Uh-huh. There were a couple of jars of pickled beets on the shelf. One of them must have fallen off and smashed. That's what we heard." He looks down at the mess and scowls. "I bet it was a mouse. Damn thing was probably scurrying along the shelf and knocked it off."

"Could a mouse do that?" I ask. The jar must have been heavy, and mice are not that big.

"I don't see any other explanation." Gregg steps out of the pantry and heads toward a closet on the other side of the kitchen. "I've seen a few around here recently. Heard scratching in the walls too. They come in from the outside when it gets too cold."

Great. Now I have to worry about mice. I shudder.

Gregg opens the closet and takes out a dustpan and broom. "I'll clean it up."

"I'll help." I go to the counter and grab a roll of paper towels from the holder, then return to the pantry. The liquid is everywhere. There must have been a lot of juice in that jar. I tear off several towels. I'm about to drop them on the floor to soak up the worst of the mess when I notice something weird. On the other side of the broken jar is a partial shoe print. I can see the ridges of the sole and curve of the heel.

I turn to Gregg and point. "Look at this."

"Huh." Gregg looks down at his feet. "Probably mine. I must have stepped in the beet juice."

"Oh." I don't remember him going to that side of the pantry. I move around the smashed jar of beets to look closer, and now I see something else. Another small square chamber on the other side and a set of narrow stairs rising into darkness.

"That's the old servants' staircase," Gregg says, coming up behind me. "When this house was built way back in the 1890s, it was common for rich folk to have live-in staff, but they didn't want them using the main stairs."

"Where does it go?" I ask, craning my neck and peering up.

"All the way to the third floor, which is the attic. That's where the servants' quarters were located. There are four rooms up there, mostly used for storage now."

"I can't imagine what it must have been like here back then," I say, unable to tear my gaze away from the worn and unloved stairs.

"Even more remote than it is now. It was one of the first summer houses built on the lake."

"And yet they still brought servants up here."

"It was a different time. The rich people didn't want to do their own housekeeping, even if it meant paying for the staff to travel with them." Gregg leans on the broom and glances back toward the shattered jar of beets. "Back then, we wouldn't have had to clean this up ourselves. Speaking of which . . ."

"Back to work." I turn away from the staircase and tear off a fresh wad of paper towels, which I use to go behind Gregg and mop up the beet juice after he removes the broken glass and slices of beetroot that rise out of the mess like small round islands. I scrub what I can off the provisions on the lower shelves but am only partly successful. The items in cardboard boxes still bear ugly red stains.

"Best I can do," I say, dumping the sodden paper towels onto the dustpan.

"Good enough." Gregg sweeps to make sure he didn't miss any shards of glass, then goes into the kitchen and drops the contents of the dustpan into the trash. He turns to me as I follow him. "Crisis taken care of. Now, where were we?"

"You were playing psychiatrist."

"Indeed. Dr. Gregg is in the house!" He gives a small chuckle. "Shall we continue?"

"Actually, I think I'm done with it." The word association game hasn't jogged loose anything meaningful, and I'm not sure that it will. Still, I was starting to have fun right before the crash sent us running in here. My pulse is racing, and my stomach is still in knots. A superstitious person might think the jar of beets smashing was a portent. The universe warning me away from Gregg. Making sure I don't do something I regret later.

Or it could just be a mouse, like he said. Coincidence.

Either way, one thing still bothers me. That footprint. I glance back toward the pantry and the servants' staircase beyond.

"Earth to Anna?"

I snap back. "What?"

"You zoned out there for a moment." Gregg comes around the island. "You feeling all right?"

"I'm fine." I look down at his shoes—a pair of black sneakers with white soles—and then I see it. Specks of red on the side of one shoe. Maybe he did step in the beet juice after all and leave that shoe print. My relief is palpable. I also wonder why I'm so on edge. Looking for mysteries where there are none. The clothes in Gregg's closet. Clothes that belonged to his dead wife but fit as if they were made for me. The early morning voices. The broken jar of beets. The answer is as obvious as it is simple. I'm in unfamiliar surroundings with a man I don't know. A man I met only twenty-four hours ago. On top of that, we're trapped by a snowstorm, and who knows how long it will be before we can get out of here? Not to mention my condition. If all that isn't enough to put me on edge, I don't know what is.

17

We go back to the living room and finish our wine, but the mood has changed. Gregg is more subdued now. He drinks slowly and stares into the fire, lost in thought. I wonder if perhaps he's disappointed that the smashed jar of beets disrupted our evening. For a while there, as we played the word association game, I was enjoying myself enough that the constant dread I've been living with since waking up in the freezing-cold water had finally eased. And Gregg was great company. Moreover, we were connecting on a personal level. For the first time since knocking on his door, I didn't feel like I was imposing.

My mind soon turns to bed, even though I've already slept through most of the evening, and it's not long before I decide to head up to my room.

The house takes on a different character at night. As I climb the main staircase, I feel it. There's a brooding melancholy about this place after the sun goes down. It weaves through the oak-paneled rooms and shadowy hallways. The air is heavy, as if an invisible blanket covers the house. Smothering. Cloying. It almost feels . . . haunted. I can't help but wonder if the spirit of Gregg's late wife lingers here, unable to leave in death the home she so loved in life.

I shudder and quicken my step, only relaxing when I reach the safety of the bedroom. The first thing I do is lock the door, then undress and go to the en suite, where I run a shower. The water is hot and steamy. It feels good on my skin, makes my scalp tingle, and I stand under it for a good ten minutes, letting the spray wash away my anxiety. Afterward, I return to the bedroom, snug and warm in my flannel PJs.

When I go to the window to close the curtains, I see that it's snowing again. Not hard yet, but enough to dash any hope that I might get out of here soon. Across the lake, I spy a pale twinkle of lights that reflect off the dark, flat, glassy surface of Gravewater Lake. This must be the house Helene said she's renting. The same house I noticed earlier on the opposite shore tucked between the trees. I think of her all alone and isolated over there, and I'm suddenly glad that Gregg is here with me. I wouldn't want to be trapped all by myself in such a remote place. It's no wonder she came over to see us earlier. She must be freaked out.

I watch the lights across the lake for a few moments more and wonder if Helene is at her window, doing the same thing. Then the chill air gets the better of me, and I close the curtains before hurrying to bed, jumping in, and pulling the covers up over me.

The piece of broken necklace I found earlier is on the nightstand. I pick it up and run my fingers over the smooth white pearl, let the strand of chain run through my fingers. It's the only clue I've found to my identity other than the bracelet with the single letter engraved on it and the clothes I arrived in.

I wonder where the rest of the necklace is. At the bottom of the lake, most likely, along with my missing slipper. I turn it over in my hand, study it, hoping for a glimmer of memory, but none comes. Frustrated, I place the chain back on the nightstand and reach for the bedside lamp, then turn it off. As I lie in the darkness, I hear a sound from the hallway beyond my room.

A creak that I recognize as the loose floorboard I stood on the night before when I snuck into the corridor.

I hold my breath and strain to listen for another sound. Someone is out there, in the hallway.

Is Gregg coming up to bed and taking a quick detour to check on me before retiring to his room? I wait for him to knock on my door, but he doesn't. Either he changed his mind and turned back toward his own room, or he's standing in the hall mere feet from my door. I listen for his bedroom door down the hall to open and close, but all I hear is the beating of my heart and the wind blowing outside. I think about the voices I heard last night. The broken jar of beets that Gregg claimed a mouse had knocked from the shelf.

A chilling thought occurs to me.

Maybe we're not alone. Maybe someone else is standing outside my door, listening.

I stay still for a few minutes more, waiting for the sound of someone walking away. But all I'm greeted with is silence.

My unease grows.

In the end, my need to know overcomes my fear. I climb from my bed as quietly as I can and go to the door, where I disengage the lock and open it a few inches to peer out.

The hallway is empty. No Gregg. No intruder.

Just lonely darkness.

I breathe a heavy sigh of relief, go to close the door again. Then I see it. A sliver of light clicks on from beneath a door farther down the hallway. A spare bedroom that I'm sure is empty.

My heart leaps into my throat. I stare at the light, not wanting to go investigate but knowing I won't be able to sleep again otherwise. I step into the hallway and creep toward the closed door with the light underneath as quietly as I can.

I stand in front of the door and look down. Weak light illuminates my socks and spills onto the carpet underfoot. I lean forward and put my ear close to the door, listen for movement from the other side. I stay like this for a minute, though it feels more like an hour.

All I hear is my own shallow breathing.

The light is still on.

I reach out to open the door. Then, as my shaking hand closes around the doorknob, the light clicks off.

I jump back in surprise.

A whimper escapes my lips.

I stand and stare at the crack under the door, heart pounding. Every fiber of my being tells me to flee. To run back to my room and barricade myself in for the rest of the night, but that will just leave me cowering and afraid as I wait for daylight.

I have to look. There is no choice.

Gathering my courage, I twist the doorknob and push the door wide.

The room beyond lies in darkness, only faint light coming in from the window and the bright white of the falling snow outside. My eyes dart around, looking for movement in the shadows. With trembling fingers, I snap on the switch beside the door, bathing the room in light.

The room is empty. There's a full-size bed against the wall to my right with a single nightstand and lamp beside it. A small white wood desk rests under the window, its surface empty, a green velvet rolling chair tucked underneath. I look back at the bed and notice that it's a platform style, with the wood extending to the floor, so nobody could be hiding underneath.

My gaze falls on a door directly across from where I'm standing. The closet. It's the only place somebody could conceal themselves. I saw the light. Saw it click off, and I'm standing in the room's only exit. If someone is in here, that's where they must be.

I want to run more than ever. My breath comes in quick gasps. My heart feels like it's going to beat right out of my chest. I say a silent prayer: *Please let this be my imagination.*

But I can't turn back. I need to look, if only for my sanity.

Quietly, gingerly, I take a step forward, then another, and soon I'm standing in front of the closet. I hold my breath and listen, straining to hear even the slightest exhalation of breath or shuffling movement that would tell me someone waits on the other side of that door.

I hear nothing.

This is it. Truth time. Bracing myself, I yank the door open and jump back, raising my arms in defense against whoever might be there. But there's no one. I'm staring at an empty closet with six velvet coat hangers pushed to one side and a cedar-scented sachet hanging from the rod.

I turn in a circle, studying every inch of the room. There's no other place someone could hide. It doesn't make sense. I saw that light click off.

What is going on?

I look at the bedside lamp. Maybe it's on a timer. That would explain the light turning on and off.

I walk over to the nightstand, look down at the outlet on the wall behind it. The lamp is unplugged. The hairs on the back of my neck stand up. If the lamp isn't on a timer, then I can think of only one explanation. Someone turned off the overhead light switch by the door.

Now I'm completely freaked out. I consider fetching Gregg, telling him what just happened. Maybe he can provide a rational explanation that I'm missing. But even as I turn to go find him, I realize I can't tell him about this. He's already commented that I'm jumpy and paranoid. Telling him that there must be somebody else in the house with us—a person who seemingly vanished from inside a room with no viable exits—will likely get me thrown out on my ass. And I have nowhere to go, no other life beyond this place.

I give the empty bedroom one last glance, then turn off the light and close the door. When I get to my room, I lock the door.

Returning to bed, I lie on my side, facing the door with my hand pushed under the pillow, and close my eyes. But even as I fall into a restless half sleep, I'm still listening, because despite all proof to the contrary, I know what I saw.

18

Anna

Day Two

There's blood all over the floor of the foyer. Lots of it. Too much to have come from one person. I stand at the bottom of the stairs, unwilling to venture any farther, and look around in horror.

"Anna." A voice echoes from somewhere in the house, drawing my name out into a singsong lilt that prickles the hairs on the back of my neck. *Ahhnnaaa.*

I stifle a scream and gather my courage, finally stepping foot into the foyer and hurrying toward the front door. I need to escape, to get out of here. I don't know why, but I know it's important, and that my life depends on it.

My feet squelch with each footfall. I look down, see that my slippers, which had once been blue, are now stained a deep red. I can feel the blood soaking through, squishing between my toes, and I try not to gag.

"Anna." The voice comes again, closer now.

I turn to see a figure at the top of the stairs. Amorphous. Undefined. It blends with the surrounding darkness.

"Where are you going, Anna?" The figure starts down toward me, its movement slow and deliberate, as if it knows I have nowhere to go. No means of escape.

"Get away from me." I turn back toward the door, faster now. My feet make wet sucking sounds each time I take a step. I slip and almost fall, even as a frantic scream wells in my throat.

A chuckle.

"Please," I beg. "Leave me alone."

I reach the door, pull it open to a wintry landscape. A thick blanket of snow covers the ground as far as the eye can see. Except for the lake. The water looks like a sheet of polished obsidian that stands in stark contrast to its bright white surroundings.

I have to go out there.

It's the only way.

"Anna." That voice again. Sibilant and menacing.

"You can't have me!" I scream, not daring to glance back into the house. But even so, I know my pursuer is close now. Right behind me. I can feel its energy. Malignant. Dead.

Another moment, and it will be upon me.

I take a deep breath and step out into the snow. I cross the deck, leaving crimson footprints in my wake.

Ahead of me is the dock. I can see a boat moored there. If only I can reach it, I'll be safe. But when I get there, the boat is gone. Vanished as if it never existed, while to my rear, the figure keeps coming.

Trapped and confused, I continue to the end of the dock.

The figure steps onto the snow-covered planks.

It advances toward me.

I teeter on the edge of the dock, glance down at the cold, dark water. When I look back, the figure is right there, so close I could touch it. Yet still I see no features. Just a black, wraithlike shape.

And now I sense something else. Movement. An arm swinging down toward me. A moment later, something heavy strikes the side of my head, sending me toppling backward.

I claw at the air, cry out in terror, even as I fall into the frigid water.

And when I do, the lake embraces me. It welcomes me as I tumble beneath its surface. I sink into the depths. And death is all around me . . .

I gasp for breath and bolt upright, expecting my lungs to be filled with water. A clammy sheen of sweat clings to my forehead despite the chill that permeates the air in the bedroom. The nightmare lingers in my memory. The shadowy figure chased me onto the dock. Slipping beneath the water.

I sit until my mind separates dream from reality and my racing heart slows. The clock on the nightstand tells me it's 5:00 a.m. There are still a couple of hours before sunrise.

Unnerved, I slip from my bed, go to the en suite, and leave the door open a crack. The glow from the night-light in the bathroom pushes back the gloom.

Then I lie back down. But I don't sleep. Not now. Instead, I lie awake until the first rays of morning sunlight peek through the curtains.

19

I rise at dawn and get dressed, because I can't take lying wide awake in bed any longer. I want coffee. Strong, hot coffee. It calls to me from the kitchen downstairs, a caffeine-infused siren song.

I slip out of the bedroom, closing the door quietly, and make my way down the hallway toward the stairs. Gregg's door is on the other side of the landing. It's closed. I cross to it and stand outside, listening. Gentle rhythmic snoring comes from within.

I turn back to the stairs, head down, then cross to the kitchen and rummage around until I find a bag of ground coffee. Five minutes later, the delicious aroma of French roast fills the air.

I pour a cup for myself and sit at the island, staring out of the kitchen window toward the lake, and I'm reminded of the terrible nightmare that woke me up in a cold sweat. Was it just a meaningless bad dream, or did it contain some deeper truth? It's impossible to know. I ended up in that lake somehow. This leads me to a chilling question. Was what happened to me something other than an accident?

Of course, I don't believe for one moment that a shapeless figure attacked me in real life, but maybe my sleeping mind was dredging up some snippet of concealed memory, albeit in the strange way that dreams often weave reality and fantasy together. My memory might be returning, taking the path of least resistance. It gives me hope and fills me with dread. What if I remember something bad? What if I remember something worse than bad?

I tell myself to calm down. I'll deal with that situation when and if it happens. And besides, there's every chance the nightmare was just what it appears to be. A bad dream that has no greater meaning than my subconscious regurgitating the unease I've been feeling about my predicament.

My coffee cup is almost empty. I jump down from the stool and pour myself another cup, then add a dash of milk and a packet of artificial sweetener that I find in the cupboard above the coffee maker.

Returning to the stool, I sit with my hands wrapped around the mug to warm my palms. Even though the house has heat, there are still cold spots. The kitchen is one of them, probably because it only has one baseboard heater on the far wall. My bedroom is another. No matter how warm the rest of the house is, that room feels chilly.

I lift the cup, take a sip, and watch a bird that has landed outside the window. It's small, with an orange-red breast and a black-and-white striped head. I marvel at how a creature so tiny can withstand such an extreme environment. My feathered visitor tilts its head, looks back at me with a beady eye. Then it lets out a series of quick chirps, spreads its wings, and takes flight.

When the bird disappears from view, I lower my gaze from the window, and in that moment, I see something else. A flicker of movement from the corner of my eye. A vague shifting of the shadows in the small and windowless chamber beyond the pantry.

I snap my head around, and my heart practically leaps into my throat.

Because someone is standing there. A burly figure whose features I can't make out, silhouetted a darker black against the gloom. Watching me.

20

A scream rises in my throat, but all that comes out is a strangled whimper. I half fall, half stumble off the stool, then rush around the island and make a beeline for the knife block sitting on the counter near the window.

The whole time I expect the figure to rush from the pantry. Attack me before I can arm myself.

But they don't.

My hand closes over the handle of the biggest knife in the block. A wide-bladed steel chef's knife that curves to a wicked-looking sharp point.

With the knife in my hand, I turn back toward the pantry, afraid of what might be there—who I might see—standing in the doorway. But there's nobody.

My first inclination is that I imagined the figure. That it was nothing more than my brain seeing familiar shapes in the abstract swirling shadows. But I know what I saw. I'm certain someone was right there. Silently watching me. But who? Why?

"Hello?" I call out into the empty darkness, hoping I'd seen Gregg, although I'm not sure why he would use the servants' staircase. "Gregg?"

No answer.

"Gregg?" I call again. "Is that you?"

Still no response. Only silence.

At least, until I hear a shuffling footfall on the stairs, followed by another.

The breath catches in my throat.

I grip the knife tightly in one hand and hurry toward the pantry. As I pass through it, I look down at the provisions on the lower shelves, still splashed with beet juice that has dried to a dark burgundy, and I falter.

A shudder runs through me. It looks so much like blood, even now.

Tearing my gaze away, I continue to the small room behind the pantry and lift my eyes to the servants' staircase, even as I fumble for the light. My fingers find the switch, and the stairs are bathed in a soft white glow.

There's nobody there.

The pent-up breath in my lungs escapes in a rapid gush of relief.

But then my eyes settle on the landing halfway up where the stairs take a ninety-degree turn. I'm not done yet. The figure could be lurking above me, just out of sight.

My stomach clenches. I don't want to continue, but I have to know. Is Gregg messing with me? Playing some ridiculous game? If so, then why?

Placing a foot on the bottom stair, I start upward to the landing.

Still no sign of the dark figure.

I climb to the next landing.

Empty, just like the one below.

To my left, the stairs keep on rising while in front of me is a plain white painted door. Nudging it open, I find myself looking down the second-floor corridor. Gregg's bedroom, the door still closed, is on the right. Farther away is the guest room. *My room.* There are other doors too. All of them are closed.

I glance toward the staircase and the unexplored space above. Gregg said there was nothing but storage on the third floor, but I need to see for myself. Make sure no one is lurking up there. Hiding from me. I need to know that I'm safe in this house. And right now, I feel anything but safe.

I contemplate going to Gregg's room and knocking to see if he's still in there, even though my rational mind is telling me it must have been him that I saw and heard. Because if it was, and he tells me why he was standing at the bottom of the stairs like that, I can stop panicking. And if it wasn't, well . . . I would feel so much better with him by my side.

But I don't. Because he might just view my claim that there's someone else in the house as unhinged. He'll think I'm nuts. That the knock I took to the head left me in a worse state than either of us previously thought. And then where would I be? He might not feel safe around a crazy person, and ask me to leave. With the bridge out and no way to reach town, where would I go?

Reluctantly, I pull the door closed and turn back toward the staircase, alone.

The stairs rise into darkness. I find another light switch and turn it on. The resulting illumination is dim, coming from a single bare bulb high on the ceiling, but it's better than nothing. I make my way up to another landing, alert for the slightest hint of danger, then turn and mount the final short flight of stairs.

At the top is another hallway. This one is narrower, the floor made of rough, bare wooden boards. There's one more light switch, which I turn on. Dust particles, disturbed by my presence, swirl in the air beneath the bulb.

Four doors lie ahead of me, two on each side.

Perfect places for an intruder to hide.

I linger at the top of the stairs, fighting the urge to flee back down to the kitchen and stay there until Gregg makes an appearance. But I saw someone. I know I did. I've come this far, so I force myself to move down the hallway, knife at the ready.

When I reach the first door, I open it and poke my head inside. Gregg said that these rooms were originally the servants' quarters. I can't imagine living somewhere like this. The room is tiny. Barely big enough to accommodate a twin bed. The ceiling follows the sloping roofline. There's a gabled dormer window caked in years of accumulated filth. It barely allows a scrap of light beyond its grimy panes. Boxes and other assorted junk pile around the walls, leaving barely enough space to walk in between. It's obvious that nobody is hiding in there. It's too cramped.

I pull the door closed and move to the next, which is pretty much the same. Boxes with their lids taped, assorted junk, and an old rocking horse with rusted springs, its body painted in garish bright colors. It looks like an antique. The sight of this long-forgotten children's toy abandoned up here unnerves me almost as much as the figure I saw. The rocking horse is out of place among the rest of the jumble. The only such artifact surrounded by less childish clutter.

I tear my gaze away from the toy and withdraw back into the hallway to explore the other two rooms.

The third chamber is as cluttered as the first two. Stuffed with outdated sticks of furniture stacked one atop the other precariously. A dresser with one empty drawer hanging open. A three-shelf bookcase coated with chipped and flaking cream-colored paint. A tarnished brass floor lamp missing its shade. The detritus of an old and well-lived-in house.

I move on to the fourth door.

This last space catches me by surprise.

It's empty.

The winter sun slants through the dormer and casts a pale skeletal outline of the leading between the panes onto the floorboards. A thick layer of undisturbed dust coats the floor. I turn back and notice that another blanket of fine dust sits atop the floorboards of the hallway. Only my own vague footprints are visible. Proof of my passage through the third floor. And proof of something else. That no one except for me has been up here in a long time.

Relieved and eager to escape the gloomy attic, I retrace my steps and practically tear down the stairs. I make my way back through the pantry and into the kitchen. But then I come to a skidding halt and raise the knife, even as I let out an involuntary scream.

Because I'm not alone after all.

21

ADRIA

Three Days Before

The last forty-eight hours since Adria met Harvey had been tense. To anyone except her, Peter would have looked like his usual charming self at the charity gala, working the room and saying all the right things to all the right people. He laughed and joked and opened wallets with his blandishing.

But Adria knew better.

She could sense the undercurrent of simmering distrust that revealed itself in his tense shoulders, the way he absently twisted the wedding ring on his finger, and the quick sideways looks he gave her every once in a while.

Ever since then, her husband had been moody and withdrawn. When they returned from the gala, he barely said a word. At least until they climbed into bed and he wanted sex, which she reluctantly let him have, if only to assuage his suspicions. But it was rough and quick, almost mechanical. Perfunctory. Almost like he was doing it just to see if she would let him, or maybe it was to make her his own again because he knew very well who she was meeting in that coffee shop and why. A last-ditch effort to reassert his authority over her. It was certainly nothing like their lovemaking of old when Peter was caring and gentle. When he considered her pleasure as much as his own.

She still remembered the trip to Nantucket he'd arranged not long after they met. It was perfect and the first time that she really felt she was falling in love. They'd stood at the rail on the ferry from Cape Cod to the little island and drunk Bloody Marys, watched as the town came into view with its iconic Brant Point Light. Then they'd spent the next forty-eight hours dividing their time between exploring the island and making love in the charming guest room at their bed-and-breakfast. The sex was better than any she'd ever had. Peter was the perfect lover. Gentle and considerate when he needed to be, and beyond passionate. She never wanted to leave. If they could just stay cocooned there in that guest room and explore the joys of each other's bodies forever, she would have been content.

And now look at them.

When she first started distrusting Peter, she had hoped it was nothing but paranoia. She possessed a natural intuition about people and situations that had served her well in her role as head of the charitable foundation, but with Peter, she was unsure. After all, that sixth sense would have kicked in right away if there was a problem with him, wouldn't it? Or was he just that good at hiding his true intentions? She had prayed for the former, but ended up reluctantly admitting to herself that it was the latter, because when she thought back to the start of their relationship, to that Nantucket trip, the signs were already there if only she could have seen them.

The whole reason for the weekend away was to meet Peter's best friend, who apparently lived on the island. She had looked forward to learning more about the man she was falling in love with, peeking behind the curtain of his life and meeting someone from his past. But when they got there, Peter's friend was a no-show. He sent them a bottle of wine and a message saying he had been called away on business and couldn't make it.

In hindsight, she suspected that there never was a friend, because at the end of that trip, on the day they were to check out, the bed-and-breakfast had slipped a folio under the guest room door. The bottle of wine was on that bill, as if Peter had arranged the wine, not some phantom friend. She had put the whole thing down to a mistake, had hardly given the bill any thought in her eagerness to believe that Peter was the one.

And that wasn't the only incident that should have given her cause for concern. He claimed to own a town house in Boston's expensive Back Bay neighborhood. A property that he was conveniently renovating for the first several months of their relationship and could not occupy. Which was why he was renting a much cheaper, cramped apartment in the less upscale Fenway district. Again, she should have been suspicious. Especially after he claimed to have sold the Back Bay property before she even saw it . . . maybe because it didn't really exist.

But now, finally, she had come to her senses, because the red flags were too frequent to ignore. Which was why she had gone to Harvey. She had to know for sure. And ever since the gala, she had been on tenterhooks, waiting for something, anything, that would tell her if Peter really was up to no good, and if so, just how bad the situation was.

Now, two days later, she had still heard nothing, and Peter's mood had only gotten worse. Which is why she had spent the day working in the suite of offices her father's company provided for the charitable foundation rather than in her more comfortable office at home. She shared that home office with Peter, whom her father had made vice president of the foundation two years before, which only made the decision easier because she was looking for a place to escape her husband more than a place to work.

To tell the truth, there wasn't much to do. A team of four full-time staff members handled the foundation's day-to-day activities, which left her and Peter with open schedules most days, despite her insistence that she be a working chief executive rather than a paid figurehead. She had finished the few tasks her staff couldn't by lunch hour and was now killing time shopping online because she didn't want to go home yet.

Then, at 4:00 p.m., when she had finally gathered the courage to face Peter and his dour mood for the evening, there was a knock at her office door.

It was Claudia Feynman, head of the company's accounting division, and the way she acted when she stepped into the office told Adria that this visit was far from routine.

"Have you got a minute?" Claudia asked, wringing her hands in an uncharacteristic show of nerves. "It's about . . ." She stepped closer to the desk, meeting Adria's gaze for a brief moment before dropping her eyes to the floor. "It's about Peter."

Adria straightened her back, sat taller in her chair. She had been waiting for something, anything, to let her know one way or the other if she could still trust him, but now that the moment might have arrived, she was overcome by a deep sense of foreboding. A trite phrase her grandmother would sometimes utter to the younger Adria popped into her head unbidden. *Be careful what you wish for.*

She told Claudia to sit down, then waited for the woman to drop a bomb.

And drop it, she did.

"I really am sorry for the intrusion," Claudia said in a breathy voice while still refusing to make eye contact with Adria. "There are some . . . um . . . discrepancies with the charitable foundation's accounting that I think you should know about."

Adria said nothing. She merely stared at the woman and waited until Claudia cleared her throat and spoke again.

"I got a phone call from Harvey Lang the day before yesterday. He's head of corporate security for the—"

"I know who he is," Adria said impatiently.

"Right. Of course you do." Claudia shifted uncomfortably in her seat. "Anyway, he wanted me to look at the foundation, and all the transactions your husband has been involved with for the past two years. He said it was just a routine random audit, but then he told me to handle it personally. Not only that, but he wanted it done right away.

Then he told me to keep it confidential. Said I wasn't to tell anyone else what I was doing, even inside the accounting department, which is highly unusual."

Get to the point already, Adria thought. Claudia was obviously nervous, but drawing it out wouldn't change whatever she had to say. Adria leaned forward, placing her elbows on the desk. "What did you find?"

"Discrepancies." Claudia finally looked up. Her face was pale. "Lots of them, involving at least a million dollars. Peter authorized donations to a charitable organization operating out of Africa. But here's the thing: The charity doesn't exist except on paper. I can't find any record of it outside of a single business registration in Nairobi that doesn't even identify it as a charitable organization. It has no website, no real-world presence. And it appears to have been set up by a shell company running out of the Cayman Islands. I haven't been able to contact any of the charity's officers, and I suspect they don't actually exist."

"What are you trying to say?" Adria asked, even though she knew very well what Claudia was saying. She just didn't want to admit it. At least until someone else said it out loud.

"I'm going to keep working on this, so I'll know more soon. And of course, I passed on my preliminary findings to Harvey," Claudia said. "But on the face of it, your husband has embezzled at least a million dollars from the foundation over the past two years."

22

ANNA

Day Two

"Whoa. Easy there." Gregg backs away from me with a mixture of surprise and fear on his face. "Put the knife down, okay?"

I don't, because an inner voice is screaming inside my head that I'm not safe, that the person I saw standing on the other side of that pantry is still in the house.

"Please, Anna," Gregg implores me. "Lower the knife."

"Where were you fifteen minutes ago?" I ask him, ignoring the request.

"What?" Gregg looks confused. He stares at me and then at the knife. "I was in the bedroom. I got out of bed, took a shower, then came down here to find a freshly brewed pot of coffee and an empty kitchen. You were nowhere in sight."

"That's because I saw someone. It was only for a moment, but . . ." I can tell from the look on Gregg's face that he doesn't believe me. "I thought it was you and went to investigate."

"It wasn't me."

"Then it was someone else."

"Anna, that's impossible. There's no one else in the house except for the two of us."

"Yes, there is. There must be," I insist. "There was a person standing at the bottom of the stairs. They vanished when I ran to get the knife, but then I heard footsteps on the servants' stairs." When I see the way Gregg is looking at me, I say, "I'm not making this up."

"We're alone, Anna." Gregg takes a breath. "Now please, for heaven's sake, put down the knife, and we'll talk about it."

"Say that you believe me."

Gregg is silent for a long moment. "I believe that *you think* someone was there. Heard what you thought were footsteps."

"I did." I spit out the words, even as I try to quell my rising frustration.

"Okay, so what did this person look like?"

"I don't know." This sounds foolish, even to me. "All I saw was a shape in the darkness."

"You didn't actually see any features? Just a vague shape."

"Yes." I feel what little credibility I might have had slipping away. "But it was a person. I'm sure of it."

"And this person just stood there, unmoving."

"Yes."

Gregg glances past me toward the pantry and the servants' stairs. "It's really dark in there when the lights aren't on. Is it possible—and I'm just asking, so don't take offense—but is it possible that you saw what you expected to see? That it was just a trick of the shadows, and you leaped to conclusions?"

"I don't know." My conviction is waning in the harsh light of Gregg's logic. "It's possible, I guess. But what about the footsteps? I didn't imagine those."

Gregg's gaze drops back to the knife, still held out in front of me at arm's length like a bayonet. "Maybe you heard me. My bedroom is right above the kitchen. You probably heard me walking around."

"No." I shake my head. "It came from the servants' staircase. I know what I heard."

"Hey, this is an old house. Sound travels in strange ways. I wouldn't give it too much thought." Gregg narrows his eyes. "You would tell me if there's more going on than just your memory, right?"

I don't know what he means by that, and I say as much.

"Well, for a start, you kind of freaked out last night when you saw that jar of beets."

"That's because I thought it was . . ." I don't finish the sentence because I realize how crazy what I'm about to say sounds.

"Thought it was what?"

"Never mind."

"And what about the noises you keep hearing? Like when you asked if I was pacing the halls in the middle of the night."

I shrug. Because what can I say that won't make this worse?

"And you're standing here in my kitchen, pointing a knife at me. A *knife*, Anna."

He's got a point. I lower the knife and go to the kitchen island, set it down on the counter.

"That's better." Gregg walks to the island and grabs the knife, then returns it to the knife block, well out of my reach. Then he goes to the coffee maker, pours himself a cup—no milk or sugar—and turns back to me. "I'm worried about you, Anna."

"You don't need to be."

"Maybe not. But when I came downstairs and couldn't find you . . ." He sips his coffee. "Anyway, you're safe, and that's all that matters."

"What does that mean?" I ask. "Why wouldn't I be safe?"

Gregg studies me over the rim of his cup. "You've had a knock on the head. For all I knew, you might've had another memory lapse and wandered off in a daze. I was about to grab my coat and go looking for you. Make sure you weren't freezing to death out in the woods."

"Well, I'm not, and I haven't forgotten anything else." I'm not sure whether to be annoyed by Gregg's attitude or flattered that he cares about me enough to worry.

"And then there's what just happened."

I'm about to respond, to continue arguing my case, but the look on Gregg's face says it all. He's right. I *was* standing in his kitchen waving a knife around. And maybe he's right about everything else. The man I saw, or thought I saw. The footsteps I thought I heard on the stairs. I pick up my mug of coffee, force myself to swallow it, even though it's cold. "Look, maybe I overreacted. I'm out of my element. Unsure of my surroundings. You would be too if you were in the same situation."

"No doubt." Gregg doesn't sound convinced by my explanation.

I don't want to keep talking about this—don't like the less-than-subtle insinuation that I'm losing my marbles—and decide to change the subject. "I went up to the third floor. There's a lot of stuff up there."

"Like I told you, it's used for storage."

"Not by you, though. It's all so outdated. And there's a rocking horse up there too. Something a child would play with, except it must be decades old. Like, almost from the Victorian era."

"I know. It came with the house. The previous occupants owned this place for a long time, and the stuff just accumulated. I suppose I should clean it out, but I figure it's not doing any harm up there. I don't use the rooms on that floor, so I've never gotten around to it."

"Who were the previous owners?" I ask. The house is big and grand, yet it's so remote that I can't imagine it was ever anything but a summer home. They must have been wealthy. Of course, that goes for Gregg too, even though I still don't know what he does for a living.

"I never met them, but from what I'm told, the house had been passed down through generations of the same family. The man who built it was a robber baron back in the nineteenth century. An industrialist who accumulated vast wealth at the expense of his workers. If I remember correctly, his name was Josephus Brand. He owned slate quarries in New York and Vermont and a mill outside of Rutland, where he turned the slate into pencils and tablets, which was apparently big business back then." Gregg looks around, almost wistfully. "They literally built this place off the sweat and toil of the masses. He even employed children to count the pencils and pack them into boxes. Worked them twelve hours a day, six days a week from what I heard."

"That's horrible," I say, aghast.

"It was a different time." Gregg pours himself a second cup of coffee. "But if it's any consolation, their fortunes waned. At least, if the condition of this place when I bought it is anything to go by. No one had lived here for over a decade. The kitchen was a complete gut job. The floorboards in the foyer were rotten and had to be replaced. All the woodwork needed refinishing, including the stairs and paneling in the living room. I repointed the fireplace and replaced all the plumbing and wiring. I also added the deck on the back and rebuilt the boat dock, which was practically falling into the water. It was a big job. Took over a year to complete."

"Which is why you haven't gotten around to the third floor yet," I say.

"Right. Couldn't face it. Thankfully, the roof wasn't leaking. It's made of tiles fashioned out of slate from Brand's quarries. It's original to the house and will probably still be here when we're long gone."

"You know a lot about the history of this house."

"It's always good to know what came before when you have a renovation job as big as this one," Gregg replies. "Cuts down on the surprises."

"I suppose."

"Okay. History lesson is over. I have some work to do for a couple of hours." He glances toward the knife block, almost as if he's contemplating removing sharp objects from the kitchen. "Will you be okay on your own for a while?"

Great. He thinks I'm going to grab the knife and go on a rampage. "Don't worry. I won't turn into a psycho while you're gone."

"That wasn't what I meant. I just want to make sure that you—"

"I'm not going to forget where I am and wander off into the woods like a mindless zombie either," I tell him in a sharp tone. "I'll be fine."

Gregg hesitates for a moment, then nods. "All right."

Coffee cup in hand, he heads for the door, and I'm alone again.

I stand there for a moment to calm down, then put my empty coffee cup in the sink and rinse it out. When I look up, a phone on the wall catches my eye. I pick up the receiver, hoping to hear a dial tone, but there's only silence.

I turn back toward the island, my gaze drawn to the pantry. Is it possible that the dark figure was nothing more than swirling shadows? The footsteps on the stairs really just the displaced sound of Gregg getting up and moving around in his bedroom? I have no choice but to consider the possibility. Or maybe I saw a ghost. If ever there was a house that should be haunted, it's this one. But not by the spirit of Gregg's dead wife, as I speculated the previous night. Now I wonder if it could be the robber baron or one of his descendants, unable to leave this mortal plane because of the evil deeds they committed in life.

That thought sends me scurrying from the kitchen and into the living room, which feels safer. I build a fresh fire and retreat to the sofa, and as I sit there, I wonder how long it will be before Gregg returns.

23

The knock at the door comes at three thirty in the afternoon, not long after Gregg and I finish a late lunch, during which neither of us mentions the morning's excitement. Me, because I don't want to make things worse between us, and him, I suspect, because he hasn't decided if I'm dangerous. When he answers, Helene is standing there with a bottle of wine gripped in her hand.

"Figured I'd come over and be social," she says, stepping past Gregg into the house without waiting for an invitation. "No point in us all sitting on our own sides of the lake in splendid isolation, right?"

Gregg doesn't answer.

Helene unzips her coat and removes it. "Is there somewhere I can hang this?"

Now Gregg finally speaks, although he doesn't sound happy. He holds out a hand. "You can give it to me. I'll hang it on the rack in the mudroom."

"Thank you." She hands him the coat and looks around. "Which way is the kitchen? Let's open this sucker."

"It's over there," I say. "First door on the right."

"Ah." Helene is off again, breezing into the kitchen, where she rummages for a corkscrew. She looks up when I follow her in, with Gregg a step behind. "You remember who you are yet, or am I still calling you *Anna*?"

"It's still Anna," I say. "Unfortunately."

"Too bad. I can't imagine what it must be like to have no past. For your life until now to be nothing but a blank."

"It's not pleasant," I say, watching her pull open another drawer.

Behind me, I hear Gregg let out a small huff of exasperation. "The corkscrew is in the top left drawer of the island."

Helene chuckles. "Always in the last place you look, right?" She looks at me. "I assume there are wineglasses around here somewhere."

"I'll get them," I say, stepping around the island and going to the cupboard Gregg took glasses from the previous evening. I glance over my shoulder to look at Helene, who is busy uncorking the wine. She appears outgoing and confident, but it feels like an act. I sense a hesitancy about her, as if she's stepping outside of her comfort zone. I wonder if Gregg has noticed it too, but it's hard to tell. He's just standing there with his arms folded, watching her. He looks annoyed.

"Got it," Helene says, as the cork comes out of the bottle with a pop. She waits for me to put down the wineglasses, then pours one for each of us.

We head into the living room.

Helene and I sit on the sofa while Gregg takes up residence in a leather chair to the right of the fireplace.

There's a moment of uncomfortable silence before Helene finally speaks. Apparently, she has used up her reserves of bravado because she sounds less sure of herself now. Almost timid. "This house is beautiful. So much bigger than the place I'm renting."

Gregg nods. "Thank you. It serves my purposes."

"Why are you renting up here in the middle of winter?" I ask her, curious.

"It's for work, mostly." Helene sets her glass down, then clutches her hands together in her lap, fingers interlaced. "I'm a writer. The solitude helps me concentrate. Of course, I wasn't expecting to get stranded by a winter storm." She looks at Gregg. "I assume the bridge is still out?"

"I'm sure it is," he replies. "The road is still unplowed."

"Gregg told me it took them weeks to repair the bridge last time," I tell her.

"Crap." Helene frowns. "I'm supposed to be here only for another ten days. But hey, if I can't leave, then whoever rented the place next can't get here either. Right?"

"Let's hope it doesn't come to that," Gregg says.

"Let's hope." Helene forces a smile. "Or I might be back before you know it, begging for scraps of food."

"If it comes to that, I've got you covered. We have a fully stocked pantry and an extra freezer full of food in the basement. Always better to be safe than sorry out here in the wilds of Vermont." Gregg sounds sincere, but he has a cold look in his eyes. Clearly, he hopes Helene won't be making too many trips across the lake.

I decide to change the subject.

"What kind of writing?" My curiosity has gotten the better of me, and I want to steer the conversation back to something more interesting than the weather. "Like a journalist?"

"Fiction." Helene pulls her hands apart and brushes an invisible strand of hair away from her face. "I'm a novelist."

"Anything we might have read?" Gregg glances toward the books on the shelf next to the fireplace.

"Oh, probably not. I mostly write romantic suspense."

"Actually, Gregg's wife used to read stuff like that. I saw a bunch of romance novels when I was browsing through the books," I blurt out, then realize what I've said. I look at Gregg. "Sorry. I didn't mean to—"

"It's fine." If my faux pas upset him, Gregg doesn't show it. "I came to terms with her death a long time ago."

And yet he won't get rid of the clothes in his closet, I think. Apparently, he can't bear looking at photos of her either. Hell, he won't even tell me her name. I wonder if he's being truthful, or just kind.

"Your wife died?" Helene says. "I'm so sorry."

Gregg nods and looks down into his wine. "I'd rather not talk about it."

Tension hangs in the air.

"This is so exciting. I've never met a real-life author before," I finally say to break the silence, then realize how stupid that statement is. I don't have any idea if I've ever met an author. I could have met hundreds of them for all I know. I try to cover my tracks. "Of course, that's not saying much."

Helene smiles. "It's okay. I get it."

"I'd love to read something you've written," I tell her. "You'll have to bring over one of your books the next time you visit us."

Helene looks sheepish. "I'm not actually published yet. I have a contract, but it's my first book. That's why I needed to get away. I'm deep in editing it right now." She glances at her wineglass, which is almost empty. "Looks like I need a refill."

"The wine bottle is in the kitchen," Gregg says, standing up. "I'll run and get it."

Helene watches him go. Then, when Gregg is out of earshot, she scoots closer to me on the sofa.

"I hope you won't think I'm overstepping my bounds," she says in a voice barely above a whisper. "But I just want to make sure that you're comfortable here. That you feel safe."

"Why wouldn't I be safe?" I ask. "Do you know something about Gregg?"

"Oh my, no. I never met him before yesterday. I didn't mean to scare you. It's just that you're here all alone with him in this house, and he's a stranger. I'm sure he's been nothing but a perfect gentleman, but it never hurts to ask."

"Gregg's been good to me. I feel perfectly safe around him."

"I'm glad to hear that. But please be careful. You never know what people are like. Who they really are."

"I will."

"And if you ever need somewhere to go, if you need help, I'm right across the lake. Come over any time of day or—" Helene falls silent and shifts back to her end of the sofa as Gregg returns with the bottle of wine.

He refills our glasses and tops up his own, emptying the bottle, which he sets aside on the coffee table.

"I hope you girls weren't talking about me while I was gone," he says with a grin as he retakes his seat.

"Of course we were," Helene says, returning his grin with a beaming smile of her own. "Who else would we talk about?"

24

By the time Helene leaves, I have a pleasant buzz from the wine. Gregg walks her to the door, then stands watching as she makes her way across the back deck and onto the dock where her boat is tied up. Once she's safely aboard, he closes the door, tells me to sit tight, and heads for the kitchen.

He comes back ten minutes later with a tray upon which he's arranged three plates. The first contains an assortment of soft and hard cheeses. The second is meat. Rolled-up slices of ham and turkey. Pepperoni and salami. The third is piled high with sliced crusty bread. Under his arm is a second bottle of wine.

He puts the tray down on the coffee table. "I figured we could pick at this while we enjoy our evening."

"You sure that's a good idea?" I ask as he pulls a corkscrew from his pocket and goes about opening the wine. I don't know how much I drink normally, but this will be our third bottle in two nights.

"It's not like we have anything better to do." He refills my glass and then his own. "Don't worry, I promise not to get you too tipsy."

I don't see how he can keep that promise. I'm already halfway there.

Gregg settles on the sofa next to me and reaches into his pocket again. "I have something for you."

He produces a small black leather-bound notebook and a silver pen.

"What's this for?" I ask as he hands it to me.

"I found it in my study and thought you might like it. You can keep it with you, and whenever something feels familiar, or you discover something new about yourself, you can write it down."

"Kind of like a diary."

"Yeah. Something like that."

"How very twentieth century."

"If you don't like it—" Gregg reaches to take the notebook back.

I don't let him. "No. I love it. You're very thoughtful."

"If you're sure."

"Quite sure." I lift my glass and swirl the crimson liquid around, then take a sip. This bottle is better than the one Helene brought over. The notes are more complex. The flavor profile more robust. It's not surprising, considering how expensive the wine must be. I suddenly realize that my ability to analyze the taste of the wine must mean that I—the *I* who knows who she is—must drink wine. It's not a big discovery, but it's a start. Maybe these small discoveries will help break the dam that's holding back my memories. I put the glass down, open the notebook, and write my first observation.

I like wine.

Then I show the notebook to Gregg. "See? I'm using it already."

Gregg smiles and looks at the charcuterie. "You should eat something. It's not good to drink on an empty stomach."

He's right. I reach over and take a piece of cheese, a slice of ham, and bread from the tray. For the next hour, we eat and drink while we talk. The conversation is light and easy. I find myself enjoying Gregg's company more and more. I was pretty lucky to find him, considering the circumstances.

When the charcuterie is nothing but crumbs, he tops up our glasses with what's left of the wine, then he stands up and extends an arm. "Come on."

I look up at him in confusion. "Where are we going?"

"To enjoy the majesty of nature." Gregg glances toward the window, and I see that not only has it stopped snowing, but the sky has cleared, and the stars are out.

"You want to go outside? It's freezing." I shake my head and look wistfully toward the roaring fire.

"It will be fine. Trust me." Gregg takes my hand and pulls me up, then guides me toward the foyer, where he hands me a coat.

Suitably bundled up and with our wineglasses in hand, we head out onto the back deck and make our way toward a semicircle of Adirondack chairs arranged around the square snow-covered lump that turns out to be a firepit. Gregg pushes away the snow and removes the cover. He turns on the propane and lights it. The flames leap into the frosty night air as he goes about brushing snow from two of the Adirondack chairs.

Warm air from the firepit wafts toward me.

"Here. Have a seat," Gregg says, offering me a chair. He waits for me to sit down before settling in the other.

"Do you sit outside in the dead of winter often?" I ask, shivering despite the firepit. I set the wineglass down on the arm of the chair and hold my hands close to the flames.

"Only with the right company," Gregg replies. "Lean back in the chair and look up at the sky. The stars."

I wonder if the right company was previously his wife, but I don't ask. Instead, I do as he says and settle into the chair before lifting my eyes toward the heavens. Now I understand and gasp at the spectacle above me. The wide band of the Milky Way arches above us like a celestial river. A billion points of light that come together to paint a shimmering ribbon across the night sky. "It's breathtaking."

"Just think," Gregg says. "Millions of years from now, after we're all long gone, those suns will still be burning."

I contemplate that for a moment. The unending cycle of the cosmos. But then my thoughts turn inward. Is there someone out there right now who loves me, misses me, looking up at those same stars? Do they wonder where I am and what happened? Or am I alone? A solitary lost vessel drifting on the sea of life with no idea how to reach port.

Or maybe I've already reached it.

This place, Gregg, could be my safe harbor.

I like that thought. It comforts me. And when he reaches across from his chair and takes my hand, all the anxiety and fear of the last few days melt away.

"This is perfect," I say, unable to tear my gaze away from the heavens.

Gregg doesn't reply. There is no need.

We stay that way for a while longer, holding hands under the canopy of stars. But then, once the wine is gone, Gregg slips his hand from mine and stands up.

"It's getting too nippy out here. Why don't we take this back inside?"

He's right. The temperature has been falling even as we've been sitting there. Who knows how much colder it will get before dawn? I pick up my wineglass and stand up, gazing out over the crystalline landscape as Gregg extinguishes the firepit. Then we go back inside.

"It's getting late, and I'm tired," I say with a yawn after we take off our coats and return the wineglasses to the kitchen. "I think I'll head upstairs."

"Are you sure?" Gregg looks disappointed. "I was thinking we could go back into the living room, enjoy the fire awhile longer."

"Thank you for tonight. It was really great." I go to give Gregg a parting hug, and he reciprocates, slipping his arms around my waist and pulling me close. Our bodies meet. This is not the polite embrace of two strangers thrown together by circumstance. My breasts press against his chest. I can feel his heart beating.

He gazes into my eyes.

For a second, the world stops.

I know what's coming next but do nothing to stop it. Maybe it's because I'm tipsy, but I want him to do it. I want to know what it feels like. Because even if I don't want to admit it, I'm attracted to Gregg, and I like the interest he's showing in me. I feel at home in his arms. A connection I desperately need to pull me back from the feeling that I'm swimming alone in the middle of a vast and empty ocean. And as I relax in his embrace, a strange feeling engulfs me. Not a memory, but a *normalness* that feels so familiar, like I've done this before, even though I can't remember when or with whom.

"Anna," he whispers in a breathless voice.

"Yes?" I reply, wishing he'd do more than talk.

And he does. His lips find mine in a lingering kiss, full of urgency and need. I melt into his arms. The world around us fades away until it's just me and Gregg, and nothing else matters.

Then, too quickly, it's over.

Gregg pulls away. Releases me from his embrace. He studies my face, silently waiting for confirmation that I'm okay with what just happened.

And I am . . . I think. But I'm also confused. Which is why all I can manage is a mumbled "Good night" before I turn and flee upstairs to my bedroom.

25

Adria

Two Days Before

The text message from Harvey Lang, the security consultant, came through on the burner phone hidden in Adria's pocket at eight in the morning, when she was in the kitchen making breakfast for herself and Peter. She knew it was the burner because she had turned the ringer off and set it to vibrate. She also made a point never to carry both the burner and her regular phone in the same pocket.

After a quick glance toward the table, where Peter was sitting with his laptop open, she pulled the phone out of her pocket, unlocked it, and checked the messages.

> Meet me this afternoon at four. Same place as before. Be careful. He is not who you think he is.

Adria stared at the message.

A finger of icy dread ran up her spine.

The toaster oven dinged, but she ignored it. How could her life have collapsed so completely in such a short time? It was bad enough that Peter was probably embezzling from the charitable foundation, but this? She couldn't tear her gaze away from the last line of the message. *He is not who you think he is.* What the hell had she gotten herself into when she married him?

"Everything okay over there?" Peter asked, poking his head up over the laptop screen.

"Yes. I'm fine." Adria snapped out of it. She tapped out a quick reply, saying that she would be there, turning away from Peter just enough to keep the screen out of his view. A moment later, three animated dots that indicated Harvey was typing a reply of his own pulsed beneath her message. Then, without warning, the dots went away. She waited, aware that Peter was still watching her. No new message appeared.

"You sure you're fine?" he asked. "You look . . . flustered."

"I'm sure." Adria put the phone back into her pocket and opened the toaster oven, pulling out half of a sliced bagel and juggling it in her palms because it was too hot. She dropped it onto a plate and turned back to Peter, forcing a smile. "You want butter or cream cheese on your bagel?"

"Cream cheese is fine. Plain." Peter glanced at his watch. "Who texted?"

"Oh, it was just the office," Adria lied. "Claudia from accounting. She has some paperwork that needs to be signed today to do with the Zimbabwe clean water project funding."

"The water wells."

Adria nodded.

"I thought that was all taken care of. The money should already be on its way."

"I guess they need something else." *Stop questioning me,* Adria thought. *I'm the one who should be asking questions.* "There's probably an issue with the transfer paperwork. You know what these international deals are like. Petty bureaucrats and red tape."

"Hmph. Do I ever." Peter looked down for a moment, then back up. "What time are you going in?"

"I don't know. Later on. Maybe I'll leave here around three."

"Great. That works for me. I'll come with you."

"What?" A glut of panic rose in Adria's throat.

"I have a few things to do around the office myself. This works out great. We can kill two birds with one stone."

You don't have anything to do around the office, Adria thought. *You barely do any work for the foundation, except siphoning off cash to your fake charity. You just want to come with me because you're suspicious.* But she couldn't say any of that. She also couldn't have Peter tagging along. She took the other half of the bagel from the toaster while she racked her brain for a reason he shouldn't come. There was only one reason she could think of, and it was pretty feeble. "You sure you want to come into the office? I'll be in and out in ten minutes. I only have to sign a couple of documents. There won't even be time for you to get anything done."

"I'm sure you can wait around for me."

He wasn't making this easy. "I thought I'd head over to the spa afterward and get my hair done. You know . . . since I'll be out already. I have an appointment at the salon across town, and I'd rather not have to drive back and pick you up."

Peter observed her for a moment longer. She thought he was going to press the issue further, but then he shrugged. "Guess I'll stay here, then."

26

Anna

Day Three

The night passes without incident. There are no creaks in the hallway outside my door, lights turning off on their own, or murmured conversations to keep me awake. The wine helps. I fall asleep quickly, consumed with thoughts of Gregg and what just happened.

When I come down the next morning, he's in the kitchen making eggs, which seems to be his routine. I pour myself a coffee from the half-full carafe and settle on a stool at the island to watch him work. Neither of us mentions the kiss. I'm not sure if we're pretending it didn't happen, or if we're taking time to ponder the new dynamic of our coexistence within this house before broaching the subject. Either way, I'm happy to put off what might be an awkward conversation, because even if I don't consider our moment of intimacy to be a mistake, I have no idea what Gregg thinks. Maybe he feels the same as me and is just as unsure how to proceed, or maybe he regrets our kiss. He told Helene that he had come to terms with his wife's death, but that doesn't mean he's ready to share himself with another woman. Especially one who comes with as much baggage as I do.

And maybe that would be for the best. Like it or not, we are going to be stuck in this house together for a while longer, and neither of us knows anything about the other. Gregg, because he won't talk about his life outside of this place, and me, because I don't remember it. Hell, I know nothing about myself. Maybe I'm a total bitch. If I have a best friend somewhere out in the world beyond Gravewater Lake, they would probably tell me that becoming entangled with this man under the circumstances is a recipe for disaster. And I would have to agree with my hypothetical friend. But that doesn't stop me from smiling when I think about the way he held me last night. The way my stomach fluttered when our lips met.

"You look happy this morning," Gregg says, glancing back over his shoulder and seeing my smile before it fades.

Shit, he caught me.

"Better than the alternative," I say, not wanting to admit the real reason to him.

"How about the notepad? Did you come up with anything else to write in it other than your love of pinot noir?" he asks, turning back to the pan and flipping the eggs with a spatula.

I assume this is Gregg's subtle way of asking me if I've remembered anything yet. I haven't and tell him so.

"Bummer." He lifts the pan and slides a golden yellow omelet onto a plate, pushes it across the island toward me along with a fork, then turns back to the stove and goes about making a second one. It only takes him a minute, and then he joins me at the island. But not before going to the refrigerator and returning with a bottle of hot sauce, which he uses to douse the top of his eggs. He offers me the bottle. "You want some?"

I shake my head, horrified. "That's a hard pass."

"Are you sure?" Gregg puts the bottle down on the counter. "Might give you another entry for that notebook."

"Yeah. Even with amnesia, I'm pretty sure I don't like hot sauce on eggs."

"Your loss." Gregg breaks off a mouthful of the sauce-laden omelet, eats it, and smacks his lips. "Speaking of the notebook, how do you feel about taking a walk after breakfast? Check out the houses on the east side of the lake and see if anything feels familiar."

"I think that's a great idea." I've been feeling frustrated with my lack of progress, and I won't jog any memories hanging around Gregg's house. But then a thought occurs to me. "There must be a foot of snow out there. It won't be easy going."

"You let me worry about that," Gregg says, cutting another wedge of omelet with the side of his fork and popping it into his mouth.

Okay, now I'm intrigued. "You have a couple of snowmobiles stashed around here or something?"

Gregg chuckles. "Nothing so cool, I'm afraid. But don't worry, you'll do fine."

I shoot him a questioning look with narrowed eyes.

He grins. "You'll just have to wait and see."

I'd rather he tell me now, but I can see that he's not going to. Gregg likes to play it close to his chest, apparently. Or maybe he just wants to tease me. I pour myself another coffee and turn my attention back to the food. Fifteen minutes later, the plates are empty, and we're heading out of the kitchen.

"It's freezing out there," Gregg says, looking at the clothes I'm wearing after we enter the foyer. "You might want to run upstairs and put on a sweater."

I do as he says and fetch the thicker of the two sweaters I borrowed from his closet. The soft wool one. I pull it over my head, then switch my socks for a warmer pair. When I go back downstairs, I find Gregg in the mudroom.

His eyes light up when I enter.

"You look . . . gorgeous."

"I don't, but thank you," I demur, although secretly I'm pleased at the way he's looking at me. Apparently, he doesn't regret our kiss. Then I notice what he has in his hands. They look like a pair of sandals with short, fat skis attached to the bottom. Another set rests alongside two pairs of ski poles leaning next to the boots I wore the last time we ventured outdoors. I stare at them. "What are those?"

"Mini ski skates. You strap them onto your boots. It will make the going easier."

"Are you sure about that?" Maybe I'm a skier, and this will come naturally to me, or I just might fall flat on my face the minute I step outside wearing those things.

"Relax. It's easy. I'll show you what to do." Gregg takes a pair of ski poles and heads toward the door. "Grab your gear and let's go."

27

We trudge across the deck and don't put on our mini skis until we reach a woodland trail that follows the curve of the lake. The snow is thinner here, only a few inches deep thanks to the tree canopy above us, and the top layer has frozen to a hard crust.

The skis are not as easy to use as Gregg makes them out to be. I almost fall flat on my ass within seconds of my feet hitting the snow and only stay upright when he grabs my arm to steady me.

"I guess you have something else for your notebook," he says after I find my balance. "You're not a skier."

"Or at least if I am, I've forgotten how to do it, along with everything else," I reply.

"Just lean forward with your upper body, and keep your weight on your heels," he tells me as I make a second clumsy attempt to wrangle the skis into some kind of forward motion. "Start with the skis in a V shape. Then extend one leg to the side, plant your pole, push off, and keep extending alternate legs. It's more like skating than skiing."

"Maybe that's why I'm not getting the hang of it," I say, adjusting my technique and seeing immediate improvement. I might not be a skier, but I must have learned to skate at some point, maybe when I was a kid.

"That's it." Gregg glides past me, making it look easy.

Which it isn't.

I'm moving forward now, but I'm hardly graceful. I grunt and curse in equal measures as I navigate the narrow trail with Gregg ahead of me. At intervals, he stops and waits for me to catch up. He refrains from commenting on my technique, even though I can tell what he's thinking by the grin on his face.

After ten arduous minutes, we reach a house tucked between the pines. Gregg's closest neighbor on this side of the lake, although it doesn't look like anyone is home. The windows are dark and impenetrable. There are no footprints anywhere, even around a stack of split logs piled up against the wall of a small utility shed. If anyone was here, they would surely use the fireplace.

"Well?" Gregg asks, peering up at the house. "Anything?"

I shake my head. The house does not look familiar.

"Guess we keep going, then." Gregg takes off again, following the trail farther around the lake.

The next house is smaller and isn't in good repair. I can see a cracked windowpane, and the shingles have lost most of their paint. I wonder if anyone even uses it anymore. Certainly, it isn't stirring any memories, so we press on.

By the time we come to the third house, my calf muscles are burning, and I beg Gregg to let us rest for a few minutes.

"I don't think I can make it all the way around the lake," I say to him. "This is hard work."

"It gets easier the more you do it," he replies. He brushes the snow off a fallen log for me to sit down, then settles beside me. "Your muscles will firm up."

I gaze out over the lake. The water sparkles under a deep blue sky. A hawk circles overhead before slipping from view behind the treetops on the opposite shore. I can see why Gregg likes it here so much, even in winter, and I tell him so.

He smiles. "I like it better with you."

"You hardly know me," I reply. "And when I get my memory back, you might not like the person I turn out to be."

"You'll still be the same person. The only difference is that we'll know what that *A* on your bracelet actually stands for."

"Maybe we guessed right, and my real name is Anna."

Now Gregg laughs. "Wouldn't that be something?" He turns to look at me. "Look, about last night—"

"The kiss."

"Yes. You practically fled upstairs afterward and said nothing about it this morning."

"What do you want me to say?"

"I don't know. That I didn't offend you."

"You didn't."

He takes my hand, and I think he's about to lean in and kiss me again, but he just stares into my eyes. "Good. But if I ever do anything to make you feel uncomfortable, just tell me, okay? I'm not exactly . . . I mean . . ."

I know what he's trying to say. His wife died, and this is as complicated for him as it is for me. We're both stumbling through this situation, not sure if we're doing the right thing. I wonder if he's going to say anything else, but he slips his hand from mine and stands up.

"Let's go as far as the next house and call it a day. There's a trail that doubles back to the house through the woods. There are a couple of summer cottages along the way. We can check them out."

"Sure." My calves feel better now, although they are still sore. I'm looking forward to a hot, soothing shower when we return. Maybe even a cup of cocoa.

We continue on. The next house doesn't jog any memories, and neither do the two cottages, which are both smaller than the lakefront properties. By the time we arrive back at Gregg's place, my calves are screaming again, and I'm happy to get the short skis off my feet before we cross the deck and go inside.

And when we do, I come to a halt.

Because from somewhere deep within the house, an alarm is going off.

28

Adria

Two Days Before

Adria left the house a little after three in the afternoon and drove downtown. But she didn't go directly to the coffee shop. Peter had mentioned nothing else about the text message or the excuse she had concocted about going into the office to sign papers. But that didn't mean he believed her. In fact, she was sure that he didn't.

Harvey had told her not to trust him, and she was going to take that advice seriously. Which was why she left so early when the drive to the coffee shop would normally take less than twenty minutes. Instead, she sent a quick text message back to Harvey explaining what she was doing and telling him to wait if she wasn't on time, then drove to the office first and parked before making a show of going into the building. If Peter had followed her, just like she was sure he had done the previous time that she met Harvey, then he would think she was telling the truth. And even if he hadn't tailed her, she was sure he would phone the office and check with reception to see if she had actually turned up there. Which is why she breezed through the lobby and said hello to the girl behind the desk before stepping into the elevator and going up to her office. She sat there for a while, counting off the minutes until she thought it was reasonable to leave again, then went back to her car and drove to the coffee shop, parking a couple of blocks away just like she had before. But when she entered and looked around, there was no sign of Harvey Lang.

She went to the counter and ordered a coffee, then settled at a table near the door and stared out the window to the street beyond. She had been right on time and was surprised that he wasn't there, already waiting. As an ex-military man, Harvey appreciated punctuality. But he was also an employee of Rhodes Enterprises, the sprawling corporation that acted as an umbrella to her family's many business enterprises. The charitable foundation technically operated outside of that corporate structure as an independent entity funded through a sizable shareholding in its parent organization. Even though Harvey had done work for the charitable foundation many times, his first duty lay with Rhodes Enterprises. And this wasn't even technically foundation business. She had asked him to investigate her husband. Maybe he had gotten held up by some developing situation at the office. But if that were the case, why hadn't he let her know?

She checked her phone just to make sure she hadn't missed a message from him, but there was nothing.

It was now 4:15 p.m.

There was only one number on the burner phone. It was his. She dialed it.

After three rings, it went to voicemail.

She hung up without leaving a message, then sat there for another ten minutes before phoning again with the same result.

Where was he?

At a quarter to five, she tried one last time, staring down into her now-cold cup of coffee, which she had been too preoccupied to bother drinking. When it again went to voicemail, she left a brief message.

"It's Adria. Call me back."

She then sent the same message via text before picking up the coffee and dumping it into a trash can near the door. Then she stepped out onto the sidewalk as the rush-hour traffic inched its way along Newberry Street and started back toward her car. This time, she saw no custom-red Mercedes sitting in traffic like it was following her, but it didn't matter. Adria couldn't shake the feeling that something was wrong. Very wrong.

29

Anna

Day Three

The alarm is shrill and insistent. A steady, high-pitched beeping that fills the house with urgency.

"What *is* that?" I ask, glancing around. I don't see any obvious signs of an emergency. No smoke from a fire or damage where someone might have broken in. "Do you have an alarm system?"

"No." Gregg appears as confused as I am. He steps farther into the foyer. "And even if I did, it wouldn't matter. We didn't lock the back door when we left."

That isn't a comforting thought. "Maybe we should have."

"Why? We're the only people up here apart from that woman, Helene, across the lake. And even if we weren't, this is middle-of-nowhere Vermont, not New York City."

"Well, something set an alarm off." The constant beeping grates on me. It sounds like it's coming from my left. The kitchen. I head in that direction and soon find the cause.

The left-side door to the closest of the two fridges stands ajar.

I hurry around the kitchen island and close it, cutting off the incessant beeping. When I turn away from the fridge, Gregg is standing in the doorway.

"See? Told you it was nothing to worry about," he says, leaning on the door surround.

But it is. Because I'm sure the fridge wasn't like that when we left. To prove it, I open the door again and wait.

A minute passes. Then two.

Gregg still stands in the doorway, silently humoring me.

At the two-minute mark, the beeping starts anew.

I close the door again and turn to him. "That proves it. We didn't leave the fridge open."

"What are you talking about? Maybe the door wasn't closed properly, and it came open again after we left the house."

I don't believe that for a moment. "We were in the kitchen longer than two minutes after you put the eggs back in the fridge. We ate breakfast right here, sitting at the island. Even if the door was only open a hair, the alarm would still have gone off, and if it wasn't, how would it come back open all by itself after we left?"

"I don't know, but it did," Gregg says in a matter-of-fact way, as if that solves the mystery. "You think someone snuck into the house after we went for our walk around the lake, and all they were interested in was the contents of my refrigerator?"

I shrug. He has a point. It sounds nutty, but I can't shake the feeling that something isn't right. I turn to the fridge again, open it, and peer inside to see if anything is missing. The problem is that I don't know what was in there to begin with, and nothing jumps out at me. I close the fridge and stand with my arms folded, trying to dispel the unease that has settled upon me.

Gregg senses my discomfort. He comes around the island and stands behind me. His arms slip around my waist. "I know you're freaked out by your situation, but you need to relax. Sometimes things like this happen. It's no big deal. I bet the fridge was closed just enough to contact the door sensor, and after we left, it swung open again. It probably happened when we opened the back door. Maybe there was a draft or a change in air pressure. I promise that you're safe here."

"Maybe."

"There's no maybe about it." He pushes my hair aside, nuzzles the nape of my neck. I feel his lips brush my skin. When he speaks again, his breath tickles my ear. "We all good here?"

I nod, because it's pointless to keep talking about something neither of us can prove either way. "I'm good."

"Wonderful." He pulls away and releases me. "Listen, I have some work to do. It shouldn't take long, but it *is* important. Will you be all right on your own for a couple of hours?"

I turn around and tell him I will. I wonder what exactly he's working on with no internet and no communication with the outside world. But I don't ask because he's made it clear that the subject is off-limits.

He studies my face for a moment. Then he turns and strides from the room.

I watch him go. The skin of my neck still tingles with the phantom touch of his kiss. I wonder where this is heading and if I should allow it to continue. I've only known him for about two and a half days, and there are so many reasons to play it safe. Keep Gregg at arm's length until the reality of my situation becomes clear. But part of me doesn't want to. I like the attention he's lavishing upon me, and I feel safe around him, despite the occasional odd occurrence in the house. And when I think about it, there's nothing about any of those incidents that proves either of us is in any danger. Gregg has an explanation for all of them. It probably was a mouse that pushed that jar of beets off the shelf. And I probably did just hear him moving around in his bedroom when I thought someone was on the old servants' stairs. And as for the refrigerator door . . . Well, maybe he's right about that too.

30

I make the cup of hot cocoa that I promised myself out on the trail, then withdraw to the living room. I wish there was a TV so I could see something of the world beyond this isolated lake, but once again I'm forced to settle for a book.

I choose a romance novel and sit down in front of the fire to read, but it doesn't hold my attention.

The notebook is in my back pocket.

I take it out and write down this latest crumb of information about myself—*not keen on romances*—before returning the book to the shelf and finding a thriller to read instead. I go back to the couch and stay there for several hours with my nose in the book.

Eventually, I come up for air and realize that Gregg has not returned. The house is eerily quiet, almost as if the building is holding its breath. I close the book and place it on the arm of the sofa, then stand and take my empty cocoa mug back into the kitchen.

There is still no sign of Gregg.

Where could he be?

His study is the obvious place, since he wanted to catch up on work.

I make my way there and rap my knuckles on the door. Two short knocks.

No answer.

I knock again, louder this time.

Still nothing.

When I try the handle, the door opens to reveal an empty room. He isn't there, and it doesn't look like he ever was. At least, not today. The office chair is pushed neatly under the desk, and the desktop is devoid of a computer or any paperwork. Also, the lights are off. The study feels . . . unused. I can't explain why I sense this. I just do.

I spot a phone on his desk. Maybe the DSL line has been repaired. I walk over and pick up the receiver, lift it to my ear. Silence. *Bummer.* Then I see something else. A small round LED display on the keypad that reads *01*. Beneath it are several buttons: *Play/Stop. Repeat. Skip. Delete.* An old-fashioned digital answering machine. *Huh.* Strange that I recognize this obsolete device but can't remember my name.

A burning curiosity overcomes me. I reach out, press Play. To my surprise, the machine actually works. And there's a message. A woman's voice, although the recording keeps cutting out, and the quality is so bad that I struggle to hear it.

Hey, it's me. I tried your cell phone, but you didn't answer. I'm on my way back from town. Storm's getting pretty bad. Snow is coming down hard. Just wanted to let you know in case I get stranded and lose cell service. See you in a few.

The message ends. I replay it, listen to it for a second time. There's no date stamp, nothing to indicate when it was left. Has Gregg kept it because it's the last tangible link he has to his dead wife? The only surviving recording of her voice? My throat tightens. I feel like I'm intruding on a private memory. A cherished moment I have no business listening to.

Uncomfortable, I turn and hurry from the office, close the door behind me. Then I search the rest of the downstairs, poking my head back into the living room, even though I just came from there, and then checking the dining room. I even look in the mudroom, wondering if Gregg stepped outside. Maybe he finished whatever work he was doing and went for a walk. But he didn't. His boots are sitting on the floor in a little pool of water where the snow melted after we returned from our trek around the lake.

I retreat from the mudroom and go to the back door, just to be sure. I peer out at the deck but don't see any fresh prints in the snow except those we made earlier. Then I go to the front door on the other side of the main staircase and check that too. As I suspected, a crisp blanket of pristine snow covers the driveway in front of the house, just as it did the last time I looked there.

I climb the stairs to the second floor and head straight for the main bedroom.

Just like the study, this door is closed. I press my ear to it and listen, but I don't hear any sound from within. Not bothering to knock this time, I try the handle.

The door opens.

I step inside to be greeted by another empty room.

What the hell? This is getting weird. Gregg is still in the house. He must be, because there's no sign that he left.

I retreat into the hallway and search the other rooms on the second floor, including a second bathroom and my bedroom. Not that I think for a moment that he would be there.

The only other place Gregg could be is on the third floor. I walk to the end of the hall and try to turn the handle, pull the door open, but it's locked. *Great.* To check the attic, I'll have to go back to the ground floor, pass through the kitchen, and then climb all the way back up two sets of stairs. My still-aching calves don't relish that idea.

A spark of frustration pulses within me.

I turn and head back down the hallway, determined to locate Gregg if it's the last thing I do. A flicker of panic extinguishes the frustration. He's my only lifeline to sanity, and it's almost like he winked out of existence. If I didn't know better, I might be tempted to believe that he was nothing but a figment of my imagination, conjured to stave off the dreadful loneliness of being trapped all by myself with a head devoid of memories in a place I don't recognize.

But Gregg is real. Because when I turn toward the stairs, he's right there, coming out of his bedroom.

A bedroom that I'm sure was empty moments earlier.

31

I stare at Gregg in open-mouthed disbelief. I know he wasn't in that room. How could he have been when I checked it myself?

He stops in the hallway, suddenly aware of my unflinching gaze. His brow creases. "What?"

"Where were you?" I ask him, although the evidence of my own eyes has already provided an answer, even if I can't reconcile it with my previous experience.

"I was in the bedroom," he replies, glancing back toward the open door. "What's the problem?"

"You weren't." I stalk down the hallway toward him. "I looked there. It was empty."

"Hey." Gregg holds his arms up. "I promise you that I was. Where else would I have been?"

"I don't know. But I couldn't find you. I checked everywhere . . . including in your bedroom."

"Maybe you should've looked a little bit harder." Gregg pushes his hands into his pockets. "You saw me come out with your own eyes."

"Well, I . . ." I falter, suddenly unsure of my own convictions. "I mean . . ."

"I was probably in the en suite. I finished my work and came upstairs to take a shower. Did you check in there?"

"Well, no." He's right. I didn't look in the en suite bathroom, but I also didn't hear the shower running. Maybe he'd already finished and was drying himself, but I'm sure the bathroom door was open and the room beyond was dark. I would have heard him in there even if I didn't see him. And there were no discarded clothes on the bed or anywhere else. Then I notice something else. He's wearing the same jeans and shirt as earlier. When I point this out, he just shrugs.

"So what? I put the same shirt back on. It was clean this morning." He takes a step toward me. "Anna, are you feeling all right? You look pale. Perhaps we should go downstairs, and I'll make you a nice hot cup of tea."

I don't want to drink tea. I want to know where Gregg was. He claims to have been taking a shower. I push past him and step into the bedroom before he can react, then make my way to the en suite.

The mirror hanging over the vanity is steamed. Droplets of water have meandered down it, leaving thin trails of clear glass among the condensation. I turn to the shower stall and open the glass door, which is also fogged. The shower tray is wet. So is the towel hanging on a hook next to the stall.

He *was* taking a shower. So how did I miss him? I'm still convinced that he was not in the en suite when I looked in his bedroom. But the proof of my own eyes doesn't lie, so what is the most logical explanation? That despite all the evidence to the contrary, Gregg is not telling me the truth about his whereabouts, or that I somehow failed to notice him in the bathroom?

"I told you, I was taking a shower," Gregg says, appearing in the bathroom doorway. He steps close to me and cups the side of my neck with his hand. The touch is soft. Almost loving. "You're jumping at shadows. Imagining things that aren't there."

"That's not true," I say in a small voice, although clearly, it *is* true.

"You were running around with a knife in your hand yesterday. For a moment, I thought you might use it on *me*. Maybe your knock to the head is worse than we thought."

"It's not," I say, not bothering to hide my irritation. I feel better today than yesterday, and certainly better than the night when I stumbled soaking wet and freezing up to Gregg's door. I would even say that I'm back to my old self, if I had any idea who she might be. "We don't even know for sure that I ever had a concussion. You're not a doctor, remember?"

"Hey, easy there." The soothing tone of Gregg's voice implies that he's being reasonable while I am not.

It irks me. I open my mouth to snap back at him, then think better of it. I won't win this argument because I probably *do* have a concussion. The difference is that I don't believe it's causing me to see and hear things that aren't there. Or in this particular instance, to *not* see someone who *was* there. Yet the wet shower stall and steamed mirror all prove Gregg is telling the truth. Regardless of how it happened, I failed to notice him in the bathroom. I drop my head, defeated. "I'm sorry. I guess I just didn't see you in there and freaked myself out."

"It's fine. I didn't mean to give you a fright," he says.

"You were gone so long. I just got jumpy."

"I won't leave you alone for that long again. Promise." Gregg kisses my forehead. "I know how hard this whole situation has been for you."

I nod.

He smiles. "Now, how about that cup of tea?"

I nod again. "Sure."

32

ANNA

I feel better after we go downstairs, and by the time Gregg has made the cup of tea, I've convinced myself that he was in the en suite all along taking a shower, and I just failed to notice him.

I drink my tea at the kitchen counter and watch while he prepares dinner, throwing a salad together and topping it with chicken he prepares in a pan on the stove. It's 5:00 p.m., and the world outside the kitchen window is cold and dark. I feel guilty about the way I've treated Gregg. Waving a knife around. Insisting that we're not alone in the house despite all evidence to the contrary, like some raving mad person. Accusing him of . . . I don't know what . . . when I couldn't find him this afternoon. I make a promise to myself that I'll do better. That I won't fall down that rabbit hole of paranoia and mistrust anymore.

"I'm sorry," I say, when Gregg glances over his shoulder toward me.

"What for?" He turns to face me, still holding the knife he's using to slice chicken. The same knife I grabbed when I thought someone was standing at the bottom of the servants' stairs and watching me.

"For acting like such an insufferable jerk. I appreciate everything you've done for me, and I'll do better from now on. Or at least, I'll try."

"There's no need to be sorry," he says, which only makes me appreciate him more. And feel worse. "But I think we should keep an eye on you, just to make sure that you're not—"

"Hallucinating?" I finish for him.

"I wouldn't put it quite like that," he replies with a chuckle. "But you obviously went through an ordeal. Who knows how that might have affected you beyond the obvious?"

The *obvious* being that I don't remember who I am. I can't deny that I've been on edge ever since waking up on the lakeshore, and if I am hallucinating, then I need to get checked out by a doctor sooner rather than later. Which leads me to my next question. "How long do you think it will be before we can get into town?"

Gregg turns back to his meal preparations. "Hard to say. If they had repaired the bridge, the plow would have been up here already."

"Unless they don't know that anyone is at the lake," I say hopefully. "Maybe we should check the bridge again."

"Honestly, I can't see the point. Last time the bridge was out, it took weeks to repair. It's only been two days since I last checked, and more snow has fallen since. It'll be a tough hike back down to the bridge, and even if we could get across the brook, we could hardly walk into town. Way too far under the circumstances."

I lapse into silence, contemplating this. Are we truly stuck here, or is he making it sound impossible to leave just to keep me here? This thought pops into my mind and terrifies me. Why would I ever think that? It's illogical. Gregg doesn't know me. Why would he want to keep me here? *I'm fine,* I tell myself. *No need to worry.* But my mind won't let it go, which is why I'm relieved when he finally turns back toward me holding two delicious-looking bowls of salad topped with hot chicken in his hands. Something else to focus on.

"There's no need to worry," he says, as if reading my mind. "If there was anything seriously wrong, anything life-threatening, we'd have known it by now, I'm sure."

I follow him to the table, hoping he's right.

As we eat, he makes small talk in an obvious attempt to lighten my mood. He tells me stories about his childhood growing up in Boston and the scrapes he got himself into. He recounts tales of his travels and spending time on the West Coast. It helps, and by the time we're clearing the plates away, I'm not mired in dark thoughts anymore.

But just to be sure, Gregg goes to the wine fridge and takes out a Bordeaux, then removes the cork. After grabbing a couple of glasses, we go into the living room and settle on the sofa. He pours the wine, and we spend another two hours drinking and talking and laughing, even though I have no stories of my own to offer. Yet somehow Gregg keeps the conversation going through a second bottle of wine, which leaves me feeling fuzzy and warm.

Every time our eyes meet, I feel a delicious shiver deep in my belly. Every time he lays his hand lightly on my knee or touches my arm, an electric current runs down my spine. I don't want the evening to end. Really, I don't want the evening *with him* to end, but the hour grows late, and I'm not sure exactly how far I want to take things. At least, that's what I tell myself.

Eventually, I put my glass down on the coffee table, declaring that I should go upstairs and crawl into bed before the room spins.

Gregg stands and reaches across me to pick it up, and when he does, I act before I can overthink what I'm doing. I slip my arms around his neck, pull him close before he knows what's happening, and our lips meet for the second time. The kiss is lingering and full of passion. I don't want it to end because in that moment, I feel safe. Gregg is the only constant in my life. The only person whom I've had any meaningful connection with—apart from a couple of brief interactions with the woman across the lake—since waking up with a blank mind.

Apparently, Gregg doesn't want it to end either. He sinks back down to the couch, so close now that I inhale his scent, woody and clean. I tug at his polo top, pull it up and off.

His hand brushes my waist, rises to cup my breast.

A jolt rushes through me at his touch. I break away, rise to my feet, and pull off my sweater to reveal the lacy white sheer bra beneath. Then I cross to the stairs, turn back with a slight smile, and beckon for him to follow me up to the bedroom.

33

ADRIA

One Day Before

Peter was back to his old self. Almost. When he came up behind her in the bathroom while she was brushing her teeth, wrapped his arms around her, kissed the back of her neck, and said good morning, it felt almost perfunctory. His lips didn't linger quite as long, and his hug lacked warmth.

Or maybe she was imagining it, looking for signs that he knew she was suspicious of him where there were none.

Adria had been on edge the previous evening after Harvey failed to show up for their scheduled meeting at the coffee shop. She had returned to the condo in Cambridge to find Peter missing, too. He hadn't shown up until nine that night, claiming he had been at the Charlton Club.

But something was wrong. He was on edge. Jumpy.

When he had asked about her afternoon, it was almost like he was studying her reaction when she replied. He didn't even mention that her hair looked exactly the same as before, even though she had claimed to have a spa appointment after going into the office. Was it because he hadn't noticed, or because he already knew it was a lie and didn't care?

The warning in Harvey's text message rolled through her brain for the hundredth time. *Be careful. Peter is not who you think he is.* The question was, Whom exactly *had* she married?

Until she heard from Harvey, that question would hang like a sword on a thread above her head. But where was the security consultant? It had been twenty-four hours since he last contacted her.

A full day.

She had checked the burner phone over and over since he'd failed to show up at the coffee shop, but nothing. If he thought Peter was such a threat, why hadn't he gotten back in contact? The previous afternoon, she had managed to convince herself that he was just held up in the office, dealing with some sudden crisis that was more important than digging into her husband's past. That he had simply forgotten about the meeting. But deep down, she knew that was not true. Harvey didn't get distracted. He also didn't leave people waiting on tenterhooks.

The dread that had been building within her ever since the coffee shop had reached a crescendo. After breakfast, she went to her home office and closed the door, then locked it before taking out the burner phone. She called Harvey one more time, but as expected, he didn't answer. Then, with no other course of action available to her, she did the only thing left. Something she had been loath to do because it would leave evidence that she was talking to him. Evidence that could tip off Peter, assuming he didn't already know about her clandestine activities with the company's head of security, which she suspected that he did.

She switched to her regular phone, called the office, and dialed Harvey's extension.

He didn't answer, so she hung up and phoned again, letting the call go through to reception this time. When she asked if Harvey Lang had come into the office yet, the woman on the other end of the phone asked her to wait, but there was something in the tone of her voice that troubled Adria. She caught the faint hesitation. The quick intake of breath before the receptionist spoke.

Then she was transferred.

But not to Harvey.

Instead, she ended up transferred to her father's personal assistant, a fearsome middle-aged woman who seemed to handle most of the delicate matters around the office, even those not in her job description.

"Chloe?" Adria said, surprised. "What's going on?"

"I've been told that you're looking for Harvey," Chloe answered.

"Yes. I had a meeting with him yesterday afternoon. He didn't show up. I've been trying to contact him ever since."

"Oh." There was a moment of silence. "I suppose you don't know yet, then."

"Know what?" From the tone of Chloe's voice, she was about to be told something bad. She braced herself. "Tell me."

"There's no easy way to say this, Adria. I know that you and Harvey have known each other for many years." Another long moment of silence. "I guess I'll just come out with it. Harvey's dead."

34

Anna

Day Four

What have I done?

Oh, fuck, *what have I done?*

Memories of the previous night come flooding back. Kissing Gregg on the couch. Leading him upstairs. Letting him peel my clothes off until there was nothing left to remove. Pulling him down on top of me. Feeling him pressing against me, and then . . . what happened next brings a flush to my cheeks. This is bad. Like, I've-completely-messed-this-up bad. I had sex with Gregg. A man I've known for only about three days. Worse, I've only known myself for the same amount of time. For all I know, there's a boyfriend waiting for me somewhere out there. A husband, or even a wife. Have I just cheated on a partner I don't even remember?

Then another thought occurs to me. I could be a mother. What kind of person am I that I would do such a thing without any regard for a family that might be out there beyond this house, worried sick about me? Or maybe I'm single, and none of that is true. After all, I might have lost my memory, but that doesn't necessarily mean I've abandoned my morals. If I had a husband or a wife, a family, would I so easily have jumped into bed with this man? There's no way to know, but I choose to believe that I'm single, because the alternative makes me a horrible person.

From off to my left comes a low snore.

It's 7:00 a.m. according to the clock on the nightstand, and I'm still lying naked in his bed. I must get out of here before Gregg wakes up and things get even more uncomfortable. I don't see my clothes anywhere. They're probably lying on the floor, out of sight. Which means getting out of bed and rummaging for them in the nude.

I cast a glance in Gregg's direction. He's still sleeping with his back turned to me. Thank heaven for small mercies. I slip out from under the covers as gently as I can, trying not to disturb him. Praying he doesn't wake up. The room is chilly. Goose bumps rise on my bare flesh. My nipples are hard, but for a different reason than seven hours ago. A memory flashes through my mind that I quickly dispel. A memory of Gregg and me, our bodies entwined.

Stop it, I chide myself. *Just find your clothes and get the hell out of here.*

And there they are, strewn across the floor at the end of the bed. All except my bra, which is dangling precariously half-off the seat cushion of a chair sitting in the far corner of the room. How did he even toss it that far?

No matter. I gather everything up, all except my panties, which appear to have fallen into a black hole. Or possibly under the bed. Either way, I'm not inclined to waste time hunting for them right now.

I tiptoe toward the door with my clothes in my arms and pull it open just wide enough to slip through. As I step into the hallway, I look back at Gregg one more time, but he hasn't moved. He's still lying on his side, facing the window.

And then I do the walk of shame back to my bedroom, which is something I imagine hasn't happened since college. If I even went to college, that is.

When I get there, I throw the clothes down in a heap on the chair and jump straight into the shower to wash away the scent of Gregg and his bed. Twenty minutes later, I'm clean and dressed but feeling no better. I don't want to be in this house. Not right now. I have to get out and find some space to think. A quiet place where I can reflect upon recent events and decide where I go from here. Where *we* go from here.

I hurry from the room, descend the stairs, and grab a coat and boots from the mudroom before heading to the back door and out onto the snow-covered deck. Then I strike out toward Gravewater Lake, the place of my metaphorical birth, and the moody pine woods beyond.

35

The world outside Gregg's house looks different at dawn. A creeping layer of mist has settled over the lake and weaves through the dark woodland that surrounds it. The sky is a featureless blanket of gray, and I wonder if there's more snow on the way. A quick glance over my shoulder toward the other side of the house confirms what I already know. The road has still not been plowed. It seems we're going to be trapped up here for a while longer.

I leave the deck behind and turn to follow the curve of the lake close to the shore, where the snow isn't as deep, going in the opposite direction from where Gregg took me yesterday. I scan the far side of the lake but see only swirling whiteness. The fog has obliterated all signs of Helene's cabin. It's a strange sensation. Almost like I exist in a tiny patch of reality beyond which there is nothing but a vast and icy void.

My thoughts turn to what happened last night. I could blame the wine, convince myself that it got the better of me and lowered my inhibitions, but the truth is that I wasn't *that* drunk. I knew exactly what I was doing when I led Gregg upstairs to his bed. When I spent the entire night there.

I don't know how this is going to change my relationship with him. He saved me from certain death, or at least a bad case of hypothermia. Welcomed a total stranger into his home and kept me safe. What happened between us might make for an uncomfortable couple of days until they fix the bridge and plow the road into town so that I can get out of here. And what if it's longer than a few days? What if Gregg is right, and it takes a week or more to fix the bridge? Just the thought of it twists my stomach into knots.

I stop and glance backward, hoping that Gregg is still sleeping and hasn't come after me. I've been walking for a while, and the house is nowhere in sight because the path has veered off from the lake and deeper into the woods. I'm surrounded by towering pine trees that point like slim wooden fingers toward the featureless sky above.

A flutter of panic seizes me until I realize that I can still just about see the lake back in the direction from which I came. I'm not lost. All I need to do is retrace my steps along the path to the shore, and the house will be right there.

But I don't want to go back yet.

To tell the truth, I'm not sure I ever want to go back, even though I know that I'll have no choice eventually. I can't hide in the woods, avoiding Gregg forever. But I *can* delay the inevitable, which is why I turn my attention frontward again, push my hands into my coat pockets, and continue deeper into the woods.

As I walk, I wonder what exactly drove me into Gregg's arms last night if it wasn't the alcohol. Am I that kind of woman? The kind who hops into bed with the first available man she meets? I might not know my real name or where I came from, but I don't think so. This is something else.

I feel safe around Gregg. Comfortable. Also, he's hot. I'd have to be blind not to notice that. Deep blue eyes; thick, dark hair; a chiseled jaw; and a body that makes me feel flushed despite the chill in the air. I once again picture him, *all* of him, as I straddle him, running my hands down his hard chest, fingers trailing down his flat stomach, soft hair tickling my sensitive fingertips, and then lower . . .

Despite the weirdness of the last few days and the odd events that seem to plague the house, I trust him. Maybe it's partly because I don't trust myself. Don't trust that the strange footsteps on the stairs, the shadowy figure beyond the pantry, and the hushed voices and phantom lights turning on and off are anything more than a product of my overworked and obviously damaged mind. Gregg is a stable force in the maelstrom of fear and doubt that has become my life. More than that, he almost feels . . . familiar. Effortless.

Up ahead, the trail narrows where a pine tree has fallen across it. A layer of snow has settled upon the horizontal trunk. I swing one leg over, disturbing some of the snow with my foot. It breaks away in a frozen chunk and shatters on the ground. I slide one hand from my pocket and grab the stump of a broken branch to balance myself as I lift the other leg. I can already feel the chill air freezing my fingers. I should have found a pair of gloves before leaving the house. I rub my hand against my thigh to clean off the flecks of bark that cling to my palm, then push it back into the warmth of my jacket.

I'm about to move forward again when I hear it.

A crunch of snow underfoot.

My head snaps around to the trail behind me. It must be Gregg. I stand still and stare down the path. But I don't see him. The trail behind me is empty.

"Hello?" I call out. "Gregg, is that you?"

My only answer is the biting wind rustling through the treetops above me and the chirp of a winter bird somewhere deeper in the woods.

I listen for another sound of movement, but the forest is quiet now.

I don't want to be out here anymore. But I don't want to go back the way I came after hearing that noise. The path ahead of me curves toward the lake again. It will take longer, but I can take it that far, then follow along the shore back to the house.

I turn and start down the path at a faster pace. It's slippery. My boots break through the crusty snow at intervals and cause me to stumble and lurch forward. I strain to listen for sounds behind me even as I move faster. My breath quickens. I'm scared. If there is another person out here and they are following me, I have nothing to defend myself with, and nobody to help me.

36

An hour ago, I was eager to escape Gregg's house. Now I can't wait to return there. The path continues through the woods, twisting and turning in a meandering route back to the lake that isn't as direct as I'd hoped.

It's just an animal, I tell myself. *There's nothing to worry about.*

I should have turned around and gone back the other way earlier. What was I thinking, straying so far from the lake house? I have no idea if what happened to me was an accident or a deliberate attempt to snuff out my existence, because I can't remember. Why didn't I consider this when I took off this morning?

I swallow my fear and keep going because there's no alternative, and soon I'm rewarded by a glimpse of the lake framed between the trees farther along the trail. It looks like a sheet of smoky glass with barely a ripple. Fog rolls across its surface and up onto the shore.

I almost faint with relief.

A few more minutes, and I can start back toward the house. I focus on the task at hand and push forward.

It's just an animal . . . Just an animal.

Finally, I step out from between the trees and onto the flat, sandy shore.

What I see stops me in my tracks.

There are graves. Lots of them.

At least thirty snowcapped headstones in various states of disrepair. Some are still standing. Others lean. A few have toppled and lie shattered on the ground. But the ones that unnerve me the most are in the lake, partially submerged with their tops sticking up. Surrounding this bizarre scene are the remains of a rough stone wall that has crumbled in places and a rusting wrought-iron gate that rises out of the lake like a decaying metal skeleton.

And now I understand how this body of water got its name.

I have stumbled upon a cemetery. A very old one.

My attention is drawn to the closest headstone, with two names engraved on it.

HENRIETTE MARIE SPAULDING

DIED FEBRUARY 16, 1827

AGED 19 YEARS.

FREDRICK THOMAS SPAULDING

DIED FEBRUARY 16, 1827

AGED 1 DAY.

My heart aches when I read it. A young mother and her newborn son who died on the same day and now spend eternity buried together. I crouch down to examine the headstone further, and that's when I hear it.

Another crunch of snow from the direction of the woods.

I stay crouched near the headstone, terrified of what I'll see when I look around.

A twig breaks, the sound sharp in the crisp morning air.

I draw in a trembling breath, try to quell the panic that threatens to overwhelm me.

Rising to my feet, I offer a silent prayer before I turn to look back at the woods.

Don't let anyone be there. Please, for the love of God, don't let anyone be there.

When I *do* turn, I think my prayer has been answered because I'm alone on the lakeshore . . . except for the silent corpses beneath my feet.

But I have that feeling of being watched. A crawling sensation that worms up my spine.

And then I see it. A flash of movement in the woods. Not an animal. Not even close. This is something far worse. A person skulking in the darkness between the trees. A man. I can tell by his height and the width of his shoulders. And he's carrying something. There's a glint, like sunlight flashing off metal.

I stumble backward. My foot catches on a half-buried headstone, and I almost fall.

Someone is out here, stalking me, and he has a knife. I'm in real danger.

The blood rushes in my ears. I need to get out of here, like, right now. Because if I don't, I'll end up joining the people who lie in these graves.

My pursuer steps out from between the trees and advances toward me, no longer trying to hide. I can't make out his features because he's wearing a thick coat with a hood and his head is bent low. But there's no doubting his intentions, thanks to the large knife in his hand.

And finally, mercifully, my legs decide to work. I turn and run, weaving through the headstones in a blind panic as a scream builds on my lips.

37

Adria

One Day Before

Adria listened to Chloe tell her that Harvey Lang was dead, but for a moment, the news didn't sink in. How could that be? She had spoken to him only a few days before, and he was fine.

"I don't understand," she said, almost in a daze. "What happened?"

There was a faint sound from the other end of the line, as if Chloe were choking back a sob. "Robbery gone wrong. Apparently, he was leaving his home to come into the office, about to climb into his car when two people jumped out of a van. They tried to rob him, and he fought back. One of the robbers had a gun and shot him. He died instantly. Bullet right through his heart."

"Robbers? He lived in Arlington. That's hardly the kind of place to get murdered by a pair of hoodlums in broad daylight while you're leaving for work." Adria could hardly believe what she was hearing. She thought back to the text message that Harvey had sent her, and how he was typing a reply that never came through. Was he doing that on his way out the door? Was that why it never got sent? Because he never got the chance to finish it? "What time did this happen?"

"Oh, I think the detective who came to the office said it was around eight in the morning, but I could be wrong. The news came as quite a shock, and to be honest, I'm still shaking even now. Why do you want to know?"

"No reason." Adria wasn't about to tell Chloe that she might have been texting with Harvey at the very moment he was killed, because then the police would want to question her. They probably hadn't bothered to look at his phone because they didn't think it was important. They believed it was a robbery, plain and simple. But if there was someone communicating with him when the crime occurred, well . . . At best, she would have to explain the message he had sent her. The one where he asked to meet and warned her not to trust her husband. At worst, Peter would find out that she had asked Harvey to look into him. Except that the phone she had been using to text Harvey was a burner. Untraceable. It wouldn't matter if the cops looked at *his* phone, because there would be nothing to identify her. For a moment, Adria relaxed. Until she remembered the voicemail she had left when she couldn't get him to pick up:

It's Adria. Call me back.

Crap. That voicemail would identify her in a heartbeat. Better hope they never listened to it.

Then another thought struck her. The timing was so convenient. Harvey being killed on the same day that he wanted to meet and tell her what he had found out about Peter. Information she was sure would cast her husband in an even worse light than the suspected embezzlement already uncovered by the audit. But it couldn't have been Peter, could it? Was he even capable of having someone killed? And besides, he was right there at breakfast with her when this occurred. *Unless he hired someone,* a small voice said inside her head. *Or a pair of someones.* "Chloe, were there any witnesses to the attack?"

"Yes. That's how they know it was two people. A woman out walking her dog saw the entire thing. Said they pulled up in a van, jumped out, and attacked Harvey. Then they jumped back into the van and sped off, leaving him bleeding on the sidewalk next to his car."

"Did she see their faces?" Adria's mind went back to the man and woman who showed up at her door looking for Peter. The man with a gun under his coat and the woman who followed her. Despite his outward appearances, Peter moved in dangerous circles. Or at least, he had at one point in time. He could very well know people willing to do this.

"No, she didn't see their faces. They were wearing masks. The police found the van a few hours later, abandoned a couple of miles away. It was stolen."

Adria found it hard to believe that the police really thought the motive was robbery, given the obvious planning that had gone into the attack. You didn't conceal your identity with a mask, then steal a van and drive around looking for a random victim, only to kill that person and dump the van minutes later just so you could steal their wallet. "How did they even get the jump on Harvey? I mean, he was ex-military. He protected people from things like this for a living. It doesn't make sense."

"I don't know. Maybe they took him by surprise. He'd hardly be expecting an attack like that out of the blue on his own street."

"Perhaps." *Or maybe he was distracted,* thought Adria. *He was looking at his phone, typing a message to me, when they rolled up, jumped out of that van, and shot him.* The thought made her feel sick. Was Harvey dead because of her? Because she asked him to look into Peter? "Do you think this was just a robbery gone wrong, Chloe?"

"Goodness. I don't know. It doesn't sound like one to me, but I'm just a personal assistant. I will say that Harvey had probably made a lot of enemies in his career, and sometimes these things come back to bite you."

"Yes, they do." Adria thanked Chloe for letting her know and hung up. She went to the office door and unlocked it, but then she hesitated. Peter was out there, somewhere else in the house, and she couldn't help wondering, Was he the enemy who came back to bite Harvey? And if so, where did that leave her?

38

Anna

Day Four

"Anna!"

I hear Gregg's voice before I see him rushing toward me along the lakeshore from the direction of the house. He's wearing jeans and a sweater with a blue polo shirt beneath. The polo's collar is creased, and I recognize it as the same one he had on last night. The shirt I peeled off him in a frenzied grip of carnal desire. His hair is messy and unbrushed, and he hasn't shaved.

Even though I might not remember, I can't imagine that I've ever been happier to see anyone in my life. I run toward him, fling my arms around his neck, then try to steer him back in the direction he came from.

"We have to go," I gasp between sobbing breaths. "He's right behind me."

"Who is?" Gregg asks. He doesn't turn around. Instead, his arms circle my waist in a protective embrace, and he peers over my shoulder.

"The man with the knife." I'm baffled by his lack of concern.

"Anna, what are you talking about?"

"A man. He was following me on the trail. He came after me with a knife." I try again to push Gregg back.

He doesn't move. "There's no one here."

"What?" I twist around and stare back toward the graveyard. Gregg is right. There *is* no one there. The man with the knife has vanished. I look up at Gregg. "He was right behind me, I swear. I thought he was—"

"Anna, I don't know what you think you saw, but—"

"No." I pull away from him. Fold my arms in indignation. "Don't tell me that I imagined this. Don't say it's only in my head, because I know that's not true. This wasn't some vague shape in the darkness. He was real. I saw him plain as day. He came after me."

I tear up. Droplets spill down my cheeks. I'm frustrated and scared, and Gregg thinks that either I'm making this up for drama or I'm crazy.

"Hey, calm down." Gregg raises his hands in mock protest. "I wasn't going to say that it was your imagination. But you have to admit, you've been having these . . ." He lets the sentence trail off and furrows his brow as if trying to think of the best way to phrase what he's going to say next.

"Having these *what*?" I snap at him.

Gregg remains silent for a moment longer, then lowers his head, avoiding eye contact when he answers. "Having episodes."

"I'm not crazy."

"I never said that you were."

"But you're implying it." I glance around, taking in the graveyard, the lake, and the dark line of trees that mark the edge of the woods. The man with the knife must still be out there somewhere because he was behind me only a minute or two ago, giving chase. For all I know, he retreated to the safety of the woods when he saw Gregg and is circling around as we stand here, positioning himself to rush from between the trees and attack while our guard is down. He could slip his knife in me before I even have a chance to react. I don't want to stay here. It's not safe. But I also want to prove that he's not a hallucination. That there really is a man with a knife. Because if Gregg doesn't believe me, he can't protect me. I steady my nerves and stride back toward the graveyard.

"Anna, where are you going?"

"Where do you think?" I glance over my shoulder and see that he hasn't moved. "To find proof that I'm not lying."

I turn my attention frontward again as I reach the graveyard. Then I stop and point down toward the snow-covered ground. "Look."

Finally, Gregg moves. He starts toward me in the resigned manner of a parent humoring an obstinate child. Shoulders slumped. Lips pressed together in a faint expression of exasperation.

I keep pointing even as he reaches me. "See!"

Gregg looks down, and I can't help but feel a swell of vindication. Because mine are not the only footprints in the snow. There are other tracks too. Larger impressions that were clearly left by a set of men's boots. I can see the well-defined tread of the soles and the curving hoof of the heels. They are obviously fresh. Even better, several of the prints overlay my own, proving that they were not already there when I stumbled upon the cemetery.

Gregg studies them, brow furrowed.

"Now do you believe me?" I ask.

Gregg looks up at me, concern in his eyes. "I do. I'm sorry for doubting you. Come on, let's get out of here."

"Please." That's the most sensible thing he's said.

Gregg takes my arm and steers me out of the graveyard. Then we start at a brisk pace, walking back toward his house, following the shore. As we go, I look back over my shoulder toward the woods, expecting to see the man with the knife, but he's nowhere in sight.

That doesn't make me feel any better.

Because I still cannot shake the prickling sensation that we're being watched. That he's out there somewhere, masked by the gloom between the trees, just waiting for a chance to strike.

39

I'm still shaking when we arrive back at the house. The whole time we were walking, I was on edge, expecting something to happen.

As soon as we enter the foyer and lock the door behind us, Gregg leads me into the living room and tells me to sit down, then settles on the couch next to me. "You want to tell me what you were doing out there?"

I really don't want to tell him, because it sounds silly, or reckless, given what just happened, but I don't think I have much choice. "I didn't want to be here when you woke up. I needed time to think. Clear my head after . . ."

"After we slept together last night."

I nod. "I drank too much wine, and I was feeling vulnerable, and you were being so nice, and—"

"Hey." He places a hand on my leg. "It's all good."

"No, it really isn't. I've ruined everything. Now we're stuck here together, and you probably regret what happened, and there's this guy with a knife in the woods . . ." The words come tumbling out, and I can feel myself close to tears.

"First off, I don't regret what happened. That's ridiculous. Second, I wanted it as much as you did, and as long as you're fine with what happened between us, then so am I. As for the man in the woods—"

"He really was there. I swear."

"I believe you."

"You do?"

"Yes. I saw the footprints. But maybe he didn't mean you any harm."

I stare at Gregg in disbelief. "How can you say that? You weren't there. You didn't see him. The way he came toward me . . . I have no doubt about his intentions."

"You really think he was trying to kill you?" Gregg doesn't sound convinced.

"Why not? For all I know, he's the person responsible for me ending up this way. Maybe he was trying to finish the job. After all, we don't know if what happened to me was an accident or if it was deliberate." Another chilling thought rattles through my mind. "I keep getting the feeling someone is watching me. This might be proof that I'm right. There's only one way he could have known that I went for a walk . . . that I was out there this morning."

"I don't know, Anna. That's a stretch. I mean, he'd have to be watching pretty much around the clock to know that you were going for a walk on your own at such an early hour. That would be a hard task for one person. And besides, it's not like we're in the city, where it's easy to stay out of sight. Anyone watching the house for that long would stand out like a sore thumb."

"Maybe he's hiding in one of the other houses around the lake. You said it yourself. Most of them are empty because the owners only use them in summer."

"And most of them also don't have a direct view of this house." Gregg sighs. "Look, Anna, just stop and think about it for a moment. If someone really is trying to finish what they started the night you woke up on the shore of the lake, then the two of you must be connected somehow. Must know each other. Since you've lost your memory, why wouldn't they just come here and say they were looking for you? Pretend to be worried. Take you back to wherever you came from. Then they would have you all to themselves and could do whatever they wanted.

It's easier than skulking around in the woods, following you with a knife."

"How would they know that I've lost my memory? Maybe they think I've told you about them and what they tried to do to me. That the only reason the police haven't shown up yet is because we're cut off up here with no way to contact the outside world. They're probably worried that I'll summon the authorities the moment we get the opportunity."

"Okay. Let's assume that you're right," Gregg says. "That means that we're both in danger, not just you."

"Then you believe me now?"

"It's plausible." Gregg stands up. "I'll make sure that all the windows and doors are locked tight, and from now on, you should stay here in the house, where it's safe. No more wandering off on your own."

"Sure." After this morning, there is no way that I'm going outside on my own again.

"And if anyone comes to the door—anyone at all, even if it's just Helene—you let me answer. Understood?"

I nod.

Gregg takes a step toward the door. "I need to take a shower. Shave. Change into some fresh clothes."

"All right," I say in a small voice. I don't want him to leave. I don't want to be alone. But I don't want to come off as needy either.

He must read the expression on my face because he says, "I won't be long. Promise. And don't worry, you're safe here."

"Okay." I watch as he makes his way toward the door. Then a thought occurs to me. "Why were you out there this morning like that, without a jacket?"

Gregg stops in the doorway and turns around. "Huh?"

"Why were you out there? I mean, don't get me wrong; I'm not complaining. You saved me, but . . ."

"I woke up, and you weren't in bed anymore. Your clothes were gone. You weren't in your room or anywhere else in the house either. I was worried, so I pulled some clothes on and went looking for you."

"Oh." That makes sense.

"Anything else?"

"No." I shake my head.

"Right." Gregg continues toward the stairs.

Something is bothering me. The way Gregg showed up at the exact moment when I was sure Knife Man was going to catch me. It feels too perfect. Does he know more than he's letting on? Does he know who I am, and who was following me?

40

"Hey." Gregg appears in the doorway. He's presentable now. Clean-shaven. Hair washed and brushed. He's also wearing a fresh pair of pants and a cream cable-knit sweater. "Feeling better?"

Not really. "I think so."

Gregg cocks his head, as if he's trying to decide if I'm telling the truth, which, of course, I'm not. Then he smiles. "Great. You hungry?"

"Starving." I follow him to the kitchen and settle into my usual spot on a stool while he throws a meal together. My mind is still on the morning's events. I don't want to talk about the man with the knife anymore. There's not much left to say, and I'd rather not keep dwelling on it. But I am curious about something else. "What's the deal with the graveyard?"

Gregg shrugs. "What do you mean?"

"How did it get there in such a remote spot, and why is it half-submerged in the lake? There must have been an earlier settlement."

"There was. A logging town that operated from the early nineteenth century until about the 1860s. They cut down the pine and used barges to float it all the way to the Missisquoi River via a canal they dug on the east side of what was called Cooney Lake back then. From there, it went to Lake Champlain to be used for construction and boatbuilding. It was a thriving community for a while."

"What happened to them?" It's hard to believe there was a whole town out there. A prosperous logging community that vanished as if it never existed. All except the graveyard. The living might have left, but the dead never did.

"Progress, I suppose. After the town was abandoned, the woodland grew up again and reclaimed everything. The canal silted and eventually dried up, which caused the lake level to rise. By the time they were building summer houses up here decades later, there was no trace of the town—probably because the buildings were made of wood—and the graveyard was half-underwater, just like it is now."

"Which must be how the lake got the name it goes by now," I say.

"Exactly. Some robber baron with a taste for the macabre decided that *Gravewater Lake* sounded better than *Cooney Lake*."

"Or maybe they just had a wry sense of humor."

"Maybe. Either way, the name stuck. There's a book in the living room that talks about the history of this area. You should take a look at it if you're interested."

I am. For all I know, I might be from this area, and maybe reading about the history of this place will jog something loose. I make a mental note to find the book.

The conversation lulls, and soon my thoughts turn back to the morning's events and the man with the knife. Gregg has checked all the doors and windows to make sure they are locked, but I still feel vulnerable.

I watch him in silence for a short while, then ask, "Do you have a gun?"

He pauses in the middle of slicing tomatoes for the sandwiches he's making and turns around. "No. I don't have a gun."

"Oh."

"But we don't need one. We're safe here," he tells me.

I disagree, but there's no point saying so because it won't change anything. Still, with no guns in the house, no alarm system, and no way to call for help if the need arises, I'm worried. Actually, I'm more than worried. I'm terrified.

Seeing the look on my face, Gregg comes over to the kitchen island and leans forward with his elbows on it. He locks eyes with me. "Anyone who tries to do you harm will have to get through me first. Understand?"

"Sure." I force a weak smile and try to put what happened on my walk out of my head. But I can't. Because Knife Man is still out there somewhere, and despite Gregg's assurances, I can't help feeling that he will be back.

41

After lunch is finished, Gregg tells me that he has work to do on the third floor. That he thinks a pipe must have frozen up there and sprung a leak because he heard water dripping above the ceiling when he was in his bedroom earlier. I volunteer to help him. But he just shakes his head, tells me that won't be necessary, and steers me toward the living room. Apparently, he works better without distractions.

"I'll try to be quick," he says before taking his leave.

I hear him pass through the mudroom and open the door leading into the home's three-car garage. A few minutes later, he returns, crossing the foyer toward the kitchen and the servants' staircase beyond with a small toolbox in one hand.

I watch him go, resisting the urge to follow along behind. He's made it clear that he doesn't want my company right now.

I pick up the book I've been reading and sit on the sofa for almost an hour with it open on my lap, but I can't concentrate. I read the words and turn the pages but don't comprehend the events detailed within. Eventually, I close the book in frustration and put it down.

I glance over the back of the sofa toward the foyer. There's no sign of Gregg. He must still be on the third floor fixing that leak.

And that's when an idea comes to me.

Gregg has been so cagey about his past, refusing to talk about his dead wife or what he does for a living. I know nothing about him beyond what I've experienced in this house. If he won't tell me, maybe I can find out on my own.

I stand and go to the door, pass through the foyer into the kitchen. At the bottom of the servants' stairs, I stand and listen, but I don't hear any banging or anything else coming from the third floor. Either the sound doesn't travel all the way down here, or Gregg isn't making any noise right now. But it doesn't matter. He isn't down here, which is perfect for what I want to do.

I hurry back through the house toward the study. Open the door and slip inside. Go to the desk and sit down. My gaze settles on the phone. When I pick up the receiver and hold it to my ear, there is still no dial tone. I return the receiver to the cradle and stare at the answering machine. The message is still there. I reach out, my finger hovering over the play button. But really, what am I going to learn by listening to that recording of his dead wife all over again?

Instead, I turn my attention to the desk drawers. The first one I try is unlocked. I open it and look inside. There's a pile of mail addressed to Gregg Fielder. I flip through the envelopes. Most of them are utility bills. Electricity, propane, water, and the phone company. I slide the pile back, careful to place the mail in the same position that I found it. The only other items in the drawer are a letter opener, three pens, and a plastic container full of paper clips. When I try the other desk drawers, they are all locked, and there is no key in sight.

Frustrated, I stand and go to the bookshelf, browsing the volumes. These are mostly business manuals, unlike the books in the living room. Thick tomes with subjects ranging from accounting and marketing to corporate law. It doesn't tell me much other than that Gregg is a businessman, which was already obvious given the size and opulence of a home he uses only when he wants to get away from the city. I turn away from the bookshelves, intending to return to the foyer, when I see it. A picture hanging on the wall next to the door. It is a finely detailed oil painting in an ornate gold frame. It looks old, and is probably worth some money, but that isn't what draws my attention.

Rather, it's the subject, a squat white lighthouse with a black catwalk that sits upon a peninsula with roiling waves breaking across it. It feels vaguely familiar to me.

I cross to the painting and find a brass plaque attached to the frame that identifies it as Brant Point Light on Nantucket Island. I lift my gaze to the painting and am overcome by a sudden sense of disorientation. I put my hand out and steady myself against the wall.

A scene flashes through my mind.

I'm leaning on the rail of a boat and looking out upon a calm, flat ocean beneath a deep blue summer sky. A man comes up alongside me, hands me a drink in a plastic cup with a celery stick poking out of it. A Bloody Mary.

"Ever wanted to be a healthy drunk?" he says, raising his voice over the breeze whipping across the rail.

I laugh and tap my drink against his, lift my gaze to look at him and . . .

And then the scene fades before I can see his face.

I stare at the painting in mute shock. Have I just experienced a memory of my life prior to Gravewater Lake? A tantalizing sliver of recollection? If only it had continued a moment longer, I would have known who my companion was. The sense of disappointment is palpable. I wonder if the man who gave me the drink is my boyfriend, or maybe my husband.

I reach out and touch the painting, feel the cracked varnish beneath my fingers, even as another tiny shard of recollection rises from my subconscious.

The drinks are long gone. I'm still at the rail, but now we are approaching a harbor lined by quaint shingled buildings. Sun glints off the waves. Pleasure craft tied to jutting docks rise and fall on the tide. And on a sliver of land to our left, a lighthouse guards the entrance to the harbor. There are people at the rail beside me, chatting excitedly and taking pictures of the lighthouse with cell phones and cameras. I sense my companion behind me, his hand resting on my shoulder.

"Breathtaking, isn't it?" he asks, his mouth close enough that I feel his breath tickling my earlobe.

"Yes," I reply. "It's beautiful. I'm so glad you invited me. This weekend is going to be perfect."

The man laughs and slips his arms around my waist. "You're perfect."

The snatch of recollection fades back into obscurity, and despite its clarity, I'm left wondering if it was real or just some fiction dredged up by my mind as I stare at the painting. It almost feels like someone else's memory that I'm experiencing secondhand. Like I'm watching a movie. But maybe that's because I'm so unmoored from my past, adrift in a vast and foggy ocean with only the barest hints of my identity to guide me.

But it's a start, and I'm eager to tell Gregg about it. All thoughts of snooping vanish from my mind. I step back out of the study, close the door behind me, and look around.

The house is silent. I assume that Gregg is still upstairs, which is where I intend to go look for him.

I cross the foyer, hurry through the kitchen and the pantry, and I'm soon at the bottom of the servants' stairs.

The light is on, casting a pale glow down through the stairwell.

I ascend with memories of the last time I climbed these stairs fresh in my mind. On the second-floor landing, I stop and listen again.

Still nothing.

The third-floor staircase is dark, which I find weird. Maybe Gregg turned the light off out of habit when he reached the top. I flip the switch and climb. Moments later, I'm staring down the same dusty corridor as before. None of the doors leading to the old servants' quarters are open.

There's no sign that Gregg is up here.

I go to the first door and open it, see the same clutter as before. In the next room, I'm confronted by the rocking horse that I found on my first visit to the third floor. I step inside the room and touch it. The horse shifts on aging springs under the pressure of my hand. It gives a rusty groan that almost sounds like the horse is alive and moaning in pain. I pull my hand away quickly, even though I know it's only the springs protesting after decades of disuse.

I shudder and retreat into the corridor, then check the next room. Gregg isn't here either. I turn my attention to the rooms on the other side of the corridor, starting with the empty one.

Still nothing.

This is getting weird.

I stare at the empty room for a moment, looking for any sign of recent activity, like maybe a disturbance of the dust coating the floor, but see nothing. I'm about to move on, close the door and check the last two rooms, when my gaze is drawn to the dormer window, and a flash of movement in the snowy landscape beyond.

Curious, I cross to the window and look down. This is the front of the house that faces the road. I see the three-car garage sitting at a right angle to the rest of the building, and the snow-covered driveway.

I see something else too.

A dark shape standing motionless in the snow and looking up at the building. He's wearing a hooded coat, not unlike that of the man I encountered earlier out at the graveyard. And even though I know it's unlikely that he can see past the grimy panes of the third-floor window into the dark room beyond, I can't help but think that he's looking straight back at me.

42

ADRIA

One Day Before

Peter found her the moment Adria left her home office. She forced a smile, tried to ignore the fear that tightened her chest when she looked at him. Was he standing in the hallway, listening at the door? Or was she being paranoid?

She held her breath and waited to see what her husband would do.

To her surprise, he was back to acting like the old Peter. He embraced her in a tight hug, kissed her, ignoring the way she tensed at his touch.

"I was thinking we should get away," he said, releasing her. "It's Friday, after all, and you've been working so much recently."

"No more than usual," Adria replied. The last thing she wanted to do was go away with him right now. But she had to play it cool just in case he really didn't know what she had been up to. And even if he did, she had a feeling it would be a mistake to antagonize him. "But I have some foundation stuff to go over this weekend. How about another time?"

"I'm not taking no for an answer." Peter folded his arms. "Go pack a bag. We're going up to the lake house."

This was bad. Peter had purchased the lake house the previous year and driven her up there on Valentine's Day as a surprise. It would be, he said, their Vermont wilderness love nest. And for the few days they were there, it was. They ate filet mignon cooked on the grill, drank copious amounts of wine, and made love. And the sex was great. Like it had been when they'd first met before life got in the way. But after that, she didn't go back until Christmas. Every time she suggested it, he had a reason why they couldn't go, even though he had made plenty of trips up to the lake house when she was up to her elbows in work and couldn't get away. Once, when she pressed him, told him that the work he was using as an excuse not to go could wait until after the weekend, Peter had snapped at her. Said that she didn't understand how much pressure he was under, even though his responsibilities at the foundation were nothing close to hers. After a while, she began to think he'd bought the lakefront property more for himself than for them.

Now, when she wished he would go there on his own, he insisted she accompany him.

"I really do have a lot planned this weekend," she said in one last futile attempt to dissuade him. "Besides, there's supposed to be a storm coming through. You really want to go up there and chance getting trapped in a blizzard?"

"We're not going to get trapped. I've already checked the weather, and the storm won't be that bad." Peter's face collapsed into a mild scowl. "I really think we need to do this for our marriage."

"What do you mean?" This took Adria by surprise. From her perspective, the problems with their marriage were Peter stealing from the charitable foundation and her suspicion—she couldn't believe she was even thinking this—that he might have been involved in Harvey Lang's death. Going up to the lake house wouldn't resolve either of *those* issues. "What do you think is wrong with our marriage?"

"Come on, Adi," he said, referring to her by the affectionate nickname he had started using a few months after they'd met. One he rarely used anymore, except when he wanted something. "You have to admit that things have been strained between us. I'm afraid we're growing apart. This will do us good. I'll even grab a couple of bottles of good wine. Maybe even some champagne. We still have a 2008 Dom Pérignon just begging to have the cork popped." He glanced toward the bedroom. "What do you say?"

What *could* she say? Adria forced a smile and nodded. "Fine. Whatever you want. Give me an hour to pack some clothes?"

Peter glanced at his watch. "An hour, and not a minute longer. It's a long drive up to the lake house, and I want to beat the weather."

"But I thought you said the storm wouldn't—"

"Go. What are you waiting for?" Peter gave her a small shove toward the bedroom door. "I'll start loading the truck."

"At least let's take the Mercedes," Adria said, her heart falling. She hated the truck. It was ugly and uncomfortable. Peter had insisted they purchase it because he claimed the roads up around the lake could get treacherous in winter, and he didn't want to risk their *good* cars. But as far as she was concerned, the Mercedes SUV, with its four-wheel drive, was more than adequate in most situations. She also couldn't see the need to have three vehicles in a place like Boston, especially since the condo had only two reserved parking spaces in the underground garage, forcing them to rent a third space at an extortionate rate from one of their neighbors who wasn't using it.

"I'm not risking the Mercedes. Not at this time of year. Last thing I want to do is skid on a patch of black ice and end up nose first in a ditch."

We could hit a patch of black ice just as easily in the truck as in the Mercedes, Adria thought, but she knew it was pointless to argue once Peter had made up his mind. Resigned to the inevitable, she turned and made her way into the bedroom. She went straight to the closet and took the burner phone out of her pocket. Harvey was dead, so there was no point in carrying it around anymore. She turned the phone off, opened her lingerie drawer, and pushed it all the way to the back, out of sight. Then she stood there, staring at the open drawer and wondering how the hell her perfect life had unraveled so quickly.

They were on the road by midday. The traffic leaving Boston was lighter than Adria expected, and they were soon out of the city and heading toward New Hampshire. Peter drove in silence, speaking only to curse out the occasional driver that cut him off or wasn't going fast enough. Adria was content to look out the window and watch the scenery roll by.

Soon after they entered Vermont, the snow started falling. By the time they were in the middle of the state, it was coming down hard enough that Peter was forced to slow down and put the windshield wipers on at their fastest setting. She almost suggested they turn back, that it wasn't worth going up to the lake house in such bad weather, but she knew he wouldn't listen any more than he had back at the condo, so she kept quiet and wondered what Peter's true motivations were. Did he really want to rekindle the romance of their first year together, or was there another reason he was so eager to escape the city? The last text message Harvey had sent her rattled through Adria's mind once again. He had told her not to trust Peter. Now she was going to spend an entire weekend alone with her husband, isolated in the middle of nowhere.

By the time they arrived at the lake and pulled up in front of the house, her nerves were shredded. After they unloaded the truck, trudging back and forth through snow that was already deep enough to bury her shoes, she took her travel bag straight upstairs to the bedroom, telling Peter that she was going to take a shower and freshen up.

Stepping inside the main suite, she slumped against the door, trying to contain her dread. The weekend stretched ahead of her like a yawning chasm. She should have fought harder not to come up to the lake. Should have done whatever it took. But it was too late now. Adria took a deep breath, held it for a few seconds, then released it slowly.

At that moment, the phone in her pocket rang. She pulled it out, hoping against hope that it would somehow be Harvey calling to tell her that there had been a dreadful mistake. That he wasn't really dead. Then she remembered. The burner phone was back in Boston, hidden at the back of a drawer. This was her actual phone. The one Peter knew about. When she looked at the screen, reality set in. It wasn't Harvey. In fact, she didn't know who it was. Because there was no number. No caller ID. Nothing.

With trembling hands she answered, lifted the phone to her ear. "Hello?"

"Adria?" asked a gruff voice.

"Yes. Who is this?"

"Are you alone?"

"Yes."

"Your husband can't hear us?"

"No. He's downstairs." Adria realized she was gripping the phone so tightly that it made her fingers hurt. She forced herself to relax. "You didn't answer my question. Who is this?"

"You can call me Frank."

That's a strange way to phrase it, Adria thought. "Frank what?"

"Just Frank. I'm an old associate of Harvey Lang. He reached out to me, asked for a favor."

"Harvey is dead," Adria said before she could stop herself.

"I know. That's why I'm calling. He gave me your number when we last spoke. Actually, he gave me two numbers, but the burner phone he provided you with is turned off, so I had no choice but to call your regular line. Now please, listen."

"How do I know I can trust you?" Adria asked. For all she knew, this was one of the men who had killed Harvey. Peter might have put him up to making the call to find out what her father's security consultant had told her, if anything.

There was a moment's pause. The man on the other end of the line took a long breath. "Because I'm with the National Security Agency, that's how."

43

ANNA

Day Four

He's found me. The thought crashes through my mind even as I stagger back from the window. Knife Man has found me.

I inhale a sharp breath and try to contain my rising panic.

Where the hell is Gregg? He promised to protect me, but now he's missing. He certainly isn't on the third floor, looking for some leaky pipe.

Gregg assured me he had checked all the doors and windows, and they were locked, but I have no proof of that other than his word. I didn't see him do it.

I step close to the window again and peer down onto the snowy driveway, and my heart skips a beat. There's a trail of footprints in the snow. A trail heading toward the front door.

I can't let him get in.

I turn and run from the room. My feet pound on the bare boards of the narrow attic hallway as I sprint toward the stairs. Dust, disturbed by my passage, rises into the air.

I fly down the first set of stairs at a breakneck pace, barely slowing to steady myself when I reach the halfway landing. On the second floor, I pause for a moment to catch my breath, then continue on. At the bottom, I skid around the corner into the pantry. My skin prickles as I enter the kitchen, expecting to see a dark shape come barreling toward me, knife in hand.

But I don't. So far, so good. My heart feels like it's going to beat right out of my chest.

When I enter the foyer, I see him.

Gregg is striding toward the front door from the direction of the main staircase.

I pull up short, almost lose my balance as my upper body continues its forward momentum.

Gregg hesitates and looks at me in mild surprise. Then he continues on without a word, even as two sharp bangs echo through the downstairs. Someone is knocking on the door.

I take another step. "Wait."

Gregg stops again, glances over his shoulder. "It's fine. I'm dealing with this. Just stay there."

"Please, don't open the door," I beg him. "What if it's the man from the graveyard? We need to make sure first."

"And how are we going to do that? You don't even know what he looks like." Gregg slips a hand into his pocket and pulls out a small black cylindrical canister with a push button on top. "Don't worry. If there's a problem, I have this."

When I don't answer, he says, "Pepper spray."

"I know what it is. I just don't think it will be much use against a man with a knife."

"Don't worry. I can take care of myself." Gregg slips the canister back into his pocket and continues toward the door.

I want to move. Want to rush forward and drag him away before something terrible happens, but my legs are locked in fright.

Gregg reaches the door and puts his eye to the peephole.

I'm not sure, but I could swear that his shoulders tense up. Then he reaches down, disengages the dead bolt, and opens the door just enough to see our visitor.

His right foot, I notice, stays firmly placed behind the door to make sure it can't be opened any wider.

I edge forward to get a better view of the man on the other side of the door. He's stocky, wearing a pair of frayed jeans that look like they've seen better days. His hood is pulled down, but I can see his face. Heavy brow. Ice-cold gray eyes. A dark growth of stubble on his chin. His hands are pushed into his pockets, making it impossible to know if he's carrying a knife.

"Figured I'd find you here," the man says in a broad South Boston accent.

When he opens his mouth to speak again, Gregg cuts in before he has the chance.

"This is Eddie," he says, shooting a quick glance over his shoulder toward me before looking back at our visitor. "He's our neighbor. You don't need to worry. He owns the house next to us on the west side of the lake, isn't that right?"

The man narrows his eyes. "Uh, yeah . . . that's right."

"Didn't think you'd come up here to the lake." Gregg is silent for a moment, then he adds, "You know, being winter and all."

"Yeah. I figured."

"How can we help you, *neighbor*?"

Eddie doesn't answer. Instead, his gaze finds me over Gregg's shoulder. "Who's the girl?"

"Just a friend who's staying here for a while," Gregg replies. "She had an accident. I'll be taking her into town just as soon as the bridge is repaired."

Eddie's gaze lingers on me, and I squirm, unnerved by the look in his eyes. "A friend, huh?"

"That's right." There's a hard edge to Gregg's voice. "Now, what do you want?"

Eddie finally looks away from me, much to my relief. "You know very well what I want."

"Right." Gregg pauses. "Your generator."

"What?"

"You wanted help to repair your generator in case the power goes out. That's what you told me back in September, right?"

"Um, sure."

"Shame we didn't sort it all out before. Could have avoided you trekking over here in such bad weather. How about I meet you over at the house later, and we'll look at it?"

"Or you could let me inside, and we'll talk about it now. You know, figure how we're going to fix this issue." Eddie places a hand on the door handle. "I won't keep you long, *old buddy*."

Gregg shakes his head. "I'm not sure I can spare the time right at this moment, what with Anna being here and all."

"Sure you can." Eddie pushes on the door, opening it wider despite Gregg's foot. "Wouldn't want to let your neighbor down now, would you?"

"I guess not." Gregg steps aside to let Eddie into the house, although from the look that passes across his face, I don't think he's pleased about it. "We can talk in the study."

"That's the spirit." Eddie waits for Gregg to lead the way, then follows along behind him toward the study. On the way past, he gives me the once-over, his gaze settling just a little too long where it shouldn't.

I fold my arms instinctively across my chest and resist the urge to shrink back. Then he continues on without saying a word. But as he passes by, I see something that makes me do a double take. A bulge under his coat that looks suspiciously like a concealed weapon.

44

Eddie and Gregg disappear into the study without a backward glance, leaving me alone in the foyer. A moment later, I hear a soft click.

Gregg has locked the study door.

I stand in the foyer and stare in disbelief toward the study, trying to make sense of what just happened, and of what I think I saw. Eddie is carrying a gun. I'm sure of it.

A frantic thought races through my mind. Could Eddie be the man with the knife? Is he the one who followed me out on the trail this morning?

But when I think about it, I realize it doesn't make sense. If he was, then Gregg would never have invited him in. Wouldn't have let him get so close to me. He knows what happened and must trust Eddie.

And despite my shock at seeing what I'm sure was a pistol tucked under his jacket, I see another flaw in my logic. If the man on the trail had a gun, why would he come at me with a knife? If he wanted to do me harm, the gun would be quicker and easier. Unless he was worried about someone hearing the gunshot. But the only other people at the lake are Gregg and Helene, neither of whom would have found me in time to see my assailant. He would have slipped back into the woods way before they reached me.

But something is off.

I struggle to believe that Eddie owns a summer house here on the lake. He looks . . . I search for the right word, then it hits me. *Uncouth.*

The way he's dressed. His mannerisms. The gun. Even his accent, which sounds distinctively working-class.

I also wonder why Gregg locked the study door and what they're talking about in such secrecy. If Eddie's generator is broken, there isn't much they can do about it from the study. And has Eddie been here all along, since before the storm? I guess he must have been, because the road still hasn't been plowed, which means the bridge is still out, so he hasn't just arrived.

Gregg insisted that nobody was up here at the lake, but that is clearly not true. First Helene shows up, and now Eddie. Was he unaware that his neighbor was here, or did he deliberately lie to me?

I won't get the answer by standing here, and the study door is mere feet away across the foyer. All it would take is going over there and pressing my ear against it. That feels wrong. I'm a guest in Gregg's house, and if he wants to talk to his neighbor in the study, who am I to question?

Except there's still that nagging sense of weirdness. The way they spoke to each other. It sounded almost . . . guarded. Like they were choosing their words carefully because I was present. But for the life of me, I can't think why.

It's too much.

So many strange things have happened over the past few days, and I want some answers.

I cross softly to the door and stand close enough that I can see where dust has settled on the lower ridges of each inset panel. A stray thought flits through my head that Gregg doesn't keep up with cleaning this place as well as he should. Maybe it's because his wife died, and she took care of that stuff. But right now, I'm not interested in dust. I have other questions.

I lean close to the door and listen, not quite pressing my ear to it yet because somehow that feels too much like I'm crossing a line with my snooping.

From somewhere on the other side, I hear a man's voice rising and falling in pitch, but I can't identify it as either Gregg or his visitor. I hear something else too. Music playing.

An acoustic guitar, to be precise.

At first, I'm baffled. Is Gregg in there serenading his buddy from around the lake? This is going from odd to ridiculous. And is there even a guitar in the study? I didn't see one when I was poking around less than an hour before. Then, when the music ends and a jabbering voice urges me to visit the biggest truck dealership in Vermont, I understand.

It's a radio.

I don't know why he even has one in this day and age. But there's no mistaking what I hear. Gregg has turned on a radio, and it's doing a fine job of masking whatever conversation is going on behind that locked door. I catch a snippet of voices once in a while, one of which I recognize as Gregg's from its timbre, but they're speaking in such low tones it's impossible to hear what either of them is saying over the din from the radio.

Even when I finally give in and press my ear against the varnished wood, it's no better. But at least it gives me fair warning when I hear the radio abruptly shut off and a flurry of movement from within the room.

They've finished their discussion, and I'm about to get caught listening.

I pivot away from the door and race toward the living room, reaching it just as Gregg and Eddie emerge. I flop down onto the sofa as if I've been there all along and twist my neck to look back toward the foyer.

Gregg is walking a step behind Eddie, almost like he wants to make sure that his neighbor goes straight to the front door and doesn't stray. And then they move beyond my limited view, but I can still hear their footfalls on the tile floor.

Neither one is talking now.

The front door opens. There's an exchange of terse goodbyes before it closes again. I hear the deadlock engage.

More footsteps, then Gregg is back. He stops in the doorway. Noticing the look on my face, he says, "What?"

"Figure out how to fix the generator?" I ask in the lightest voice I can muster.

"We figured it out. Yes." Gregg enters the room and comes over to the sofa, then sits down next to me. "I don't think Eddie will be back."

"Why would you say that?" If Eddie really is our neighbor, if it wasn't him who followed me this morning—and I'm still not completely sure either way—then there's safety in numbers. Not least because Eddie has a gun.

"No reason. I just thought you might be uneasy around him." Gregg's palm lands on my leg. He squeezes my knee. "After what you've been through and all."

"That depends if he had anything to do with what happened this morning by the lake."

"Eddie?" Gregg shakes his head. "I promise you it wasn't him."

"How long have you known him?" I ask.

"A few years. He's a little rough around the edges, but you don't need to worry about him."

"And you didn't know he was up here at the lake until now?"

"No."

"You saw that he was carrying a gun, right?"

Gregg shrugs. "I didn't." He studies me for a few seconds. "Look, Anna, I know how jumpy you are, but you need to stop this. Eddie had nothing to do with what happened earlier today. Neither did I, in case you're wondering. Whoever that guy with the knife was, he's probably long gone by now. It was likely a hunter passing through, or some random stranger who was surprised to see you out there in such a remote place at this time of year."

"Or it was the person who did this to me," I say with more than a little indignation. "Caused me to lose my memory. Tried to kill me."

"There's no proof that anyone is trying to kill you." Gregg lifts his hand from my knee. "For all you know, what happened was an accident.

Maybe you're staying at one of the other houses around here and fell off a dock, bumped your head."

"With my slippers on and no coat?"

Gregg sighs with exasperation. "I don't know. Maybe. That's a whole lot more believable than someone trying to kill you for no reason."

"Until I get my memories back, we won't know what reason someone might have to want me dead," I snap back at him. "And maybe that's the point. Whoever did this to me knows I'm still alive and has come back to finish the job." I glare at Gregg. "What were you and Eddie talking about in that study? Because I find it really hard to believe you were discussing his broken generator."

"But it's the truth."

"With the radio on to mask your voices," I say. "Who even owns a radio these days?"

"Anna, you're being ridiculous." Gregg shakes his head. "The radio was already on. I was looking for that leaky pipe and couldn't find it. I came back downstairs and went into the study. That's when I put the radio on. A few minutes later, Eddie knocked on the door. I was going to answer it when you showed up."

"You weren't on the third floor. I went up there looking for you. And we didn't pass each other on the back stairs, so how did you end up in the study?"

"For heaven's sake. I came down to the second floor and went to my room to see if I could still hear the dripping from above. Then I used the main staircase. You were probably going up while I was coming down."

That's convenient, I think. "And the toolbox? Where's that?"

"Back in the garage. Stop being so goddamned paranoid."

The accusation hits me like a slap in the face. "I'm not paranoid. Something is going on here, and I want to know what it is right now."

"There's nothing going on. All I've done is try to help you, and this is the thanks I get?" Gregg jumps to his feet. "This conversation is over."

"Damn right it is." Now it's my turn to jump up. I storm toward the door.

"Where are you going?" Gregg calls after me.

"Upstairs to my room." I step into the foyer and make for the staircase. "I need some time alone."

"Anna, wait. Please come back. There's no need for this." Gregg sounds despondent.

But I don't go back, because I still think he's lying about his conversation with Eddie. I'm the only other person in this house with him, and I have no idea who I am, so what exactly were they hiding from me? And why?

45

Adria

One Day Before

An icy dread enveloped Adria. She could hardly believe what she was hearing. "Why is the NSA interested in my husband?"

"We're not," Frank replied, if that was even his real name, which Adria guessed it wasn't. "Harvey Lang is an old friend. We worked together at the same agency many years ago. I owed him some favors, and he called one in, that's all."

"What agency?" Adria asked. "Harvey was in the military before he worked for my father's company."

"Harvey did a lot of things before he worked for your father, most of which I'm not at liberty to divulge. Now, please, can we get back to the point in hand?"

"Fine." Adria was more interested in what the man on the other end of the line had to say about her husband than Harvey Lang's past, anyway. "Should I be worried about Peter?"

"I think you should be careful, if that's what you're asking. There are a lot of red flags in your husband's past, mainly because he doesn't appear to have one."

"I don't follow."

"It's simple. Peter Bailey didn't exist until five years ago. He has what we in the trade call a legend. A cleverly crafted false identity, complete with fake documents to back it up. Driver's license. Passport. Credit cards."

"You're saying that my husband is a spy?"

"No. What I'm saying is that your husband used the Social Security number of an infant with the same name who died a few months after birth to invent a new identity for himself. An infant who, had he lived, would have grown up to be roughly the same age as Peter is now."

Adria could hardly believe what she was hearing. "How is that possible?"

"If you know what you're doing, it's easier than you would think."

"If Peter didn't exist five years ago, then who was he before?"

"A good question. Harvey sent me a photograph of your husband, and I used some of my resources at the agency to run a facial comparison—off the books, mind you. We got a partial match with a man who vanished almost twelve years ago. Now, I stress that it's only a partial match because of the low quality of the older photograph, so it doesn't mean that they are necessarily the same person, but if this man and your husband are the same, then he's wanted for questioning in a California homicide."

"What?" Adria felt suddenly lightheaded. She went to the bed and sat down. "Is my husband a murderer?"

"I never said that. The facial match was only fifty percent. The original photograph was grainy, and the subject was not looking at the camera head-on. It's also the only image of Nick Blakely that exists, so we can't run another comparison. Just like Peter, Nick only has a short history, popping up for a few years, then vanishing again."

"You think my husband has created false identities before," Adria said.

"If they're the same person, then yes. But here's the thing. Nick Blakely was renting a room from a couple in Santa Barbara, California. Jess and Rob Cody. He passed himself off as a financial adviser and offered to help manage their assets. Around the time that Nick Blakely moved out of Jess and Rob's home, they allegedly went on a month-long trip that took them across the country and abroad. Their family and friends even received postcards sent from various places that seemed to confirm as much. But then the postcards stopped, and the couple was never seen again. Eventually, their home went into foreclosure and sold. When the new owners decided to add a lanai and started digging the foundation, they came across skeletal remains."

"Jess and Rob Cody," Adria said.

"Yes. Forensic examination dated their deaths to around the time that Nick Blakely ceased to exist. And when investigators looked at the Codys' finances, they found Nick had been siphoning money out of their accounts and into one that he controlled. An account that was emptied shortly before he disappeared."

"How much money?" Adria asked, a prickle running up her spine.

"Half a million, give or take. The detectives working the case concluded that Jess and Rob grew suspicious of their tenant and financial adviser and were about to discover his deception. That was when they went missing."

"I don't believe this." Adria put her head in her hands, fighting the hysteria that threatened to overwhelm her. "My husband really is a murderer."

"Keep in mind, the facial recognition wasn't conclusive," Frank told her. "Nick and Peter might not be the same person."

Adria lifted her head, composed herself as best she could. "If they are the same person, where was he in the years between living as Nick and claiming to be Peter?"

"Who knows? Presumably he set up another false identity, but he could have lived for a while on the money he stole from Rob and Jess."

"Or he could've been scamming someone else."

"It's possible," Frank admitted.

"Or it might all be coincidence," Adria said, clutching at straws.

"That's also possible. But regardless of Peter's prior identity, it doesn't change the fact that your husband is not who you thought he was."

"Which means I'm in danger."

"It means that you should be careful, yes." Frank cleared his throat. "You said your husband was downstairs. I assume you're at home right now?"

"No, we're up at our lake house in Vermont."

"Vermont, huh? Sounds remote."

"It is."

"And it's just the two of you?"

"Yes."

"Then you need to be especially careful. I'll see if I can open a back channel to the Santa Barbara Police Department and get more information about their homicide, pass on my findings without involving the NSA in this. But I warn you, there's no guarantee that anything will come of it. The chances are that you're on your own, at least for now."

"I understand," Adria said with a rising sense of dread. "If you find out anything else, you will let me know?"

"Absolutely. You have my word. In the meantime, I'd like to send you the photograph of Nick Blakely. Do you have a secure email address, one that your husband can't access?"

"You can use my company address," Adria said, giving him her charitable foundation email address. "He never goes in there, and I'm not even sure he knows the password."

"Good. I'll send it as soon as I get a chance. In the meantime, keep your head down. Don't antagonize your husband," Frank said. "And get out of that lake house and back to Boston at the first opportunity."

That won't be easy, thought Adria. *Not with the blizzard, and Peter being so stubborn.*

"Did you hear me?" Frank asked when she didn't answer.

"Yes. I'll do my best."

"Good." Frank told her to be careful one more time, then hung up.

Adria cradled the phone in her hand and stared at it. All the evidence pointed to Peter being a killer, no matter what the man from the NSA who called himself Frank said about the facial recognition not being conclusive. She knew in her heart Peter was responsible for Harvey Lang's death, even if he hadn't committed the act himself. The question was, Had he also killed that couple in California? Maybe when she saw the photograph of Nick Blakely, she would find out. In the meantime, she had to act as if everything were fine. Adria was no actress. How was she going to manage that when all she wanted to do was get as far away from him as possible?

She wiped away a tear and was about to stand up when the bedroom door opened, and Peter strode in. He looked at her, then at the phone. "I thought you were going to take a shower. I've made us a light dinner. What were you doing?"

"Nothing," Adria said, thinking quickly. "Work called about the water well project. I'll take my shower now, then I'll be down."

"Don't take too long." Peter stepped toward her, reached down, and snatched the phone from her hand before she could stop him. "And from now on, no more work calls. This is supposed to be a romantic getaway."

"What are you doing?" Adria jumped up, tried to take her phone back.

Peter held it out of reach. "Not so fast. I'm making a new rule. No phones at the lake house. We're up here for each other. The outside world can wait."

"But—" Adria tried to swallow her rising panic.

"No buts. Take your shower, and I'll see you downstairs." Then Peter turned on his heel and stomped from the room, taking Adria's only lifeline away with him.

46

Anna

Day Four

I pace back and forth in my room, angry with Gregg and myself. I hate how my damaged mind refuses to work like it should. I feel as if I'm trapped at the bottom of a dark pit with no way to climb out. The blank canvas of my past is just waiting to be filled with every paranoid delusion my brain can conjure. It's hard to separate fact from fiction, fantasy from reality, when the anchor of what went before has been snatched away.

I could howl with frustration.

Why aren't my memories returning? Other than a few brief flashes of familiarity and vague snippets devoid of context, like when I was looking at the lighthouse painting in Gregg's study and saw myself at the rail of a boat drinking a Bloody Mary with an unknown man, I've got nothing. The truth of my situation lies buried within the subconscious depths of my mind, tantalizingly out of reach, yet there for the taking if only I could grasp it. In the absence of this knowledge, I lurch from one fevered delusion to another, trying desperately to make my world whole again. To fill the gaps in a jigsaw puzzle missing most of its pieces.

Am I really in danger?

My gut says yes, but it's impossible to gauge from which direction that danger might come when I have no clue how I came to be in this situation. Which leaves me distrusting everyone, including Gregg.

Maybe I was too harsh on him downstairs. I shouldn't assume that he's keeping things from me just because I couldn't find him on the third floor, or because Eddie doesn't fit my preconceived notions of the type of person who would own a second home on Gravewater Lake. Yet I can't help the way I feel. This is the second time Gregg has gone missing inside the house, almost like he vanished into thin air, even though his explanations sound reasonable. Then there's Eddie. He gives me the creeps. The way he looked at me. The concealed gun beneath his jacket. How he was dressed.

But Eddie and Gregg are only the tip of a metaphorical iceberg. I'm scared of everything. I'm even scared of myself. It's not just that I don't know *who* I am, but I also don't know *what kind of person* I am. For all I know, I deserve what's happening to me. What if I get my memories back and discover that there's something terrible lurking in my past? Then again, what if I *never* get my memories back and have to go through the rest of my life not knowing? I'm not sure which of those scenarios terrifies me more. But I know one thing. Living in constant fear is exhausting.

I go to the bed and lie down on my side, facing the window. It is getting dark outside. The sun has slipped low on the horizon and is casting shadows through the trees and into my room, throwing long fingers of golden light across the floor. I watch for a while as the sky grows dark, then close my eyes. I remind myself that I'm safe inside the house. That the doors are locked, and our gruff visitor is gone. That Gregg is not my enemy. And it works. The fear and anger slowly ebb, or at least retreat enough that they aren't at the forefront of my thoughts, and I fall into a broken and fitful slumber . . . only to be woken sometime later by a gentle knock at my door.

"Anna?" Gregg's voice drifts into the darkened room.

I roll over on the bed, sit up, but don't answer.

"I'm sorry about earlier. I know how scared you are, and I didn't mean to make it worse."

I hear the bedroom door handle rattle as he tries to open it, only to discover that I've locked it from the inside. He gives up, and for a moment I think he's walked away, but then he speaks again.

"I made you a light dinner. Figured you must be hungry. I'll leave it out here in the hallway if you want it." There's a momentary pause, then: "I found the book you're reading in the living room, so I brought that up too, just in case you get bored and want something to do."

My heart melts a little at his kindness and obvious attempt to make up. I almost respond but still can't bring myself to do so, because then I'll end up opening the door, letting him in, and I'm not ready for that yet. I need more time to sort out my emotions. Because my relationship with Gregg is complicated. Sometimes I trust and want to be near him, like when I went to his bed last night, and then there are times when I think he's lying to me. Or at least holding back. These pendulum swings of emotion keep me off-balance. Just when I think I've figured Gregg out, something else happens.

I just don't know what to think anymore, so I don't answer, and soon Gregg retreats.

After five minutes of silence, I turn on the bedside lamp and walk to the door. I linger there a moment, listening, but hear nothing on the other side. When I disengage the lock and open it, there's a wooden tray sitting on the floor in the hallway. Upon it is a plate with a salmon fillet, green beans, and baby potatoes slathered in melting butter. Hardly what I would call a light dinner. It feels more like the sort of meal a person would make if they had a hot date coming around. The glass of red wine that accompanies it does little to dispel that notion. The final item on the tray is my book, with a slip of folded paper inserted into it to save my place.

The pendulum swings again, and I almost step into the hallway, go to the top of the stairs, and call for Gregg to come back. But I resist the urge and pick up the tray instead, then return to the solitary confines of the bedroom, where I close and lock the door.

47

I eat the meal, which is delicious, and drink the glass of red wine, which takes the edge off. After I finish, I gather the empty plate and wineglass and put them back onto the tray. I consider taking it downstairs, using it as an excuse to end my self-imposed solitude while saving face, but I don't. Apparently, I have a stubborn streak. Good to know. Instead, I pick up the book he brought up for me and go back to the bed, where I settle down to read.

When I open it, the slip of paper falls out onto the comforter, and for a moment I wonder if he wrote a note on it—maybe an apology or some other sweet message to coax me out of my funk—but when I unfold it, there's nothing.

I swallow my disappointment and focus my attention on the written word instead. As I fall into the story, all thoughts of Gregg and our disagreement fade into the background.

A couple of hours and many chapters later, my eyes are sore, and I'm overcome by a deep weariness. I set the book aside on the nightstand and stand up, then undress before heading into the en suite.

Five minutes later, I'm in the shower and relishing the drumbeat of hot, soothing water on my bare skin. By the time I step out, the water has turned from scalding hot to tepid, and the small room has taken on the appearance of a steamy sauna.

I dry off quickly, brush my teeth, and wrap a towel around myself, then step back out into the bedroom. The flannel pajamas Gregg loaned me the first night I was here are folded at the end of the bed, but before I can reach them, I hear a soft knock at the bedroom door.

"Anna," Gregg says from out in the hallway. "I'm going to bed now. I guess you're still mad at me, but I just wanted to say good night."

I'm not mad at him. Not anymore, thanks to the current disposition of my wildly swinging emotions, and I don't want him to go to bed thinking otherwise. But even so, I hesitate to respond, because I'm so confused. At times, like earlier today, I think Gregg is part of the problem. That he's lying to me. But then I wonder if I'm being ridiculous. Looking for deceit where there is none. Maybe Gregg really is just trying to help me. That's the problem with having no memory. No past. You don't have a compass upon which to gauge your present. That same blank past has left me lonely and vulnerable, like a barren island amid a swirling tempest. Strangely, I didn't feel that way last night when I was in his bed, even if I was a little drunk. I felt safe because I wasn't alone in this strange place. True, I was horrified this morning when I woke up. Mortified that I climbed into Gregg's bed so easily—but was it really that bad? Especially with another long, dark night stretching ahead of me. A night I don't want to spend by myself. I fear that more than I fear Gregg.

"Anna?" Gregg is still there. "I guess I'll see you in the morning."

"Wait." I clutch the towel, gripping the loose ends tight to my chest, and hurry to the door, where I disengage the lock and swing it open.

He looks mildly surprised that I answered, especially when he sees that I'm wearing nothing but a damp towel. He takes a small step backward, as if expecting me to berate him.

"Hey," I say, ignoring the tingle when his eyes drop from my face to the curve of my body beneath the towel. "Thanks for the meal and the wine. They were delicious."

"You're welcome." He forces his gaze back up and smiles. "Does this mean we're friends again?"

"Maybe." Overcome with a sudden urge not to let him leave, I let the towel shift just a little lower to reveal the barest hint of cleavage. "I don't suppose there's any wine left in that bottle you poured earlier?"

"I think there might be," Gregg says, but he makes no attempt to go back downstairs and get it. At least until he realizes that it might be his ticket into the bedroom. He tears his eyes away from me and turns toward the stairs. "I'll be back in a few."

"Don't be long," I say as he starts down the hallway, then I saunter back into the bedroom, all thought of sleep now gone.

Gregg is back barely a minute after he left, clutching the bottle of wine in one hand and a second glass in the other.

He crosses to the vanity, where the meal tray sits, and pours me a glass of wine, then does the same for himself. When he turns around, I'm behind him, still wrapped in my towel. I pick up my wineglass, take a sip, then set it down again and move close enough to stand on tiptoe and kiss him.

Our lips meet.

His arms slide around my shoulders even as I wrap mine around his waist with the towel held in place only by the pressure of my body pressed against his. And when I move, releasing that pressure ever so slightly, the towel falls away, leaving me standing unclothed in his embrace. And this time, I don't second-guess myself. Don't wonder if there's a husband or boyfriend somewhere that I'm about to betray. A family I don't remember. Not because I'm a bad person, but because right here and now, I don't care. I want Gregg. I'm not going to feel guilty when I wake up in bed next to Gregg tomorrow morning. I'm not going to flee before he stirs, racked by embarrassment or shame. This time, I'm owning it.

48

My eyes snap open in the darkness. Something has pulled me from a deep sleep. A stray sound I don't recognize. The clock on the nightstand tells me it's the middle of the night. Gregg is lying on his side to my left, facing away from me and snoring. Irregular breathy rumbles that sound almost like distant thunder. He's stolen most of the covers while we were sleeping, wrapping them around his body like a wrinkled shroud and leaving me with the corner of a thin sheet. Which wouldn't be so bad if I wasn't naked, and the room wasn't cold as the Arctic. Goose bumps pepper my skin, but that isn't what woke me. It was something else.

At first, I'm not sure what roused me from sleep. The wind is whistling outside, but no more so than it ever does. Nothing appears to be out of place. The dark outlines of the wine bottle and two empty wineglasses are visible across the room on the vanity, silent witnesses to my earlier seduction. Gregg's clothes drape over the chair where he left them.

The house is quiet and still.

Except that isn't quite true. Because when my eyes drift sideways to scan the rest of the room, I see it.

The bedroom door is open a couple of inches. It shouldn't be. Gregg closed it when he returned with the wine. I assumed it was locked, but when I think back, I don't remember checking. In the heat of my desire, there was only one thing I could think about.

My heart leaps into my throat.

I'm acutely aware of my nakedness. Not for the first time since arriving in this house, I'm overcome by the conviction that we are not alone. That someone was in here, watching me while I slept. Standing over the bed and looking down at me. An image of Knife Man flashes through my mind. An ominous figure clutching a sharp blade, ready to plunge it into my chest. A scene right out of a nightmare. But this is no product of a fevered slumber. It's real, and I'm awake. Which is why I can't tear my eyes away from that door, and the thin sliver of blackness that cloaks the dark hallway beyond.

Then, as I watch, the door swings slowly shut, closing upon itself with a faint click.

49

Adria

One Day Before

Adria spent the rest of the day thinking about the phone call with the NSA agent, Frank, and what he had told her. She was desperate to check her email and see if he had sent the photo of Nick Blakely, but Peter had taken her phone, and she knew he wouldn't give it back. He either genuinely wanted the weekend to pass without distractions, or he was trying to isolate her for more nefarious reasons.

There was one other way that she could check her email. The slim laptop tucked into the front pocket of her travel bag. If he saw it, Peter would probably try to take that away from her as well, which is why she had no intention of letting him see it. She would bide her time and wait for an opportunity to look at it when she was alone. But up at the lake house, that was proving hard to do.

Peter fawned over her like they were on a first date. He barely let her out of his sight for the rest of the day. In the evening, he cooked a meal and opened a bottle of wine, then led her upstairs to the bedroom. She knew what he wanted instantly by his flirty demeanor. He pulled her close and kissed her, tugged at the hem of her top, and lifted it over her head.

The last thing she wanted was sex, but she was also afraid of Peter, so for the second time in three days, she let him have his way. But to her surprise, even his lovemaking was like times of old. Gone was the rough and frenzied assault on her body that she had endured a few days before. If she pushed the thoughts of his transgressions aside, ignored that she was sharing her bed with a man she suspected of murder and embezzlement, she could almost believe that everything was just fine, and there was no cause for concern.

Except she couldn't do that, which was why, after he fell asleep naked and semi-inebriated atop the covers, she lay awake for a long time, listening to him snore. Then, when she was sure that he wouldn't wake up, she swung her legs off the bed and pulled on a robe.

She crossed to the walk-in closet where she had put her travel bag earlier in the day, removed the laptop from its pouch, then snuck from the bedroom and headed downstairs. Sitting on the couch in the living room with the laptop in front of her on the coffee table, she opened the computer and went straight to her email.

There were six messages. Three from the office, a pair of spam emails, and a message from a Gmail account that identified the sender simply as Frank, with the subject line:

> From a friend.

She opened the email. There was a brief message.

> Photo attached. Jess and Rob Cody, right and left, with Nick in the middle.

She downloaded the attachment and clicked on it, then leaned close to the screen to study the grainy photograph that opened in her image viewer. If she was expecting to see Peter staring back at her, she was disappointed. The photograph appeared to have been taken at night inside what looked like someone's living room. Jess and Rob, the murdered couple, stood on each side of a tall, thin man in his midtwenties wearing a white T-shirt and jeans. All three of them had their arms around each other and appeared to be laughing, although the image, which was probably shot with a standard 35mm film camera, appeared to have been taken in low light, and the grain made it hard to see fine details.

The figure in the middle, whom Frank had identified as Nick Blakely, was looking sideways at Jess with a big grin on his face. He certainly didn't look like the sort of person anyone would hire as a financial adviser, but Adria had to admit that even in the poorly exposed photograph, he bore a resemblance to her husband.

But no matter how hard she looked, she could not be certain. There just wasn't enough detail. She sat back on the sofa and stared at the image, as if looking at it longer would somehow bring the details into sharper focus. It was pointless. If the NSA's facial recognition software couldn't even say that it was Peter with more than 50 percent accuracy, then how was she expected to do any better?

She yawned and sank back into the cushions, suddenly feeling tired. But she didn't want to go back to bed. Couldn't bring herself to climb between the sheets and lie next to a man who just might have murdered the people in that photograph. Not to mention Harvey Lang, who was simply doing her a favor. And if Peter had done those things, how many other people had he killed in the years between?

Stop it, she chided herself. *You don't even know if it's Peter in that photo.* Which was true, but it didn't stop the thought from repeating in her mind like a morbid earworm.

She glanced toward the window, watched the snow tumbling from the dark sky. Like it or not, she was trapped up here. The road from the lake to the closest town could be closed for days during a blizzard, and the storm was worse than Peter had made it out to be. Was this all part of his plan? Get her stranded up here so she couldn't keep digging into his past? If so, what was his endgame?

She dragged her gaze away from the window and back to the laptop. The screen saver had come on. An undulating vortex of swirling colors. She was about to sit up straight and tap the keyboard to get rid of it and take another look at the photo when a voice spoke from behind her.

"Adria, I woke up, and you weren't in bed. What are you doing down here? It's two in the morning, for heaven's sake."

She turned to see Peter standing in the doorway with his arms folded and a look as hard as granite on his face. Then he stepped into the room and advanced toward her.

50

Anna

The bedroom door has barely clicked closed when I push the covers back and jump out of bed, my terror overcome by a determination to figure out what is going on in this house, once and for all.

The frigid air raises goose bumps on my exposed skin, and I grab a robe from a hook in the bathroom, then pull it on as I rush toward the door.

From somewhere behind me, Gregg stirs, mumbles something incoherent, but I ignore it. Trying to explain what I saw will only waste valuable time, and he won't believe me, anyway. He never does. I don't need to be told all over again that it's only my imagination when I know otherwise. This is my opportunity to prove it.

The empty wine bottle is still sitting where we left it earlier, and I scoop it up, feeling bolder now that I have a weapon with which to defend myself.

I reach the door and fling it open without allowing myself time to think. The hallway beyond is mired in darkness. I rush out just in time to see a glimmer of light from another door farther down the hallway. A thin sliver that quickly vanishes as the door closes.

I hesitate, overcome by a sense of danger. If someone really is in the house with us, should I be chasing them armed with nothing but an empty wine bottle? What if their intentions stretch to more than just watching us? It's almost enough to make me run back into the bedroom, slam the door, and lock it. But if I don't follow through, find out who is in that room, I will never know—truly know beyond a shadow of a doubt—that what I'm experiencing is real and not just some lingering effect of the bump on my head.

"What's going on?" comes a voice from behind me in the bedroom.

It's Gregg, who has woken up. I hear movement as he climbs out of bed. It galvanizes me into action.

"There's someone in the house with us," I say, even as I start down the hallway with renewed determination, wine bottle gripped tightly and ready to swing at the slightest provocation.

"Anna, wait." There is panic in Gregg's voice.

I have no intention of waiting. This is the same door that I saw a light beneath a few days before. There is no doubt in my mind that an intruder is on the other side. What other explanation is there? I'm not hallucinating. It isn't a remnant of some forgotten dream forcing its way into my waking consciousness. This is *real.*

With a shaking hand, I reach out and grip the door handle, fling the door wide open, and step inside with the wine bottle heavy in my other hand.

And I see . . . nobody.

The light is still on, but the room is empty. Or at least, it appears that way . . . which is impossible, because doors don't just close on their own.

"Anna, what are you doing?" Gregg appears in the doorway behind me, wearing nothing but a pair of boxer shorts. He looks flustered. Out of breath.

"I told you; someone was here." I look around the room. At the desk and chair on the opposite wall. The bed, which would be great to hide beneath except for the bed frame that goes all the way to the floor. And finally, the closet.

It's the only place an intruder could conceal themselves. I move farther into the room, take a step in that direction, but Gregg beats me to it.

He weaves around me and goes to the closet door, pulls it open, then quickly sticks his head inside before turning to me, a faintly smug look on his face. He moves aside. "Empty."

I'm overcome by a pulsing sense of déjà vu. This is the second time I've been sure someone was in this room, and on both occasions, I was wrong. I struggle to understand how that could be. The window is closed and latched from the inside, and the only other way out is through the door we came in.

I saw someone come in here. Saw the door close. It wasn't a well-timed breeze because the air in the hallway is thick and still. Yet my eyes don't lie. We're the only people in here.

Did I see a ghost? That sounds even more ridiculous than a vanishing intruder. Although a supernatural cause for the events in this house would certainly go a long way toward explaining them, even without my memories, I know that I'm smarter than that. There is no such thing as ghosts. They are the product of superstitious people, creating a flawed narrative to reason away what they don't understand. So where does that leave me? Conflicted and unnerved.

"Come on." Gregg reaches out and turns off the light, then places a guiding hand on my arm and steers me back into the hallway. "There's nothing in here. Let's go back to bed."

I tense, waiting for the lecture that I'm sure will come. Waiting for him to tell me that it was all in my head, or that I dreamed everything. But he says nothing. Instead, he just leads me back to the bedroom and closes the door, engaging the lock.

Then he turns and kisses me.

This reaction surprises me. It feels like a deliberate distraction. I hesitate for a moment before relaxing and returning his kiss. If he's trying to stop me from thinking about the phantom closing doors, this should do the trick nicely.

His hands find the belt keeping the robe closed, and he tugs at it until the robe falls open. He slips it from my shoulders, lets it drop to the floor so that I'm naked and exposed to his gaze. He pushes me back onto the bed, then positions himself above me. We make love for the second time that night.

51

Anna

Day Five

I sleep fitfully and wake early. The bedroom is cloaked in darkness, and at first, I think it's still the middle of the night, but when I look at the clock on the nightstand, I realize my mistake. It's 6:30 a.m. I lie there awhile longer, hoping I'll fall back to sleep, but when the first light of dawn seeps in through the bedroom's east-facing window, I reluctantly climb out of bed, making sure not to disturb Gregg, and hurry from the room.

After finding some clothes in the main bedroom's closet and getting dressed, I head downstairs to the kitchen, where I brew a pot of coffee, then sit at the table with my hands wrapped around the mug for warmth. By the time I'm on my second cup, I hear movement from upstairs. Gregg is awake.

That gives me an idea. After everything he's done for me, I want to do something for him. I go to the fridge, grab a carton of eggs and a pack of bacon. Then I make a hearty breakfast for both of us. I cut thick slices of bread from a sourdough loaf and toast them, then pour two glasses of orange juice, which I put on the table.

By the time he comes down, the food is about ready.

"You weren't in bed when I woke up. I thought you might have done something foolish," he says, stepping into the kitchen, "like taking another early morning walk."

"Nope. Learned my lesson there." I glance over my shoulder and smile at him. "Thought I'd make up for yesterday by cooking breakfast."

"You didn't need to do that."

"I know, but I wanted to. Unless you're not hungry. Then I'll just eat it all myself."

"Not so fast," Gregg says with a chuckle. He walks around the island, comes up behind me, slips his arms around my waist. "It's been a long time since a woman cooked for me. I intend to enjoy every mouthful."

"Good." I twist around and place a lingering kiss on his lips. "Sorry for being so dramatic last night. I was scared."

"Which you had every right to be under the circumstances. I shouldn't have been so snippy with you. I can't imagine what it must be like to have no memory of your past and no idea who you are or where you're from."

"It's not much fun," I tell him in one of the most blatant examples of understatement he'll probably ever hear. "But I'm glad I'm not going through it alone."

"Me too," Gregg replies, then glances toward the pans on the stove. "You should probably get back to that before it burns."

"Right." I wriggle from his embrace and turn my attention back to the stove. "You might not let me stay here anymore if I turn out to be a horrendous cook."

"I don't think there's any danger of that."

"What, of me being a dreadful cook, or of you kicking me out?"

Gregg laughs. "Most definitely the latter. I guess we'll find out about your cooking skills soon enough. Which means I should probably go back upstairs and freshen up. It was all I could do to pull on some pants and a shirt and rush down here when I saw you were missing."

"You've got five minutes," I tell him. "Better make it quick."

"Gotcha. No time for a shower, then." He's already on his way back toward the stairs.

"I could use a shower too," I call after him with memories of our lovemaking the night before still fresh in my mind. "Maybe we can share one later and do our bit for the environment. Save some water."

"Always happy to help the environment," he says, starting up the stairs. "And I can't think of a better way to do it than taking a shower with you!"

52

By the time Gregg comes back down, breakfast is on the table. He eats heartily, even stealing a slice of bacon from my plate when I proclaim that I'm too full to finish it. Afterward, he sits back in his chair with a hand on his stomach and tells me that if I keep making meals like that, I can stick around as long as I like. Apparently, I've passed the culinary test, even if it was just a couple of slices of toast and some fried food. I almost pull out the notebook he gave me and add *maestro in the art of breakfast* to the slim list of facts I've discovered about myself, but then decide that even a woman with no memory should be able to fry a decent egg.

I stand to clear away the plates, but Gregg jumps up. "Not so fast. You cooked. I'll take care of the dishes."

I sink back down onto the chair and watch him rinse everything off and load the dishwasher. When he turns back to me, I raise the issue of the heating, or rather the lack of it, in my bedroom.

He nods in agreement. "I noticed that too. You should have said something earlier. I'll go down into the basement and check the furnace valves to make sure they're all open. Don't want you turning into a Popsicle up there."

I almost tell him that I won't, as long as he's in bed next to me, but I bite my tongue. Instead, I just say, "Thank you."

He nods again, then dries his hands on a dish towel before striding toward the foyer. I follow along behind and watch as he goes to the door behind the stairs that leads into the basement. I have no intention of following him down there. My level of tolerance for spiders and other creepy-crawlies is even lower than it is for a freezing bedroom. Instead, I go into the living room.

The book I'm reading is still upstairs on the nightstand, and I don't feel like expending the energy to get it. Instead, I find the local history book that Gregg told me about and pull it down from the shelf. I settle on the sofa and browse through the first quarter of the book that mostly talks about the original inhabitants of the area. Indigenous people like the Abenaki, who were eventually driven out by foreign invaders—mostly the Dutch, English, and French. But it's when I reach the chapters detailing the later history of the area, from around 1805 onward, when the first logging camp was established, that my interest is piqued. The first several pages contain nothing but dry accounts of the first settlers, but then I find a series of plates reproduced from old daguerreotype photographs taken by none other than the pastor who ran the church that must once have been associated with the graveyard. Apparently, his interests extended to the newly invented art of photography when he wasn't saving souls.

And there it is. A church with rough stone walls and a wooden tower.

It sits on a plot of land with trees on both sides. Behind it, a good way distant, lies the graveyard, sitting high and dry with the flat waters of what was then Cooney Lake farther away still. I study the photo, fascinated, and notice the outlines of several small wooden structures dotted among the trees on each side of the church. They are almost impossible to make out because the edges of the photograph are so blurry and dark, but I assume them to be the dwellings of loggers who toiled to send wood downriver to Burlington.

On the following pages, I find several more photographs, some of which depict the daily lives of the men and women who made this remote patch of land their home for so many years. They sit on the stoops of small wooden huts, cook over open fires, or pose with large crosscut saws with a handle on each end that must have required two people to use.

I stare at the rugged faces of these long-dead pioneers, wondering how many of them remain in the partially submerged cemetery only a short distance from the house. It's a creepy thought, and I close the book with a shudder.

A few minutes later, Gregg returns.

"I checked the valves, and they were all open," he says. "The furnace is working just fine. I don't know why the second floor is so cold on your side of the house. Maybe the vents are closed on the baseboard heaters."

"No, they're not." I already checked that when I realized how cold the room was.

"Then I've got nothing. We'll probably need a plumber to check it out. Maybe there's an airlock in one of the pipes. It happens once in a while. But who knows how long it will be before we can get someone up here to fix it."

"That's all right." I've managed so far. Still, it would be nice not to freeze my ass every morning when I get out of bed. "You did your best."

Gregg observes me for a long moment, then says, "Maybe you should sleep in my room from now on, where it's warmer. You won't have to worry about being alone at night, then, either."

"Was that your plan all along?" I say with a laugh. "Turn the heating off to my room so that I'll have to hop into bed with you every night?"

An unreadable expression passes across Gregg's face, but it's quickly gone. His lips curl up into a lopsided half smile. "I would never do such a thing."

"Pleased to hear it." Even if he didn't sabotage the heating to get me into his bed, I get the impression that he isn't exactly put off by it.

Gregg claps his hands together and glances toward the cold hearth. "Now we've settled that, how about I make it nice and cozy in here and build a fire? Then I've got some chores to do around the house if you're okay entertaining yourself for a while."

"Sure." I watch Gregg build a fire, then take his leave. I pick up the history book again and start to read with my legs curled under me and my back against a soft cushion. I stay that way for the next several hours, only seeing Gregg a couple of times when he sticks his head inside the living room to check on me. At one point, he goes outside with a snow shovel and clears the back deck and a wide path down to the lake. It looks like hard work. I watch for a while, happy that it's him out there and not me, then go back to my book.

By early evening, the sky has grown dark, and the house has taken on the moody character that older dwellings often do when night falls. I'm relieved that nothing untoward has happened. It's nice not to feel on edge, if only for a while.

But all that soon changes.

My eyes are weary, so I close the history book and place it down on the sofa. I've been so engrossed in reading that I didn't realize how much time had passed. My stomach growls. It's been hours since I last ate. I look over my shoulder toward the foyer, looking for Gregg, hoping that he's going to make dinner.

At that moment, I hear the screen door leading out to the deck bang closed.

Was Gregg still outside in the dark?

I stand and stretch, working the kinks out of my stiff muscles, then head to the foyer. There's no trace of him. *That's weird.* Maybe he was going outside again instead of coming in.

I go to the back door, open it, expecting to see Gregg. Instead, a piece of paper flutters to the ground at my feet. I stare at it for a moment, confused, then bend down and pick it up. The paper is yellow with light lines ruled across it. It's a sheet torn from a legal pad and folded in half. I open it. A message written in bold block lettering stares back at me.

YOU CAN'T HIDE FOREVER.

53

I stand rooted to the spot and stare at the note in horror. Who would have left this? The world closes in until there's nothing left but me and that dreadful threat. I stumble. My legs give way beneath me.

"Whoa, easy there." Strong hands slip under my arms, pull me upright before I can sink to the floor.

It's Gregg.

After several deep breaths, when my composure has returned, I look down at the note, which is still in my hand. I was gripping it so tightly when I was about to faint that I crumpled it.

"What's that?" Gregg asks, finally releasing me.

I turn to him and hold the sheet out, smoothing it as best I can. "This was left between the doors."

He takes it and studies the note, lips pressed into a tight line. He says nothing.

When a full minute passes, I can't take it any longer. "Well?"

"Well, what?"

Really? He has to ask? I point toward the sheet of paper, jabbing at it with my finger. "That. It's a threat. Proof someone wants me dead."

Gregg nods thoughtfully. "Maybe."

"There isn't any *maybe* about it. You keep telling me it's all in my head. That I'm imagining things. This proves that I'm not. Someone is after me, just like that day at the graveyard. Knife Man was real. *This* is real."

"Hey, calm down. I'm not saying that it isn't." Gregg folds the note, then steps around me and goes to the still-open door. He stares out through the screen, across the deck and into the night. "Did you see anyone?"

"No." I shake my head. "I heard the screen door bang closed and thought it was you."

"Me either." Gregg steps back and closes the door, locks it.

If only he hadn't shoveled the back deck, there would be footprints in the snow. More evidence of my unknown stalker. Or maybe they wouldn't have been bold enough to come up to the door like that and leave a trail . . . leave the note. A part of me wishes they hadn't, because until now, I could try to kid myself that Gregg was right even if I didn't really believe it, and it was all nothing but paranoia. Good luck with that now.

I realize that I'm shaking.

He folds the note again so that it's a quarter of its original size, then tucks it into his back pocket before wrapping his arms around me in a tight embrace. "I won't let anyone hurt you. Promise."

"Thank you." I press against his chest, feel the rhythmic beat of his heart, which is comforting.

At that moment, there's a knock at the door.

In an instant, the fear ratchets up a notch. My stomach clenches.

Gregg releases me and turns away.

"Don't." I grab his arm, hold him back. "That must be them. They left the note, and now they've come around to the front door to finish the job. To kill me."

Another knock echoes through the foyer, louder this time.

Gregg shakes free of my grip. "Don't be ridiculous. If someone was coming to kill you, they wouldn't knock first."

That makes sense . . . sort of. But it does nothing to ease my fear. Not that it matters. Gregg is already striding across the foyer and past the stairs toward the front door. He turns the dead bolt, reaches for the doorknob before I can get there to stop him.

When he opens it, a familiar figure is standing on the other side.

Eddie is back, and this time he doesn't wait for an invitation before pushing his way into the house.

54

Adria

The Day She Found Out

Adria snapped the laptop closed a moment before Peter reached the sofa.

He glared at the computer. "I thought we agreed there would be no electronic devices this weekend. No work. Nothing to distract us."

Adria hadn't agreed to any such thing. Peter had just taken her phone and announced it. But she had no intention of arguing with him. "I couldn't sleep, so I thought I'd come down here and check my emails. You were out to the world. I figured it wasn't a big deal."

"What sort of emails?"

"Just work stuff," Adria replied, praying that Peter wouldn't reach for the computer, lift the lid, and look. Because then he would see the photograph, which was still open in the image browser. And if the smiling twentysomething in that old picture standing between a pair of murder victims was him, if he thought she knew about his past, what would he do then?

But Peter didn't open the laptop. He just shook his head, as if he was disappointed. "I don't know what I'm going to do with you. It's like an addiction. You just can't stop working. That's why we've been having so many issues in our marriage. You realize that, right?"

"We haven't been having issues," Adria protested, even as a thought ran through her head: *Except for the money you've been embezzling from the foundation.* And there was so much more, like the Social Security number he was using. The one that belonged to the real Peter Bailey, who had been dead for almost as long as her husband had been alive. He had been lying to her since the day they'd met. But worse than all that was the photo on her laptop. The man who looked like her husband and had in all likelihood killed Rob and Jess Cody when they caught him doing to them the same thing that Peter was doing to her. But she wasn't going to mention any of that. Instead, she stood up and forced a yawn. "We can talk about this in the morning. Let's go back to bed. What do you say?"

"I don't want to go back to bed." Peter rubbed his temples, kneading them with his thumb and forefinger as if he had a headache. "I want you to stop disobeying me."

"You want me to do what?" This was too much. Adria's trepidation turned to anger. The words were out of her mouth before she even realized what she was saying. "How dare you speak to me like that!"

"I'll speak to you any way I want to." Peter's eyes flashed, his face twisting into a demonic scowl. Then he lunged for the computer before Adria could stop him, scooped it up off the coffee table. "And if you won't do as I say, then I'll have to make you do it the hard way."

"Wait." Adria could hardly believe what was happening. This was a side of her husband she had never seen before, as if he no longer cared about hiding his true self. That there was no point in pretending anymore. And if that was true, then how much danger was she in, trapped in the house alone with him?

Peter ignored her protest. He drew his arm back and threw the computer with all his might.

The laptop sailed through the air, flipping end over end. It hit the wall near the fireplace with a sharp crack. The screen broke away and flew in one direction. The rest of the laptop went in the other.

Adria stared at the destroyed computer in silent shock. Who the hell was this man she had let into her life? He had never shown her this side of himself before, and it was terrifying. If she needed proof Peter was dangerous, this was it. But when she turned toward him, the anger had drained from his face.

"I'm sorry," he said in an almost childlike voice. "I shouldn't have done that."

Adria realized she was shaking. She tried to stop, couldn't. She blinked moisture from her eyes and swallowed.

Peter took a step forward, put an arm around her waist, then steered her toward the stairs. "Come on, let's get you back into bed. Everything will be better in the morning, I promise."

55

Anna

"What are you doing back here?" Gregg asks in a gruff voice as Eddie pushes past him.

"Well now, that's no way to speak to an old friend, is it?" Eddie lifts his arm to show Gregg the six-pack of canned beer he's carrying. "Figured we could hang out and catch up for a few hours. Maybe cook up some hamburgers to go with these. You know, since you haven't bothered to take care of that issue yet, like you promised."

"I told you . . . I'll get to it when I can." Gregg looks down at the six-pack. "And I don't need your beer."

"Seriously?" Eddie pushes the door closed with the toe of his boot, cutting off the biting wind that whips into the foyer. "It's your favorite. You've never turned it down before."

Gregg casts a furtive glance back toward me. "Maybe my tastes have changed. I appreciate the finer things in life now."

"Yeah? Like what?"

"Like a good wine."

Eddie looks at him as if he's speaking a foreign language, then he grins and slaps Gregg on the back. "Guess tonight we're going old-school, then."

Eddie starts toward the kitchen. As he passes me, he grunts a barely audible hello. My eyes drop to his coat, where I saw the bulge of a gun the last time he was here. If he's carrying, I see no evidence of it now. Another thought occurs to me. Was it Eddie who left that note? It's convenient that he showed up at the front door mere minutes after I found the sheet of paper at the back door. Then again, Eddie seems more concerned with Gregg than me, so maybe not.

Gregg hasn't moved. He stands like an island near the door, silently watching Eddie's back with a scowl on his face. Finally, when his *friend* enters the kitchen, he follows along.

"I'm sorry about this," he says as he walks past me. "I'll get rid of him as quickly as I can."

I'm not sure that's going to be easy, considering Eddie's mood. He seems hell-bent on hanging out for the evening, although I can't imagine for the life of me why. Gregg doesn't want him here. It's clear that there's animosity between them.

When I enter the kitchen, Eddie has set the six-pack down on the island; he pulls one loose, then pops it open. I notice that it's the same brand that Gregg has in the smaller beverage fridge under the island counter. A cheap domestic light beer.

Eddie takes a swig and smacks his lips. "That hits the spot." He rips another can free and holds it out to Gregg. "Here."

"I told you already, I don't want it," Gregg says, making no move to accept the beer.

"And I don't want to drink alone." Eddie presses the can into his hand. He looks at me. "You want one as well, sweetheart?"

"No." I bristle at being called *sweetheart*. I might not remember who I am, but I'm pretty sure I'm not the kind of woman who likes strange men referring to her in that manner. I take a step toward the taller built-in wine cabinet. "Thanks, but I'll stick with the red."

Eddie shrugs. "Suit yourself."

I turn my back on the men and open the wine cabinet, looking for a screw top. After pulling out all the drawers in the warmer bottom half of the fridge, which is dedicated to red wines, I don't find one. In the end, I settle on a 2012 French Cabernet Sauvignon. It's probably expensive, but since most of the other vintages are older, some by many years, I figure Gregg won't complain about my choice. Besides, he's opened several bottles since I've been here, so he clearly doesn't mind drinking his collection.

When I turn around again, Gregg is sipping his beer straight from the can and glaring over the rim at Eddie, who doesn't appear to notice.

A weighty silence fills the air.

I open the drawer that I saw Gregg remove the corkscrew from a few days earlier and go to work opening the wine. The cork comes out with a bright pop. I find a glass and give myself a generous pour.

Eventually, after finishing one beer and crumpling the can, then opening a second one, Eddie speaks again. "You know, I've been thinking. Yesterday, you told me you haven't seen Ricky in over a year. That the two of you don't talk much anymore. But here's the thing, see, you were always so close. Kind of like brothers. Seems strange to me that you'd fall out like that."

I'm confused. I thought they were talking about fixing Eddie's generator, not discussing some guy I've never heard of. I look between the two men until my gaze falls on Gregg. "Who's Ricky?"

"Nobody. He's not important. Just someone I used to know."

"That's kind of harsh, don't you think?" Eddie shakes his head. "What would Ricky say if he heard you talking like that?" He looks at me. "He's Gregg's cousin. They grew up together." He turns his attention back to Gregg. "Right?"

"Yeah." Gregg shifts from foot to foot, looking uncomfortable. "We used to be tight. But Ricky, well, he took a wrong turn somewhere along the way. Fell in with a bad crowd. Got himself into trouble."

"And you were always there to bail him out," Eddie says with a chuckle that almost comes across as menacing. "And I mean that literally. Just couldn't help trying to do the right thing by him, no matter how many times he let you down. I admire you for that. I really do."

"Not anymore. That's all in the past."

I listen to this exchange with a growing sense of foreboding. Gregg claims that he's only known Eddie for a few years. That they only met after he bought the lake house. But the way they're talking sounds like they've known each other for much longer. I don't know what to make of it. I want to ask, but now isn't the right time. Not with Eddie standing there. I don't like the man. He gives me the creeps. He reminds me of a spider waiting for its prey to make the wrong move, to get stuck in its web so it can pounce. I don't think Gregg will be honest with me while Eddie is around.

As if to prove me right, Gregg clears his throat and changes the subject, leaving my questions about Ricky in the dust. "I don't know about the pair of you, but I'm starving. How about I get those hamburgers going, and we can eat?" He looks at Eddie. "I'm sure you don't want to waste your entire evening over here."

Eddie just shrugs and crushes his second can, then drops it onto the countertop without even trying for the recycling bin in the cabinet below. "I appreciate the concern, but I'm good." He opens another beer and takes a long swig, then smiles. "It's not like I have anything better to do."

56

Gregg takes a package of hamburgers out of the freezer along with some buns, then heads for the garage to cook them on the propane grill, which he says has been stored there for the winter. Eddie doesn't show much inclination to join him, so I tag along, mostly because I can't abide the thought of spending even a minute alone with the man.

It's the first time I've been in the garage, and I notice that two of the three bays are empty. An older-model black truck with a dent in the passenger-side door occupies the third. It feels about as out of place in this home as the domestic light beer in Gregg's fridge.

"If you take a look at the back bumper," he says, noticing the way I look at it, "you'll find a sticker that reads, *My other car is a Ferrari*."

"Really?" I take a faltering step toward the truck, then stop.

"No. It's a joke. I'm not that crass. I only bring the truck up here in winter. Four-wheel drive is better on the icy roads, and I can throw firewood in the back without worrying about making a mess. And before you ask, even the truck won't make it into town on an unplowed road with the bridge out."

I wasn't going to ask. But I do have one question. I glance over my shoulder to make sure we're still alone, then turn back to Gregg. "Can we talk about Eddie?"

"Wondered how long that would take." Gregg hits a button on the wall and lifts the closest garage door. He pushes the grill as near to the opening as he can while keeping it under cover, then opens the lid and lights it. As if his actions need an explanation, he says, "Just to be safe. Don't want to end up gassing ourselves if there's a leak." When he sees the look on my face, he touches my arm. "Don't worry. Whoever left that note is probably long gone by now, and even if they aren't, I'm here. No one is going to hurt you."

I nod, forcing myself to calm down. "About Eddie . . ."

"What about him?"

"You said you've only been friends for a few years, since you bought this house, but he seems to know a lot about you and your cousin."

"So?"

"I don't know. I just think it's odd."

"Not really. I've brought Ricky up here before. He and Eddie have met a few times. I've also done my fair share of griping to Eddie about my cousin and the scrapes he's gotten himself into, mostly when I've had a few too many. I kind of consider myself a big brother to my cousin. He didn't have a great upbringing. Our families didn't have a lot of money when we were growing up. Cash was tight. I chose to make an honest living. Earn my money the right way. Ricky walked a different path."

"I'm sorry," I say, laying a hand on Gregg's arm. "That must've been hard for you."

"It was. But hey, whatever doesn't kill you only makes you stronger." When my face falls again, he throws me an apologetic look. "Hell. That was a poor choice of words, since someone might actually be trying to kill you."

"It's fine." I glance back toward the door that leads into the house. "I know you must feel bad for Ricky, but you should also feel proud that you didn't let adversity get in your way. Look at everything you have. The money you've made. I mean, unless it was your wife that had the—" I stop myself before I put my foot in it any further.

Gregg doesn't reply right away, then he says, "Like any good marriage, it was a joint effort."

A lump rises in my throat. "You must miss her a lot."

"I've had my moments," he says, then adds, "but honestly, since you came along, it's like she isn't gone at all."

It takes a few seconds for what he said to sink in. When it does, I'm not sure how to respond.

But it doesn't matter because Gregg has already moved on.

"Grill's up to temperature," he announces, tearing open the package of frozen hamburgers and throwing five of them on to cook—presumably two each for him and Eddie, and one for me. "And it's about time. I'm famished."

57

Eddie finally leaves two hours later after demolishing the rest of the six-pack he brought with him and another beer that he grabs from the small beverage fridge. Gregg doesn't try to keep up but rather helps himself to one more beer and sips it slowly. He sits across the table from Eddie while we eat and watches him with a stony expression that makes me wonder just how good the friendship between these two men really is.

Conversation is stilted, and by the time Eddie steps across the threshold and out into the wintry night, I'm ready to see the back of him. If he is the author of the note, he doesn't show it.

As he departs, he locks eyes with Gregg and says, "This was fun. I'll be back again real soon."

Gregg doesn't respond. He just observes Eddie with a tight-lipped stare.

Eddie lingers a moment with his hands pushed deep into his coat pockets, then turns and walks away.

I go to the window and watch as he trudges down the driveway in calf-deep snow and is finally swallowed up by the darkness.

"You okay there?" Gregg asks, coming up behind me and wrapping me in a quick embrace.

"Not sure." I break away from him and head toward the living room. When I look back, he's standing there like some schoolboy who's just been snubbed at recess by his best friend. I wonder if he expected me to turn and kiss him instead of walking off, but after the uncomfortable evening with Eddie and our conversation in the garage, I don't feel like playing the female lead in an illusion of domestic bliss. After all, I barely know this man. Heck, I barely know myself.

I flop down onto the sofa and stare at the flames that dance and leap in the hearth.

Gregg appears in the doorway. He watches me for a moment before speaking. "You want another glass of wine?"

"I don't think so." I drank the first one quickly, hoping it would take the edge off everything that has happened today. It didn't. The second one went down harder. I ended up nursing it through the meal and the interminable conversation afterward, mostly because I had a deep sense that I should keep my wits about me. Now, I'm tired and just want to put this day behind me.

Gregg takes a step inside the room, hesitates. "I'm sorry about this evening. I promised you that Eddie wouldn't be back."

"It's not your fault," I say. "It's not like you invited him over here or anything."

"I know, but even so. . ." Gregg folds his arms. "If he shows up here again, I'll tell him he's not welcome."

"You don't need to do that on my account. He's your friend."

"Out of circumstance, not choice. Honestly, he's not the kind of guy I want to hang out with."

"Can't pick your neighbors, right?"

"Something like that." Gregg looks toward the kitchen. "I'll go stick a cork in that wine and put it back in the fridge."

"Right." I watch him go, then relax back into the soft cushions of the sofa. I close my eyes. And in that moment, I'm hit by an overwhelming sense of déjà vu, swiftly followed by a scene from another time and place that bullies its way into my mind.

A man stands on the sidewalk in front of a different home. His face is out of focus, his features blurry in the same way that people in dreams are sometimes unrecognizable. Yet somehow, he reminds me of Eddie. He's gruff. Overbearing. More than that, he's menacing.

I shrink back from him, consider stepping around him and running for the door and the feeling of safety locking it behind me would bring, but I can't because he's too close and would likely grab me if I tried. And there's something else too. He has a gun beneath his jacket. The bulge is unmistakable.

My eyes widen, but he does nothing to hide it, almost as if he wants me to know that the gun is there.

I don't know what to do, but he's clearly here for a reason, and the only way I'll get rid of him is to find out what that reason is, so I ask what he wants.

He glances over my shoulder, as if he's expecting to see someone else. Then he says, "I'm looking for your husband."

I gasp and open my eyes. The scene that just played through my mind feels like a half-remembered dream, the events jumbled together out of sequence. But that's not what scares me. It's the last thing that *Eddie but not Eddie* said to me.

I'm looking for your husband.

Is this another resurfacing memory, or just a cruel trick of my tired mind playing on my unease? If it's the former, then someone really is out there looking for me. Then another thought enters my head. A worse thought. The man in the flashback felt an awful lot like Eddie. Maybe there isn't a husband out there searching for his missing wife. Maybe he knows exactly where his wife is because . . .

"All done." Gregg saunters back into the room and stands near the sofa. When he notices the look on my face, he frowns. "Something wrong?"

I shake my head, forcing myself to calm down. "Nothing's wrong. I'm okay."

"You don't look okay." He comes around the sofa and sits down. "What is it? You can tell me."

I want to tell him. I really do. Because carrying the weight of all the fears and suspicions that plague me is a burden that I have no desire to shoulder alone. But Gregg is a part of those fears, and I waft between needing him right there next to me, trusting him, and thinking that he's at least partially responsible for whatever is going on here. And then there's my newest suspicion, brought on by the weird flashback I've just experienced. *Am I his wife?* If that's true, then I'm in more danger than I could ever imagine, because it means that Gregg knows who I am and has been lying to me all along. I turn to look at him, study his face for a moment to see if I can read anything behind those piercing blue eyes, but all I see is concern.

"Well?"

"There's nothing to tell," I say to him. "I'm good. I swear."

Gregg doesn't look convinced. "If you're sure."

"I'm sure." I'm also feeling tired and can't wait to put this evening, that terrible note, and Eddie's unannounced visit behind me. "If you don't mind, I think I'm going to hit the sack. Get an early night."

Gregg looks at his watch. "It's only nine thirty."

"I know, but it's been one hell of a day, and I was awake so early this morning. If you're not ready for bed yet, I can go up on my own." Despite Gregg's earlier suggestion that we both sleep in his room from now on, I'm having second thoughts. I don't want to be alone, but there are those nagging suspicions I can't get out of my head, which is why I add, "It might be better if I sleep in the guest bedroom again tonight, anyway."

"You mean, like, by yourself?"

I nod. "I know it's cold up there, but I'll be fine once I'm under the covers."

"I don't understand," Gregg says, his face dropping. "After what happened last night, the night before . . . after what we did . . ."

"It's nothing to do with that," I tell him quickly, even as a memory of climbing onto the bed, straddling him, giving myself to him flashes through my head. And I mean it. But I also can't tell him the truth, so I end up feeding him the only excuse I can think of, which sounds feeble even to me. "I don't want to impose upon you, that's all."

"That's ridiculous. It's not an imposition, and you're not sleeping in that freezing room all by yourself," Gregg replies. "Not now that I know the heating's broken. And with everything that's happened, I don't think you should be alone, anyway. My bed is perfectly big enough for the both of us."

"Gregg—"

He shakes his head and raises a hand to mollify me. "And you don't need to worry. I'll be the perfect gentleman if that's what you want. Scout's honor."

What else can I say? He hasn't left me any choice, and I'm still freaked out by that warning—*You can't hide forever*—so I force a smile and agree. I only hope that I won't come to regret it later.

58

Adria

The Day She Found Out

With her phone gone and the laptop shattered, Adria felt more trapped than ever. She spent most of the day trying to avoid Peter, which turned out to be easier than she thought. He spent most of the morning outside chopping wood. Then, after eating a light lunch during which he barely spoke, he locked himself in his study for the next several hours.

Adria cocooned herself in the living room and tried not to think about her dire situation. But it was no good. Even as the shadows grew longer and day turned to night, her thoughts kept returning to what the man from the NSA had told her. In particular, his suspicion that Peter and the man named Nick in the old photo—a man suspected of murder in California—were the same person. And in doing so, a memory dislodged itself. A recollection of an earlier time and place.

◆ ◆ ◆

"They delivered the wrong food," Peter said, staring at the Chinese takeout order with a scowl.

"Really? What did they give us?" Adria leaned over the kitchen counter to study the contents of the white cardboard containers.

"Kung pao shrimp." Peter huffed with displeasure. "It should be lo mein."

"Bummer." Adria bit her bottom lip. "Hate to say this, but I have a nut allergy."

"That's just great. Those idiots could have killed you." Peter threw up his arms.

"Don't be so dramatic." Adria smothered a grin. "It's only a mild allergy. At worst, I'll get itchy for a day or two and break out in hives. Hardly the end of the world."

"Yeah, well, even so." Peter was already stuffing the food containers back into the bag.

"What are you doing?"

"What do you think I'm doing? Taking it back to get what we ordered. The place is just around the corner. You can't eat this, and they'll take forever to redeliver, especially on a Saturday night."

"It's fine." Adria's stomach rumbled, reminding her she'd skipped lunch. "I'll just eat the fried rice and crab rangoon."

"It's not fine. I'll fix this." Before Adria could respond, Peter had grabbed the food, scooped up his keys, and made for the door. "Back in twenty."

A moment later, from the direction of the hallway, she heard the elevator bell ding. She imagined Peter stepping inside, face like thunder, with the food bag dangling from one hand. She felt sorry for whoever was behind the counter at that Chinese restaurant when he got there.

Then she realized something.

She was alone.

He'd never left her alone in his apartment before.

Adria wasn't normally one to snoop, but now she was overcome with curiosity.

Peter was charming and talkative, but he never spoke about his past. Never talked about friends or family, or even his exploits before they were together. The only thing he had shared was about his living arrangements, and she suspected that was only because he didn't want her to think his cramped apartment on Commonwealth Avenue near Fenway Park was where he lived by choice. A week after they started dating, he'd told her he was forced to move out of his upscale town house in the Back Bay while it underwent renovations that might take several months. Something to do with the electrical and heating system that Adria didn't quite understand.

But beyond that . . . zilch. Nada. Barely a nugget of information about Peter or his past.

Which was why she wouldn't miss this opportunity to discover more about him. After all, she'd told him plenty about her life. She'd even told him about her past boyfriends . . . at least, some of them.

Adria glanced around with her hands on her hips.

The apartment was small, with a narrow breakfast counter separating the kitchen and living room.

The appliances looked old. A compact electric range that was missing a knob. A cream-colored refrigerator with chrome handles and rust on the bottom corner of the freezer compartment door. A cheap-looking microwave that took up precious counter space. There was no dishwasher.

The living room doubled as a dining area, with a round pine table and two chairs on one side and a dark gray love seat, a particleboard coffee table, and a small black leather side chair on the other. There was no TV, nor any art on the walls. Nothing to personalize the space. The bedroom was at the rear of the apartment, behind the kitchen, next to a small bathroom.

Adria wandered back there, glancing briefly toward a queen bed that took up most of the floor space. A bed she was sure they would share later in the evening when dinner was over. There was no TV here either. But there was a desk and chair in the corner, upon which sat a slim laptop, a laser printer, and a phone charging station.

She settled at the desk and wiggled the mouse, hoping the computer would wake up and allow her access, but all she got was a lock screen asking for a password.

Bummer.

She didn't know Peter well enough to guess what it might be. Which was crazy. Shouldn't she at least know enough about him to hazard a guess, even if it was wrong? His birthday—he hadn't even told her when that was—or the name of his childhood pet dog? She was sleeping with the man, after all. Allowing him to share her most intimate moments.

Frustrated, Adria stood up and wandered back into the main living area.

A bookcase crammed with books stood on the far wall of the living room, next to the sofa. Most of them were nonfiction. The Art of Conversation. American Social Classes. A Thousand Conversation Starters for Any Occasion. How to Connect with People. The Power of Charm. A Regular Guy's Guide to Making Money. The Stock Market for Beginners. The Complete Guide to Investing in Art and Collectables. *And the dubiously titled* Fake It Until You Make It.

A weird combination of interests.

Adria went to pull out Fake It Until You Make It, *but then a fiction book caught her eye. A spy thriller with a fat spine.* Code of Deceit *by Michael Larsen. She'd read the book a few years ago, and it was comforting to know they shared the same taste in fiction, if nothing else.*

She drew it from the shelf and noticed a flap of paper sticking out from between the pages. A bookmark advertising the book's release ten years earlier. There was a second folded slip of paper there as well, tucked between the same two pages. A flyer advertising a meet and greet and author signing at Wanderlust Books, an independent bookstore in Santa Barbara. Curious, she flipped to the front of the book. On the title page, she found what she was looking for.

To Nick. Happy reading, mate! Michael Larsen.

Adria stared at the inscription.

Why did Peter have a book signed to someone named Nick?

Scenarios ran through her mind. Maybe he got it signed for a friend and never got around to giving it to them. Or he found it in a used bookstore. Maybe he bought it online without realizing it was inscribed to a stranger. She wondered what other surprises might be in the bookcase.

But there was no time to find out.

Peter was home. She could hear him fumbling to slide his key into the front door lock.

Adria snapped the book closed and slid it quickly back into the bookcase, then turned toward the door just as Peter entered with a bulky brown paper bag clutched in his hands.

He held it up with a flourish.

"Your dinner awaits, my lady," he said in a ridiculous, over-the-top British accent so bad, she couldn't help but giggle. "I hope you weren't too bored while I was gone."

"No." Adria glanced back at the book sitting snug on the shelf. "Not too bored."

Adria gasped as the implications of the memory hit her. *Nick. The book on Peter's shelf was addressed to Nick.* An icy shiver sent the hairs on the back of her neck standing up. Was she remembering it right? If so, then it added weight to her previous suspicion that Peter was not only lying to her about his identity but might also be a murderer. That realization made her stomach churn. She rose from the sofa, paced back and forth. Wished she could contact the NSA guy, Frank, and tell him what she had remembered. He would surely know what to do. But it was impossible without her cell phone. Maybe she could ask Peter for it back, tell him she had to make an important call? But he would never believe her, wouldn't let her have it, so what was the point?

She was trapped.

Adria turned back to the sofa, defeated. Better to play it dumb. Pretend she didn't suspect her husband of those awful things, at least until they got back to the city.

She went to sit down.

At that moment, the light flickered once, twice, and went out.

Adria froze, caught by surprise.

From somewhere beyond the room, a door slammed.

Peter stomped through the foyer and into the living room, cursing under his breath.

"What's wrong?" she asked, even though it was obvious.

"Power's gone out," Peter said, toggling a light switch up and down as if to prove the veracity of his statement. "A line must have come down in the storm. Who knows how long it will take to fix it? I'll have to go fire up the beast."

"How about we wait a few minutes? See if it comes back on," Adria said. *The beast,* which was what Peter called the old generator that had been on the property for decades, was in a utility shed on the side of the house behind the garage. The generator was unreliable and hard to start. It was even harder to keep running for any length of time. But under the circumstances, there would be no choice if the power stayed off.

"Yeah. It's not coming back on anytime soon." Peter turned and headed back toward the foyer and the mudroom beyond, where he kept his boots and coat.

A few minutes later, Adria heard the back door open. There was a swell of howling wind before the door closed again, cutting it off.

She was alone in the house.

It would take at least a half hour to get the generator working, maybe longer, because it always did.

That presented her with an opportunity.

Peter spent a lot of time on his own up at the lake house, and she suspected that if there was any evidence of his true identity and past exploits, it would be here. The obvious place to find it was the study that her husband had claimed for his own when they'd first bought the property. As a bonus, she might also find the cell phone he had confiscated from her the day before.

But she had to be quick because it might be her only chance. With a pounding heart, Adria rose from the couch and made her way through the dark foyer to the garage, where she grabbed a hammer, a screwdriver, and a flashlight. Then she hurried back inside to discover the secrets her husband was keeping.

59

Anna

Day Five

When I told Gregg that I was tired, I meant it, but now that we're in bed, I lie here staring into the darkness because I can't find the off switch for my mind. Gregg had no such trouble falling asleep. After making sure the doors and windows downstairs were locked tight and coming up to bed, he'd escorted me to his bedroom, as if afraid that I would change my mind at the last second and make a mad dash for the guest room. He even volunteered to fetch my PJs and looked disappointed when I let him. His dismay only grew when I took them into the main bedroom's en suite with me and changed in there. After the passion of the last two nights, he clearly viewed my actions as a rebuff. When we climbed into bed, he lay there for a while, casting me furtive glances, probably in some vain hope that he'd misread my mood. Then, when it became clear that he hadn't, he scooted farther down under the covers and turned on his side with his back to me after mumbling a quiet good night.

Now he's dead to the world and snoring lightly.

I look sideways at him.

Gregg is nothing more than a vague lump in the darkness facing the other way, with the covers pulled up all the way to his shoulders.

I think back to the newly surfaced flash of memory and wonder if I'm correct in my suspicions about Gregg. The memory was clearly triggered by Eddie and my sense of déjà vu. If he and the unknown man in my flashback—assuming that's what it is—are the same, then I've known Gregg for a lot longer than a few days. This would explain why I've so easily fallen into his arms, but chillingly, it might also explain how I ended up on the shore of Gravewater Lake. If Gregg is lying about knowing me, then the only logical conclusion is that he is the one I should fear. I think back to the message on the answering machine in the study. Was that me? I'm sure I would recognize my own voice, but then again, the quality of the recording was so bad that I might not. And what about the note? If Gregg is behind what's happening to me, if he was trying to scare me into staying, would he have had time to leave it, then get back inside before I found it? I don't have an answer for that. Then there's Eddie. I'm not sure how he fits into any of this, but I know one thing. I need to be careful, because if the man I'm sharing a bed with has reason to want me dead, he could try again at any time.

Of course, all this is pure speculation. Gregg might be just what he seems. A concerned stranger who only wants to help. And that message might really be the last connection to his dead wife and nothing to do with me. But regardless, I can't let my guard down, because there is still the note.

Which is why I'm still awake two hours after I told him I wanted an early night. I despair of ever falling asleep in this house again, but I tell myself that it's okay. I've slept next to Gregg for the past two nights, and he's done nothing to me—at least, nothing I didn't want him to do. If he intended to kill me in my sleep, I would be dead already.

I close my eyes and take several deep breaths, inhaling slowly as I count to four, then holding the air in my lungs as I count off another four seconds, before releasing it in a slow and steady stream. After I've done this for a few minutes, the voice in my head quiets down, and I start to relax. Until . . .

60

The sound of breaking glass snaps me back to reality in an instant. I sit up, strain my ears to listen. When I feel Gregg move beside me, I glance toward him. "Did you hear that?"

"Yeah, I heard it." He pushes himself up onto his elbows, then swings his legs off the bed. "I'll go look."

"Don't go out there," I say, suddenly glad that he's here with me despite my earlier suspicions. "It's not safe. That sounded like glass breaking. It might be whoever left that message."

"There's only one way to find out." Gregg is already pulling on his pants. He slips a sweater over his head, then heads toward the door. "Stay here."

"Alone?" I'm overwhelmed by a sudden panic.

"You'll be fine."

I wish I believed that. Despite talking about it earlier, we have nothing with which to defend ourselves. Not even an empty wine bottle this time.

But Gregg is one step ahead of me. He takes a detour to the walk-in closet and goes inside, then reappears a moment later holding an aluminum baseball bat.

"I won't be long," he says, crossing to the bedroom door and gripping the handle.

"Wait." I jump up and go to him, throw my arms around him in a quick embrace. For all I know, he's the person who did this to me, caused me to lose my memory, but right now he's something else. My defender against whatever unknown dangers might lurk beyond the safety of the bedroom. "Please be careful."

"I will." He opens the door and steps out into the hallway beyond, looking left and right as he does so. Then he goes to pull it closed. "Lock the door."

"What if you need to get back in?"

"I'll be fine." Gregg hoists the baseball bat. "I know how to use this."

There's something in the way he says it that makes me shudder. Does he mean that he used to play on a Little League team growing up, or is there some darker meaning to his words? I step back so that he can close the door, and then I lock the door and retreat to the bed, climb back in, and sit with the covers pulled against my chest.

Ten minutes pass, and Gregg is still not back.

The silence is excruciating.

I imagine him creeping through the house, baseball bat at the ready, even as a shadowy figure comes up behind him and . . .

Two heavy thumps from below make me jump.

I draw a quick breath and hold it, waiting for what might happen next. Afraid of what I might hear. Conflicting scenarios crash through my mind, each one worse than the last. Did Gregg find someone skulking around in the darkness and swing at them with the bat? Is he grappling with them out there right now, desperately trying to save himself . . . and me? Or were those thuds the sound of his lifeless body tumbling down the stairs after he ended up on the wrong end of an intruder's knife?

It's too much to bear.

There have been no more noises from below, but that isn't necessarily a good thing.

I climb back out of bed and go to the window, pull the curtains back to look outside. I'm not sure what I expect to see—maybe an intruder fleeing the scene of the crime, or a line of fresh footprints that would tell me there really is someone else in the house. But there is just the unbroken expanse of a snow-covered back deck lit by the pale light of the waxing moon. I can see where Gregg cleared a path from the back door the previous afternoon, and it hasn't snowed since. I see it cutting across the deck toward the shore. Beyond that is the lake, and farther away still, the black line of trees that crowd the opposite shore. Somewhere over there in that Stygian gloom is Helene's cabin, but the lights must all be off because there is only darkness.

I let the curtains fall back into place and stand for a moment, wondering what to do next. The house is quiet, and I'm worried about Gregg. I go to the door and reach for the handle, then hesitate. He told me to stay here and keep it locked, but if something really has happened to him, then I can't see the point of cowering here and waiting for Knife Man to come for me.

I disengage the privacy lock and open the door.

The hallway beyond is empty.

I step into it and start toward the stairs, ignoring the prickle of fear that runs up my spine. And then, suddenly, I realize that I'm not alone anymore. There's someone climbing the stairs, their footfalls heavy and deliberate.

I freeze, caught between standing my ground and fleeing back to the relative safety of the bedroom. But there's no time to do anything as a dark figure appears.

"I told you not to leave the bedroom," says a familiar voice.

I slump with relief. It's only Gregg. "I was afraid something had happened to you."

"That's no excuse." He comes toward me with the bat swinging at his side. "Do you ever do anything you're told?"

"I heard thumps from downstairs," I say, as if that is the only answer his question requires. "Is everything okay?"

Gregg frowns. "Not so much. The breaking glass that we heard . . . it was a tree branch. Came right through the living room window. Must've come loose in the wind and fell."

"Really?" I step past him toward the stairs.

"Uh-huh." He turns and follows me. "Where do you think *you're* going?"

I ignore his question and start down the stairs. When I reach the bottom, I go straight to the living room and stop.

There's glass scattered across the floor under the now-busted center pane of the three-pane leaded window. Some of it is still attached to the bent and broken strips of leading that kept the diamond-shaped glass pieces in place and gave the window its distinctive Tudor look.

I hear Gregg enter the room behind me, and I turn around to face him. "I thought you said a tree branch fell and broke the window? I don't see one."

"Because I already got rid of it," he says, lingering in the doorway.

"Oh." I step closer to the window and peer down through the shattered opening. The snow on the deck beneath it has been trampled, but I don't see any sign of a branch. When I pull my head back inside, I see what looks like dirty boot prints on the floorboards underneath the window among the broken glass.

"You should go back upstairs where it's warmer," Gregg says. "You'll catch your death down here right now dressed like that."

"What are you going to do?" I don't want to leave him down here on his own, but Gregg is right. I'm wearing nothing but the flannel pajamas, which are warm enough under normal circumstances but aren't holding up well against the frigid air blowing in through the shattered window.

"Put a board over that window to stop any further damage. It shouldn't take me too long, and then I'll come back to bed."

"I can help you," I say.

But Gregg just shakes his head. "I'm pretty sure there's a piece of wood the right size in the garage. I'll just lean it up there and screw it to the window frame. By the time you've changed into something warmer and come back down here, I'll be done."

"If you're sure."

“I’m sure.” Gregg steps aside to let me pass, then watches as I climb the stairs. As I make my way along the hallway, I hear him go into the garage. A minute later, I’m back in the bedroom. I lock the door behind me, then sit on the bed and wait for him. My thoughts turn to the missing tree limb. Even if he removed it from the window, there should have been some sign of it on the deck outside. Maybe I missed seeing it in the darkness, but what about the dirty boot prints on the floorboards beneath the broken window? I didn’t notice if Gregg was wearing boots or not, but I feel like I’m missing something. And then I realize. The boot prints aren’t facing the window. They are facing away from it and into the room. As if someone had climbed in from the outside.

61

I'm still sitting on the bed half an hour later when Gregg returns. He discovers the door is locked, knocks quietly, and calls my name.

When I open it to let him in, he steps inside and locks it again, then leans the baseball bat against the wall. "I thought for a minute you might have fallen asleep already, and I'd be forced to spend the rest of the night in that freezing guest bedroom."

"I've just been sitting here waiting for you," I tell him in the lightest voice I can manage, but I don't mention my observation about the footprints beneath the window. I'm more certain than ever that something strange is going on inside this house and that Gregg is right in the middle of it. I also don't believe that a tree limb broke the window. If it had, wouldn't there be some evidence left behind, like broken twigs or pieces of scraped-off bark, even if the limb itself was gone? "Did you fix the window?"

"Not exactly pretty, but it's sealed up tight." Gregg pulls the sweater over his head, then discards it on a nearby chair. "We shouldn't have any more trouble. Honestly, I'm just glad that I was here when it happened. Otherwise, it might have been open to the elements for days, or even weeks, before the caretaker discovered it under the circumstances. The damage could have been catastrophic."

"Has anything like this ever happened before?" I ask, climbing back into bed.

Gregg shakes his head. "Not since I've owned the place."

He finishes undressing and slips in next to me, again wearing only his boxer shorts. I wonder if he gets cold sleeping like that, or if he just has a hardy disposition. Or maybe he's still hoping that something will happen between us. But I make it quite clear that nothing has changed when I reach out and turn off the bedside light, then slide down under the covers with my back to him.

I feel his weight shift on the mattress. I'm sure that if I roll over right now, I'll find him lying there in the darkness, watching me with those icy blue eyes. It's a creepy feeling. Then his weight shifts again, and the sensation passes. A few minutes after that, he snores.

I pull the covers up to my chin and make myself as small as possible, then lie there staring at the door and the baseball bat that sits beside it. If someone tries to break into the room, Gregg has put it down too far away to be of any use. They would be upon us before I even make it halfway there.

I try to tell myself that it's fine. That we're alone in the house. That it really was just a broken tree limb that came through the window and that Gregg made those boot impressions when he was taking care of it. I'm sure that Gregg didn't search the house from top to bottom looking for an intruder, either because he believes it was a branch that busted the window or because he's lying about what really happened.

I'm never going to fall back to sleep while I'm thinking like that. Not in a million years. I climb back out of bed as softly as possible, making sure I don't disturb Gregg, and hurry across the room to retrieve the baseball bat, which I then lean within easy reach against my nightstand. The only question is, Am I protecting myself from an external threat, or one who's already in the room with me?

Stop it, I chide myself. *Gregg isn't the enemy here.*

And it's true at face value. He's done nothing but try to help me. Look after me. I'm basing all my suspicions on my dislike of Eddie and a vague recollection that might have nothing to do with Gregg, even if it is a surfacing memory of my past. For all I know, Gregg is exactly who he appears to be—a caring stranger who took me into his home.

There might be a husband I don't remember out there somewhere. A husband who got himself into a lot of trouble and could already have been murdered by whoever came after me with a knife by the lake and left that note at the back door. The same person who tried to kill me once before but instead left me without a past.

And yes, if that's true, then it makes me a terrible person for sleeping with Gregg, but perhaps that's the point. Lacking any memories upon which to set my moral compass, I've invented a scenario that relieves me of guilt.

I'm never going to get any sleep at this rate. The various thoughts churn inside my head in a raging storm of conflicting possibilities until all I want to do is scream with frustration. There's no way to know which of them is correct, or if any of them are. And beneath it all is the fear that has become my constant companion.

But even that can't keep my exhaustion at bay forever, and eventually I fall into a fractured sleep that carries me through until dawn . . . only to be broken by an echoing boom that sends me scrambling, still half-asleep, for the baseball bat.

Then I see Gregg standing at the bedroom window and looking out at the lake, even as I realize the boom didn't come from within the house. It came from somewhere outside.

And it sounded very much like a gunshot.

62

Adria

The Day She Found Out

Adria hurried through the darkened foyer with the hammer and screw-driver in hand, and into the study. The flashlight beam cut a swath of light into the gloom. She went to the desk and tried the drawers. There were three on each side. Five were unlocked, but the bottom right drawer refused to open. She looked around for the key, but of course, Peter wouldn't be stupid enough to leave it lying out in the open.

She had to know what was in that drawer.

Taking the screwdriver, Adria inserted it into the gap between the drawer and desk frame, then pried it up. At first, the drawer refused to budge, but then on the second attempt, it flew open with a splintering crack.

Inside was a black metal safe box. She pulled it out onto the desk, then went to lift the lid. Locked. The key was probably in the same place as the one that unlocked the desk drawer. She had no choice. Picking up the hammer, she brought it down as hard as she could: once, twice, three times. On the fourth go, the lock barrel gave way.

Adria lifted the lid to find a small red jewelry box. Inside were a pair of wedding rings and an engagement ring. There were initials inscribed on the inner rim of the wedding ring: *R & J.*

Setting the rings aside, she rummaged through the other items in the safe box. The first thing she found was an expired California driver's license. The name on it sent chills down her spine.

Nick Blakely.

Her husband's face—younger but definitely him—looked back at her from the license photo. For a moment, Adria couldn't breathe. Her universe crashed down around her. It was him.

She dropped the driver's license as if it had scalded her and dove back into the box.

There was another driver's license, this time from Oregon and issued nine years ago, which also bore her husband's photograph, but the name was different. Neil Carmichael.

Horrified, she rummaged through the rest of the items in the box. An old speeding ticket and bill of sale for a truck, both in fake names. Then she found the newspaper clippings. A bunch of them. Articles from ten years earlier that detailed the disappearance of the couple in California, Jess and Rob Cody. Beneath the clippings were postcards, just like the ones Frank from the NSA had said Blakely sent to make people think Rob and Jess had just gone on an extended trip. At least, until their remains were found in a shallow grave behind their old house. She picked up a postcard and read it.

Having so much fun here in Key West! Not sure when we will get back. Please take good care of Charlie Cat for a little longer!

Love, Jess and Rob

Adria was overcome with the notion that she had entered some crazy alternate reality. Despite everything that she'd found, a part of her wanted to believe that it was a coincidence. But she knew better.

"You shouldn't be looking at that stuff. It's mine."

Adria dropped the postcard and looked around.

Peter was standing in the doorway with a crazed look on his face.

"I'm sorry. I was just . . ."

"Snooping," Peter said, finishing the sentence. "You were just snooping."

Adria jumped up from the chair. "You killed them, didn't you? That couple. Jess and Rob. That's why you have those rings. You killed them."

"That was a long time ago and nothing to do with you." Peter advanced toward her.

Adria looked around, desperate. A large panoramic window took up one wall of the office, overlooking the snow-laden deck and the dark lake beyond. But there was no escape that way. No door leading to the outside. And her husband was blocking the only other way out of the room.

But there was the hammer.

She turned to grab it off the desk where she had put it down after breaking open the box.

Peter realized what she was doing and lunged forward.

But she was too quick. She snatched the hammer up in one hand and swung it even as Peter closed the gap between them.

He twisted sideways, ducked under the blow, and almost lost his balance as the hammer whistled harmlessly inches above his head. But it was all Adria needed. Before her husband could regain his balance, she darted around him and sped toward the door and out into the foyer.

From somewhere behind her, she heard a screech of rage.

"Bitch!" Peter's voice boomed out. "I'm going to kill you for that."

Adria didn't pay him any heed. Obviously, he was going to kill her. That was where their relationship had been going since the first day they'd met. She just hadn't realized it.

She veered toward the front door and the truck parked outside in the driveway. But then it dawned on her. *The keys.* She didn't have the keys, and there was no time to look for them. They might even be in Peter's pocket. Which meant that if she ran out that door, tried to make it down the driveway, he would catch up with her in a heartbeat. He might even run her over with the truck and then claim it was an accident.

There was no way in hell she was going out the front door.

Which left only one other option. She changed course and ran for the back door as Peter came out of the study.

She reached the door, twisted the handle, but it wouldn't open. She tugged in a blind panic, but it still wouldn't budge. Then she saw the dead bolt. She had forgotten about it in her haste to escape. Relieved, she disengaged the lock, then flung the door wide and ran out onto the deck beyond.

Clouds scudded above her in the night sky, hiding the moon. Snow was still falling. It stung her cheeks and arms with tiny pinpricks of freezing pain, but she ignored it.

Their dock wasn't far away, maybe fifty feet. In summer, a boat would be tied there, but not right now. They always took it out of the water before winter.

Which left the woods as her only option.

So that was where Adria went. She fled through the darkness toward the shore. It was hard going, especially as she wasn't wearing boots. There were at least twelve inches of snow piled on the deck.

But Peter had no such problem.

As she approached the shore, she risked a glance over her shoulder and saw him trudging through the snow at a fast pace, gaining with every step.

Adria turned and ran toward the trees, following a narrow path that wound through the dark woods.

"There's nowhere to go, honey!" Peter called out from somewhere behind her, his voice faint as the shifting wind snatched it away. "Might as well give up now and make it easier on yourself."

Adria didn't respond. What was the point? Instead, she barreled on through the pitch-black woods, moving as fast as she dared.

At one point, her foot snagged a root, and she almost fell, managing to save herself at the last moment.

Close behind her, she heard pounding footfalls.

Peter, better equipped to be outside thanks to his heavy boots, was catching up fast.

Another few minutes, and he would be upon her.

Then she saw it.

Another boat dock that belonged to one of the other houses. It jutted out into the lake. And there, at the end, against the odds, was a rowboat tied to the dock as if it were waiting for her.

She mouthed a silent prayer and sprinted forward with renewed hope. If she could get to that boat, it would buy her time, because the one place Peter couldn't follow her was out onto the lake.

She reached the dock and started down it, trying to keep her balance as she navigated the icy, snow-covered boards. At one point, her feet slipped out from under her. The hammer fell from her grip. She put her arms out to break her fall, then pushed herself back up and kept going, leaving the hammer buried in the snow. There was no time to look for it.

Jumping into the boat, she tugged at the ropes securing it to the dock, trying to release the knots. Her fingers were numb with cold. She could barely feel them. The frigid air burned her lungs.

The bow knot loosened, and the rope slipped free.

She stumbled to the stern and worked on the second rope, frantically pulling at the knot as Peter stepped onto the dock and closed the gap between them. She looked back down, focused her attention on the rope, and finally loosened the knot enough to untie it. When she looked back up, Peter was almost upon her. And as if that weren't bad enough, he clutched the hammer she had dropped when she slipped.

Shit.

She reached down and grabbed one of the oars lying in the bottom of the boat. Then, as she was about to push off, a hand grabbed her hair and yanked her head back hard.

Peter stood on the dock above her, his face contorted with rage.

"Just where do you think you're going?" he growled in a voice she hardly recognized as he swung the hammer down toward her.

63

Anna

Day Six

"Was that a gunshot?" I grip the baseball bat in my hands so tightly that my knuckles turn white.

For a moment, Gregg says nothing. He just continues to stare out the window and across the lake, where the dawn sun is sending golden rays over the treetops. Then he nods. "Probably someone shooting at a coyote, or maybe a fox that was sniffing around their chickens. There are other houses and cabins scattered all around the area. In the right conditions, you can hear a gunshot from miles away, especially out in the wilderness like this where it's so quiet."

"Then whoever fired that gun wasn't anywhere near the lake?"

"I guess they could have been, but probably not." Gregg turns from the window and heads for the en suite. "It's still early, and I doubt you got a whole lot of sleep last night. Why don't you hop back into bed while I take a shower? Then I'll go downstairs and leave you in peace. When you're ready to get up, I'll make us some breakfast while you do whatever you girls do in the bathroom to make yourselves pretty. Sound like a plan?"

"Sure." Going back to sleep is the last thing I want to do under the circumstances. Between the tree limb breaking the living room window in the middle of the night—assuming that's what really happened—and the gunshot that sounded way too close to be some random person miles away defending their livestock, I'm just about as wide-awake as I think I'll ever be. But I'll take an hour of solitude away from Gregg because I'm not sure how I feel about him right now.

I go back to bed, then watch Gregg disappear into the bathroom and close the door. I hear the toilet flush and then the shower running.

Fifteen minutes later, Gregg reemerges. His hair is damp, and the boxer shorts are gone. I lie there with my eyes half-closed and pretend to be sleeping even as I watch him move around the room. He's in no hurry to get dressed, and I feel uncomfortable spying on him even though it's hardly the first time I've seen him naked. I close my eyes the rest of the way and listen as he goes about his business. Soon I hear the rustle of fabric and the chink of a belt being done up. Then the bedroom door opens and closes again, and I'm finally alone.

I lie there for another hour, content to be warm under the blankets. Finally, when the need for caffeine overwhelms my reticence to leave the snug cocoon of the bedroom, I rise and make my way into the walk-in closet to borrow yet another outfit from Gregg's dead wife. And then, as I'm pulling a stunning designer red and cream jacquard knit sweater over my head, a thought hits me. I take a fresh look around the closet and realize that I love the style of *everything* in here. It's all my taste. Which brings me right back to wondering if Gregg has been lying to me since the moment I stepped into this house. But that's not something I want to think about right now, so I take a deep breath and push the thought aside, then hurry from the room.

It's then that I hear them. Voices from the floor below.

I can't make out the words, but it sounds like two people having a conversation. Or more accurately, arguing, because I detect the distinct cadence of a confrontation. I assume one of them is Gregg. There's only one person the other voice could belong to, and my heart falls.

Eddie is back.

I stop at the top of the stairs and listen, but I still can't make out what they are arguing about, so I descend toward the ground floor, figuring I'll know soon enough.

But when I'm only halfway down, the voices stop.

I stop again, expecting the conversation to resume. When it doesn't, I continue down and head toward the kitchen, expecting to see Gregg and Eddie there.

To my surprise, I find only Gregg.

He's at the coffee maker, pouring himself a cup. When he sees me coming, he smiles. "Cup of joe?"

"Sure. Who were you talking to?" I ask, looking around to see if Eddie is somewhere else, like maybe in the butler's pantry, although I don't know why he would be.

"I wasn't talking to anyone," Gregg replies, taking a second mug from the cabinet and pouring me a cup. He places it in front of me on the island along with a carton of half-and-half and a glass sugar bowl.

"Yes, you were. I heard you when I was coming down the stairs. It sounded like an argument." This isn't the first time I've heard him talking to someone, only for Gregg to claim that he wasn't. "Where's Eddie?"

Gregg leans on the counter and looks at me with a furrowed brow. "Eddie isn't here, and I wasn't arguing with anyone. You probably heard me singing to myself."

"Singing?" That's ridiculous. I might not have been a guest in this house for very long, but I've never heard Gregg even hum a tune, let alone walk around singing. "There were two voices. I know what I heard."

"Apparently not. There's no one here except you and me, so who would I be arguing with?"

Since there's no sign of Eddie, I don't have an answer for that. I stay silent.

"That's what I thought." Gregg observes me for a moment longer with narrowed eyes, then his face relaxes. He turns to the kitchen counter behind him and picks up a plate upon which sit two fluffy croissants and a butter knife. He sets the plate down on the island and then does the same with a ceramic butter dish and a half-empty jar of strawberry preserves. "I know it's not much of a breakfast, but I didn't know when you were going to come down. There's one for each of us. Hungry?"

I was when I left the bedroom, but now my appetite has deserted me. In its place is a gnawing unease that sits in the pit of my stomach. I'm sure that Gregg is lying . . . again. But I have no proof. Except for how the croissants are arranged on the plate, pushed to one side as if there used to be a third. And where that missing croissant would have been, only flaky crumbs remain . . . and a faint smear of strawberry preserves on the knife.

64

After drinking my coffee and forcing down half a croissant, I leave Gregg in the kitchen and go into the living room. So much has happened over the last forty-eight hours, and none of it is good. The man with the knife. Gregg's mysterious disappearances. Eddie showing up on the doorstep, not once but twice. That threatening note. A tree branch breaking the window in the middle of the night. The gunshot. I feel like I'm standing in the eye of a hurricane, with ever-worse events swirling out of control around me.

I look at the busted window. Gregg has secured a piece of plywood over the hole. It isn't a great fit, obscuring the panes on each side and blocking most of the light, which leaves the room in partial darkness. A few remnants of the window itself lie strewn across the floor. Shards of glass that Gregg missed when he was sweeping up. I spot a small strip of the leading, twisted and bent, near the baseboard.

The boot prints are gone.

I'm reminded of my suspicions from the night before. How those prints looked more like someone climbing inside than Gregg dealing with a broken tree limb. I decide to look outside, figuring that if there is a large branch lying somewhere nearby, then it will support Gregg's version of events.

I return to the foyer and stick my head inside the kitchen, but Gregg isn't there. As usual, he's MIA. If I didn't know better, I might think I'm sharing the house with a ghost. He has a habit of disappearing the moment I turn my back. But in this case, it works in my favor because I don't want him to see me going outside.

Crossing to the mudroom, I find a coat and a pair of boots, then step out the back door and onto the deck. The frosty air hits me right away, and I draw in a sharp breath.

Ahead of me is the path down toward the lake that Gregg cleared through the snow, but that isn't where I'm going. Instead, I turn left toward the living room window. The snow here, next to the house, is trampled and crushed into a hard-packed frozen surface as if someone, or more than one person, has walked back and forth. I look for an individual boot print that might match what I remember of those on the inside, but the snow is so disturbed that none remains. I also don't see any sign of a fallen tree limb, even when I brave the slippery, trampled path to the window. In fact, the closest tree is at least fifteen feet away and shows no signs of any damage that I can see. The faint sliver of hope that I was wrong, that Gregg wasn't lying, evaporates. I'm sure that if I ask him about it, he will just provide some flimsy excuse like he dragged it off into the woods—highly unlikely in the middle of the night—or that he chopped it up for firewood before I came downstairs this morning. Which is why it's not even worth confronting him.

Frustrated, I turn back toward the door, and that's when I hear the low drone of an outboard motor. I glance toward the lake and see a small motorboat heading for Gregg's dock. Helene is sitting at the rear of the vessel with her hand on the tiller.

By the time I cross the deck and step onto the dock, the boat is pulling up alongside it. She secures it with ropes and climbs out.

"Just the person I was coming to see," she says, approaching me. "And here you are." She glances around. "Where's Gregg?"

"I don't know," I reply. "Somewhere in the house, I guess."

Helene steps closer and lowers her voice. "Good. I'd rather talk to you alone. How are you doing?"

"Good enough, I guess, for someone who doesn't know who they are."

"Memory still hasn't returned, huh?"

I shake my head. "Not so far."

"That's too bad. I have to admit, I've been worried about you." She glances around again. "When I heard that gunshot this morning, I figured I'd better come over here and check on you."

"That's so thoughtful, but it wasn't anything to do with us. Gregg said it was probably someone miles away shooting at a fox or something."

"Didn't sound like it was miles away," Helene replies. "Too loud. I thought it came from somewhere around the lake." She locks eyes with me. "Do you believe everything Gregg says?"

"I don't know. I suppose . . . well . . ."

The way I hesitate and the look on my face apparently tell Helene all she needs to know. "What's the deal here, Anna? Is there something going on with Gregg? You can talk to me. I won't say anything to him, I promise."

"I'm not sure what's going on with him," I admit, wanting to unload all my concerns and frustrations but wary of doing so to a stranger. I know less about Helene than I do about Gregg. I want to trust her, but I'm not sure I trust anyone right now. "He's been acting strange. Sometimes I think I'm just being paranoid because of my situation and it's all in my head, but at other times . . ."

Helene picks up where I left off. "You think that he's not being truthful?"

I nod.

"Want to tell me more about it?"

"I don't know. Maybe." I bite my bottom lip. "But what if I'm wrong?"

"Do *you* think you're wrong?"

This time, I shake my head.

Helene is silent for a moment. Then she clears her throat. "Look, I meant it when I said that I'm concerned about you. I also understand why you're hesitant to talk behind Gregg's back. He took you in, after all. Helped you. But that doesn't mean that he's being straight with you.

Honestly, there's something about the man that I just don't like. I'm not sure you should stay here with him anymore. I think you should come back with me."

Helene's offer takes me by surprise. It also provides me with a way to put some distance between myself and Gregg, at least until I figure out if he can be trusted. "You really wouldn't mind me staying with you for a few days? It's such an imposition."

"Nonsense. To be honest, I'd love the company. I rented the cabin for the solitude so I can finish editing my book, but it still gets lonely. And there're two bedrooms, so we won't be on top of each other. You can gather your belongings and come with me right now. What do you say?"

I think about her offer for a moment, then make up my mind. But before I can say yes, I hear a door slam. When I glance over my shoulder and back toward the house, I see Gregg striding toward us across the deck. And he doesn't look happy.

65

Gregg is at the dock before I know it. "Helene, what a lovely surprise. What brings you across to our side of the lake?"

"I was just telling Anna that I heard a gunshot this morning. It was a little unsettling. I was worried about the two of you and thought I'd come over and see if you were both all right."

"We're fine, as you can see. Like I told Anna this morning, it was probably just someone shooting at a coyote or some other critter that strayed too close to their house." Gregg looks at me, then back at Helene. "Was that the only reason you came over here?"

"Well . . ." Helene hesitates, no doubt sensing the undercurrent of animosity in Gregg's voice. Then she takes a deep breath and straightens her back, raising herself up to her full height. "I also thought that Anna might like to come and stay with me for a while to give you a break from looking after her. It's no trouble, and there's plenty of—"

"That won't be necessary, but thank you." Gregg steps close and puts his arm around me, his hand resting on my shoulder. "We're getting along just fine, and she's no bother at all. In fact, I quite like having her around."

"I'm pleased to hear that." Helene makes eye contact with me, then looks back at Gregg. "I just thought that Anna might prefer some female company."

"Oh, I think Anna's enjoying *my* company just fine." Gregg squeezes my shoulder. "Aren't you?"

"Well, I—" Gregg's fingers dig into my flesh, and even though he's still looking at Helene with an expression of blank neutrality, I'm sure it's a warning. Or maybe a threat. "I guess I'm fine where I am right now."

"See?" Gregg beams. "It's all good."

"Is that right?" Helene asks me. "You can come with me now. Climb in the boat and get away from here. Just say the word."

If only it were that easy. I won't be free of Gregg even if I go with her. He will be right there, just a short distance away around the lake, and will know exactly where I went. I don't know if he's dangerous, but I'm not sure it's a good idea to push him and find out. After all, he could come for me at any time, and that would put Helene in danger too. I can't do that to her. Which is why I shake my head and say, "I appreciate the offer, Helene, but honestly, I'm good staying here with Gregg."

"I'm glad that's settled." Gregg's hand falls away from my shoulder. "Now if you don't mind, Helene, I think we'll be getting back to the house. I would invite you in for a coffee, but we have a lot to do today. I'm sure you understand."

"Loud and clear." Helene presses her lips together, then turns toward the boat, steps down into it, and unties the rope holding it against the dock. She looks back up at us one more time, perhaps hoping that I've changed my mind. Then she starts the outboard motor and steers away from the dock without another word.

I watch the boat plow through the water toward the other side of the lake, leaving a trail of frothy, churning blackness in its wake. And as it goes, I'm overcome by an overwhelming conviction that, along with it, goes my last chance to escape Gregg and whatever he might have in store.

66

No sooner are we back inside the house than Gregg makes his way toward the kitchen. He hasn't spoken a word to me, and I wonder if he's angry, so I follow along behind.

"Are you okay?" I ask him, standing on the opposite side of the kitchen island and watching as he rinses the coffee mugs from earlier before putting them in the dishwasher.

"Why wouldn't I be?" He glances back over his shoulder and flashes me a brief smile that quickly fades.

"I don't know. You weren't exactly friendly to Helene." I'm glad the kitchen island is between us—a barrier in case his apparent good humor is nothing but a temporary veneer.

Gregg wipes his hands on a dishcloth, then throws it down on the counter and turns to face me. "She was meddling. Trying to drive a wedge between us."

"I'm sure that's not true. She was just trying to be helpful," I say.

"Is that what you think?" He comes closer. "She suggested you're not happy here. That you would rather be over there on the other side of the lake with her instead of me. You are happy here, aren't you, Anna?"

I open my mouth to reply but can't find my voice, so instead I nod, even as I press my trembling hands down onto the counter in front of me, palms down to steady them.

Gregg isn't fooled. "Then you *would* rather be over there with Helene." A flash of disappointment crosses his face. "I can't believe it.

After all I've done for you. After everything we've done together." A vein pulses at the corner of his left eye. "We shared a bed. We—"

"I know what we did," I say quickly, interrupting him. I need to save this before he loses his temper, which won't be long, judging by the look on his face. That's why I step around the island and go to him, wrap my arms around his neck and kiss him, because it's the only thing I can think of to do. "See? I'd rather be here."

Gregg observes me for a few seconds, then he breaks contact and turns away. "Your hands are cold. I'm not surprised, going outside like that without wearing gloves. I'll make a cup of hot cocoa to warm you up."

I don't really want cocoa at this time of the morning. It feels more like a drink for a cold winter's evening. But I also want to keep on his good side, so I agree.

He starts toward the pantry, then looks back over his shoulder. "Why don't you go into the living room and make yourself comfortable? I'll bring it to you."

"Sure." I'm happy to do that. The less time I spend in Gregg's presence right now, the better. I'm not looking forward to another night in this house, sharing a bed with him and pretending that we're in some sort of budding relationship. The sooner I regain my memories and find out if he was involved with what happened to me, the better. I want to trust him, put my concerns to rest about the events of the past few days, but it's hard to do that given the way he's been acting. I didn't imagine his hostility toward Helene, or the way his fingers dug into my shoulder—a silent warning.

I sink down onto the sofa, close my eyes, and try not to let the hopelessness of my situation overwhelm me. A couple of minutes later, I hear movement. When I open my eyes, Gregg is there holding out a mug with steam curling up from it.

"I even put some marshmallows on top," Gregg says. The simmering menace I detected out on the dock is gone now, replaced by an expression that reminds me of an expectant schoolboy presenting his teacher with an apple. "To make it extra special."

"Looks wonderful," I say, taking the mug and inhaling the sweet aroma of liquid chocolate. Five small marshmallows bob on the surface of the drink. I look up at him and force myself to smile. I almost ask if he's joining me—which is the last thing I want at that moment—then think better of it.

"Okay, then." Gregg rubs his hands together and edges toward the door. "I'll leave you to it. If you need me, I'll be in the kitchen."

"Sure." I wait for him to leave before blowing on the cocoa and taking a sip, sucking a marshmallow up along with it and burning my tongue. I blow on the cocoa some more, waiting for it to cool down, then drink about half of it before the sweetness overwhelms me and I set the mug aside.

I lean back on the sofa and stare at the large abstract painting hanging above the fireplace. I feel a strange affinity with the swirling brushstrokes, chaotic and raw, almost as if the artist peered inside my soul and rendered my fears and frustrations in thick impasto swooshes. A melee of jumbled colors and abstract shapes that holds my attention in an almost hypnotic torpor.

I want to look away, to pick up the mug and drink the rest of my cocoa, but my eyelids are growing heavy. They droop, and I force them back open, fighting a deep weariness that presses down upon me. I shift on the sofa, sink lower until my head rests against a cushion. And then, like a paper lantern snatched up on a stirring breeze, I float away into unconsciousness.

67

I wake with a crick in my neck thanks to the way I'm lying across the sofa, a sore throat, and no sense of how much time has passed. I blink a few times to clear my vision and sit up, rubbing my neck even as I reach for the half-drunk mug of cocoa, which, to my surprise, is now stone-cold. A slimy film has formed across the surface of the liquid, trapping the remaining marshmallows. They look like small white islands in a muddy sea. I wrinkle my nose and put the mug back down, then stand up and wander into the foyer.

Silence presses around me. The house feels empty.

"Gregg?" I call out to the empty air.

No reply.

I call his name again with no response, then make my way into the kitchen, where I grab a glass from a dish rack next to the sink and fill it from the tap. I gulp the water down and refill the glass, then drink some more to soothe my throat before placing it in the sink.

The clock on the stove reads 11:48 a.m. I stare in disbelief. I was out cold for almost two hours. Dead to the world. How is that even possible? I mean, sure, I haven't been sleeping well the last several nights—who would under the circumstances?—but I'm not tired enough to pass out like that in the middle of the day.

Something is wrong.

I look around the kitchen, not entirely sure what I'm searching for. And then my eyes settle upon the island cabinet hiding the trash and recycling cans. The cabinet door, affixed to a pullout metal caddy, is open a few inches. Still not sure what I expect to find, I pull it all the way out and flip open the lids of both containers. The recycling bin contains nothing but a couple of empty wine bottles, some crumpled beer cans, and a plastic egg carton.

The trash is a different story.

There, sitting atop cracked-open eggshells, coffee grounds, and used paper towels, are the discarded husks of several teal blue gelcaps. I pluck one out from among the trash and study it. One end has been cut off to leave a small round hole through which someone, presumably Gregg, squeezed out the contents to leave the empty capsule puckered in upon itself like a tiny, deflated football. I turn it over in my palm. There is no drug name printed on the capsule, nothing to identify what it once contained. When I look at the others, they are the same. Five of them in total.

I drop the lid back on the trash and push the cabinet closed but keep the capsule I salvaged. A creeping suspicion dances around the edge of my mind. I need to find where Gregg got the gelcaps. I open the drawer above the trash cabinet but see nothing other than collected junk that people throw into such kitchen drawers on the off chance they will someday need it. A package of AAA batteries with two missing. Menus for a pizza place and Chinese restaurant that I assume must be in the closest town across the washed-out bridge. Corks from wine bottles, some of them stained red on one end from the wine they once stopped from escaping. But no bottles of gelcaps.

I close the drawer and move on to the next, only to find it crammed with kitchen utensils. I see a meat thermometer, kabob skewers, and other culinary items, but again, no pill bottle.

I repeat the process, going through the drawers and cabinets without success, until I come to a tall pantry unit sitting between the double refrigerators and the wine fridge. I open the lower cabinet and find only kitchen appliances on the shelves. A blender, Crock-Pot, and air fryer. But when I turn my attention to the upper cabinet, I see it.

A small white plastic bottle with a childproof lid tucked in among two piles of folded dishcloths. It looks out of place in the cabinet, as if someone hid it there deliberately, and when I pick it up and read the label, I understand why.

Sleeping pills.

With a quickening heart, I twist off the lid and scatter the contents on the kitchen counter. Small teal oval gelcaps identical to the one I took from the trash. I read the instructions on the back of the container, see that the recommended dose is one gelcap. There were five in the trash, and it doesn't take a genius to figure out where the contents of those capsules ended up.

In my cocoa.

Thank goodness I only drank half of it, or I would probably still be snoring away on the sofa.

I scoop the capsules back into the container with shaking hands and return it to where I found it. Push it down between the dish towels.

A dark rage seethes within me. Is this the first time Gregg drugged me, or has he done it before? Is this what he did to me on the night I lost my memory? Because I'm more certain than ever that he's the reason I woke up freezing and alone on that lakeshore with no knowledge of who I am or how I got there. I'm also certain that he tried to kill me, which means I wasn't a stranger to him when I stumbled up to his door. Or should I say, *our* door? Because the suspicion that formed in my mind yesterday evening when Eddie triggered what I now believe was a repressed memory has snapped into unwavering certainty.

There's a reason the clothes in that closet upstairs fit me so well. The bras. The shoes. All of it. There's a reason I felt comfortable enough around Gregg to sleep with him so easily. And why he won't talk about his dead wife.

Because she's not dead.

I'm right here.

Which begs the question: Why didn't he finish me when he realized I'd survived his first attempt? He's had enough opportunities. I've been living in this house with him for days with no clue who I am. He could have killed me at any time. Instead, he engaged in mind games. Tried to scare me and convince me he was a good guy. Tried to make me think I was crazy.

And I almost fell for it. Almost . . .

Not anymore. I want answers, and the only way to get them is to find Gregg. I leave the kitchen and cross back into the living room, where I pluck the poker from the fireplace tool set. I might be angry, but I'm not stupid. I have no intention of facing him unarmed.

Then I spin on my heel and sprint from the room.

Gregg isn't downstairs. If he was, I would have heard him. Not only that, but he would never have let me discover the sleeping pills he used to drug me.

I start up the main staircase, then make a beeline for the main bedroom, which I figure is the most likely place I'll find him. But it appears to be empty when I step inside.

Unless . . . I turn toward the en suite and the walk-in closet with the poker gripped tightly in one hand. The closet is the closer of the two, so I go there first. When I step inside, it's empty. I'm about to turn around and check the en suite, but then something catches my eye.

Both sides of the large walk-in closet are lined with clothes racks. A bench sits in the middle. And at the end is a floor-to-ceiling shoe rack with square cubbies. The last time I was here, everything was in order. But now the shoe rack looks weird. It's not flat against the wall like it was before. It's sitting at an angle, and I can see a crack of light shining from behind it.

I stand and stare, trying to understand what I'm seeing. Then I go to the rack and grab it with my free hand. It swings inward on soft hinges, and I suddenly realize what I've been looking at. A false door . . . and behind it, a hidden room.

68

I stand on the threshold of the concealed room and stare in disbelief, even as the purpose of the hidden space dawns on me.

It's a panic room—a place where people hide when there's an intruder in the house or some other life-threatening situation.

The space is maybe six feet wide by twelve feet long, with a second door at the other end—no doubt also concealed from the outside—that must exit into one of the other bedrooms on this floor. My mind darts back to the light under the door of the unoccupied bedroom a few nights ago. There are no windows. A pair of neon lights on the ceiling provide the only illumination.

Is this where Gregg has been going whenever he pulls a vanishing act? I have to assume that the answer is yes. The question is, Why?

I glance over my shoulder to make sure that I'm still alone, then step into the room.

A bed stands against the wall to my left. The covers are pushed back, and there's a head-shaped dent in the pillow as if someone has lain on it recently. Next to the bed is a metal desk upon which sits a keyboard, mouse, and a large monitor. A slim desktop computer rests on the floor. Farther away, on the other side of the room, is a partition behind which I can see a toilet and a small washbasin. A pair of hard plastic chairs separated by a small table sit against the wall opposite the desk. There's also a compact dormitory-style refrigerator.

The furniture in the room doesn't alarm me. The signs of recent habitation do. Because there's an empty soup can with the lid pried back sitting on the table next to a dirty spoon. There's more food waste too, spilling out of a white plastic trash bag. A couple of crumpled chip bags. More soup cans. Empty soda bottles. Even worse, there's a pile of dirty clothes sitting in the corner near the door next to a large ratty-looking backpack. A couple of pairs of jeans. T-shirts. Men's underwear and socks.

I glance toward the bed and the crumpled sheets, the head-shaped impression on the pillow, and I grow cold. There's only one explanation for what I'm seeing.

Someone has been living here.

Hiding in this room the whole time I've been in the house.

I stifle a cry even as I think back to all the strange incidents. The voices in the night. The smashed jar of beets. The footsteps on the stairs. Phantom lights turning on and off. The feeling of being watched. The door that closed by itself. Gregg claimed we were alone in the house, but we weren't. He must have known there was someone else here all along but let me think I was going crazy. That I was hallucinating because of the bump I took to the head. As the owner of the house, he would know about this room, so although someone could hide out here from me, there would be no hiding from him.

I want to run. To put as much distance between this dreadful place and myself as I can. But then my gaze settles upon the desk, and I see something I recognize. A folded sheet of yellow notepaper sitting next to the computer monitor. The same sheet that was left inside the screen door. The one Gregg took from me and slipped into his pocket. If I open it, I know what I will find. A threatening message: *You can't hide forever.* I thought it was meant for me, but was it really intended for whomever has been hiding in this room?

I tear my eyes away from the note, let my gaze drift higher. And when I do, I see something else. Equipment sitting on a shelf above the monitor. Two black boxes. The bigger box connects to a thick bundle of cables that runs up into the ceiling. Another cable runs down to the computer. It's the DSL router.

A voice inside my head urges me to get the hell out before it's too late. Before whoever has been living in this room comes back. But I don't. Not yet. Because even though Gregg claimed the internet was down, I'm not sure I believe a word he's told me since I got here. Not after finding this room. And if he *was* lying about the internet, then the computer might be my salvation. I can connect with the outside world. Call for help.

I cross to the desk and touch the mouse.

The monitor springs to life.

What I see on the screen sends a chill down my spine.

Video feeds arranged in a grid pattern that show every room of the house. This isn't a regular computer. It doubles as a monitor for the surveillance system, presumably meant to allow occupants of the panic room to see what is going on in the rest of the house. I see the living room, the kitchen, and several bedrooms, including Gregg's. One in particular draws my attention. A feed labeled *BR4*. It's the guest bedroom where I've been sleeping. Even on the thumbnail, I can tell that the camera's field of view captures the entire space.

I double-click on it, and the feed jumps to full screen.

From the high angle of the video, I figure the camera must be mounted near the ceiling in the corner next to the door. I certainly didn't see a camera there; otherwise, I would never have slept in that room. But there *is* a smoke detector. The perfect place to conceal a surveillance camera.

A camera that has been observing my every move. Like when I get undressed or take a shower . . . or have sex, like I did with Gregg on that very bed.

And all the while, there was someone in this room, watching.

I feel physically sick. Just the thought of a stranger watching Gregg and me in our most intimate moments makes me want to curl into a ball and cry. And it's not just one camera. Nowhere in this house is private. The cameras are everywhere, including in Gregg's bedroom, which is where we first made love.

But I can't think about that right now. It's not safe for me here. I minimize the app showing the surveillance feeds and open a web browser. If I can find a website for the local police department, I might be able to contact them through it. Ask them to send help. But when the browser opens, it just displays a message saying that there's no internet connection. When I look down at the task bar, the internet icon tells me the same thing. It's then that I notice the blinking red light on the router. Either it's out because of the storm, or Gregg has disabled the phone lines. Either way, it doesn't matter. I'm not using this computer to summon help.

Which means I need to get out right now.

I turn to leave, but then a thought occurs to me. Maybe whoever has been living in this room has a cell phone, and it might still be here. If I can find that phone and make it to somewhere that has service, I can call the police. I look around, checking the desk, the bed, and the table, but find nothing. Then I see the backpack lying next to the pile of dirty clothes in the corner. Maybe there's a phone in there. I go to it and kneel, then unzip the bag. But when I look inside, it's not a phone that I find but money. Lots of it. Fifty- and hundred-dollar bills in neat bundles.

I pull out a couple of bundles and study them. There must be thousands of dollars. No . . . tens of thousands. There's only one reason I can think of that it would be here. Whoever has been hiding in this room stole it. If so, then Gregg is harboring a fugitive. After all, it would be pretty hard for someone to be in your house like that and go unnoticed, even in a concealed room. That raises a disturbing question. Is Gregg connected to the money too? And what about me? Maybe the three of us robbed a bank, and I got injured somehow and lost my memory. But that doesn't explain how I ended up on the lakeshore, or why Gregg would bring us here to his own house.

Unless it isn't *his* house.

Now I really want to get out of here, cell phone be damned.

I stuff the money back into the backpack and zip it closed. When I go to stand up, I spot something else. A cardboard box pushed under the bed with what looks like picture frames stuffed into it. I grab the box and pull it out.

It *is* full of picture frames. At least ten of them. Some are small. The type meant to be displayed on a table or a shelf. A few are bigger and had probably hung on a wall. I lift one out and study it, then put it back and look at another one, then another. And at that moment, my suspicions about Gregg and this house snap into focus. Because all the picture frames contain photos of the same two people. A slim woman of about my build with long dark hair whom I guess to be in her late forties, and a man of about the same age with thin graying hair, sagging jowls, and glasses.

He looks nothing like Gregg, and I'm sure the woman in the photos is not Gregg's dead wife. In fact, I suspect he doesn't even have a dead wife, and that the clothes I've been borrowing belong to the woman in these pictures. If I need any proof of that, she's wearing in one photo the same sweater I wore yesterday.

But that's not all I see. The last photo in the box is a wedding picture showing the couple in a flowing white bridal gown and a black tux. And there, written in gold embossed lettering on the print, are the words:

Gregg and Sara Fielder, October 7, 1997

69

Run! The thought flashes through my mind even as I flee the panic room. *Run as far and as fast as you can from this place!*

I enter the bedroom, half expecting to find Gregg—the fake Gregg—there waiting for me, but he isn't. The house still feels empty, and I'm not complaining. I hurry toward the bedroom door, but then stop and turn around. The baseball bat Gregg armed himself with before checking the house after we heard the window break is still sitting next to the bed. I have the poker, but the bat is a much better weapon. I cross the room and toss the poker onto the bed, then pick up the baseball bat before making my way to the door and out into the hallway.

Seconds later, I'm descending the stairs at a breakneck pace, not bothering to be stealthy because there's no point. Either fake Gregg is somewhere in the house waiting for me, or he isn't.

Reaching the foyer, I cross to the mudroom, stuff my feet into what must be Sara's boots, and snatch a coat from a hook. Then I'm at the back door and out onto the deck even as I pull it on.

Then I remember the truck. I turn and step back into the house, run through the mudroom and out into the garage.

Gregg's truck is still there, just as it was when we were out here grilling hamburgers. I rush over to it, try the driver's side door. Locked.

Shit.

I go to the passenger side and try again.

Still locked.

Turning, I sprint back into the mudroom and look around, frantic. There is a keyholder next to the door, but the only keys hanging on it are for the house. Nothing that looks like car keys.

Double shit.

The keys could be anywhere, and I don't have time to search the house from top to bottom looking for them. For all I know, Gregg has them in his pocket. He wouldn't be stupid enough to leave me an easy means of escape, even if he did claim that the truck can't handle the amount of snow on the unplowed road. Then there's the washed-out bridge—assuming Gregg wasn't lying about that too.

Not that it matters. I won't be escaping in the truck. That much is obvious.

Which leaves only one place to go.

Helene's cabin.

There's safety in numbers. Two of us stand a better chance of survival than one. And if I'm lucky, she'll have something there that we can use to defend ourselves with. Something better than my baseball bat, like a gun. Still, I'll have to be careful and keep my wits about me on the way there, because I don't just need to worry about Gregg. There's also Eddie, who I'm sure is mixed up in this somehow. And whoever has been living in that panic room. I don't believe for one second that Gregg was sitting in there eating cold soup straight out of a can and sleeping in there when I wasn't around. Then another thought occurs to me. What if it's *Eddie* who was in that room?

I stop at the edge of the deck and think about that for a moment. Gregg said that Eddie was a neighbor. That makes more sense than the alternative. After all, he showed up at the front door, not once, but twice. If he was hiding in the panic room, why would he reveal himself in such a brazen way? What would be the point? And he brought beer too, just like a real neighbor. Where would he get a six-pack if he was spending all his time in that secret room? I reluctantly dismiss Eddie as the phantom houseguest, at least for now.

I step off the deck, then stop again because I remember something else Gregg said about Eddie. That he owns the next house on the west side of the lake, which is the same direction that I went when I stumbled across the old graveyard . . . and crossed paths with Knife Man. I have no idea if Eddie really owns a house there—I didn't notice anything that would lead me to believe any of the homes I passed were currently occupied—but I'm not taking any chances. Even if he isn't hiding out in that panic room, he still scares me. I turn in the opposite direction, following the same route Gregg and I took when we went out on the short skis, and set off at a brisk pace.

I don't know how far it is to Helene's cabin, but I figure it must be at least a mile, maybe two. It would be quicker to cut straight across the lake by boat, but there isn't one, so I have no choice but to take the long way around.

I follow the path close to the lake where there's less snow, and the going is easier, at least until the primitive trail that loops around the lake curves away from the shore. I step away from the path and stick to the edge of the lake.

That's when I notice it. Something in the water up ahead.

A rowboat. It's caught in the reeds where the woodland meets the water, sitting at an angle with its stern half-submerged.

Something stirs within me. A faint pulse of familiarity, as if I've seen this boat before.

I come to a halt and look around, gripping the baseball bat tightly in one hand. Satisfied that I'm still alone, I turn my attention back to the boat, which is about ten feet away, with its bow wedged between the trunks of two small pine trees growing at the water's edge. If it wasn't for that, the vessel might have floated free and sunk already.

I step closer to the water's edge and push through a couple of bushes that have lost their leaves, ignoring the branches that scrape at my hands. And now I see why the boat is sitting at such a weird angle. The stern end is full of water. When it first got stuck on the shore, the boat was probably still floating, but I suspect that the weight of snow that accumulated in the hull during the storm pushed it low enough to slip beneath the surface. Then the water in the hull froze. Now a sheet of ice locks the boat in place. And stuck in that ice is an object I recognize only too well.

A fluffy red slipper identical to the one I was wearing when I stumbled, confused and frozen, up to Gregg's door on the night that this nightmare began.

70

I stare at the slipper. The missing twin to the one I was wearing when I woke up on the shore of the lake. I was in this rowboat. I don't know how or why, but clearly something bad happened, and I fell overboard, leaving it behind. And I was out on the lake; otherwise, the empty boat wouldn't have subsequently floated here and become stuck.

But where did I come from? It must have been one of the houses around the lake. The most likely candidate is Gregg's house, or at least the house I believed to be his before I found those hidden photos in the panic room. Maybe something happened between us, and I fled and found this boat tied to the dock. After all, there's no boat at the end of his dock now. I assumed it had been moved out of the water for the winter, but maybe that isn't correct. Did I jump into the boat to escape him, then fall into the lake and hit my head, only to wash up on the shore with no memory of who I am or how I got there?

But the question is, What would have caused me to flee in such a panic during a snowstorm in the middle of the night?

The obvious answer makes my stomach churn. Maybe he did something to the real owners of the house. For all I know, Gregg and the unknown man who has been hiding in the panic room killed them. Then I remember Eddie, and how he was asking about Gregg's cousin, Ricky. Another piece of the puzzle clicks into place. What if the man in the panic room is Gregg's cousin? That still doesn't explain why he was hiding, or why there's a bag of cash. Was all this a home invasion gone wrong? Did Gregg and Ricky come here to steal from the real owners of the house I've been living in for the last several days and end up killing them? Is that why I fled? I might not know much about myself, but I'm pretty sure that a double murder would repulse me.

And how does Eddie fit in to all this?

They clearly knew each other, but I didn't get the sense that Gregg was his friend. Actually, just the opposite. He couldn't wait to get rid of him.

I won't find the answers standing out here, looking at this boat. It's told me about as much as it can. My best option is to keep going. Get to Helene's, and hope that she has a weapon with which we can defend ourselves, or maybe even a car so that we can try to drive out of here, unplowed roads or not.

I turn and make my way back, then continue on toward Helene's cabin. After a couple of minutes, I come across a house. The closest one on this side of the lake. I know that it's empty because we checked it when Gregg and I skied through here. There are a few more houses farther along the trail that have been closed for the winter too.

Something is different. I can still see the ski trail I left in the snow a couple of days before when I walked up to the house to check it . . . alongside several more recent tracks.

A faint hope ignites within me.

Someone else is up at the lake.

My heart leaps. Maybe they have a way to get out of here. A snowmobile or some other vehicle that can handle the rugged terrain. Maybe the bridge has been repaired.

I change course and head toward the house, climb the steps onto the porch.

But when I reach the front door, something is wrong. The frame is damaged, like someone pried it open to gain access.

This wasn't the homeowners. They aren't here . . . someone else is. I can think of only one person: Gregg. But why would he break into another house on the lake?

A voice inside my head screams, *Run. For God's sake, run!*

But I don't because I have to know. What is he up to, and why did he drug me? He thinks I'm out cold next door, so as long as I'm quiet and careful, he will never know that I've been here.

With trembling hands, I push the door open and listen, the bat gripped tightly in my hands.

Silence.

There is no sound of anyone moving around inside.

No voices.

The home is dark, probably because the owner disconnected the electricity for the winter. I wish I'd brought a flashlight, but even if I hadn't been in such haste to escape that panic room and flee to safety, I wouldn't have thought to bring one. It is daylight, after all.

I almost call out into the darkness to see if I'll get a response but think better of it. If Gregg is inside the house, I don't want to alert him.

Slowly, cautiously, I step across the threshold, ready to swing the bat if someone comes charging at me out of the blue. But no one does.

I start along a narrow hallway. To my left, stairs lead up into darkness. To the right is an archway that opens into a large living room. The curtains are drawn. A big-screen TV is mounted above a wide fireplace. I see a sofa and chair covered in white sheets to keep the dust at bay while the owners are away. Strangely, a third chair is uncovered. A musty odor like mothballs hangs in the air.

I continue down the hallway past the stairs until it opens up into a well-appointed kitchen with a breakfast nook that overlooks the woods, and a formal dining room to the right.

I look around the kitchen but see nothing unusual. Nothing out of place. Until I turn toward the dining room.

And there he is.

Eddie.

He's lying on the floor atop a bloodstained sheet that probably came from the chair in the living room. He won't be paying us any more unannounced visits. At least, if the bullet that entered through his forehead and removed the back of his skull has anything to say about it.

71

I stifle a scream and take a step back, even as the full horror of what I'm looking at dawns upon me. Someone murdered Eddie, and I can think of only one person who could have done it. The man who claimed his name was Gregg. A man I slept with. Willingly gave myself to.

I double over and retch, trying not to look at the grotesque tableau on the bloodied sheet in front of me. I can't stay here, should never have entered this house. If Gregg finds me here, I'll end up the same way as Eddie. But even before the last heave has racked my body, I hear a sound to my rear. A door opening.

I force myself to straighten up and spin around to see Gregg standing at the back door, his eyes wide with surprise. He is wearing a pair of old jeans and a black sweatshirt, both of which are dirty. Dirty snow encrusts his shoes.

He's holding a coil of orange polyester rope.

"You shouldn't be here," he says in a low voice as he enters the room.

"Don't come near me." I raise the bat and take a step back. "I'm warning you."

"Anna, you don't understand."

"I understand well enough." My hands are shaking. My voice sounds feeble, and I realize that I'm close to tears. "You killed the couple who own the house we've been staying in. Lied about your name and pretended it was your home. You killed Eddie."

"Please. Put the bat down. The people who own that house aren't dead, I promise you."

"Just like *he* isn't dead?" I risk a quick glance sideways at Eddie. "You told me there weren't any guns in the house."

"And it was the truth."

"Then why is half of Eddie's skull missing?" I practically scream, glancing at the corpse and realizing my mistake when bile rises in my throat, thick and acidic. I swallow and look away again.

"Eddie was carrying," Gregg says, as if that's all the explanation I need. "And as for the couple who own the place we've been staying in, they're just fine down in Connecticut at their other house. They know nothing about what's been going on here." Gregg's arms are at his sides, but he's tense, balling his hands into fists, then relaxing them over and over. "Please, give me a chance to explain. It's not what you think."

"Bullshit. I found the panic room. The bag of money. The photographs you hid so I wouldn't see them. Someone's been living in there. They were watching us on those cameras. When I undressed for bed. Took a shower. *All of it.*" A sob escapes my lips. "When we made love."

"Anna—"

"All this time, you had me thinking I was crazy, that I was imagining things, and I wasn't. The footsteps I heard. The jar of beets. The figure I saw at the bottom of the servants' stairs. All of it. There really *was* someone else in the house." Anger replaces the fear, at least temporarily. My voice rises to a screeching crescendo. "You *fucking* drugged me!"

"I had no choice." Gregg's eyes flick toward Eddie and back again. "I needed to take care of this, and I couldn't have you wandering around looking for me while I did it."

Thank goodness I drank only half the cocoa, or I'd still be dead to the world. "It wasn't the first time you drugged me, was it?"

Gregg says nothing, but the look on his face is the only answer I need.

"That's what I thought."

"Anna, I swear I'm not going to hurt you, but it's not safe here. You have to leave right now. Go back to the house and wait there." Gregg takes a step toward me. "Let me take care of this situation, and then I'll tell you everything you want to know. Cross my heart."

"I don't believe you." I back away from him again. "Who was in that panic room?"

"Damn it, Anna, that's not important right now." Anger flashes in Gregg's eyes. "We don't have time for this. Please, do as I say." He takes another step toward me, holds out his hand like he wants me to take it and let him lead me away.

As if! I'm doing no such thing. If I do, I'll be the next one lying dead on a sheet in a pool of blood.

Gregg takes another tentative step. Then he lunges forward without warning, hoping to catch me off guard.

A surge of fear-fueled adrenaline explodes in my veins.

I swing the bat with all the strength I can gather.

Gregg twists and tries to duck, but it's too late. There's nowhere for him to go. The bat slams into the side of his skull with a sickening crunch.

His head snaps around. Spittle flies from his lips. He grunts in pain. Then his legs give way, and he crumples to the floor next to the man he killed.

72

I stand over Gregg with the bat raised, ready to hit him again if he so much as twitches a finger, but he doesn't move. Judging by the trickle of blood that seeps from his hair behind his ear and down onto his cheek, he won't be, at least anytime soon. I can't even see him breathing. Is it possible to kill a man with one whack of a baseball bat? I have no idea, but I'm not about to kneel and check his pulse. Screw that. If he's dead, then I'll deal with the repercussions later when I'm far away from this horror show.

Speaking of which, it's time I get out of this place.

I edge around Eddie's body, making sure not to step anywhere near the blood-soaked sheet, and as I do, a thought occurs to me. *How did Eddie even get here?*

Despite the terror that twists my stomach, I pause and look down at him. It doesn't take a genius to figure out what killed Eddie, but now that I look closer, I see something else. An ugly bruise that darkens his cheek. The skin is split too, and his left eye is swollen. His jaw sits at a strange angle, like it's dislocated.

He must have been hit by something hard and heavy.

Something like . . . I look down at the baseball bat in my hands. It only took one blow to put Gregg down. In the hands of a man stronger than me, the bat could do much more damage. And now I remember the window that broke in the middle of the night, and how Gregg took the baseball bat with him to check it out. There were footprints on the floorboards under the window, as if someone in heavy boots had climbed in. Boots like the ones that Eddie is wearing.

Did Gregg go downstairs and catch Eddie breaking in? My mind flies back to the two thuds that I heard that night. The ones that drew me from the bedroom and sent me looking for Gregg. Were they the sounds of Gregg hitting Eddie? That would explain why there was no sign of the branch he claimed broke the window, because there was no branch. Instead, he must have knocked Eddie out and moved him before I came downstairs. Then, at some point, he broke into this house and brought him over here.

I avert my gaze from the dreadful corpse, and then I see something else. A chair around the kitchen table has been moved. There's a roll of silver duct tape on the table, and more on the legs of the chair, as if someone had been sitting on it with their ankles bound. I assume that Eddie's hands were also bound, but I'm not willing to investigate further.

Because one more chilling thought has occurred to me. Gregg was in his bedroom with me when I heard that gunshot, which means he couldn't have killed Eddie.

The man who was hiding in the panic room. He must have been the one who brought Eddie over here after Gregg incapacitated him with the baseball bat. And it was he who put that gaping hole in Eddie's head. Lashed him to a chair and murdered him.

It's the only explanation.

It also means that I'm not safe.

I need to get out of here right now.

The back door is still open. It's also closer than the front door through which I entered. I want to spend as little time in this house as necessary, so that's where I go. But as I pass through the kitchen, I see a tub of bleach sitting on the floor alongside a pair of yellow dish gloves and several rolls of paper towels. It's pretty obvious what Gregg intended to do with those.

And if I need any further proof of his macabre undertaking, I get it the moment I step outside. There's a blue plastic tarp spread on the ground alongside a pile of rocks. That must be why Gregg was carrying rope. He was going to drag the body out here, probably on that sheet, then wrap it up in the tarp along with the rocks to weigh it down. After that, Eddie would be, as the clichéd phrase goes, swimming with the fishes.

And if I had drunk that whole mug of cocoa, he would have finished his task and been back before I ever woke up. Then what would have happened? Would he have killed me next and dumped my body in the water too? I think I know the answer to that, and this time, the lake would not have given me up so easily.

73

I shudder at the thought and keep moving, turning down the side of the house and running back toward the lake. It's more important than ever that I reach Helene's cabin and contact the outside world. Get the police up here.

I reach the shore and keep going. Every once in a while, I glance back over my shoulder toward the murder house, but neither Gregg nor anyone else is pursuing me.

It takes a good forty minutes before Helene's cabin comes into view. It's much smaller than Gregg's house on the opposite shore—or rather, I remind myself, the house that belongs to the couple in the wedding photo. The real Gregg and his wife, Sara, who might or might not also be dead.

The cabin has two stories and a rustic front porch that overlooks the lake. The exterior walls are clad in unpainted shaker shingles that have turned silver from years of exposure to the elements. A stone chimney rises on one side of the building.

I know it's the right place because I recognize the boat tied up at the dock as the same one that she used to come across the water when she visited us.

I slump with relief and start toward the front door, but before I've made it even halfway there, I'm hit with a weird flash of recognition. I've been here before.

I stop and stare up at the building, trying to reel in the impression of familiarity, to bring it into focus, but the sensation has passed, replaced again by the frustrating blankness of my mind.

I start walking again and mount the porch steps to the front door.

I knock.

There's no answer.

I cast a quick look back down the trail but see no one.

That doesn't mean it will stay that way.

I knock again.

Come on, where are you, Helene?

There's a window on each side of the door. I go to one and cup my hands against the glass to peer inside. I'm ready to bang on it if I see any sign of movement. All I see is an empty living room with a small couch covered by a red and green throw.

I go back to the door and grab the knob. Try to turn it.

Locked.

A swell of panic engulfs me.

I don't have time for this.

I step back down off the porch. Helene must be around here somewhere because the boat is tied to the dock. There are also two cars covered in snow parked on the side of the house. A shiny black Audi roadster, and a green VW Bug.

I walk past the cars to the back of the house and see a pair of sliding glass doors that lead out onto a deck overlooking the woods beyond. I step up onto the deck and try the closest door. It slides sideways, and I'm in.

There's still no sign of Helene, but the sound of running water from upstairs tells me why. She's taking a shower.

I don't want to scare her when she comes down, but I also don't want to wait outside. I compromise and put down the baseball bat, leaning it against the wall near the sliding door.

The cabin has an open floor plan, with a living room, a kitchen, and a small dining table. There's a desk against the wall under the stairs in a nook. A laptop sits on the desk next to a stack of papers and several books. I wander over to take a look, but when I get there, something else catches my eye.

A silver pearl necklace, or rather, the broken half of one, sitting on the desk next to the computer. I stare at it in disbelief. Because I recognize this necklace. The other half is across the lake, lying on the nightstand next to my bed.

74

I pick up the piece of jewelry and turn it over in my hands. Study it. There's no doubt that it's the missing section of the broken necklace I found on the shore.

How did it get here? Unless . . .

I think back to the strange feeling of familiarity that came upon me as I approached the cabin. Have I been here before? Is it this house, and not the one across the lake, that I came from prior to whatever misfortune robbed me of my memories? If so, why didn't Helene recognize me that first day when she knocked on Gregg's door? I don't have the answers to any of these questions, and I suspect that until my memory returns, it will remain that way.

The shower is still running. I almost go to the stairs and climb them, call out to Helene, and let her know I'm here. Ask her about the broken necklace. But something stops me. Call it a premonition, or maybe some kind of sixth sense, but I'm overcome with the notion that it would be a bad idea.

I turn to the other things on the desk. The pile of paperwork, the books, and the laptop. That same intuition tells me that these items are important, but I don't know why until I focus on the stack of paperwork and realize that it's a laser-printed manuscript. This must be the book Helene has been working on.

I pick up the cover page and read it: *Body of Lies by Alex Moore*. A pen name, perhaps? I set the cover sheet aside and flick through the manuscript. It's a thriller. Or, more accurately, one of those women's fiction thrillers that combines psychological suspense with romance. I browse through the pages, stopping here and there and reading the start of different chapters.

And when I do, something jars loose inside my head. I recognize this book, which is impossible because it's an unpublished manuscript. Yet when I read the words on those pages, I feel an overwhelming sense of familiarity. Even more so than the feeling I got when I was approaching the cabin.

I turn more pages, skimming the text faster and faster. And then I realize something else. This manuscript doesn't just invoke a vague sense of familiarity within me. I know the story. The *entire* story. Every word. It bursts through the brick wall of my amnesia.

A woman named Adria gets into a relationship with a man named Peter, who isn't all he claims to be. She's rich. He's not. But he pretends he is and convinces her to marry him so that he can live the life he wants. And when she discovers his duplicity, he tries to kill her.

How could I know this? It doesn't make sense.

I turn to another chapter. Pick up the first page. Read it. Adria and Peter on a ferry crossing to Nantucket. She's standing at the rail. He hands her a Bloody Mary and makes a joke about healthy drinking. And there's the lighthouse sitting on Brant Point with the town of Nantucket behind it.

I drop the page in shock.

It flutters to the floor and lands under the desk.

I paw through the rest of the manuscript like a madwoman, pushing pages aside until I come to another chapter. Adria is in front of her condo, talking to a man and woman who are looking for her husband. A man with a gun under his jacket.

I gasp in disbelief.

It's no wonder this manuscript feels so familiar. The flashbacks I've been having that I thought were surfacing memories are nothing of the sort. They are chapters from this book. It wasn't me who visited

Nantucket. It was the fictional Adria. Just like it wasn't Eddie who cornered me on the sidewalk in my flashback but a fictional goon.

I don't need to keep reading because I know what I will find. More chapters that I believed were memories were really just the pages of this book. And not just a book . . . an unpublished manuscript. Why is *this* what I'm remembering?

I look at the laptop computer. The screen is dark. There's a mouse sitting next to it. I touch the mouse, and the screen lights up and asks for a PIN. My fingers go to the keyboard and tap in four numbers before I even think about it, almost like a habit, or muscle memory.

5698.

To my surprise, the screen unlocks, and I find myself staring at another manuscript in a word processor. And not just any manuscript. The same manuscript. Except that the names have been changed. Instead of Adria and Peter, the main characters are called Marcia and Trevor. There are other changes too. Instead of the Blackberry Adria uses to call her husband when the ruffian corners her, Marcia uses an iPhone. I spot more updates, big and small. Someone, presumably Helene, has retyped and edited the manuscript to make it current. I wonder how long ago the original was written, and why Helene is rewriting it. What is my connection to this manuscript? For that matter, what is my connection to Helene? If I'm remembering the plot of this book, I must have seen it before, which means I must know her. Why didn't Helene say something when she came to the house?

I turn my attention from the computer to the stack of hardcover books sitting next to the printed manuscript. I pick up the top one and look at the cover. It's another romantic thriller. *Devil Swept Away* by Alex Moore. I put it down and look at the next book, and the next. They are all thrillers by the same person. Helene, or Alex as she apparently goes by when she's writing, is prolific. I pick up a fourth book and turn it over to look at the back, hoping to find a bio or some other nugget of information about Alex Moore.

And when I do, I get a shock.

There isn't an author bio on the back of the book. There's a full-page photograph. But it isn't Helene staring out from that dust jacket. It's me.

I'm Alex Moore.

75

No wonder I recognize the manuscript sitting on the desk, and the events contained within. Helene didn't write it—I did. I turn my attention back to the computer, scroll up through the manuscript on the screen until I get to the cover page.

The Lies That Kill
by
Helene Carter

What the hell? I stare in shock. Is she really trying to steal my book? Is that why I ended up in the lake? Did Helene try to kill me so she could take credit for my work? If so, how does Gregg, or whatever his real name is, fit into all this? Are they working together? And what about Eddie and whoever has been living in the panic room? My head is spinning. None of it makes sense.

I turn back to the original manuscript, hoping it will help me remember something else. It doesn't, but I see something else. A yellow legal pad I hadn't noticed before. It's tucked under a small pile of papers. I reach out, hands trembling, and slide it free. And when I do, my suspicion is confirmed. The topmost sheet has been ripped off, leaving a jagged line of torn paper. A tear that I'm sure will match the sheet I found tucked inside the screen door. A sheet of paper with a threatening note written on it. This is proof positive. The note wasn't meant for Gregg or whoever was in that panic room, like he must have thought. It was from Helene.

At that moment, I hear a sharp voice behind me.

"What are you doing here?"

I spin around to find Helene standing there, hands on her hips. Her hair is wet and her face is rosy. I was so engrossed that I didn't notice the shower wasn't running anymore.

I glare at her. "What did you do?"

Helene looks at the laptop screen. "From the looks of it, you already know."

"You stole my manuscript. That much is obvious. That still doesn't explain how I woke up on the shore across the lake with no memories. I'm assuming that had something to do with you too."

Helene stares at me for a long moment, as if she's trying to decide if I'm on the level, then she shakes her head in disappointment. "Alex, I didn't think you were this dumb. You can drop the act. We both know you're faking." Her face creases into a scowl. "What, did you think that pretending to lose your memory—playing happy family with that guy across the lake—would protect you?"

"I'm not faking. I really have lost my memory. I notice you didn't deny trying to kill me. If I could remember, then why would I come back here instead of trying to escape? Or calling the police?"

Helene looks surprised. "Huh. That's a good point. I actually think you might be telling the truth. I was wondering what you were up to. You and Gregg shacking up over there like he's your boyfriend or something. All that crap about the bridge being out and us being stranded here."

"The bridge isn't out?" This is news to me. Not that I'm surprised that Gregg lied to me about it. Nothing else he said was the truth. He clearly just wanted to keep me here to stop anyone finding out that he was living in that house, pretending to be someone he wasn't. I've got a pretty good idea that whatever he's up to, it is far from legal.

"No. At least, not when I drove up here. Honestly, I had no intention of staying. I figured I'd take care of you, make it look like an accident, and everything would be good. I'd leave, then come back a few days from now, and find the tragic scene. The brilliant author Alex Moore accidentally drowned at the lake house she was renting to work on her next novel. Except you were harder to kill than I thought. You got away in that damn rowboat. Kind of ironic that you fell overboard, anyway."

I can't believe what I'm hearing. "Why would you even want to kill me? Who are you? I don't understand."

"Right. The memory thing again. Pretty convenient that you've forgotten how you treated me for the past five years. The big *New York Times* bestselling author who won't even give her assistant's manuscript the time of day. What was it you said about my book? Let me think. Oh, that's right. You said the writing was clunky, and the story was unbelievable. Told me I was a talentless hack, and that I should stick to doing what I was good at. Like pretending to be you and posting stupid crap on social media. Replying to your fan emails. Sending out autographed copies of your books and scheduling book signings. You didn't give a damn about my ambitions. Just brushed them aside like I was nothing. I came to you looking for guidance, and you crushed me."

"Helene, I really don't remember any of—"

Except that's not true. Not anymore. Helene's vitriolic outburst has finally shattered the last vestiges of my memory loss. The memories come flooding back in a torrent. I don't remember everything. Not yet. But I remember enough. Like how she came to me with that manuscript she'd been working on, and it really was bad. The last thing I wanted to do was crush her. I gave her advice. Marked it up, made suggestions for improvement in the plot and character development. Tried to help her. Encourage her.

"I never said you were a talentless hack. That's not a thing I would ever say. I even offered to work on it with you."

"I didn't want your pity, Alex." Helene clenches her jaw. "I wanted you to tell me that my writing was good."

But it wasn't, I think, even though there's no way I'm about to argue the point with her. Instead, I say, "I still don't understand, Helene. This all happened . . ." I think a moment. "Two years ago? You never came back to me with anything else. I thought you'd given up on writing."

"You didn't even bother to ask. That's the worst part. And there you were with all those bestsellers. It was like everything you touched turned to gold. And me . . . I couldn't even get anyone to read my stuff. All I got was rejection after rejection.

"Then I found that old manuscript. The one you wrote when you were nineteen. Genre trash, like all your other books. But that wouldn't stop people from buying it, putting it on the bestseller lists, which is ridiculous. It's like talent just doesn't matter. I have a master's in creative writing. What do you have? A stupid degree in art history that has *nothing* to do with being a writer." Helene laughs, the sound shrill. "It was like a slap in the face. I labored for three years on my manuscript, writing and rewriting. And you dashed off this stupid romantic suspense novel while you were still in college and didn't even do anything with it. Just threw it in a drawer and left it there to rot for fifteen years because you didn't think it was good enough. Do you know how arrogant that was?"

The memories are coming faster now, bombarding me even as I listen to Helene's tirade. I guess all I needed was to confront the lunatic who almost killed me.

I take a step toward her. "It wasn't arrogance, Helene. I was so young. It really wasn't a good book."

Helene's face flushes with anger. When she speaks again, her voice is like thunder. "Then why the fuck did they agree to publish it?"

76

I stare at Helene in shocked silence, trying to figure out what she means but coming up blank. No one has offered to publish the manuscript because nobody has seen it. I shake my head in confusion. "I don't know what you're talking about, Helene," I say. "I've never sent that manuscript out. You said so yourself."

"No. You didn't, but *I* did."

"What?" I can't believe what I'm hearing. "You sent it out?"

Helene nods. "I typed up a digital copy, made a few edits, and changed the title, then sent it to agents."

"You stole my book and submitted it under your own name?"

"Sure. I figured you weren't ever going to do anything with it, anyway, so what was the harm?"

"Because it's stealing, Helene. That's the harm. Why would you do something like that?"

"You had no interest in helping me. Regardless of what you said, I knew you weren't ever going to be the mentor I wanted you to be," Helene says. "But in the end, you did help me because they wanted your manuscript . . . I mean, my manuscript. Can you believe that? I finally got an agent and a publishing deal. A big one. They loved the book. And everything would have been just fine. I wasn't going to publish under my own name, of course. That would have been too obvious, and with the number of books that come out every year, you would never even have known. I mean, what are the chances that you would ever stumble across it? Read it? Pretty slim, in my estimation." Helene looks at the printed manuscript on the desk. "But then, out of the blue, you decided to come up here and rewrite it yourself. After all those years the manuscript sat forgotten in that drawer, you suddenly wanted to publish the damn thing."

Another memory comes crashing back. Finding the cabin for rent online. Booking it for a month so I could immerse myself in the landscape of the story while I rewrote it. Using the lake and the cabin as inspiration. And I remember something else too. Helene telling me that the novel was too different from my previously published books. That it was too immature, and I should cancel the cabin rental. Forget about that old manuscript.

Now I understand what this is all about. It makes perfect sense. "There couldn't be two identical novels sitting on bookstore shelves written by different authors."

"Exactly. The publisher would find out. They would want their advance money back. Everyone would know what I'd done. I'd be sued. Bankrupted. My career would be ruined."

"So you decided to kill me instead?"

"I didn't want to, Alex. You have to believe that. I'm not a monster. But I had no choice. If it came out that you wrote the book and not me . . . That's not something a person can ever come back from. I wouldn't even be able to get another assistant job, let alone become a published author. Besides, I'd already spent a big chunk of the advance paying off my credit cards. Student loans."

"You could have come to me, told me what you'd done. I would have helped you." I'm not sure if this is true, even though I want to believe it. Would I have been sympathetic to her plight after she stole my manuscript and claimed it as her own? It's a pretty big violation of my trust. But I have no intention of admitting that to Helene. It doesn't matter because she doesn't believe me.

"Yeah, right. You would have told my publisher. That's what you would have done."

"You don't know that."

"Yes, Alex, I do. That's what anyone would have done. Which is why I was forced to take matters into my own hands, even though I hated to do it."

"Okay, I get that," I say in a last-ditch attempt to mollify her, "but you don't need to kill me. Not now. You can have the book. It's yours. Take it."

Helene observes me with narrowed eyes, maybe trying to decide if I'm serious. Then she huffs. "Nice try, Alex, but we both know you're lying. The first chance you get, you'll turn me in."

"I won't. I swear."

"Yes, you will. Besides, I don't need you to give me the manuscript like I'm some sort of charity case. I can just take it, which is perfect because my editor wants more changes to the version that *I* turned in. Lots of them. Guess my rewrites weren't up to scratch. Figures, huh? But who cares? You've pretty much completed your little do-over of the original manuscript, so now I have your wonderful edits, and my name is on the title page. I bet they'll just lap those up. Once you're finally out of the way, that is."

My jaw drops. She really is nuts.

I open my mouth to tell her as much, but at that moment, another memory explodes in my head, dousing my senses and dragging me back to the past.

◆ ◆ ◆

Helene shows up unannounced at the cabin with a bottle of wine in one hand and a cardboard box full of looseleaf pages in the other. I've been editing all day, updating the manuscript of the first book I wrote, getting it ready for publication. I'm exhausted. I ask her what she's doing here.

"Publisher needs these signed by next week," she says, holding up the box, which contains what the industry calls tipped-in pages. Loose sheets that are printed separately from the rest of the book. Once I sign them, they'll

go back to the printer to be bound into an autographed limited edition. Helene steps past me into the cabin. "I know you won't be back by then, so I thought I'd drive them up to you." She lifts the bottle of wine. "Figured we could celebrate your new project at the same time. I'm sure it's going to be wonderful."

We spend the next two hours talking. She opens the wine in the kitchen and brings me a glass. I drink it. She brings me another. I drink that, too. And then, it happens. My vision blurs. I'm having trouble walking. This is not a normal reaction to a couple of glasses of wine. I look at Helene, confused. Mystified. I expect her to help me. Can't she see what's going on?

She doesn't help. Instead, she just smiles and pulls a small orange pill bottle out of her pocket.

She leans close. "Prescription painkillers. And wow, did you take a lot of them."

She heaves me up and starts toward the door.

We go outside, and she steers me to the dock.

"Such a shame. All that success, and you went and did a thing like this. Overdosed on opioids, then threw yourself into the lake. Drowned. And no one even knew that you were struggling with depression."

Even in my addled state, the words strike fear into my heart. She's going to kill me.

I try to pull away, but her grip is like a vise, so I do the next best thing. I pretend the drugs are working faster through my system than they really are. I let my legs go slack, slump as if I'm about to pass out. This does the trick. Helene lets go and puts her arms under my armpits instead. She drags me along backward toward the end of the dock.

I bide my time.

Then, when she stops, I gather all my remaining strength and push myself up, twist out of her grasp, and shove her backward. She stumbles, almost falls in the water herself, then lands on her ass with a grunt.

There are two boats tied to the dock. One of them only has an outboard motor, and I don't have the keys. But the other, smaller, boat has oars. They are sitting across the seats, just waiting for me. I half jump, half fall into the rowboat and untie the mooring ropes, even as Helene gets to her feet. Another second, and she'll be upon me. I grab an oar and push off. Start rowing.

Helene stands at the end of the dock and watches me with a desperate look on her face. "What are you doing? There's nowhere for you to go. Just come back here!" she calls out—the midnight breeze snatching the words away and making them hard to hear.

I have no intention of going back. But the drugs she dosed me with are taking their toll now. By the time I get to the middle of the lake, my arms feel like lead, and I can barely keep my head up. Then, even as I struggle to stay awake, the oars slip from my hands, and I slump sideways.

The next thing I know, I'm tumbling into the water and sinking beneath its cold, dark surface.

◆ ◆ ◆

I gasp and lean against the desk as the memory recedes. The sudden recollection is overwhelming. Visceral. My chest heaves. What is it about people drugging me? First Helene, then Gregg. Everyone up here at this lake is nuts. Talk about bad luck. I escaped one murderous psychopath only to wander, with no memory of who I was, up to the door of another.

I look sideways at Helene. She tried to kill me once. There's no reason she won't try again. I have to talk some sense into her. Make her see that murder isn't the answer. But at that moment, the full desperation of my situation dawns on me. Because in the heat of our exchange, I've forgotten about Gregg. I've forgotten about the mystery person in the panic room. Helene might have wanted me dead, but there could be someone else out there willing to kill us both. A brief question runs through my head: *Why?* If I woke up next to the lake with no memory because of Helene, then what the hell did I walk into when I stumbled, freezing and scared, to Gregg's door? Had I even met him before that night? I ponder this for a moment, then decide it can wait until later.

"We can't stay here. It's not safe." I look nervously toward the glass slider. "We have to go. Right now."

Helene doesn't move. "What are you talking about?"

"Gregg. He's not who we thought he was. He's been lying all along. There was someone else in the house too, hiding in a room upstairs. I think they might have been involved in some kind of crime. They've already killed one person, and they won't hesitate to kill us."

A faint smile plays across Helene's lips. "Pathetic. You're supposed to be an acclaimed author, and that's the best you can come up with? It doesn't even sound plausible to me."

"I'm serious. Please, Helene, you have to believe me," I implore her, even as the ludicrousness of the situation occurs to me. I'm trying to save the life of a woman who tried to murder me. "They *will* kill us."

Helene shakes her head. "I'm sorry, Alex, but the only person who's dying today is you."

Then she lunges forward.

This time, I'm expecting her.

The baseball bat is where I left it a few feet away, leaning against the wall near the sliding glass door. I dodge sideways out of Helene's path in the nick of time. I feel a soft stirring of the air as she careens past me and slams into the desk, sending manuscript pages and a couple of my hardcover books tumbling to the floor.

She pushes herself up and turns toward me with a screech, but my hands have already closed over the handle of the baseball bat. I scoop it up and swing it in a wild, flailing arc.

Helene jumps back, and I miss her. I would swing again, but my grip on the bat is loose, and it rips from my hands and continues its inertia-driven trajectory until it slams into the wall near the desk.

But it buys me the time I need to escape.

I pull the sliding glass door open, then flee out onto the deck and around the house toward the driveway. I don't know where I'm going, but anywhere is better than here. Maybe I can head toward the graveyard and find the ruins of that old church in the woods, hide there until I come up with a plan to escape this dreadful place.

I don't make it that far.

As I sprint past the Audi, I catch a blur of movement off to my left. A firm hand grips the collar of my coat, spinning me around. Another hand grasps the back of my head, fingers lacing into my hair and tugging painfully. Then I'm slammed forward headfirst into the car, and everything goes black.

77

I awake to a world of pain. A pulsing ache throbs at my temples, making it hard to think. I force my eyes open, wincing as a stab of discomfort drills down behind my right cheek. Even though I can't see my eye socket, I can tell that it's puffy and swollen.

At first, all I see are hazy abstract shapes, but when I blink, my vision clears, and a face comes into view.

Helene's face.

She's staring at me, mouth open and lips curled back, her eyes wide and unblinking. My first instinct is to back away, but it's not that simple. Something is wrong. My surroundings don't make sense. Everything is off-kilter. Turned sideways. I take a moment to realize why, and when I do, fear clutches at my heart.

I'm lying on the floor atop a worn Oriental rug a few feet away from Helene, who still hasn't moved. A crimson pool is spreading on the floor between us and soaking into the edge of the rug, turning it almost black. A pool that looks very much like the beet juice I mistook for blood in the pantry. Except this time, I'm not mistaken. Helene isn't moving because she can't, thanks to the knife that's buried in her chest up to the hilt.

I whimper and try to push myself up, even as a new drumbeat of agony flares inside my head. I cry out and sink back down with a sob, then try to crawl away from her across the floorboards instead. But I don't get far.

A heavy foot pushes into my back, denying my escape.

"Welcome back, sunshine," says a deep baritone voice from above me.

I twist and roll over onto my back, look up into the face of a man I don't recognize. He's wearing a heavy coat and black gloves. His boots are crusted with dirty snow just like Gregg's were. This must be the man who was living in the panic room, but I still don't know who he is.

I try to ask, but my throat is bone-dry, probably thanks to how long I was unconscious and the side effects of the drugs in my cocoa. All that comes out is a rattling whisper barely loud enough to be heard.

I swallow, ignoring the pinpricks of discomfort at the back of my throat, and try again. "Who are you?"

"It isn't important who I am," he says, looking down at me like I'm something he just scraped off his shoe. "You, though, that's another matter. Bestselling author Alex Moore, up here at the lake to finish her latest book, only to find out that her assistant is a psychotic bitch with an axe to grind."

"How do you know—"

"Come on, Alex, are you really that dumb? How do you think I know? I went back to the house to see what was keeping Michael. Figured he was taking his time because he didn't want to help dispose of Eddie. Instead, I found him on the floor with his head cracked open. It didn't take a genius to figure out you were responsible. I mean, who else could it have been? Lucky for me, you left a pretty obvious trail announcing where you'd gone in the snow. I followed it all the way here." He glances at Helene. "I have to say, it was quite an interesting conversation the two of you had."

"Michael?"

"Oh, that's right. He told you his name was Gregg." My captor kneels down next to me and brushes a strand of hair from my face. I shudder at his touch, but he doesn't seem to notice and just continues talking. "I'm sorry my cousin dragged you into this. He should never have let you inside the house. But it's just like him, trying to help a wounded soul. Too much empathy. That's his problem."

It only takes a moment for this to sink in, and then I know exactly who my captor is. "You're Ricky, the guy Eddie was looking for."

"Very good."

"What did he want with you?" I ask more to buy time than because I care about the answer. I'm thinking about the knife a few feet away, still embedded in Helene's chest. My gaze shifts to it for just a moment, as I sum up my chances of grabbing it before Ricky can react.

He's way ahead of me. "Don't even think of trying for the knife. You just lie there nice and still, like a good girl. If I see even a twitch from you, you'll regret it. Understand?"

When I nod, it seems to satisfy him.

"Good girl." He touches my cheek. "You're a smart one. I tried to tell Michael that, but he wouldn't listen, even when your assistant started showing up unannounced. Couldn't figure out what her deal was at the time. But I guess she thought you might not have drowned in the lake and had escaped. Then Eddie showed up. What a mess. And on top of that, my stupid cousin fell for you. I told him we should just kill you, then come over here and do the same to the woman, get rid of anyone who'd seen you, but he wouldn't let me. He even chased after you that morning in the graveyard, which was stupid. He should have just stayed out of it and let me take care of business; then we wouldn't be in this situation.

"Still, it was entertaining enough watching the pair of you go at it. Especially in the bedroom. Thank heavens the people who own that house put cameras everywhere. Gave me something to do while I was stuck in the panic room. I can see why Michael liked you so much. Shit, if I was in his place, I might even have taken you to bed a couple of times before I killed you, just for the hell of it."

I cringe with horror at the full implication of what Ricky just said. Until now, I'd clung to a slight hope that whoever was in that panic room hadn't watched everything Gregg—or rather, Michael—and I did together. Hadn't watched us having sex.

Even through the terror, I feel violated.

Ricky isn't done, though. "Even when everything went to shit, when we needed to get rid of Eddie's corpse, he wouldn't kill you. Wanted to drug you instead. And yet here you are. He couldn't even do that right. Still, it's turned out okay in the end. I thought we'd have three bodies to get rid of, but thanks to your crazy assistant, it will only be one. And a good thing too, because gathering those rocks to sink Eddie in the lake really did a number on my back."

Ricky intends to kill me. That much is clear, but I still don't know what he's talking about, and I say as much.

"Isn't it obvious? You girls clearly had issues. The woman already tried to kill you once. All I gotta do is make it look like the two of you got in a tussle that ended in a neat little murder-suicide." Ricky clears his throat. "Now, before we end this thing, I just need you to tell me. Did you call anyone before I got here?"

So that's why he's kept me alive this long. I was wondering about that. Still, he should know the answer already. "You heard the argument between me and Helene. What do you think?"

"I heard only part of the argument. I have no idea what you did before I got here, so I'll ask you again. Did you call anyone?"

I stay mute. I wouldn't tell him even if I had. I'm as good as dead already, so why bother?

He's still one step ahead of me. "How about we make a deal? You tell me the truth, and I'll make sure you don't suffer too much. Refuse to tell me, and well . . ."

The implication is hard to miss. But I'm damned if I'll make it easy on him, so I reply, "I called the police. They're on their way right now, so you'd better leave me alone and get out while you still can."

Ricky studies my face for a moment, then he cocks his head and smiles. "Good. You didn't call anyone."

"You want to bet on that?" I'm not sure how I could have called anyone, unless there really *is* cell service here at the lake, and Michael lied to me.

I try to push myself up.

"Yeah, I would." Ricky puts a hand on my shoulder and forces me back down. "I've played a lot of poker in my time, sunshine. Gotten pretty good at it, and you're a horrible liar. If you were sitting opposite me in a game with that look on your face and you raised, I'd call your bluff in a heartbeat." He climbs to his feet with a weary sigh. "Guess it's time to finish this thing."

My throat tightens at those words. I look up and meet Ricky's gaze, hoping to see a shred of humanity in those eyes, some speck of hope that he can be reasoned with, but they stare back at me, black and cold. Emotionless. And in that moment, I realize . . . I'm about to die, and there isn't a thing I can say or do to stop it.

78

"Ricky! Don't do it!" A voice booms out from somewhere behind us. It's Michael, a.k.a. Gregg. I thought I'd killed him with the baseball bat, but apparently, I didn't. Relief floods over me. And not just because I don't know how I would have lived with myself if I'd killed a man, but because his appearance buys me more time to figure a way out of this madness. I turn my head to look at him, ignoring the sharp pain in my neck.

Michael looks the worse for wear. An ugly bruise has blossomed on his cheek, and dried blood mats the hair above his ear where I hit him. It looks painful, and I should know, because my face throbs where Ricky slammed it into the side of the car after I fled from Helene.

"Crap." Ricky looks almost disappointed. "Figured you'd be out cold for a while longer."

"So you could kill more people without me getting in your way?"

"Something like that." There's a gleam in Ricky's eyes. "Look, cuz, I know you like the girl—hell, she's cute as can be—but she's also a witness. She's seen our faces. Knows who we are. We let her go, and she'll run straight to the cops."

"How do you know she hasn't called them already?" Michael asks. "That Helene woman must have a cell phone around here somewhere."

"You think I'm an idiot and didn't already check that?" Ricky is keeping one eye on his cousin and the other on me. "She hasn't. Trust me."

Michael looks past me toward Helene's body, and for a moment, I see sadness in his eyes. Then it's gone. He turns his attention back to Ricky with a shake of his head. "You just can't help yourself, can you?"

"I told you. No witnesses."

"Damn it, Ricky. *I told you* after that mess you made in Boston that I'd only help if you do what I say. What part of that didn't you understand?"

"You weren't there. That guy in Boston had it coming," Ricky says in a tone that reminds me of a petulant child. He positions himself between me and Helene. "It was his own fault."

"Christ, you're unbelievable." Michael's voice rises a note. "He walked in on you and Eddie robbing his business. You didn't have to shoot him."

"That wasn't me. It was Eddie. He was the one with the gun."

"It doesn't matter who pulled the trigger. You were both there committing a crime with a firearm. You're as guilty as him in the eyes of the law. Do you understand what that means, cousin? Twenty years to life. That's what it means."

"Not if we reach Canada first and disappear."

"Which you just made a lot harder by killing Eddie and Helene." Michael glares at his cousin. "Damn it, Ricky. All you had to do was lie low and keep out of sight until we could get you to the border."

"It wasn't my fault Eddie showed up, sniffing around. What else was I supposed to do?"

"That's the problem. It's never your fault. Maybe if you hadn't stiffed Eddie and run with his share of the cash, he wouldn't have been looking for you." Michael shakes his head. "I told you not to kill him. Just take him over to that house and tie him up. Keep him there out of sight."

"And then what?" The petulance is back.

"I don't know. But I'd have thought of something. Given him his money and said you're sorry for double-crossing him. Sent him on his way."

"Yeah, like he'd have just accepted my apology. That ain't Eddie, cuz. Besides, we need the cash for Canada. All of it. That's why I took Eddie's share. He's the one who got us into this by killing that guy."

"There's no *we*. We already talked about this. I'm not ruining my life by fleeing to Canada with you. I agreed to hide you. Help you get over the border. That's it. And as for killing people, look at yourself. You murder Anna, that's a triple homicide. They'll come after you with everything they've got, and it won't be the state police. It'll be the feds, because your crimes crossed state lines. You'll spend the rest of your life behind bars. You can forget about parole—not with so much blood on your hands. Think about that a minute."

"I already have. Double homicide. Triple homicide. What's the difference?"

"The difference is, I won't let you kill Anna."

"That's so cute. You're going to save your girlfriend." Ricky gives a derisive snort. "You don't even know her real name. It's Alex, you idiot, not Anna. Alex Moore. Apparently, she's a famous author. And no one's going to be pinning a triple homicide on either of us. She and her assistant have some sort of crazy rivalry going on. That Helene woman already tried to drown her once. That's how she ended up at our door in the first place. All we have to do is make it look like they got into an argument—which they did, by the way—and Helene pulled a knife. They fought. Alex got a hold of it, killed her assistant in self-defense."

"And what about Anna?" Michael asks. "What happens to her in this little murder fantasy?"

"Easy." Ricky puts a hand in his pocket, comes out with a bottle of prescription pills. "Painkillers. Strong ones, like the doctors give out. Get you hooked on. I found them in the bathroom." He looks down at me. "All we have to do is get her to write a little note, saying how sorry she is for everything that happened, and that she can't go on anymore."

"Then you feed her the pills," Michael says.

"See, now you're getting it."

"You can go to hell." I glare up at Ricky. "I'm not writing any suicide note."

"Meh." Ricky shrugs. "Doesn't matter. I can always type something up on that laptop of yours . . . or not. Who cares? When the cops come looking and find you dead of an overdose, your assistant with a knife in her chest, they'll put two and two together and get five. Assume it was a murder-suicide. Nice and neat." He nods toward Helene. "Your prints are already on the knife, by the way. I took care of that while you were still out for the count.

"And as for Eddie, I bet no one even knows that he came up here. We sink him deep enough in the lake and clean up the mess in that house, they'll never find him. He'll disappear forever. And trust me, no one is going to shed a tear. The man had a lot of enemies."

"I won't let you kill her." Michael looks at me. Then his gaze darts briefly toward the discarded baseball bat lying on the floor near the desk. A swell of hope rises inside me, until I realize that I'm not the only one who caught the glance.

Ricky reaches inside his jacket and pulls out a gun. Eddie's gun. "Don't even think about it, cuz. I'd hate to do it, but if you leave me no choice, I'll put you in the same watery grave as Eddie."

"You won't shoot me," Michael says, although I can see from the look on his face that he isn't so sure about that. "Put the gun down before you do something you'll regret."

"Are you going to help me finish this thing?"

"What do you think?"

Ricky lets a slow stream of air out through his nose. "Figured you'd be like that." He raises the gun.

Another few seconds, and Michael will be dead. Then it will be my turn. I have to do something. Ricky is standing between me and Helene, but he isn't paying me any attention now. The knife is still sticking out of her chest, frustratingly out of reach. Unless . . . I gather my strength and push myself up on my elbows, then lunge for the knife.

It only takes a moment for Ricky to realize what I'm trying to do. He lands a vicious kick, catching me in the stomach with his foot. The air rushes from my lungs. I fight the urge to double over from the pain.

From the corner of my eye, I glimpse movement.

Ricky is lowering the gun toward me. Apparently, in the heat of the moment, he's abandoned the idea of staging my death to look like a squabble gone wrong between me and Helene.

"No!" Michael cries out.

I sense, rather than see, him dive forward toward his cousin.

The momentary distraction is all I need. My hand closes over the knife handle. I tug at it. For a second, the knife refuses to move, and I panic, thinking it's stuck, but then it slides out of Helene's chest with a wet slurp that makes my stomach churn.

I twist around and raise the knife, then slam it down into the only part of Ricky's body that's within reach. His left foot. There's a moment of resistance, then the knife blade slices through his flesh and buries itself in the floorboards, pinning Ricky in place.

He howls in pain, but the cry is quickly drowned out by another, more deafening noise, as Ricky pulls the trigger and shoots me.

79

Michael hits Ricky in a waist-high tackle and sends him flying backward just as the gun goes off. Instead of crashing through my skull, the bullet grazes my upper arm and smacks into the floorboards beneath me.

It still hurts like crazy, though.

I cry out and clutch my wounded arm, then stagger to my feet. Michael is straddling Ricky, who is flat on his back next to Helene's corpse. Ricky's foot is no longer impaled by the knife, which remains embedded in the floor, pinning his empty boot. His foot, which ripped free when his cousin knocked him to the floor, is a mangled, bloody mess. The gun is lying a couple of feet away, knocked from Ricky's grasp when he hit the floor.

Michael pulls his arm back, hand clenched into a fist, and delivers a crushing blow to Ricky's jaw. Then another. Ricky goes limp, eyes rolling up into their sockets. When Michael lifts his arm for a third punch, face contorted with rage, I cry out to stop him.

"Enough. He's out cold. You can stop now."

Michael brings his arm back farther, and for a moment, I think he's going to ignore me and land another left hook on his incapacitated cousin. But then the fight goes out of him.

He lowers his arm and stands up, then turns to me. "Are you okay?"

I nod, even as a tear winds its way down my cheek.

Michael's gaze drops to my injured arm, and the blood seeping through my fingers, then back up to my swollen and bruised face. "You don't look okay. God, I'm so sorry, Anna . . . Alex."

"I'll live," I tell him through gritted teeth. *Unlike Helene.* Despite everything she tried to do to me, all the craziness, I can't help but feel sad that she's gone. We were friends, or at least, that's what I'd believed. I trusted her with so much of my life. And to die in such a horrific way . . . it's almost more than I can bear. Tears are flowing, hot and wet, and I have to remind myself that I'm crying for a woman who wanted me dead. Despite this, it takes all my willpower to pull myself together and focus on the present. "What happens now?"

"We put an end to this madness, like I should have done right from the start." Michael fishes in his pocket and pulls out a cell phone. When he sees the look on my face, he says, "Sorry for lying to you about the cell service, but I didn't know what else to do, what with Ricky in the house. I promised to help him. Thought I could manage the situation. Guess that was pretty dumb of me."

"You stopped him from killing me, so . . ." I trail off, not sure how to express the conflicting emotions swirling inside my head. Everyone I've met since waking up on the shore of this lake was lying to me. Half of them wanted to kill me. Which is ironic, considering the type of books that I write. I'm literally caught up in a real-life thriller, just like those I put on paper. In the end, I settle for a simple "Thanks."

"You're welcome." Michael goes to the gun, picks it up, and looks at me. "Just in case Ricky wakes up. Don't want him giving us any more trouble."

"Right." It's weird, but I actually trust Michael. I know he won't hurt me. In a strange way, despite his deceit, I feel closer to him than ever. Because when it really mattered, he came through. He fought his cousin to save my life. Chose me over his family, no matter how depraved that family member might be. I realize that he might have been making that choice all along—protecting me from Ricky and keeping his lunatic cousin at bay—but he risked everything for me today. Ricky could just as easily have shot him as me. Without thinking, I blurt, "I got my memory back. Well, most of it."

"I'm pleased to hear that." Michael nods slowly, then looks down at the phone. "Suppose I'd better make that call."

"To whom?" I ask, my gut clenching. Am I going to end up surrounded by people worse than Ricky? "Some sort of gangland fixers who can come up here and make all this vanish like it never happened?"

"Gangland fixers?" Michael almost laughs. "Not quite. Figured 911 might be more appropriate."

I draw in a sharp breath as relief washes over me. After the events of the last several hours, I can't believe that I'm actually going to get out of here. That I will be okay. The implications for Michael are much worse. "But that means—"

"I know what it means. I'll end up in jail. But they'll put Ricky where he belongs too, and I think that's for the best." Michael dials, then puts the phone on speaker. As it rings, he smiles and looks at me. "I wish we'd met under better circumstances, Alex Moore. I think we would have been good together."

So do I, I think with a tinge of yearning for what might have been. *So do I.*

80

I open my eyes at the sound of footsteps entering the room. This has been a regular occurrence over the last five days since I've been in the hospital. Nurses coming in to take my vitals or haul me off for more tests. Doctors stopping by to see how I'm doing, and a steady stream of worried visitors. Everyone from family—my parents, who come in separately because they are divorced and can't stand to be in the same room together; two sisters; and a brother—to neighbors, my literary agent who drove all the way up from New York, and even the young woman who works at my favorite coffee shop down the street from the mock Tudor in Newton Centre that I bought with the proceeds from my first major book deal many years ago.

But it's none of those people.

Detective Matt Flynn stands at the end of my bed, his hands resting on the rail. He has already paid me three visits, the last of which was only yesterday.

"Missing me already, Detective?" I ask with a pained smile. My face still feels like a truck ran into it, and in a way it did, except it was my Audi roadster.

"Hardly. This case is like trying to unravel a bowl of cold spaghetti. But it's still my job." He chuckles at his own joke. "The doctors tell me that your memory has returned completely, so I have a few more questions for you."

My memory *has* returned, and it's not playing tricks on me anymore, like it did with the flashbacks. I thought they were real, but they turned out to be brief snippets of the novel I was working on. Which makes sense, because I was so engrossed in that book right before Helene showed up and tried to kill me. The mind is a strange thing. It can believe the imaginary almost as easily as reality. And I spent a lot of time in that imaginary world. Months. In the absence of memories, my subconscious filled in the blanks with my writing. Of course, not all of it was the book. In hindsight, I can see where my real experiences bled through. Like when I remembered going to Nantucket. Sure, it was in the book, but I really had gone there. I drew from my visit when writing that chapter, and my mind did the same thing, mixing fact and fiction. It was the same with the necklace. The one Helene ripped off my neck. I used it in the book because it was one of my favorite pieces of jewelry, and I like dropping little tidbits of my life into my fiction. But none of that will help the detective. "I've already told you everything I know."

Flynn shrugs. "Just crossing t's and dotting i's. Between your assistant trying to kill you to steal your manuscript, and the mess you stumbled into in that house across the lake, there's a lot to get straight. The DA is going to ask some tough questions. I want to make sure I have the right answers."

"Makes sense. But I have some questions of my own first," I say. I'm still not sure about exactly what I ended up in the middle of, and I'm getting fed up with the stock answer of *I'm not at liberty to divulge that information*. "Otherwise, my memory might not be as good as the doctors think it is."

"Are you blackmailing me, Miss Moore?"

"No. I'm saying that instead of a one-sided interrogation, it's about time we had a meaningful exchange of information. I think I'm entitled to know what was going on at that house, since *my* life was in danger."

"You know what was going on in that house probably better than I do. Otherwise, I wouldn't need to keep coming here with more questions."

"But there's still a lot that I don't understand, like who Ricky and Eddie robbed, and why Gregg—I mean Michael—agreed to help his cousin escape. After all, he tried to keep me safe when Ricky was pushing to kill me, tried to stop his cousin from committing more murders. He doesn't seem like the criminal type."

"I'm sorry, Miss Moore, but—"

"Don't tell me again that you're not at liberty to discuss the case. I'm not some newshound hanging out in front of the precinct with a TV camera. I'm a victim in all of this. I have a right to know what I got myself involved with."

"Well, that's debatable." Detective Flynn stares at me for a moment, rubbing the stubble on his chin. Then he sighs. "Look, if I answer your questions, what I tell you must remain confidential, at least for now."

"Fair enough."

"And then you'll answer *my* questions?"

"I already told you that I would."

"Right." The detective falls silent for a few moments, as if he's trying to decide if he really wants to enter into this bargain. Then his shoulders slump. "Ricky Sullivan and his associate Eddie Miller were a real pair of rotten apples. They grew up in the South Boston projects, which is where they first met when they were kids. Life was hard, and money was tight. By the time they were teenagers, the two of them were getting into trouble. Petty theft. Drugs. Extortion. They even ran with a gang for a while, until they got caught robbing a liquor store and ended up serving two years apiece. It would've been longer, except they weren't armed.

"When Ricky got out, he tried to go straight with the help of his cousin Michael, who was about the only person in his family who gave a damn about him. And it worked for a while. Then he fell back into his old habits. And every time Ricky messed up, Michael was there to bail him out, sometimes literally. He did a pretty good job of keeping Ricky on the straight and narrow, enough to avoid him going back to prison."

"Then how did they end up hiding out at that house on the lake?" I ask.

"Because Eddie showed up out of the blue with a scheme to rob this guy he was working for who owned an auto repair shop. The owner liked to employ ex-cons. You know, give them a second chance and all that. Eddie went to work there as a mechanic, a skill he'd learned behind bars. He told Ricky that the repair shop was a front for laundering Irish Mafia drug money, and that they kept large amounts of cash in a walk-in safe behind the office. It would be an easy score. Said he knew the combination because he'd seen the repair shop's owner open the safe late one evening when he didn't realize Eddie was still there. It was supposed to be a simple job. Break into the place after hours, and clean out the safe. No one would ever know who pulled the heist, and it wouldn't be reported to the police because of the stolen money's illegal origins."

"Except the business owner walked in on them," I say. This much I already know from Michael's conversation with Ricky at the lakeside cabin.

The detective nods. "Pretty much. There was a confrontation. Eddie shot and killed him. After that, they panicked and hid the money in a storage unit that Ricky's friend was renting. They intended to come back and split it up later, after the heat died down."

"But Ricky didn't wait that long. He went back there and took it, then asked his cousin for help."

"Pretty much."

"That still doesn't explain how they ended up at the lake house in Vermont."

The detective scratches his head. "Because that's where Michael was living. I mean, not up at the lake—he couldn't afford a house like that—but in the town nearby. Guess he wanted to put South Boston and all the trouble that went with it behind him. And he did a pretty good job of that for a while. He was working as a carpenter, built up a nice little business. The home's owners hired him to do renovations after they bought the place. He also had a side hustle as a caretaker, looking after the summer homes in the area during the winter months when the homeowners weren't there."

"And they hired him for that too."

"Yup. Which made it the perfect hideout. He had access, and it was empty all winter. Even better, he could put it back to rights when he left, and nobody would be any wiser."

"That's why the DSL didn't work," I say. "He must have disabled it so the owners couldn't remotely access the cameras inside the house and see what was going on."

"Nope. The camera system is on a hardwired closed loop. Ethernet cable. It's there so that occupants of the panic room can see what's happening in the rest of the house during an emergency. That's why the cameras are concealed. To stop home invaders from finding and disabling them. Michael cut the DSL line when you showed up to keep you from contacting the outside world and alerting someone to his and Ricky's presence."

"Why did the owners even have a panic room?" I ask, shuddering when I think about the discoveries I made there.

"It was already there when the current homeowner purchased the place. The previous owner, a New York millionaire whose business practices were more than a little shady, put it in many years ago in case anyone with bad intentions came looking for him or his family." Detective Flynn pushes his hands deep into his pockets. "It was a perfect place for Ricky to conceal himself when you showed up, because he didn't want anyone to see his face. Of course, he wasn't too happy about being stuck in there for days on end."

"That makes sense. I just have a few more—"

"I think I've answered enough of your questions, Miss Moore. Now it's time that you answer mine."

"Please, just one more," I beg him.

"Fine. One more, and that's it."

"Thank you." I push myself up in the bed and prop a pillow behind my head. "What will happen to Michael now?"

"Do you care?"

"I'd like to know. He deceived me and hid his cousin from me, which made me think that he might be responsible for my memory loss, that he might have tried to kill me, and put me in even more danger from the real culprit. My crazy assistant. But he also protected me from his homicidal cousin, who was just as much a threat as Helene, probably more so. When it mattered, when everything came to a head, he stopped Ricky and turned him in. He picked me, even though he knew it would result in his own arrest. So yes, I care."

"Whatever. He's looking at a bunch of charges. Aiding and abetting a fugitive, false imprisonment, and trespassing. Maybe even a few counts of accessory to murder for Eddie Miller and Helene Carter."

"But they'll take the good things he did into account too, right? Like keeping me safe from Ricky and turning his cousin in when things got out of hand."

"I'm sure the district attorney will consider all his actions, good and bad, when she makes her decision on what charges to file." Detective Flynn removes a compact voice recorder from his pocket. "Now, if you don't mind, it's my turn to ask some questions."

81

It's been three weeks since I was released from the hospital, and I'm putting my life back together. Part of that is realizing that none of what happened at Gravewater Lake was my fault. Another part is learning to trust people again. Which is why I'm sitting at a table near the window in Café Dissetante, a popular new restaurant located in the North End, a district of Boston—the city that's been my home for the past twelve years.

Across the table with a Cobb salad in front of her is my oldest friend, Jasmine. She's known me since we were studying art history together at college and I was pounding out pages of my first manuscript in every spare moment. The same manuscript that I eventually gave up on and threw in a drawer for Helene to find years later and steal.

"I still can't believe Helene did that to you," Jasmine says, picking up her fork and poking at the salad. "You think you know someone, and then . . ."

"Tell me about it. I've been thinking about her a lot over the last month," I admit, gazing absently out the window to the bustling street beyond. "I should have seen what was happening, been there for her."

"Just don't, okay?" Jasmine glares at me across the table. "That woman was a lunatic. She tried to kill you and steal your book. The last thing she deserves is your sympathy."

Jasmine is right, of course. There was something broken deep within Helene. A festering rot that ate her from the inside out. Nothing

I said or did could have stopped that. Still, maybe if I'd seen her true nature earlier, recognized the danger, I might have avoided a lot of pain. But Helene wasn't the only one responsible for the events at Gravewater Lake. Gregg, or rather Michael, and his psychotic cousin played a significant role too.

As if reading my thoughts, Jasmine says, "I can't believe you escaped Helene only to end up sharing a house with a pair of killers."

"Michael isn't a killer," I correct her. "Everything bad that happened was because of his cousin, Ricky."

"Whom he was hiding from the police." Jasmine shakes her head. "I don't get it. If Michael isn't like his cousin, if he's really a good guy, then why go out of his way to help someone like that?"

"Like you said, he's a good guy," I reply. I've thought a lot about Michael since escaping that lake and regaining my memory. At first, I was mad at him, but I soon came to realize that he was in an impossible situation. I showed up at his door unannounced in the middle of a snowstorm, freezing cold, wet, and with no memory of who I was. He could hardly send me away, but bringing me inside was just as dangerous. And once I was in the house, he had another problem. Even though he was the caretaker of the property, he couldn't fetch help and risk his cousin being discovered. And he wasn't supposed to be living there. It would have raised questions he wasn't prepared to answer, so he made the best of a bad situation. And even if things went sideways at the end, his intentions were noble.

"That isn't an answer."

"But it's the truth," I say. "Michael probably should have cut Ricky loose right from the start, but they were family, and that meant something. He thought his cousin was redeemable. You can't blame him for trying to help."

"It sounds like he tried to help one too many times," Jasmine says. "There comes a point when you just have to walk away and let people suffer the consequences of their mistakes."

"Maybe, but in a strange way, it worked out for the best. If Michael hadn't taken Ricky to that house, if they weren't hiding there, there wouldn't have been anyone home when I woke up on the lakeshore. Who knows what would've happened then? I might have stumbled all the way back to Helene and given her the opportunity to finish what she started. Or more likely, I'd have died out in that storm. Frozen to death. I know it sounds crazy, but if it wasn't for Michael and his doomed effort to save his cousin at all costs, I might actually be dead now."

"You have an odd perspective on life." Jasmine can't help a small laugh. "I get the impression that *you think* Michael is redeemable."

I shrug. "I'm not sure what to think, Jaz, but there was definitely a spark between us. If things had gone differently . . ."

"But they didn't."

"No. Still, I hate to think of him going to prison when all he was doing was trying to help."

Jasmine rests her arms on the table and leans toward me. "There's nothing you can do about that. It's not your problem."

"Actually . . ."

Jasmine's eyes shrink to narrow slits. "What did you do?"

"Nothing much." I look down at my food. "I wrote a letter to the district attorney in his defense."

"You did what?" Jasmine's voice rises an octave in pitch. Disbelief passes across her face.

"Don't make a big deal of this, please? I couldn't just sit back and let him take the blame like that. All that stuff in the newspapers about how he kept me at the lake house against my will. They want to charge him with false imprisonment. Can you believe that?"

"Yes. Because it's true. He told you the bridge was out, which it wasn't. And he chopped down a tree right before the bridge to keep the plow away."

"Which he could have cut up at any time with the chain saw in the garage."

"I don't believe this. You're impossible." Jasmine takes a breath. "Okay, fine. Let's forget about the bridge and the tree. What about the rest of it? He lied about how far away the closest town was. He disabled the internet. He did everything he could to keep you inside that house until he could get his cousin to the Canadian border. If that isn't keeping you a prisoner, then what is?"

"You're supposed to be on my side."

"I am. Always. It's just . . ." Jasmine's expression softens. "What's done is done. How about we change the subject?"

"I'd like that."

"Tell me about the book. There must be a lot of interest after what happened. I guess if nothing else, your ordeal will be good for business."

"It's a little early for that," I say. "I barely finished the rewrite a couple of days ago. It probably won't come out for another year or more."

"I thought you were pretty much done with that when you went up to the cabin."

"I was. But after what happened, my editor, Meghan, thought it would be a good idea to change some of the details. Like making the fictional lake and house in the book more closely resemble the real ones. I even used the floor plan of the real house. I changed the main characters too. Adria shares a lot of my features, and Peter now looks a lot like Michael. Eddie was a no-brainer for the bad guy who comes looking for Peter."

"Just like he came looking for Ricky," Jasmine says.

"Right. The story itself is different, of course, but Meghan thinks the changes will drive sales. What happened to me generated a lot of buzz, and it makes for good talking points for interviews and at book signings."

"You know what would be even better?" Jasmine's excitement is palpable. "Writing a book about what really happened. The whole plot is already there. It wouldn't have to be autobiographical. You could still make it fiction. You could even call it *Gravewater Lake*, just like in real life. Think about the hype *that* would generate, and people love that whole *based on a true story* stuff."

My editor at the publishing house has already come up with the same idea, tactfully suggested through my agent, but I'm not sure I'm ready to immortalize my ordeal in four hundred pages. It's too soon. And besides, I don't know how the story ends yet—there's still Michael. Which is why I just smile and say, "We'll see."

82

Eighteen months later

I pace back and forth between the stacks of books outside one of the three private meeting rooms in the public library in Burlington, Vermont. From inside the room, I can hear the woman who asked me to come here, Hilary Wharton, talking to her book club, who has been reading my latest novel, *Body of Lies*, which shot to the top of the bestseller lists. And the irony is that it might not have gone so far if it weren't for the publicity around Helene trying to steal my old manuscript and pass it off as her own. I mean, sure, every book of mine hits a bestseller list or two. But this one is different. It was the first book I ever wrote, back when I was nineteen and didn't have a clue what I was doing, and I'm not sure it would've done so well even with rewrites had it not been for the publicity surrounding the events at Gravewater Lake.

"I hope all of you did as I asked and stopped reading this month's book club selection before the end," Hilary says. "Because as you know, we have a very special speaker with us today, and she has agreed to read the last exciting chapter of her latest bestseller, *Body of Lies*, to you in person. We are so excited to have her here and honored that she has taken time out of her book tour to be with us today. Please give a big book club welcome to bestselling author Alex Moore."

There's a burst of applause.

That's my cue.

I step from between the rows of shelves and open the meeting room door, my heart aflutter.

Six rows of strangers, all with expectant looks on their faces, sit facing me on hard plastic chairs, at least fifty of them.

I resist the urge to turn around and flee, because at the heart of it, all of us authors are introverts. We hide behind our creative endeavors and let the words speak for themselves, content to be known by only a pen name or some other anonymous moniker that keeps us suitably distanced from the realities of stardom. We are known by our words and not our faces. And that's fine with me. Except that sometimes, you have to take a deep breath and own the words you put on the page. Which is how I ended up here.

The room falls quiet. Everyone is holding their breath, waiting to hear the first words out of my mouth.

I give them what they want. The last chapter of the book that almost got me killed, not once, but twice.

Adria: The Day She Found Out

The hammer swung down toward Adria's head. The boat bobbed and shifted beneath her, threatening to pitch both of them into the water. Then she remembered the oar, still gripped in her hand. She placed her other hand on it, then swiped upward with all the strength she had left.

The oar slammed into Peter's arm a split second before the hammer would have struck her skull. He let out a pained yelp and staggered back, letting go of her hair. Then he slipped and fell, landing on his back with a thud.

That was all she needed.

Adria dropped the oar into the oarlock and reached for the other one, even as the boat drifted a few feet away from the dock. If she could row across the lake, get to the other side quickly enough, she might survive. It would take Peter twice as long to walk around, especially in the middle of the storm, as it would take for her to row.

She sat in the boat and gripped the oars, dropping them into the water and pulling forward.

The boat moved farther from the dock. Another few strokes, and she would be out of his reach. But Peter had regained his footing. He lunged forward with the hammer still in his hand and launched into the air.

For a second, Adria thought she was safe. That he wouldn't make it across the gap between the dock and the rowboat, but then he landed in the stern with a grunt and dropped to his knees.

Adria stopped rowing and tugged to release an oar, but in her panic, she couldn't figure out how to open the oarlock.

Peter tried to stand up.

The boat rolled over a swell, and he dropped back down, almost losing his balance.

Adria saw her chance.

Instead of trying to unhook the oar, she gripped the sides of the rowboat and swayed.

The boat pitched to the left, then to the right.

Peter cursed and pushed himself back up. He swung the hammer clumsily in a last-ditch attempt to stop her from tipping the boat.

Adria leaned quickly back, avoiding the deadly blow. But she wouldn't be so lucky the next time. He was too close to miss twice. She rocked the boat again, sending it into another violent roll as Peter lunged forward with the hammer held aloft.

For a moment, he hung in the air as the boat rolled out from under him.

The hammer fell toward her in a deadly arc.

Adria braced herself for the blow that she knew was coming. Then, as the boat tipped back in the other direction, Peter lost his balance and pitched sideways with a startled cry.

He hit the water hard and went under, only to appear seconds later, spluttering and clawing at the side of the boat. Trying to climb back in.

Now Adria managed to release the oar. She jumped up in the still-swaying boat and stood over him. "I don't think so!"

She lifted the oar and swung with all her might.

It caught Peter above the ear, sent his head snapping sideways.

For a few seconds, he held on, fingers still curled around the gunwale. Then his eyes rolled up into their sockets, and his hands fell away limply into the water.

Adria watched him bob up and down in the freezing water, torn between doing the right thing and letting him drown.

But unlike her husband, Adria wasn't a killer.

She cursed under her breath and reached down to grab his collar. Stop him from slipping under.

Then she paddled clumsily toward the shore, where she used the mooring ropes to tie him up before staggering back to the house to find her phone and call for help. Peter's reign of terror was over for good, and Jess and Rob's killer would finally pay for his murderous crimes.

"The end." I close the book and look up to find a sea of faces, every last one of them hanging on my words. When I finish reading, there's a moment of silence before the applause begins.

I've barely taken a breath when Hilary steps up to the mic and says that I will sign copies of my book. All they have to do is form an orderly line and tell me to whom they would like the dedication made.

I spend the next fifteen minutes scribbling messages and signing my name in black permanent marker until I stop to sip from a bottle of water on the table in front of me. And then, when I glance up, I see a familiar face at the back of the line. Someone I'm sure is not part of this book club, and I wonder how he knew I was even here.

83

"Hello, Alex," Michael says in a baritone voice that I never thought I'd hear again. "It's been a while."

"Not long enough," I reply, even though deep down, I don't mean it. He looks the same, but different. His hair is longer, and there are faint lines at the corners of his eyes that weren't there before. But he's still as handsome as ever. Deep blue eyes, chiseled jaw, rugged good looks. A sudden image of the two of us back at the lake house pops into my head. Of sharing his bed.

I blush and look down, thankful that the line of autograph hunters has dispersed. Only Hilary and an employee of the library remain, deep in conversation at the back of the room. They pay us no attention. "I thought you were still in prison."

Michael drops his gaze to the floor. "By rights I should be for at least another eight months, but they let me out early for good behavior."

You should have been in prison for a lot longer than that, I think. Michael's two-year sentence surprised me when I heard about it. That was back when the events at Gravewater Lake were still all over the news, mostly thanks to me being a minor celebrity. I can still remember the headlines:

Bestselling Author Survives Murderer on the Run After Assistant Tries to Kill Her

And:

> Murderer's Cousin Cuts Plea Deal in Gravewater Lake Killings Case to Testify Against Him, Receives 24-Month Reduced Sentence

"I never thanked you for what you did," Michael says.

"I don't know what you mean." I pick up a small stack of hardcovers that I brought along in case anyone in the book group didn't already have a physical copy and move them to the other side of the table. It's more of a nervous distraction than because they need to be there.

"Yes, you do," Michael replies. "The letter you wrote to the district attorney telling her you didn't consider yourself a prisoner. That keeping you in that house protected you from Helene and saved your life. It went a long way to getting the false imprisonment charge dropped."

"I just told the truth as I saw it," I say, toying with the silver bracelet on my left wrist. The same bracelet with the engraved letter *A* that I woke up wearing on that freezing lakeshore the night we first met. I don't know why, but I've worn it a lot since then. Perhaps to remind myself to be thankful I survived that dreadful ordeal, or maybe because a part of me has missed Michael, and I'll always associate the bracelet with him. He did, after all, give me the name *Anna* after seeing the engraved *A* and guessing it was my first initial. He got my name wrong, of course, but . . . "No big deal."

"Well, I'm still grateful." Michael looks at the stack of hardcovers. "So, this is the book that brought you to my door?"

"Yes." The novel, my original version of it, not the one Helene butchered, has been number one on the bestseller lists for twelve weeks already, which is longer than any of my previous novels. Again, mostly thanks to the news frenzy surrounding the events at that lake. "Although it wasn't really *your* door, as I later came to find out."

"Touché. If I buy a copy, will you sign it?"

"That *is* the point of having them here," I say, pulling a book from the stack. "But you don't need to buy a copy. Consider it a gift for saving my life."

"Doesn't seem like much compensation, considering," Michael says with a grin.

"What else do you want, then?"

"How about you buy me a coffee?" he asks. "There's a cute coffee shop just down the street. I saw it when I was coming here."

"You want *me* to buy *you* a coffee?"

"Or I can buy you one. It doesn't really matter who pays. I'd just like a chance to spend some time with you." When he sees the look on my face, he adds, "You did agree that we would have been good together if we'd met under better circumstances. I figure this counts as *better circumstances*."

I laugh despite myself. "It would be hard to find worse circumstances."

"So, what do you say?"

I don't reply. Instead, I think for a moment, then open the book, write a quick inscription, and sign it. I close the book again and push it across the table toward him.

Michael nods. "I guess your silence is my answer."

"Actually, I wrote my answer inside the book."

Michael picks it up and goes to open it, then changes his mind and tucks it under his arm instead.

"You don't want to see what I wrote?"

"Oh, I really do," he replies. "But I'll wait until I'm outside. That way, if you said yes, I won't make a fool of myself by grinning like the Cheshire Cat, and if you said no, then I'll spare you the miserable sight of my bitter disappointment."

Then he turns and walks toward the library doors, without so much as a backward glance.

ACKNOWLEDGMENTS

Whenever we sit down at the start of a new literary journey, it feels like a long and lonely road ahead, but the truth is that a novel is never a solitary affair. After the long hours spent putting words on the page (and sometimes deleting them for better words), a whole army of wonderful people jump in to make the story shine.

Thanks as always to our marvelous literary agent, Liza Fleissig, who keeps us on our toes, and to our publisher, Thomas & Mercer, who put our story out into the world and let it fly free.

Thanks also to Charlotte Herscher, developmental editor extraordinaire, who made this book so much better with her shrewd observations and sharp eye for detail. A big thank-you to the rest of the editorial team, from proofing to copy editing, who make the manuscript shine.

Thank you to everyone at Amazon Publishing, who work tirelessly behind the scenes to make each book a success, from layout and cover design to marketing and production. And a big thank-you to our editor, Alexandra Ţorrealba.

Finally, a big thanks to you, our readers. We hope you enjoy reading this book as much as we enjoyed writing it!

ABOUT THE AUTHORS

A.M. Strong is the coauthor of nine novels, most recently *The Last Girl Left* and *I Will Find Her. Gravewater Lake* is his second psychological thriller. A native of the United Kingdom, Anthony now splits his time between Florida and the coast of Maine. He also writes under the pen name Anthony M. Strong. For more information, visit www.amstrongauthor.com.

Sonya Sargent is the coauthor of nine novels, most recently *The Last Girl Left* and *I Will Find Her. Gravewater Lake* is her second psychological thriller. A native of Vermont, Sonya now splits her time between sunny Florida and the beautiful coast of Maine. For more information, visit www.twistedthrillers.com.